A talent emerges. . . .

Suddenly Cal pushed himself off the bench he'd been leaning against and came to stand in front of me. "What do I have behind my back?" he asked.

My brow creased for a second, then I said, "An apple. Green and red." It was as if I had seen it in his hand.

He smiled, and his expressive, gold-colored eyes crinkled at the edges. He brought his hand from around his back and handed me a hard, greenish red apple, with a leaf still attached to its stem.

Feeling awkward and shy, aware of everyone's eyes on me, I took the apple and bit it, hoping the juice wouldn't run down my chin.

"Good guess," Raven said, sounding irritated. It occurred to me that she was probably jonesing for Cal big time.

"It wasn't a guess," Cal said softly, his eyes on me.

• • •

SWEEP

SWEEP

Cate Tiernan

BOOK OF SHADOWS
THE COVEN
BLOOD WITCH

speak
An Imprint of Penguin Group (USA) Inc.

BOOK ONE

SWEEP
BOOK OF SHADOWS

All quoted materials in this work were created by the author.
Any resemblance to existing works is accidental.

Book of Shadows

SPEAK
Published by the Penguin Group
Penguin Group (USA) Inc., 345 Hudson Street, New York, New York 10014, U.S.A.
Penguin Group (Canada), 90 Eglinton Avenue East, Suite 700, Toronto, Ontario, Canada M4P 2Y3
(a division of Pearson Penguin Canada Inc.)
Penguin Books Ltd, 80 Strand, London WC2R 0RL, England
Penguin Ireland, 25 St Stephen's Green, Dublin 2, Ireland (a division of Penguin Books Ltd)
Penguin Group (Australia), 250 Camberwell Road, Camberwell, Victoria 3124, Australia
(a division of Pearson Australia Group Pty Ltd)
Penguin Books India Pvt Ltd, 11 Community Centre, Panchsheel Park, New Delhi - 110 017, India
Penguin Group (NZ), 67 Apollo Drive, Rosedale, North Shore 0632, New Zealand
(a division of Pearson New Zealand Ltd)
Penguin Books (South Africa) (Pty) Ltd, 24 Sturdee Avenue, Rosebank, Johannesburg 2196, South Africa

Registered Offices: Penguin Books Ltd, 80 Strand, London WC2R 0RL, England

Published by Puffin Books, a division of Penguin Young Readers Group, 2001
Published by Speak, an imprint of Penguin Group (USA) Inc., 2007
This omnibus edition published by Speak, an imprint of Penguin Group (USA) Inc., 2010

5 7 9 10 8 6

CIP DATA IS AVAILABLE

Produced by 17th Street Productions,
an Alloy company
151 West 26th Street
New York, NY 10001

17th Street Productions and associated logos
are trademarks and/or registered trademarks of Alloy, Inc.

Speak ISBN 978-0-14-240986-2
This omnibus ISBN 978-0-14-241717-1
Printed in the United States of America

With love to my life supports
Christine and Marielle

BOOK OF SHADOWS

1

Cal Blaire

><"Beware the mage, and bid him well, for he has powers beyond your ken."

—WITCHES, WARLOCKS, AND MAGES, Altus Polydarmus, 1618 ><

Years from now I'll look back and remember today as the day I met him. I'll look back and remember the exact moment my life began to include him. I will remember it forever.

I wore a green tie-dyed T-shirt and jeans. My best friend, Bree Warren, arrived in a peasant shirt and a long black skirt down to her violet toenails, and of course she looked beautiful and sophisticated.

"Hey, junior," she greeted me with a hug, even though I'd just seen her the day before.

"See you in AP calc," I told Janice Yutoh, and met Bree halfway down the front steps. "Hey," I said back. "It's hot. It's supposed to be crisp on the first day of school." It wasn't even eight-thirty, but the early September sun was burning whitely, and the air felt muggy and still. Despite the weather I felt excited, expectant: A whole new year was starting, and we were finally upperclassmen.

"Maybe in the Yukon Territory," Bree suggested. "You look great."

"Thanks," I said, appreciating her diplomacy. "You too."

Bree looks like a model. She's tall, five-nine, and has a figure most girls would starve themselves for, except Bree eats everything and thinks dieting is for lemmings. She has minky dark hair that she usually gets styled in Manhattan, so it falls in perfectly tousled waves to the base of her neck. Wherever we go, people turn their heads to look at her.

The thing about Bree is that she knows she's gorgeous, and she enjoys it. She doesn't shrug off compliments, or complain about her looks, or pretend she doesn't know what people are talking about. But she isn't exactly conceited, either. She just accepts what she looks like and thinks it's cool.

Bree glanced over my shoulder at Widow's Vale High. Its redbrick walls and tall Palladian windows betrayed its former incarnation as our town courthouse. "They didn't paint the woodwork," she said. "Again."

"Nope. Oh my God, look at Raven Meltzer," I said. "She got a tattoo."

Raven's a senior and the wildest girl in our school. She has dyed black hair, seven body piercings (that I can see, anyway), and now a circle of flames tattooed around her belly button. She's amazing to look at, at least for me—Ordinary Girl, with my long, all-one-length, medium brown hair. I have dark eyes and a nose that could kindly be described as "strong." Last year I grew four inches, so I'm five-six now. I have broad shoulders and no hips and am still waiting for the breast fairy to show up.

Raven headed to the side of the cafeteria building where the stoners hung out.

"Her mom must be so proud," I said cattily, but inside I admired her daring. What would it be like to care so little about what other people thought of you?

"I wonder what happens to her nose stud when she sneezes?" asked Bree, and I giggled.

Raven nodded to Ethan Sharp, who already looked wasted at eight-thirty in the morning. Chip Newton, who's absolutely brilliant in math, way better than me, and our school's most reliable dealer, gave Raven a soul handshake. Robbie Gurevitch, my best friend after Bree, looked up and smiled at her.

"God, it's so weird to see Mary K. here," said Bree, glancing around and running her fingers through her wind-tossed hair.

"Yeah. She'll fit right in," I said. My younger sister, Mary Kathleen, was headed toward the main building, laughing with a couple of her friends. Next to most of the freshmen, Mary K. looked mature and together, with grown-up curves. Stuff just comes easily to Mary K.—her hip but not-too-hip clothes, her naturally pretty face, her good but not perfect grades, her wide circle of friends. She's a genuinely nice person, and everyone adores her, even me. You can't help it with Mary K.

"Hey, baby," said Chris Holly loudly, coming up to Bree. "Hey, Morgan," he said to me. Chris leaned down and gave Bree a quick kiss, which she caught on her lips.

4 book of shadows

"Hey, Chris," I said. "Ready for school?"

"Now I am," he said, giving Bree a lustful smile.

"Bree! Chris!" Sharon Goodfine waved, gold bangles clinking on her wrist.

Chris grabbed Bree's hand and pulled her toward Sharon and the other usuals: Jenna Ruiz, Matt Adler, Justin Bartlett.

"Coming?" Bree asked, falling behind.

I made a wry face. "No, thank you."

"Morgan, they like you fine," Bree said under her breath, reading my mind as she often did. She'd dropped Chris's hand, waiting for me while he went on ahead.

"It's okay. I need to talk to Tamara, anyway." Bree knew I didn't feel comfortable with her clique.

She paused another moment. "Okay, see you in homeroom."

"See ya."

Bree began to turn away but stopped, her mouth dropping open like someone in Acting 101 doing "dumbstruck." I turned and followed her gaze and saw a boy coming up the steps to our school.

It was like in a movie when everything goes into soft focus, everyone becomes silent, and time slows down while you figure out what you're looking at. It was just like that, watching Cal Blaire come up the broad, worn front steps of Widow's Vale High.

I didn't know then that he was Cal Blaire, of course.

Bree turned back toward me, her eyes wide. "Who is *that?*" she mouthed.

I shook my head. Without thinking, I put my palm to my chest to slow my heartbeat.

The guy walked up to us with a calm confidence I envied.

I was aware of heads turning. He smiled at us. It was like the sun coming out of the clouds. "Is this the way to the vice principal's office?" he asked.

I've seen good-looking guys before. Bree's boyfriend, Chris, in fact, is really good-looking. But this guy was . . . *breathtaking*. Raggedy, black-brown hair looked as if he hacked at it himself. He had a perfect nose, beautiful olive skin, and riveting, ageless, gold-colored eyes. It took me a second to realize he was speaking to us.

I gazed at him stupidly, but Bree sparkled. "Right through there and to the left," she said, pointing to the nearest door. "It's unusual to transfer as a senior, isn't it?" she asked, studying the piece of paper he held out to her.

"Yeah," the guy said. He gave a half smile. "I'm Cal. Cal Blaire. My mom and I just moved here."

"I'm Bree Warren." Bree gestured to me. "And this is Morgan Rowlands."

I didn't move. I blinked a couple of times and tried to smile. "Hi," I finally said in a near whisper, feeling like a five-year-old. I'm never good at talking to guys, and this time I felt so overwhelmed and shy that I couldn't function at all. I felt like I was trying to stand up in a gale.

"Are you seniors?" Cal asked.

"Juniors," Bree said apologetically.

"Too bad," Cal said. "We won't have classes together."

"Actually, you might have some with Morgan," Bree said, with a cute, self-deprecating laugh. "She's taking senior math and science."

"Cool," Cal said, smiling at me. "I better check in. Nice meeting you. Thanks for your help." He turned and strode to the door.

"Bye!" Bree said brightly.

As soon as Cal passed through the wooden doors into the school building Bree grabbed my arm. "Morgan, that guy is a god!" she squealed. "He's going to school here! He'll be here all year!"

The next moment found us surrounded by Bree's friends.

"Who is he?" Sharon asked eagerly, her dark hair brushing her shoulders. Suzanne Herbert jostled her, trying to get closer to Bree.

"Is he going to school here?" Nell Norton asked.

"Is he straight?" Justin Bartlett wondered aloud. Justin's been out of the closet since seventh grade.

I glanced at Chris. He was frowning. As Bree's friends reviewed the meager info, I stepped back, out of the crowd. I drifted to the entrance and put my hand on the heavy brass handle, swearing I could still feel the warmth from Cal's touch.

A week passed. As usual, I felt a tingle in my chest as I walked into physics class and saw Cal there. He still looked like a miracle sitting in a dinged-up wooden desk. A god in a mortal place. Today he was focusing his beam on Alessandra Spotford. "It's like a harvest festival? Up in Kinderhook?" I heard him asking her.

Alessandra smiled and looked flustered. "It's not till October," she explained. "We get our pumpkins there every year." She tucked a curl behind her ear.

I sat down and opened my notebook. In one week Cal had become the most popular guy at my school. Forget popular; he was a celebrity. Even a lot of the boys liked him. Not Chris Holly or any other guy whose girlfriend was salivating over Cal, but most of the others.

"What about you, Morgan?" Cal asked, turning to me. "Have you been to the harvest festival?"

Casually I flipped to the current chapter in our textbook and nodded, feeling a rush of giddiness at hearing him say my name. "Pretty much everyone goes. There's not a lot else to do around here unless you go down to New York City, and that's two hours away."

Cal had spoken to me several times over the past week, and each time it had gotten a little easier for me to reply to him. We had physics and calculus together every day.

He turned in his desk to face me fully, and I permitted myself a quick glance at him. I don't always trust myself to do this. Not if I want my vocal cords to work. My throat tightened right on schedule.

What was it about Cal that made me feel like this? Well, he was gorgeous, for one obvious thing. But it was more than that. He was different than the other guys I knew. When he looked at me, he really looked at me. He wasn't glancing around the room, checking for his buds or trolling for prettier girls or sneaking quick looks at my breasts— not that I have any. He wasn't self-conscious at all, and he wasn't keeping score socially the way everybody else does. He seemed to look at me or Tamara, who was in advanced classes, too, with the same frank intensity and interest that he looked at Alessandra or Bree or one of the other local goddesses.

"So what do you do for fun the rest of the time?" he asked me.

I looked back down at my textbook. I wasn't used to this. Good-looking guys usually only talked to me when they wanted a homework assignment.

"I don't know," I said mildly. "Hang out. Talk to friends. Go to movies."

"What kind of movies do you like?" He leaned forward as if I were the most interesting person in the world and there was no one he would rather be talking to. His eyes never left my face.

I hesitated, feeling awkward and tongue-tied. "Anything. I like all kinds of movies."

"Really? Me too. You'll have to tell me which theaters to go to. I'm still learning my way around."

Before I could agree or disagree, he smiled at me and turned to face the front of the room as Dr. Gonzalez walked in, thumped his heavy briefcase on his desk, and began to call roll.

I wasn't the only person Cal was charming. He seemed to like everybody. He talked to everyone, sat by different people, didn't show favorites. I knew that at least four of Bree's friends were dying to go out with him, but I hadn't heard of any successes so far. I did know that Justin Bartlett had struck out.

2

I Wish

><"Beware the witch, for she will bind you with black magick, making you forget your home, your loved ones, yea, even your own face."
—WORDS OF PRUDENCE, Terrance Hope, 1723><

"You have to admit he's good-looking," Bree pressed, leaning against my kitchen counter.

"Of course I admit it. I'm not blind," I said, busily opening cans. It was my night to make dinner. The washed, cut-up chicken was sitting naked in a large Pyrex dish. I dumped out a can of cream of artichoke soup, a can of cream of celery soup, and a jar of marinated artichoke hearts. Voilà: dinner.

"But he seems like kind of a player," I continued mildly. "I mean, how many people has he gone out with in the last two weeks?"

"Three," said Tamara Pritchett, unfolding her long, skinny frame onto the bench in our breakfast nook. It was Monday afternoon, the beginning of the third week of school. I could safely say that Cal Blaire's arrival in the sleepy town of Widow's Vale was the most exciting thing that had happened since the Millhouse Theater burned to the ground two years ago. "Morgan, what *is* that?"

"Chicken Morgan," I said. "Delicious and nutritious." I reached into the fridge for a Diet Coke and popped the top. Ahhh.

"Toss me one of those," Robbie said, and I got him one. "How come when a guy dates a lot, he's a player, but if a girl does, she's just picky?"

"That is so not true," Bree protested.

"Hello, girls and Robbie," my dad said, wandering into the kitchen, his brown eyes somewhat vague behind his glasses. He was wearing his usual uniform: khaki pants; a button-down shirt, short sleeved because of the weather; and a white T-shirt underneath it. In the winter he wears the same thing except with a long-sleeved shirt and a knit sweater vest over it all.

"Hey, Mr. R.," Robbie said.

"Hi, Mr. Rowlands," Tamara said, and Bree waved.

Dad glanced around distractedly, as if to make sure that this was really his kitchen. With a smile at us he wandered out again. Bree and I shared a grin. We knew that soon he'd remember what he had come in to get, and he'd return for it. He works in research and development at IBM, and they think he's a genius. Around our house, he's more like a slow kindergartner. He can't keep his shoes tied, and he has no concept of time.

I stirred the mixture in the glass pan and covered it with foil. Then I grabbed four potatoes and scrubbed them in the sink.

"I'm glad my mom cooks," Tamara said. "Anyway, Cal has

gone out with Suzanne Herbert, Raven Meltzer, and Janice." She ticked off the names on her fingers.

"Janice Yutoh?" I squealed, putting the dish in the oven. "She didn't even tell me about it!" I frowned and added the potatoes. "God, he sure doesn't have a type, does he? It's like one from column A, one from column B, one from column C."

"That dog," said Robbie, pushing his glasses up on his nose.

Robbie was such a close friend, I hardly noticed it anymore, but he had terrible acne. He had been supercute until seventh grade, which made it all the harder on him.

Bree wrinkled her forehead. "The Janice Yutoh thing I can't figure out. Unless she was helping him with his homework."

"Janice is actually really pretty," I said. "She's just so shy, you don't notice it. *I* can't figure out Suzanne Herbert."

Bree almost choked. "Suzanne is gorgeous! She modeled for Hawaiian Tropic last year!"

I smiled at Bree. "She looks like Malibu Barbie, and she's got the brain to match." I ducked as Bree tossed a grape at me.

"Not everyone can be a National Merit Scholar," she said snippily. She paused and then said, "I guess none of us are wondering about Raven. She goes through guys like Kleenex."

"Oh, and *you* don't," I teased her, and was rewarded by another grape bouncing off my arm.

"Hey, Chris and I have been together for almost three months now," Bree said.

"And?" Robbie prompted her.

Self-righteousness mixed with rueful embarrassment crossed Bree's face. "He's bugging me a little," she admitted.

Tam and I laughed, and Robbie snorted.

"I guess you're just picky," Robbie said.

My dad wandered into the kitchen again, got a pen from the pen jar, and headed out again.

"Okay," Bree said, opening the back door. "I better get home before Chris freaks out." She made a face. "Where have you *been?*" she said in a deep-voiced imitation. She rolled her eyes and left, and moments later we heard her temperamental BMW, Breezy, take off and chug down the street.

"Poor Chris," Tamara said. Her curly brown hair was escaping from her headband, and she expertly twisted it back underneath.

"I think his days are numbered," Robbie said, taking a sip of soda.

I pulled out a bag of salad and ripped it open with my teeth. "Well, he lasted longer than usual."

Tam nodded. "It might be a record."

The back door flew open and my mom staggered in, her arms full of files, flyers, and real estate signs. Her jacket was wrinkled, and it had a coffee stain on one pocket. I grabbed the stuff from her hands and set it on the kitchen table.

"Mary, mother of God," my mom muttered. "What a day. Hi, Tamara, honey. Hey, Robbie. How have you two been? How's school so far?"

"Fine, thanks, Mrs. Rowlands," Robbie said.

"How about you?" Tamara asked. "You look like you've been working hard."

"You could say that," my mom said with a sigh. She hung her jacket on a hook by the door and headed to the cabinet to fix herself a whiskey sour from a mix.

"Well, we better head out," Tamara announced, picking up her backpack. She kicked Robbie's sneaker gently. "Come on, I'll give you a ride. Nice seeing you, Mrs. Rowlands."

"See you later," Robbie said.

"Bye, guys," my mom said, and the back door closed behind them. "Gosh, Robbie's getting tall. He's really growing into himself." She came over to give me a hug. "Hi, sweetheart. It smells great in here. Is it chicken Morgan?"

"Yep. With baked potatoes and frozen peas."

"Sounds perfect." She drank from her glass, which smelled sweet and citrusy.

"Tiny sip?" I asked.

"No, ma'am!" Mom replied, as she always did. "Let me change, and I'll set the table. Is Mary K. here?"

I nodded. "Upstairs with some of the Mary K. fan club."

Mom frowned. "Boys or girls?"

"I think both."

Mom nodded and headed upstairs, and I knew that the boys, at least, were about to get the boot.

"Hi. Can I sit here?" Janice asked at lunch period the next day, pointing to an empty spot on the grass of the school's courtyard next to Tamara.

"Of course," Tamara said, waving a handful of Fritos. "We'll be even more multiculti." Tamara was one of the very few African Americans in our overwhelmingly white school, and she wasn't afraid to joke about it, particularly with Janice, who was sometimes self-conscious about being one of very few Asians.

Janice sat down cross-legged with her tray balanced on her lap.

"Excuse me," I said pointedly. "Is there any interesting . . . news you'd like to share?"

Confusion crossed Janice's face as she chewed the school's version of meat loaf and swallowed. "What? You mean from class?"

"No," I said impatiently. "Romantic news." I raised my eyebrows.

Janice's pretty face turned pink. "Oh. You mean Cal?"

"Of course I mean Cal!" I practically exploded. "I can't believe you didn't say anything."

Janice shrugged. "We just went out once," she said. "Last weekend."

Tamara and I waited.

"Can you embellish, please?" I pressed after a minute. "I mean, we're your friends. You went out with the single best-looking guy on the planet. We deserve to know."

Janice looked pleased and embarrassed. "It didn't really seem like a date," she said finally. "It's more, like, he's trying to get to know people. Know the area. We drove around and talked a lot, and he wanted to know all about the town and the people...."

Tamara and I looked at each other.

"Hmmm," I said finally. "So you're not hooking up or any-thing?"

Tamara rolled her eyes. "Be blunt, why don't you, Morgan?"

Janice laughed. "It's fine," she said. "And no. No hooking up. I think we're just friends."

"Hmmm," I said again. "He *is* friendly, isn't he?"

"Speak of the devil," Tamara said softly.

I looked up to see Cal ambling toward us, his lips curved in a smile.

"Hey," he said, crouching on the grass next to us. "Am I interrupting anything?"

I shook my head and drank my soda in an attempt to look casual.

"Are you getting settled in?" Tamara asked. "Widow's Vale is pretty small, so it probably won't take you long to figure out where everything is."

Cal smiled at her, and I blinked at his supernatural face. By now I expected to have this reaction when I was around him, so it didn't bother me as much.

"Yeah. It's pretty here," Cal said. "Full of history. I feel like I've gone back in time." He looked down at a patch of grass, absently stroking a blade between his fingers. I tried not to stare, but I found myself wanting to touch what he touched.

"I came over to ask if you guys would come to a party this Saturday night," Cal said.

We were all so surprised that we didn't say anything for a second. It seemed gutsy for a relative stranger to throw a party so soon.

"Rowlands!" Bree called from across the lawn, then came and sank down gracefully on the grass next to me. She gave Cal a beautiful smile. "Hi, Cal."

"Hey. I've been going around inviting people to a party this Saturday," Cal said.

"A party!" Bree looked like this was the best idea she'd ever heard. "What kind of party? Where? Who's coming?"

Cal laughed, leaning back his head so I could see the strong column of his throat, with its smooth tan skin. In the vee of his shirt hung a worn leather string with a silver pendant dangling from it, a five-pointed star surrounded by a circle. I wondered what the symbol meant.

"If the weather's all right, it will be an outdoor party," Cal said. "Mostly I just want to have a chance to talk to people, you know, not at school. I'm asking most of the juniors and seniors—"

"Really?" Bree's lovely brows arched.

"Sure," Cal said. "The more the merrier. I figured we could meet up outside. The weather's been beautiful lately, and there's this field right at the edge of town over past Tower's market. I thought we could sit around and talk, look at the stars...."

We all stared at him. Kids hung out at the mall. Kids hung out at the movie theater. Kids even hung out at the 7-Eleven when things got really slow. But nobody ever hung out in the middle of an empty field out past Tower's market.

"This isn't the kind of thing you usually do, is it?" he asked.

"Not really," Bree said carefully. "But it sounds great."

"Okay. Well, I'll print up some directions. Hope you guys can come." He stood smoothly, gracefully, the way an animal rises.

I wish he were mine.

I was shocked that my brain had formed the thought. I'd never felt that way about *anyone*. And Cal Blaire was so out of my league that wanting him seemed stupid, almost pathetic. I shook my head. This was pointless. I would just have to snap out of it.

When he was gone, my friends turned to one another excitedly.

"What kind of a party is this?" Tamara wondered out loud.

"I wonder if there'll be a keg or something," Bree said.

"I think I'm going out of town this weekend," Janice said, looking half disappointed, half relieved.

The four of us watched as Cal approached Bree's other

friends, who were hanging out on the benches at the edge of the school grounds. After talking to them, he headed to the stoners clustered by the doors to the cafeteria. The funny thing was, he looked just like each crowd he spoke to. When he was with the brains, like me and Tamara and Janice, he was totally believable as a gorgeous, brilliant, deeply inquisitive scholar type. When he was with Bree's friends, he looked cool, casual, and hip: a trendsetter. And when he was standing next to Raven and Chip, I could totally imagine him as a stoner, smoking pot every day after school. It was amazing how comfortable he was with everyone.

On one level I envied it since I'm comfortable with only a small group of people, my good friends. In fact, my two closest friends, Bree and Robbie, I've known since we were babies and our families lived on the same block. That was before Bree's family moved into a huge modern house with a view of the river and long before we'd split up into different cliques. Bree and I were two of the only people at our school who managed to be close despite belonging to different groups.

Cal was . . . universal, in a way. And even though I was nervous, I wanted to go to that party.

3

The Circle

><"Roam not at night, for sorcerers use all phases
of the moon for their craft. Be you safe at
home till the sun lights the sky and drives evil
to its lair again."

—NOTES OF A SERVANT OF GOD,
Brother Paolo Frederico, 1693><

I am casting the net. Pray for my success, that I may increase our number and find those for whom I search.

The porch light cast a shadow across our lawn. Before me, on the crunchy, dried-out autumn grass, a smaller, darker me walked to my car.

"What's wrong with Breezy?" I asked.

"She's making a weird pinging noise," Bree said.

I rolled my eyes, hoping she could see me. Bree's expensive, sensitive car was always doing one thing or another. So much for fancy engineering.

I opened the driver's side door and eased onto the cool vinyl seat of Das Boot, my beautiful white '71 Chrysler Valiant. My dad likes to joke that my car weighs more than a submarine, so we named it Das Boot, the German word for *boat* and the title of my dad's all-time favorite movie. Bree climbed in the other side, and we waved good-bye to my dad, who was putting out the trash.

"Drive carefully, sweetheart," he called.

I started the engine and glanced out my window at the sky. The waning moon was a thin, sharp crescent. A wisp of a dark cloud drifted across it, blotting it from the sky and making the stars pop into prominence.

"Are you going to tell me where Chris is?" I asked as I turned onto Riverdale Drive.

Bree sighed. "I told him I'd promised to go with you," she said.

"Oh, jeez, don't tell me," I groaned. "I'm afraid of driving by myself at night; is that it?"

Bree rubbed her forehead. "Sorry," she muttered. "He's gotten so possessive. Why do guys always do that? You go out with them for a while, and suddenly they own you." She shivered, though it was barely chilly. "Turn right on Westwood."

Westwood headed right out of town, northward.

Bree waved the piece of paper that had the directions. "I wonder what this will be like. Cal is really . . . different, isn't he?"

"Uh-huh." I took a swig of seltzer, letting the conversation die. I was reluctant to talk to Bree about Cal, but I wasn't sure why.

"Okay, okay!" Bree said excitedly a few minutes later.

"This is it! Stop here!" She was already scrambling out of her seat belt, grabbing her macramé purse.

"Bree," I said politely, looking around. "We're in the middle of freaking *nowhere*."

Technically, of course, you're always somewhere. But this deserted road on the outskirts of town didn't feel like it. To the left were acres of cornfields, tall and awaiting harvest. To the right was a wide strip of unmowed field edged by thick woods that led back toward town in a large, ragged vee.

"It says to park under that tree," Bree instructed me. "Come on."

I eased Das Boot off the side of the road and glided heavily to a stop beneath a huge willow oak. That was when I saw moonlight glinting off at least seven other cars that hadn't been visible from the road.

Robbie's distinctive red VW Beetle sat glowing darkly like a giant ladybug under the tree, and I saw Matt Adler's white pickup, Sharon's SUV, and Tamara's dad's station wagon edged up neatly next to them. Parked in a sloppy circle around them were Raven Meltzer's battered black wreck, a gold Explorer that I recognized as Cal's, and a green minivan I thought belonged to Beth Nielson, Raven's best friend. I didn't see any people, but there was a somewhat trampled path through the tall, dried grass toward the woods.

"I guess we're supposed to go there," Bree said, sounding uncharacteristically unsure. I was glad she was here with me and that Chris wasn't. If I'd had to come by myself, I might not have had the nerve to show.

We followed the path of beaten grass, the cool evening breeze filtering through my hair. When we reached the edge of the woods, Bree pointed. I could barely make out the pale gleam of her finger in the forest darkness. Looking ahead, I saw it: a small clearing and shadowed shapes standing around a low fire ringed with stones. I heard low laughter and smelled the delicious scent of wood smoke coiling through the newly crisp air. Suddenly an outdoor party seemed like a brilliant idea.

We stepped carefully through the woods toward the fire. I heard Bree swearing under her breath—her chunky platform sandals weren't the best shoes for nighttime hiking. My own clogs were cheerfully crunching twigs underfoot. I heard a crashing sound behind us and startled, then saw it was Ethan Sharp and Alessandra Spotford, lurching through the forest after us.

"Watch it!" Alessandra hissed at Ethan. "That branch hit me right in the eye."

Bree and I emerged into the clearing. I saw Tamara and Robbie and even Ben Reggio from my Latin class. I went over to join the three of them as Bree split off from me to stand by Sharon, Suzanne, Jenna, and Matt. The firelight cast a soft golden glow on everyone's faces, making the girls look prettier than usual and the guys look older and mysterious.

"Where's Cal?" Bree asked, and Chris Holly straightened up from where he was crouched by an ice chest, a beer in his hand.

"Why do you want to know?" he said unpleasantly.

She ran her fingers through her hair. "He's our host."

Cal appeared almost silently from the edge of the clearing. He was carrying a large wicker hamper, which he set down next to the fire. "Hi," he said, looking around at us and smiling. "Thanks for coming. I hope the fire will keep you warm."

I pictured myself snuggling up to him, his arm around my

shoulders, feeling the heat of his skin slowly seep through my fleece vest. I blinked quickly, and the image was gone.

"I brought some stuff to eat and drink," Cal said, kneeling and opening his basket. "There's food in here—nuts, chips, corn bread. There's stuff to drink in the coolers."

"I should have brought some wine," Bree said, and I blinked in surprise to see her standing right there. Cal smiled at her, and I wondered if he thought she was beautiful.

For the next half hour we hung out and talked, sitting around the fire, maybe twenty of us altogether. Cal had brought some delicious apple cider spiced with cinnamon for people who didn't want beer, which included me.

Chris sat next to Bree, his arm around her shoulders. She wasn't looking at him but sent me irritated glances from time to time. Tamara and Ben and I sat with our knees touching. One of my arms was almost too warm from the fire, and the other was pleasantly chilly. From time to time Cal's voice flowed over me like the night air.

"I'm glad you all came tonight," Cal said, coming over to kneel next to me. He spoke loud enough for everyone to hear. "My mom knew people here before we moved, so she has a bunch of friends already, but I thought I'd have to celebrate Mabon by myself."

Bree smiled and leaned forward. "What's Mabon?"

"Tonight is Mabon," Cal said. "It's one of the Wiccan sabbats. Kind of an important day if you practice Wicca. It's the autumnal equinox."

You could have heard a leaf land at that moment. We were all looking at him, his face golden and flame-colored, like a mask. Nobody said anything.

Cal seemed aware of our surprise, but he didn't look embarrassed or self-conscious. In fact, he plowed on. "See, usually on Mabon you have a special circle," Cal continued, crunching into an apple. "You give thanks for the harvest. And after Mabon you start looking forward to Samhain."

"Sowen?" Jenna Ruiz said faintly.

"*S-a-m-h-a-i-n,*" Cal clarified. "Pronounced Sow-en. Our biggest holiday, the witches' new year. October 31. Most people call it Halloween."

Silence, broken only by the crackling of the logs as they burned.

Chris was the first to speak. "So, what, man?" he said with a nervous laugh. "You saying you're a witch?"

"Well, yeah, actually. I practice a form of Wicca," Cal said.

"Isn't that like devil worship?" Alessandra asked, wrinkling her nose.

"No, no. Not at all," Cal responded in a way that wasn't the least bit defensive. "There is no devil in Wicca. It's about the tamest and most inclusive religion there is, truthfully. It's all about celebrating nature."

Alessandra looked skeptical.

"So, anyway, I was hoping to find a few people to make a circle with me tonight."

Silence.

Cal looked around, absorbing the surprise and discomfort in almost every face but showing no sign of regret. "Listen, it's not a big deal. Making a circle doesn't mean you're joining Wicca. It doesn't mean you're going against your religion or whatever. If you're not into it, don't worry about it. I just thought some people might think it's cool."

I looked at Tamara. Her dark brown eyes were wide. Bree

turned to me, and we shared a glance that communicated a whole conversation's worth of ideas. Yes, we were both surprised and a little skeptical, but we were both intrigued, too. Bree's look told me she was interested, she wanted to hear more. I felt the same way.

"What do you mean, a circle?" It was a few seconds before I recognized the voice as my own.

"We all stand in a circle," explained Cal, "and join hands, and give thanks to the Goddess and the God for the harvest. We celebrate the fertility of the spring and summer and look forward to the barrenness of winter. And we walk in a circle."

"You're joking," Todd Ellsworth said, sipping his beer.

Cal looked at him evenly. "No, I'm not. But if you're not into it, that's fine."

"Jesus, he's serious," Chris said to no one in particular.

Bree deliberately shrugged his arm off her shoulders, and he scowled at her.

"Anyway," Cal said, standing up. "It's almost ten. Anyone who wants to stay is welcome, but you're also welcome to leave. Thanks a lot for coming and hanging out, either way."

Raven stood up and walked over to Cal, her dark, heavily outlined eyes on his. "I'll stay." She turned a disdainful face to the rest of us, as if to say, "You wankers."

"I think I'm gonna go home," Tamara whispered to me, and stood up.

"I'm going to stay for a while," I said softly, and she nodded, waved good-bye to Cal, and left.

"I'm outta here," said Chris loudly, throwing his beer bottle into the woods. He got to his feet. "Bree? Come on."

"I came with Morgan," Bree said, moving closer to me. "I'll go home with her."

"Come on with me now," Chris insisted.

"No, thanks," Bree said, meeting my eyes. I gave her the slightest smile of encouragement.

Chris swore, then crashed off through the trees, muttering. I reached over and squeezed her arm.

I cast a glance at Cal. He was sitting with his knees bent and his elbows resting on them. There seemed to be no tension in his body. He just watched.

Raven, Bree, and I stayed. Ben Reggio left. Jenna stayed, so of course Matt stayed, too. Robbie stayed: good. Beth Nielson stayed, and so did Sharon Goodfine and Ethan Sharp. Alessandra hesitated but stayed, and so did Suzanne and Todd.

When it looked like everyone had left who was going to, there were thirteen of us standing there.

"Cool," Cal said, standing. "Thanks for staying. Let's get started."

4

Banishing

><"They dance skyclad beneath the blood moon in their unholy rites, and beware to any who bespy them, for you will turn to stone where you stand."

—WITCHES, WARLOCKS, AND MAGES,
Altus Polydarmus, 1618><

While we milled around uncertainly, Cal took a stick and drew a large, perfect circle in the ground around the fire. Before he joined the two ends of the circle, he gestured us inside, then closed the circle as if he were shutting a door. I felt a bit like a sheep inside a pen.

Then Cal took out a box of salt and sprinkled it all around the drawn circle. "With this salt, I purify our circle," he said.

Bree and I glanced at each other and smiled tentatively.

"Okay, now, let's join hands," Cal said, holding out his hands. A wave of shy self-consciousness washed over me as I realized I was standing closest to his left hand. He reached for my hand and held it. Raven went to Cal's other side, taking his right hand firmly.

Bree was on my other side, then Jenna and Matt, Beth, Alessandra, Todd, and Suzanne. Sharon, Ethan, and Robbie made up the other side, and Robbie held Raven's other hand.

Cal lifted my hand, and our arms were raised to the narrow patch of clear sky above us. "Thanks to the Goddess," Cal said in a strong voice. He looked around the circle at the rest of us. "Now you guys say it."

"Thanks to the Goddess," we said, though my voice was so low, I doubt I added anything. I wondered who the Goddess was.

"Thanks to the God," Cal said, and again we repeated it.

"Today day and night are balanced," Cal continued. "Today the sun enters the sign of Libra, the balance."

Todd chuckled, and Cal slanted his eyes at him.

I seemed to grow a billion extra nerve endings in my left hand. I tried not to think so much about whether I was holding Cal's hand too tightly or loosely, whether my hand was clammy from nervousness.

"Today the dark begins to dominate the light," Cal said. "Today is the autumn equinox. It's the time of harvest, when crops are gathered. We give thanks to the Earth Mother, who nourishes us." He looked around the circle again. "Now you guys say 'blessed be.'"

"Blessed be," we said. I was praying my hand didn't all out start sweating in Cal's. His was rough and strong, gripping mine as hard as possible without hurting it. Did my hand feel pathetically limp in return?

"It's the time to gather the seeds," Cal said in his calm

voice. "We gather the seeds to renew our crops for next year. The cycle of life continues to nourish us." He looked around the circle. "Now we all say 'blessed be.' "

"Blessed be," we said.

"We give thanks to the God, who will sacrifice himself in order to be reborn again," Cal said. I frowned, not liking the word *sacrifice*. He nodded at us.

"Blessed be," we said.

"Now let us breathe," Cal said. He bowed his head and closed his eyes, and one by one we did the same.

I heard Suzanne drawing in exaggerated-sounding breaths and opened my eyes a slit to see Todd smirking. Their reactions irritated me.

"Okay," Cal continued, opening his eyes after a few minutes. He seemed either unaware of or was deliberately ignoring Todd and Suzanne. "Now we're going to do a banishing chant, so we'll move widdershins—that means counterclockwise. You'll catch on."

Cal's body pushed me gently counterclockwise, and two seconds later we were all doing a Wiccan version of ring-around-a-rosy. Cal chanted, over and over so that we all learned it and could join in:

> "Blessed be the Mother of All Things,
> The Goddess of Life.
> Blessed be the Father of All Things,
> The God of Life.
> Thanks be for all we have.
> Thanks be for our new lives.
> Blessed be."

It felt less weird after a couple of minutes, and soon I felt oddly exhilarated, practically running in a circle, holding hands under the moon. Bree looked so happy and alive that I couldn't help smiling at her.

A while later—it could have been two minutes or a half hour—I noticed I was starting to feel dizzy and strange. I'm one of those people who can never go on merry-go-rounds, roller coasters that do inversions, or anything that goes around in circles. It's an inner-ear thing, but the bottom line is I throw up. So I was starting to feel kind of iffy but didn't feel quite like I could stop.

Just as I was wondering what we would be banishing, Cal said, "Raven? What would you get rid of if you could? What do you banish?"

Raven smiled, and she looked almost pretty for a moment, like a regular girl. "I banish small minds!" she called gleefully.

"Jenna?" Cal asked as we moved in our circle.

"I banish hatred," Jenna said after a pause.

She glanced at Matt. "I banish jealousy," he said.

Holding tightly to Cal and Bree's hands, I raced in a circle around the fire, someplace between running and dancing, simultaneously pushed and pulled. I began to feel like a sliver of soap at the bottom of a bathtub whirlpool, going around and around, out of control. But I wasn't getting sucked toward the drain. Instead I was rising up through the ribbed circle of water, rising to the top, held in place by centrifugal force. I felt light-headed and weirdly happy.

"I banish anger," Robbie called out.

"I banish, like, school," Todd said.

What an idiot, I thought.

"I banish plaid golf pants!" said Alessandra, and Suzanne giggled.

"I banish fat-free hot dogs," Suzanne contributed. I felt Cal's hand tighten a bit around mine.

To my surprise, Sharon went next with, "I banish *stupidity*."

"I banish my stepmother!" Ethan yelled, laughing.

"I banish powerlessness," cried Beth.

Next to me Bree shouted, "I banish fear!"

Was it my turn? I thought dizzily.

Cal squeezed my hand hard. What was I afraid of? Right then, I couldn't remember any of my fears. I mean, I'm afraid of all kinds of things: failing tests, speaking in public, my parents dying, getting my period at school when I'm wearing white, but I couldn't think of how to phrase those fears to fit in with our banishment circle.

"Um," I said.

"Come on!" Raven cried, her voice tearing away, lost in the whirling circle.

"Come on," said Bree, her dark eyes on me.

"Come on," Cal whispered, as if he were enticing me into a private space with him alone.

"I banish limitations!" I blurted out, unsure where the words had sprung from or why they felt right.

Then it happened. As if obeying a director's cue, we threw our hands apart from one another, up in the air, and stopped where we stood. In the next instant I felt a piercing pain in my chest, as if my skin literally ripped open. I gasped, clutched my chest, and stumbled.

"What's with *her?*" I heard Raven say as I sank to my knees, pressing hard on the center of my chest. I felt dizzy, sick, and embarrassed.

"Too much brew," Todd suggested.

Bree's hand touched my shoulder. I sucked in breath and rose unsteadily to my feet. I was sweating and clammy, breathing hard, and felt like I was about to faint.

"Are you okay? What's the matter?" Bree put her arm around me and shielded me with her body. Thankfully I leaned into her. A cloudy mist swam before my eyes, turning everything around me into a heat mirage. I blinked and swallowed, wanting childishly to cry. With each breath I took, the pain in my chest was lessening. I became aware that the members of the circle were gathered around me. I felt their gazes on me.

"I'm okay," I said, my voice low and raspy. Heat came off Bree's tall, thin body in waves, and her dark hair was stuck to her forehead. My own hair hung around me in long, limp strands. Although I was sweating, I felt cold, chilled to the bone.

"Maybe I'm coming down with something," I said, trying to speak more strongly.

"Like witchitosis," Suzanne said sarcastically, her tanned face looking plastic in the moonlight.

I stood up straighter and realized the pain was almost gone. "I don't know what that was—a cramp or something." I broke away from Bree and tried a shaky step. And that was when I noticed something was wrong with my eyes.

I blinked several times and looked up at the sky. Everything was brighter, as if the moon had blown into fullness, but it was still just a sharp-edged crescent, a cream-colored sickle in the sky. I glanced at the woods and felt drawn into them, as if into a 3-D photograph. I saw every pine needle, every acorn, and every fallen twig in sharp relief. I closed my eyes and realized I could hear each separate sound of the night: insects, animals, birds, my friends' breathing, the delicate swoosh of my blood moving through my veins. The drone of crickets splintered into a thousand pieces—the music of a thousand separate beings.

I blinked again and looked at the faces around me, dim but utterly distinct in the firelight. Robbie and Bree wore expressions of concern, but it was Cal's face that held my eyes. Cal was gazing at me intently, his golden eyes seeming to strip through my skin to the bones underneath.

Abruptly I sat down on the ground. The earth was slightly damp and covered with a thin layer of decaying leaves. The crunching sound was incredibly loud in my ears as I tucked my legs beneath me. Instantly I felt better, as if the ground itself were absorbing my shaky feelings. I looked deeply into the fire, and the timeless, eternal dance of colors I saw there was so beautiful, I wanted to cry.

Cal's deep voice floated toward me as clearly as a whisper in a tunnel, as if his words were meant for me alone, and they found me unerringly even as the group dissolved into talking.

He said the words under his breath, his gaze fixed on my face. "I banish loneliness."

5
Headachy

>< "A witch may be a woman or man. The femi-
nine power is as fierce and terrifying as the
masculine power, and both are to be feared."
—THERE ARE WITCHES AMONG US,
Susanna Gregg, 1917 ><

I saw something last night—a flash of power from an
unexpected source. I can't jump to conclusions—I've
been looking and waiting and watching for too long to
make a mistake. But in my gut I feel she's here. She's
here, and she has power. I need to get closer to her.

On Sunday morning I woke up feeling like my head was
packed with wet sand. Mary K. stuck her head in my door.

"Better get up. Church."

My mom brushed past her into my room. "Get up, get up,
you lazy pup," she said. She threw open my curtains, flooding

my room with bright autumn sunlight that pierced my eyeballs and stung the back of my head.

"Ugh," I moaned, covering my face.

"Come on, we'll be late," said my mom. "Do you want
waffles?"

I thought for a minute. "Sure."

"I'll put them in the toaster for you."

I sat up in bed, wondering if this was what a hangover felt
like. It all came back to me, everything that had happened last
night, and I felt a rush of excitement. Wicca. It had been strange
and amazing. True, today I felt physically awful, foggy-headed and
sore, but still, last night had been one of the most exciting
times of my whole life. And Cal. He was . . . incredible. Unusual.

I thought back to the moment when he looked at me so
intensely. I thought at the time he'd been talking to me alone,
but I later realized he wasn't. Robbie had heard him banish
loneliness, and Bree had, too. On the way home Bree had
wondered aloud how a guy like Cal could possibly be lonely.

I swung my feet over to the chilly floor. It was really autumn,
finally. My favorite time of year. The air is crisp; the leaves change
color; the heat and exhaustion of summer are over. It's cozier.

When I stood up, I swayed a bit, then clawed my way to
the shower. I stepped under the wimpy, water-saving shower-
head and turned it to hot. As the water streamed down on
my head, I closed my eyes and leaned against the shower
wall, shivering with headachy delight. Then something shifted
almost imperceptibly, and suddenly I could hear each and
every drop of water, feel each sliding rivulet on my skin, each
tiny hair on my arms being weighted down by wetness. I
opened my eyes and breathed in the steamy air, feeling my
headache drain away. I stayed there, seeing the universe in

my shower, until I heard Mary K. banging on the door.

"I'll be out in a minute!" I said impatiently.

Fifteen minutes later I slid into the backseat of my dad's Volvo, my wet hair sleeked into a long braid and making a damp patch on the back of my dress. I struggled into my jacket.

"What time did you go to bed, Morgan? Didn't you get enough sleep last night?" my mom asked brightly. Everyone in my family except me is obnoxiously cheerful in the morning.

"I never get enough sleep." I moaned.

"Isn't it a beautiful morning?" my dad said. "When I got up, it was barely light. I drank my coffee on the back porch and watched the sun come up."

I popped the top off a Diet Coke and took a life-giving sip. My mom turned around and made a mom face. "Honey, you should drink some orange juice in the morning."

My dad chuckled. "That's our owl."

I'm a night owl, and they're larks. I drank my soda, trying to swig it all down before we got to church. I thought about how lucky my parents are to have Mary K. because otherwise it would seem as if *both* of their children were total aliens. And then I thought how lucky they are to have *me* so that they'll really appreciate Mary K. And then I thought how lucky I am to have *them* because I know they love me even though I'm so different from the three of them.

Our church is beautiful and almost 250 years old. It was one of the first Catholic churches in this area. The organist, Mrs. Lavender, was already playing when we walked in, and the smells of incense were as familiar and comforting to me as the smell of our laundry detergent.

As I passed through the huge wooden doors, the numbers 117, 45, and 89 entered my mind, as if someone had drawn them on the inside of my forehead. How weird, I thought. We sat down in our usual pew, with my mom between Mary K. and me so we wouldn't cut up, even though we're so old now that we wouldn't cut up, anyway. We know about everyone who goes to our church, and I liked seeing them every week, seeing them change, feeling like part of something bigger than just my family.

Mrs. Lavender began to play the first hymn, and we stood as the processional trailed in, the altar boys and the choir, Father Hotchkiss and Deacon Benes, Joey Markovich carrying the heavy gold cross.

Mom opened her hymnal and began flipping pages. I glanced at the hymn board at the front of the church to see what number we should be on. The first hymn was number 117. I glanced at the next number—45. Followed by 89. The same three numbers that had popped into my brain as I first entered the church. I turned to the correct page and began singing, wondering how I had known those numbers.

That Sunday, Father Hotchkiss gave a sermon in which he equated one's spiritual struggle with a football game. Father Hotchkiss is very big on football.

After church we stepped out in the bright sunlight again, and I blinked.

"Lunch at the Widow's Diner?" said Dad, as usual, and we all agreed, as usual. It was just another Sunday, except that for some reason I had known the numbers of the three hymns we would sing before I had seen them.

6

Practical Magick

>< "They keep records of their deeds and write them in their books of shadows. No mere mortal can read their unnatural codes, for their words are for their kind alone."

—HIDDEN EVIL, Andrej Kwertowski, 1708 ><

I am not psychic. Life is packed with weird little coincidences. I'll just keep telling myself that until I believe it.

"Where are we going?" I asked. I had changed out of my Sunday dress into jeans and a sweatshirt. My headache was gone, and I felt fine.

"An occult bookstore," Bree said, adjusting her rearview mirror. "Cal told me about it last night, and it sounded great."

"Hey, speaking of occult, you know something weird?" I asked. "Today in church I knew the numbers for the hymns before I saw them on the board. Isn't that bizarre?"

"What do you mean, you knew them?" Bree asked, heading out of town on Westwood.

"These numbers just popped into my head for no reason, and then when we got into church, they were up on the board. They were our hymn numbers," I said.

"That *is* weird," said Bree, smiling. "Maybe you heard your mom mention them or something."

My mom is on the women's guild at church and sometimes changes the hymn numbers or polishes candlesticks or arranges the altar flowers.

I frowned, thinking back. "Maybe."

Within minutes we were in Red Kill, the next town to our north. When I was little, I had been afraid of going to Red Kill. The name itself seemed to be a warning of something awful that had happened there or would happen there. But actually, a lot of towns in the Hudson River Valley have the word *kill* in them—it's an old Dutch word meaning "river." *Red Kill* simply means "red river"—probably because the water was tinted from iron in the soil.

"I didn't know Red Kill had an occult bookstore. Do you think they'll have stuff about Wicca?" I asked.

"Yeah, Cal said they have a pretty good selection," Bree answered. "I just want to check it out. After last night I'm really curious about Wicca. I felt so great afterward, like I just did yoga or had a massage or something."

"It *was* really intense," I agreed. "But didn't you feel yucky this morning?"

"No." Bree looked at me. "You must be coming down with something. You looked awful on the way home from the circle last night."

"Thanks, how comforting," I said flatly.

Bree pushed my elbow playfully. "You know what I mean."

We sat in silence for a couple of minutes.

"Hey, do you have plans tonight?" I asked her. "My aunt Eileen's coming over for dinner."

"Yeah? With her new girlfriend?"

"I think so."

Bree and I wiggled our eyebrows at each other. My aunt Eileen, my mom's younger sister, is gay. She and her longtime partner had broken up two years ago, so we were all happy she was finally dating again.

"In that case, I can definitely make dinner," said Bree. "Look, here we are." She parked Breezy at an angle against the curb, and we got out, walking past the Sit 'n' Knit, Meyer's Pharmacy, Goodstall's Children's Shoes, and a Baskin-Robbins. At the end of the row of stores, Bree looked up and said, "This must be the place." She pushed against a heavy double-glass door.

Glancing down, I saw a five-pointed star within a circle painted on the sidewalk in purple—just like Cal's silver pendant. Gold lettering on the glass door said Practical Magick, Supplies for Life. I wondered about the odd spelling of the word magic.

I felt a bit like Alice about to go down the rabbit hole, knowing that simply entering this store would somehow start me on a journey whose ending I couldn't predict. And I found that idea irresistible. I took a deep breath and followed Bree inside.

The store was small and dim. Bree moved ahead, looking at things on the shelves while I hovered by the door and gave myself time to adjust after the bright autumn sunlight outside. The air was heavy with an unfamiliar incense, and I imagined that I could almost feel the coiling smoke brushing against me and winding around my legs.

After blinking a few times, I saw that the shop was long and narrow, with a very high ceiling. Wooden shelves that looked homemade lined the walls and divided the store into halves. The half I could see down was floor-to-ceiling books: old, leather-bound volumes, bright-covered modern paper-backs, cheesy pamphlets that looked like they had been pho-tocopied at Kinko's and stapled by hand. I read some of the hand-lettered category signs: Magick, Tarot, History, Womancraft, Healing, Herbs, Rituals, Scrying . . . and within each category there were subcategories. It was all very orderly, though it didn't give that impression at first.

Just looking at the books' spines, I felt that my mind was blooming like a flower. I hadn't known books like this ex-isted—ancient volumes describing magic and rituals. I was seeing a whole new world.

Bree wasn't in sight, so I walked down the aisle and headed for the other side of the store. She was looking at candles. One large shelf unit was like candle mania. There were huge pillar candles; tiny little birthday-style candles; candles in the shape of people, men and women; nice dining-table tapers; star-shaped votives: You name it, this store had it.

"Oh my God." I pointed to a candle in the shape of a life-size penis. At least I assumed it was life-size. I hadn't seen one up close since Robbie had flashed my class in first grade.

Bree giggled. "Let's get a bunch of these for tonight. They would make dinner really festive."

I laughed. "My mom would keel over."

Most of the other candles were pretty, hand dipped in graduating shades of color, some in earth tones, some in rainbow colors. A little rhyme came into my head: *Firelight, my soul is bright.* I didn't know where it came from—probably some Mother Goose book I had when I was younger. It reminded me of how I had felt the night before, looking into the fire at the circle.

"Are you looking for anything in particular?" I asked. Bree had moved to examine shelves of glass jars, each filled with herbs or powders. One section was called essential oils, with row after row of tiny dark brown glass vials. The air was heavy with scent there: jasmine, orange, patchouli, clove, cinnamon, rose.

"Not really," Bree said, reading jar labels. "Just checking it out."

"I think we should maybe get a book on the history of Wicca," I suggested. "For starters, anyway."

Bree looked at me. "You're getting into this, huh?"

I nodded self-consciously. "I think it's cool. I'm curious to learn more about it."

Bree smiled at me. "You're sure it's not just a crush on Cal?"

Before I could answer, she was studying a small bottle and opening it. The scent of roses after a summer rain filled the air.

I was about to say that wasn't it at all. Instead I stood there, staring at my clogs. I did have a crush on Cal. Though I knew better than anybody he was out of my league, I was drawn to him. What a pair we would make: Cal, the most beautiful person in the world, and Morgan, the girl who had never been on a date.

I stood still and silent in the aisle of Practical Magick, overwhelmed by a strange sense of longing. I longed for Cal, and I longed for . . . this. These books and these smells and these things. New emotions—passion; yearning; gnawing, inexplicable curiosity—were waking up inside me, and it was thrilling and threatening at the same time. One part of me wished they would go back to sleep.

I looked up to try to explain some of it to Bree, but now she was bent intently over the jewelry case, and I had no idea how to put my feelings into words.

As I was gazing blankly at the labels on the packets of incense, I felt a slight prickling on the back of my neck. I looked up and was startled by the intent gaze the store clerk had fastened on me.

The clerk was an older guy, maybe in his early thirties, but with short gray hair that made him appear older than he probably was. And he was looking at me with a focused, unmoving stare, as if I were a new kind of reptile, something incredibly interesting.

Most guys don't look at me that way. For one thing, I'm usually with either Bree or Mary K. Bree is straight-up gorgeous, and Mary K. is totally cute. I'd heard that a guy in my class, Bakker Blackburn, was thinking about asking her out. Already Mom and Dad had started instituting rules about dating and going steady and all that stuff—rules they hadn't needed to worry about with me.

I turned my back to the clerk. Had he mistaken me for someone he knew? Finally Bree came up and tapped me on the shoulder.

"Find anything interesting?"

"Yeah, this," I said, pointing to a package of incense called Love Me Tonight.

Bree smiled. "Ooh, baby."

Laughing, we headed for the bookshelves and started reading titles. There was a whole shelf of books labeled Books of Shadows. One by one I opened them, and they were all completely blank, like journals. Some were like cheap notebooks; some were fancier, with marbled endpapers and deckle-edged leaves; and some were bound in gold-stamped leather, oversize and heavy. I felt sudden distaste for the girlish, pink vinyl-covered journal I'd been keeping since ninth grade.

Fifteen minutes later Bree had chosen a couple of Wiccan reference books, and I had settled on one about a woman who had suddenly discovered Wicca when she was in her thirties and how it had changed her life. It seemed to explain Wicca in a personal way. The books were kind of expensive, and I don't have Bree's access to parental credit, so I was getting only one.

We headed to the counter.

"This it for you?" the store clerk asked Bree.

"Uh-huh." Bree dug in her purse for her wallet. "We can swap books when we're finished," she said to me.

"Good idea," I said.

"Do you have everything you need for Samhain?" the clerk asked.

"Samhain?" Bree looked up.

"One of the biggest Wiccan festivals," the clerk said and pointed to a poster tacked to the wall with rusty thumbtacks. It depicted a large purple wheel. At the top it said The Witches' Sabbats. At eight points around the wheel were the names of Wiccan celebrations and their dates. Mabon appeared at nine o'clock on the wheel. At about ten-thirty was the word *Samhain,* October 31. My eyes scanned the wheel, fascinated. Yule, Imbolc, Ostara, Beltane, Litha,

Lammas, Mabon, Samhain. The very words were strange and also somehow familiar and poetic-sounding to me.

Tapping it with his finger, the clerk said, "Get your black and orange candles now."

"Oh, right," Bree said, nodding.

"If you need more information, there are a couple of great books about our festivals, sabbats, and esbats," said the clerk. He was speaking to Bree but looking at me. I was dying for the books but didn't have enough money with me.

"Hang on—let me get them." Bree followed him back to the bookshelves to get the ones he recommended.

I heard a lightbulb flickering overhead and felt the spiral of incense smoke rising above its little stand. As I stood there, it seemed as if everything around me was actually vibrating, almost. As if it was full of energy, like a beehive. I blinked and shook my head. My hair suddenly felt heavy. I wished Cal were there.

The clerk returned while Bree continued browsing. He stared at me. The silence was so awkward I broke it. "Why is magic spelled with a K here?" I heard myself asking him

"To distinguish it from illusionary magic," he responded, as though it was very strange of me not to know this.

He went right back to his silent stare. "What's your name?" he finally asked me in a soft voice.

I looked at him. "Um, Morgan. Why?"

"I mean, who are you?" Though soft, the soft voice was quietly insistent.

Who am I? I frowned at him. What did he want me to say? "I'm a junior at Widow's Vale," I offered awkwardly.

The clerk looked puzzled, as if he were asking me a question in English and I was insisting on answering in Spanish.

Bree came back, holding a book called *Sabbats: Past and Present,* by Sarah Morningstar.

"I'll get this, too," she said, sliding it onto the counter. The clerk silently rang it up.

Then, as Bree took her paper bag, he said to me, "You might be interested in one of our history books." He reached for it beneath the worn wooden counter.

It's black, I thought, and he pulled out a black-covered paperback. Its title was *The Seven Great Clans: Origins of Witchcraft Examined.*

I stared at the book, tempted to blurt out, "That's mine!" But of course it wasn't mine—I had never seen it before. I wondered why it seemed so familiar.

"It's practically required reading," the clerk said, looking at me. "It's important to know about blood witches," he went on. "You never know when you might meet one."

I nodded quickly. "I'll take it," I said, and fished out my wallet. Buying it cleaned me out entirely.

When I had bought my books, we took our bags and stepped again into the sunny day. Bree slipped on her sunglasses and instantly looked like a celebrity going incognito.

"What a cool place, huh?"

"Very cool," I said, though for me that didn't express even a tiny part of the emotions storming in my chest.

7

Metamorphosis

><"In many villages, innocents turn to their local witch as a healer, midwife, and sorceress. I say, better to submit to the will of God, for death must come to all in time."

—Mother Clare Michael,
from a letter to her niece, 1824 ><

I can't stop thinking about *Practical Magick* and the strange mixture of fear and familiarity I felt there. Why did the names of the esbats and festivals feel like deeply buried memories? I never gave much thought to the possibility of past lives, but now, who knows?

"Morgan! Mary K.!" my mom called from downstairs. "Eileen's here!"

I rolled off my bed, marked my place in the book, and put it on my desk next to my journal, trying to pull myself back into the regular world. I was blown away by what I had been reading—about Wicca's roots in pre-Christian Europe thousands and thousands of years ago.

My brain still felt glazed as I padded downstairs in my socks just as my dad came in the front door with bags of food from Kabob Palace, Widow's Vale's only Middle Eastern restaurant. The smell of falafel and hummus started bringing me back to my senses.

I went into the living room, where the rest of the group was already gathered.

"Hi, Aunt Eileen," I said, and hugged her hello.

"Hi, sweetie," she said. "I'd like you to meet my friend, Paula Steen."

Paula stood up as I turned toward her, a smile already on my face. The first impression I had was of animals, as if Paula were covered with animals. I stopped dead and blinked. I mean, I saw *Paula:* She was a bit taller than I am, with sandy hair down to her shoulders and wide, pale green eyes. But I also saw dogs and cats and birds and rabbits all around her. It was weird and scary, and I felt an instant of panic.

"Hi, Morgan," Paula said, her voice friendly. "Um, are you okay?"

"I'm seeing animals," I said faintly, wondering if I should sit down and put my head between my knees.

Paula laughed. "I guess I can never quite get all the fur off," she said matter-of-factly. "I'm a vet," she explained, "and I just came from a Sunday clinic." She looked down at her skirt and jacket. "I thought with enough masking tape, I might be presentable."

"Oh, you are!" I said, feeling stupid. "You look fine." I shook my head and blinked a couple of times, and all the weird afterimages were gone. "I don't know what's wrong with me."

"Maybe you're psychic," Paula suggested easily, as if she

were suggesting that maybe I was a vegetarian or a Democrat.

"Or maybe she's just a weirdo," Mary K. said brightly, and I aimed a kick at her leg.

The doorbell rang, and I ran to get it.

"What's she like?" whispered Bree, stepping into the foyer.

"*She's* great. *I'm* a freak," I whispered back as Bree hung her jacket on a peg.

"You can explain later," she said and followed me into the living room to meet Paula.

"Okay!" my mom announced a few minutes later. "Why don't you all come in and sit down? Food's ready."

Once we were seated and served, I thought back to what I had said. Why had I seen those images of animals? Why did I say anything?

In spite of my weirdness, dinner was great. I liked Paula right away. She was warm and funny and obviously crazy about Aunt Eileen. I was happy to have Bree there, talking to everyone and teasing Mary K. She felt like one of us, one of our family. Once she told me that she loves coming to our house for dinner because it feels like a real family. At her house it's usually just her and her dad. Or just her, eating alone.

As I was helping myself to more tabouli, I looked up and absently said, "Oh, Mom—it's Ms. Fiorello."

"What?" my mom asked, dipping her pita bread into some hummus. Just then the phone rang. Mom got up to answer it. She talked in the kitchen for a minute, then hung up and came to sit back down. She looked at me.

"It was Betty Fiorello," she said. "Had she told you she was going to call?"

I shook my head and applied myself to my tabouli.

Bree and Mary K. started humming the theme from *The X-Files*.

"She *is* psychic!" Aunt Eileen laughed. "Quick, who's going to win the play-offs for the World Series?"

I laughed self-consciously. "Sorry. Nothing's coming to me."

Dinner went on, and Mary K. teased me about my supernatural brain powers. A couple of times I felt my mother's eyes on me.

Maybe since I had been in the circle, since I had banished limitations, something inside me was opening up. I didn't know whether to feel glad or terrified. I wanted to talk to Bree about it, but she had to get home right after dinner.

"Bye, Mr. and Mrs. Rowlands," Bree said, putting on her jacket. "Thanks for dinner—it was great. Nice meeting you, Paula."

Later, after Aunt Eileen and Paula left, I went upstairs and did my calculus homework. I called Bree, but she was watching a football game with her dad and said she'd talk to me the next day.

Around eleven I got a weird urge to call Cal and tell him what was going on with me. Luckily I realized how completely insane this was and let the urge pass. I fell asleep with my face against the pages of *The Seven Great Clans*.

"Welcome to Rowlands Airlines," I intoned on Monday morning as Mary K. slid into the car, trying to hold her cardboard tray level so the scrambled eggs didn't slide into her lap. "Please fasten your seat belts and keep your seat in its upright and locked position."

Mary K. giggled and took a bite of her sausage patty. "Looks like rain," she said, chewing.

"I hope it does rain so Mr. Herndon won't clean his stupid gutters," I said, steering with my knees so I could open a soda.

Mary K. paused, her eyes narrowed. "Um, okaaay," she said in an exaggerated soothing tone. "I hope so, *too*." She continued chewing, giving me a sidelong glance. "Are we back to *The X-Files* again?"

I tried to laugh, but I was puzzled by my own words. The Herndons were an old couple who lived three houses down. I hardly ever thought about them.

"Maybe you're metamorphosing into a higher being," my sister suggested, opening a small carton of orange juice. She took a deep swig, then wiped her mouth on the back of her hand. Her straight, shiny, russet-colored hair swung in a perfect bell to her shoulders, and she looked pretty and feminine, like my mom.

"I'm already a superior being," I reminded her.

"I said higher, not superior," Mary K. said.

I took another drink and sighed, feeling my brain cells waking up. Another one of these and I would feel ready to face the day. Cal would be at school. Just the idea that I would see Cal soon, be able to talk to him, made me so pleasantly nervous that my hands tightened on the steering wheel.

"Um, Morgan?" Mary K.'s voice was tentative.

"Yeah?"

"Call me old-fashioned, but it's traditional to stop for red lights."

I snapped to attention, leaning forward, tensed to brake. Looking back quickly, I saw that I had just breezed through the intersection of St. Mary's and Dimson, right through a red light. At this hour of the morning there was always traffic. It was amazing we hadn't gotten into an accident—no one had even honked.

"Jeez, Mare, I'm sorry," I said, clutching the steering wheel. "I was daydreaming. Sorry. I'll be more careful."

"That would be good," she said calmly. She scooped up the last of her scrambled eggs and shoved the tray into my car's trash bag.

We managed to get to school without my killing us, and I found a great parking spot practically right outside the building. Mary K. was immediately surrounded by a gaggle of friends who ran over to greet her. Mary K. had arrived: The party could begin.

I saw Bree and Robbie hanging out not by the stoners, not by the nerds, not by the cool kids, but in a completely new area around the old cement benches that face each other across the brick path by the east-side door. Raven was there, Jenna and Matt, Beth, Ethan, Alessandra, Todd, Suzanne, Sharon, and Cal. Everyone who had done the circle Saturday night. My heart started a slow, dull pound.

Before I got there, Chris walked up and spoke to Bree. Frowning, she headed off with him, talking intently as they walked away.

"Hey, Morgan," said Tamara, walking up to me. I glanced over at Cal. He was talking to Ethan.

"Hi," I said. "How was your weekend?"

"Okay. I called you on Sunday, but I guess you were at church. How was the circle? What happened after I left?"

I grinned. "It was really neat," I said. "We just made a circle and went around the fire. We talked about things we wanted to get rid of."

"Like . . . pollution or what?" asked Tamara.

"Pollution!" I said. "That would have been a good one. I

wish I'd thought of it. No, stuff like anger and fear. Ethan tried to banish his stepmother."

Tamara laughed, and Janice walked up and joined us.

"Hi," she said, pushing her glasses up on her delicate nose. "Listen, Tam, I have to go put a proof up on Dr. Gonzalez's board. Want to come?"

"Sure," said Tamara. "Coming, Morgan?"

"No, that's okay," I said. They walked off, and I headed over to the east-side benches.

"Hey, Morgan," Jenna said, sounding friendly.

"Hi," I said.

"We're talking about our next circle," Raven said. "That is, if you've recovered." Today Raven was wearing a boned maroon corset, a black skirt, black ankle boots, and a black velvet jacket. Eye-catching.

I felt my cheeks heating up. "I'm recovered," I said, playing with the zipper of my hooded sweatshirt.

"It's not unusual for a sensitive person to have some kind of reaction to circles at first," said Cal in his low voice. The timbre of it fluttered in my chest. "I did myself."

"Ooh, sensitive Morgan," said Todd.

"So when's our next circle?" asked Suzanne, flicking back her surfer-blond hair.

Cal looked at her evenly. "I'm afraid you're not invited to our next circle," he said.

Suzanne looked shocked. "What?" she said, forcing a laugh.

"No," Cal continued. "Not you, nor Todd. Nor Alessandra."

The three of them stared at him, and I felt fiercely glad. I remembered how snide they had been on Saturday night. They were part of Bree's clique, and it was unthinkable that someone would stand up to them, would cut them out of something. I was enjoying it.

"What are you talking about?" Todd asked. "Didn't we do it right?" He sounded belligerent, as if trying to cover up embarrassment.

"No," Cal said calmly. "You didn't do it right." He offered no other explanation, and we all stood there, waiting to see what would happen next.

"I don't believe this," said Alessandra.

"I know," Cal said. He sounded almost sympathetic.

Todd, Alessandra, and Suzanne looked at each other, at Cal, and at the rest of us. No one said anything or asked them to stay. It was very odd.

"Huh," said Todd. "I guess we know when we're not wanted. Come on, ladies." He offered his arms to Alessandra and Suzanne, and they had no choice but to take them. They looked humiliated and angry, but they had brought it on themselves.

Daringly, I gave Cal a look of thanks, and he kept his eyes locked on mine for several beats. I couldn't look away.

Suddenly Cal pushed himself off the bench he'd been leaning against and came to stand in front of me. "What do I have behind my back?" he asked.

My brow creased for a second, then I said, "An apple. Green and red." It was as if I had seen it in his hand.

He smiled, and his expressive, gold-colored eyes crinkled at the edges. He brought his hand from around his back and handed me a hard, greenish red apple, with a leaf still attached to its stem.

Feeling awkward and shy, aware of everyone's eyes on me, I took the apple and bit it, hoping juice wouldn't run down my chin.

"Good guess," Raven said, sounding irritated. It occurred to me that she was probably jonesing for Cal big time.

"It wasn't a guess," Cal said softly, his eyes on me.

That afternoon when Mary K. and I got home, we found out that Mr. Herndon from down the street had fallen off a ladder while cleaning his gutters. He had broken his leg. Mary K. started calling me the Amazing Kreskin. I was so freaked out, I called Bree and asked if I could come over after dinner.

8

Cal and Bree

><"There exist Seven Houses of Witchery. They keep to themselves, marrying within their clans. Their children are most unnatural, with night-seeing eyes and inhuman powers."
—WITCHES, MAGES, AND WARLOCKS,
Altus Polydarmus, 1618 ><

There's a spark there. I wasn't wrong. I saw it again today. But she hasn't recognized it yet. I have to wait. She needs to be shown, but very carefully.

Bree answered the door. The night air was brisk, but I was comfy in my sweater.

"Come on in," she said. "Want something to drink? I've got coffee."

"Sounds good," I said, following her to the Warrens' huge, professional-style kitchen. Bree poured two tall mugs of coffee, then added milk and sugar.

"Your dad here?" I asked.

"Yep. Working," she said, stirring. "How unusual."

Mr. Warren is a lawyer. I don't get exactly what he does, but it's the kind of thing where he and a bunch of other lawyers defend big corporations from people who sue them. He makes tons of money but is hardly ever around, at least now that Bree's older.

Five years ago, when Bree was twelve and her brother, Ty, was eighteen, Bree's mom took off and divorced Bree's dad. It was a huge scandal here in Widow's Vale—Mrs. Warren moving to Europe to be with her much younger boyfriend. Bree's seen her mom only once since then and hardly ever talks about her.

Upstairs, in Bree's large bedroom, I dove right in. "I think I'm losing my mind. Do you think the circle was dangerous or something?" I sat nervously upright in her tan suede beanbag chair.

"What are you talking about?" Bree asked, leaning back against the pillows of her double bed. "All we did was dance around in a circle. How could it be dangerous?"

So I told Bree about my newly discovered sixth sense and that it had started after Saturday night. In a rush I told her how I had felt sick Sunday and saw animals around Paula. How I knew about Cal's apple and Mr. Herndon. I reminded her about Mom's phone call.

Bree waved her hand. "Well, if that stuff was happening to me, I might be a little weirded out, too. But I have to tell you—listening to you talk about it, it seems like you might be kind of overreacting," she said gently. "I mean, you might have heard your mom mention the hymn numbers. We already talked about that. Then the phone call—Ms. Fiorello calls your mom all the time, right? God, she's called every time I've been at your house! I can't explain seeing the animals—except maybe your subconscious picked up the scent of all the vet stuff somehow. And the other things—maybe it's just a bunch of weird coincidences all at the same time, so it adds up and freaks you out. But I don't think you're going crazy." She grinned. "At least, not yet."

I felt a little reassured.

"It's just that it's all at once," I explained, "and this whole Wicca thing. Have you been reading about it?"

"Uh-huh. So far I like it. It's all about women," Bree said, and laughed. "No wonder Cal is into it."

I smiled wryly. "Too bad for Justin Bartlett."

"Oh, Justin's dating someone from Seven Oaks," Bree said dismissively. "He can't hog Cal, too. Hey, remember all those Books of Shadows we saw at Practical Magick?"

"Uh-huh," I said.

"They're for witches," Bree said cheerfully. "Witches write down things in their Books of Shadows. Like a diary. They keep notes of spells and stuff they try. Isn't that cool?"

"Yeah," I agreed. "Do you think local witches go there to buy them?"

"Sure," said Bree.

I drank the coffee, hoping it wouldn't keep me up. "Do you think Cal keeps a Book of Shadows?" I asked. "With notes about our circles?" I was leading up to telling Bree about my feelings for Cal, but I was self-conscious. This was bigger and harder to explain than any shallow crush I'd ever had. And even though Bree had named it so casually in Practical Magick, she didn't know how much I liked Cal, how deep my feelings were.

"Ooh, I bet he does," Bree said with interest. "I'd love to see it. I can't wait for our next circle—I already know what I'm going to wear."

I laughed. "And how does Chris feel about this?"

Bree looked solemn for a moment. "It doesn't really matter. I'm going to break up with him."

"Really? That's too bad. You guys had so much fun over the summer." I felt a nervous flutter in my stomach and shifted back in the beanbag chair.

"Yeah, but number one, he's started being a jerk, bossing me around. I mean, screw that."

I nodded in agreement. "Number two?"

"He hates all this Wicca stuff, and I think it's cool. If he isn't going to be supportive of my interests, then who needs him?"

"Too true," I said, looking forward to having her around to hang out with more often, at least until she found his replacement.

"And number three . . . ," she said, twining her short hair around one finger.

"What?" I smiled and drained the last of my coffee.

"I'm totally and completely crazy about Cal Blaire," Bree announced.

For several long moments I sat there, encased by the beanbag. My face was frozen, and so was the breath in my lungs. So much for being the Amazing Kreskin. Why hadn't I seen this coming?

Slowly, slowly, I released my breath. Slowly I drew it in again. "Cal?" I asked, trying to sound calm. "Is that why you want to break up with Chris?"

"No, I told you—Chris is being an ass. I'd break up with him anyway," Bree said, her dark eyes shining in her beautiful face.

Inside my brain, nerve impulses were misfiring frantically, but a new thought managed to formulate. "Is that why *you* like Wicca?" I asked. "Because of Cal?"

"No, not really," Bree said thoughtfully, looking up at the paisley fabric on her bed's canopy. "I think I'd like Wicca even without Cal. But I'm just—falling for him in a big way. I want to be with him. And if we have this huge thing in common . . ." She shrugged. "Maybe it'll help us get together."

I opened my mouth, fearing that a thousand mean, angry, jealous, awful words were about to fly out. I shut it with a snap. So many pained thoughts were swirling in my head that I didn't know where to start. Was I hurt? Angry? Spiteful? This was *Bree*. My best friend for practically my whole life. We had both hated boys in fourth grade. We had both gotten our periods in sixth grade. We'd both had crushes on Hanson in eighth grade. We'd both sworn those crushes to eternal secrecy in ninth.

And now Bree was telling me she was crazy about the only guy I'd ever felt serious about. The only guy I'd ever wanted, even if I knew I couldn't have him.

I should have predicted it. My own feelings had blinded me. Cal is unmistakably gorgeous, and Bree falls in love easily. Obviously Bree would be attracted to him. Obviously Chris would be no competition for a guy like Cal.

Bree was so perfect. So was Cal. They would be awesome together. I felt like I was going to throw up.

"Hmmm," I murmured, my mind racing hysterically. I tried to take a sip from my empty mug. Cal and Bree. Cal and *Bree*.

"You don't approve?" she asked with raised eyebrows.

"Approve, disapprove, what does it matter?" I said, trying to hold my face in some normal position. "It just seems like he's gone out with a couple of different people already. And I think Raven's trying to get her claws into him, too. I don't want you to get hurt," I heard myself babbling.

Bree smiled at me. "Don't worry about me. I think I can handle him. In fact, I *want* to handle him," she joked. "All over."

The forced smile froze on my face. "Well, good luck."

"Thanks," Bree said. "I'll let you know what happens."

"Uh-huh. Um, thanks for listening to me," I said, getting to my feet. "I better get home. See you tomorrow."

I walked out of Bree's room, her house, stiffly and carefully, as if I were trying not to jostle a wound.

I started Das Boot's engine, then realized that chilly tears were sliding down my cheeks. Bree and Cal! Oh God. I would never, ever be with him, and she *would*. It was a physical pain inside my chest, and I cried all the way home.

9
Thirsty

><"Each of the Seven Houses has a name and a craft. An ordinary man has no hope against these witches: better to commend yourself to God than to engage in battle with the Seven Clans."
—THE SEVEN GREAT CLANS,
Thomas Mack, 1845 ><

Am I losing my mind? I'm changing, changing inside. My mind is expanding. I'm seeing in color now instead of black and white. My universe is moving outward at the speed of light. I'm scared.

The next day I woke early after thrashing unhappily all night. I'd had horribly vivid, realistic dreams, mostly featuring Cal—and Bree. I had kicked off my covers and was freezing now, so I grabbed them and burrowed under again, scared to go back to sleep.

Lying in bed, I watched my windows as they gradually grew lighter. I almost never saw this time of morning, and my parents were right: There was something magical about it. By six-thirty my parents were up. It was comforting to hear them moving in the kitchen, making coffee, shaking cereal into bowls. At seven Mary K. was in the shower.

I lay on my side and thought about things. Common sense told me Bree had much more of a chance with Cal than I did. I had no chance. I wasn't in Cal's league, and Bree was. Did I want Bree to be happy? Could I sort of live vicariously through Bree if she went out with Cal?

I groaned. How sick is *that*? I asked myself.

Was I okay with Bree and Cal going out? No. I would rather eat rats. But if I *wasn't* okay with it and they *did* get together (and there was no reason to assume they wouldn't), then it would mean losing Bree's friendship. And probably looking pretty stupid.

By the time my alarm went off for school, I had decided to perform the supreme sacrifice and never let Bree know how I felt about Cal, no matter what happened.

"Some people are coming over to my house on Saturday night," Cal said. "I thought we could do a circle again. It's not a holiday or anything. But it'd be cool for us to get together."

He was hunkered down in front of me, one tanned knee showing through the rip in his faded jeans. My butt was cold as I sat on the school's concrete steps, waiting for the classroom to open up for the math club meeting. As if in recognition of Mabon, last week's autumnal equinox, the air had suddenly acquired a deeper chill.

I let myself drift into his eyes. "Oh," I said, mesmerized by the minute striations of gold and brown circling his pupils.

On Tuesday, Bree had broken up with Chris, and he

hadn't taken it well. By Wednesday, Bree was sitting next to Cal at lunch, showing up at school early to talk to him, hanging out with him as much as she could. According to her, they hadn't kissed yet or anything, but she had hopes. It usually didn't take her very long.

Now it was Thursday, and Cal was talking to me.

"Please come," he said, and I felt like he was offering me something dangerous and forbidden. Other students walked past us in the thin afternoon light, glancing at us with curiosity.

"Um," I said in that stunningly articulate way I have. The truth was, I was dying to do another circle, to explore Wicca in person instead of just reading about it. I felt thirsty for it in a way that was unfamiliar to me.

On the other hand, if I went, I would see Bree go after Cal, right in front of me. Which would be worse, *seeing* her do it or *imagining* her doing it?

"Um, I guess I could," I said.

He smiled, and I literally, *literally* felt my heart flutter. "Don't sound so enthusiastic," he said. I watched in complete amazement as he picked up a strand of my hair that fell near my elbow and gently tugged on it. I know there are no nerve endings in hair, but at that moment I felt some. A hot flush rose from my neck to my forehead. Oh, Jesus, what a dweeb I am, I thought helplessly.

"I've been reading about Wicca," I blurted out to him. "I . . . really like it."

"Yeah?" he said.

"Yeah. It just . . . feels right . . . in some way," I said, hesitating.

"Really? I'm glad to hear you say that. I was worried you would be scared off after the last circle." Cal settled next to me on the steps.

"No," I said eagerly, not wanting the conversation to end. "I mean, I felt crappy afterward, but I felt ... alive, too. It was ... like a revelation for me." I glanced up at him. "I can't explain it."

"You don't have to," he said softly. "I know what you mean."

"Are you—are you in a coven?"

"Not anymore," he said. "I left it behind when we moved. I'm hoping that if some people here are into it, we could form a new one."

I drew in a breath. "You mean, we could just ... do that?"

Have you ever seen a god laugh? It makes you catch your breath and feel hopeful and shivery and excited all at the same time. That's how it was watching Cal.

"Well, not right away," he clarified with a smile. "Typically you have to study for a year and a day before you can ask to actually join a coven."

"A year and a day," I repeated. "And then you're ... what? A witch? Or a warlock?" The names sounded overly dramatic, cartoony. I felt like we were conspirators, the way we were speaking softly, our heads bent toward each other. His silver pendant, which I now knew was a pentacle, a symbol of a witch's belief, dangled in the open vee of his shirt against his skin. Behind Cal, I saw Robbie enter the classroom where the math club was meeting. I would have to go in a minute.

"A witch," Cal said easily. "Even for men."

"Have you done that yet?" I asked. "Been initiated?" The words seemed to have a double meaning, and I prayed I wouldn't blush again.

He nodded. "When I was fourteen."

"Really?"

"Yeah. My mom presided. She's the high priestess of a coven, the Starlocket coven. So I had been studying and learning about it for years. Finally, when I was fourteen, I asked to do it. That was almost four years ago—I'll be eighteen next month."

"Your mom is a high priestess? Does she have a new coven here?" Outside, it was getting dark, and the temperature was dropping. Inside, the math club meeting had already started, and it would be warm and well lit. But Cal was out here.

"Yes," Cal said. "She's pretty famous among Wiccans, so she already knew a bunch of people here when we moved. I go to her circles sometimes, but they're mostly older people. Besides, part of being a witch is teaching others what you know."

"So you're actually a—witch," I said slowly, taking it in.

"Yep." Cal smiled again and stood up, holding out his hand. Awkwardly I let him pull me to my feet. "And who knows?" he said. "Maybe this time next year, you will be, too. And Raven and Robbie and anyone else, if they want."

Another smile and he was gone, and then it really was dark outside.

10

Fire

><"If a woman lies with a witch of the Seven Houses, she will bear no child except he wills it. If a man lies with a witch of the Seven Houses, she will bear no child."

—THE WAYS OF WITCHES,
Gunnar Thorvildsen, 1740 ><

Tonight I sent a message. Will you dream of me? Will you come to me?

"The movie is supposed to be great. Don't you want to see it? And Bakker's going to be there," Mary K. said. She came through the bathroom that connected our two rooms, pulling on her shirt. In front of my full-length mirror she turned, looking at herself from all angles. She gave her mirror image a big smile.

"I can't," I said, wondering why my fourteen-year-old sister had gotten not only her share of the family chest but my share, too, apparently. "I'm going to a party. Where are you all meeting?"

"At the theater," she said. "Jaycee's mom is driving us. Do you like Bakker? He's in your class."

"He's okay," I said. "He seems like a nice guy. Cute." I had a thought. "I heard he's been crushing on you. He's not being too—pushy, is he?"

"Uh-uh," Mary K. said confidently. "He's been really sweet." She turned to look at me as I stood in my underwear in front of my open closet. "Where's the party? What are you going to wear?"

"At Cal Blaire's house, and I don't know," I admitted.

"Ooh, that new senior," said Mary K., coming over to shove clothes around. "He is so hot. Everyone I know wants to go out with him. God, Morgan, your clothes really need help."

"Thank you," I said, and she laughed.

"Here, this is good," she said, pulling out a shirt. "You never wear this."

It was a dark olive green, thin, stretchy top that my other aunt, Margaret, had given me. Aunt Margaret is my mom's older sister. I love her, but she and Aunt Eileen haven't talked in years, ever since Eileen came out. Since Aunt Margaret had given me the sweater, I felt disloyal to Aunt Eileen when I wore it. Call me oversensitive.

"I hate that color," I said.

"No," Mary K. said emphatically. "It would be perfect with your eyes. Put it on. And wear your black leggings with it."

I scrambled into the shirt. Downstairs, the doorbell rang, and I heard Bree's voice. "Oh, no way," I protested. The shirt barely came down to my waist. "This isn't long enough. My ass will be hanging out."

"So let it," Mary K. advised. "You have a great ass."

"What?" Bree came in. "I heard that. That shirt looks great. Let's go."

Bree looked amazing, like a glowing topaz. Perfect, flyaway hair accentuated her eyes, making them striking. Her wide mouth was tinted a soft shade of brown, and she was almost quivering with energy and excitement. She wore a clingy brown velvet top that accentuated her boobs and low-slung drawstring pants. A good three inches of tight, flat stomach showed. Around her perfect belly button she had put a temporary tattoo of sun rays.

Next to her I felt like a two-by-four.

Mary K. shoved the leggings at me, and I put them on, no longer at all concerned about how I would look. A plaid flannel shirt of my dad's completed my ensemble and covered my butt. I brushed my hair while Bree tapped her feet with impatience.

"We can take Breezy," she said. "She's working again."

Minutes later I was sitting on a prewarmed leather seat as Bree stomped on the gas and flew down my street.

"What time do you have to be home?" she asked. "This may go till late." It was barely nine o'clock.

"My curfew's at one," I said. "But my folks will probably be asleep and won't know if I'm a little later. Or I could call them or something." Bree never has to call home and check with her dad about anything. Sometimes they seem more like roommates than father and daughter.

"Cool." Bree tapped her brown fingernails against the steering wheel, took a turn a bit too fast, and headed out Gallows Road to one of the older neighborhoods in Widow's Vale. Cal's neighborhood. She already knew the way.

*   *   *

Cal's house was awesome, huge, and made of stone. The wide front porch supported an upstairs balcony, and evergreen vines climbed up the columns to the second floor. The front garden was lush and beautifully landscaped and just on the verge of wildness. I thought of my dad humming as he pruned his rhododendrons every autumn and felt almost sad.

The wide wooden door opened in answer to our knock, and a woman stood there, dressed in a long linen dress the dark purple-blue of the night sky. It was elegant and simple and had probably cost a fortune.

"Welcome, girls," the woman said with a smile. "I'm Cal's mother, Selene Belltower."

Her voice was powerful and melodious, and I felt a tingling sense of expectation. When I got closer to her, I saw that Cal had inherited her coloring. Dark brown hair was swept carelessly back from her face. Wide, golden eyes slanted over high cheekbones. Her mouth was well shaped, her skin smooth and unlined. I wondered if she had been a model when she was younger.

"Let me guess—you must be Bree," she said, shaking Bree's hand. "And *you* must be Morgan." Her clear eyes met mine, her gaze seeming to pierce the back of my skull. I blinked and rubbed my forehead. I was actually physically uncomfortable. Then she smiled again, the pain went away, and she ushered us inside. "I'm so glad he's made new friends. It was hard for us to move, but my company offered me a promotion, and I couldn't say no."

I wanted to ask what her job was or find out what had happened to Cal's dad, but there was no way to ask without being rude.

"Cal's in his room. Third floor, at the top of the stairs,"

said Ms. Belltower, gesturing to the impressive carved stair-case. "Some of the others are here already."

"Thanks," we both said a bit awkwardly as we climbed the dark, wooden staircase. Beneath our feet a thick flow-ered carpet cushioned our steps.

"She doesn't think it's weird to let a bunch of girls into her teenage son's bedroom?" I whispered, thinking about how my mom kicks boys out of Mary K.'s room at home.

Bree smiled at me, her eyes shining with excitement. "I guess she's cool," she whispered back. "Besides, there's a bunch of us."

Cal's room turned out to be the entire attic of the house. It went from front to back, side to side, and there were small windows everywhere: some square, some round, some clear, some made of stained glass. The roof itself was pitched steeply and rose to about nine feet in the center, only about three feet at the sides. The floor was dark, unpol-ished wood, the walls unpainted clapboards. In one small gable was an antique desk with school textbooks on it.

We dropped our jackets on a long wooden bench, and I kicked off my clogs, following Bree's example.

A small working fireplace was set into one wall. Its plain mantel was covered with cream-colored candles of various sizes, maybe thirty of them. Pillars of candles stood around the huge room, some on black wrought-iron stands, some on the floor, some atop glass blocks or even set on top of stacks of ancient-looking books. The room was lit only by candlelight, and the wavering shadows thrown on every wall were hypnotic and beautiful.

My eyes were caught by Cal's bed, standing off in a larger

alcove. I couldn't help staring at it, feeling frozen to the spot. It was a wide, low bed of dark wood, mahogany or even ebony, with four short bedposts. The mattress was a futon. The bedclothes were of plain, cream-colored linen, and the bed was unmade. As if he had just gotten out of it. Lit candles burned brightly on low tables at either side.

In the far alcove against the back wall of the house, bathed in shadows, the rest of the group was gathered. When Cal saw us, he came over.

"Morgan. Thanks for coming," he said in his confident, intimate way. "Bree, nice to have you back."

So Bree had been in his bedroom.

"Thanks for inviting me," I said stiffly, pulling my flannel shirt closer around me. Cal smiled and took both of our hands, leading us to the others. Robbie waved when he saw us. He was drinking dark grape juice from a wine goblet. Beth Nielson stood next to him, her hair newly bleached pale blond. She had medium brown skin, green eyes, and a short-cropped Afro that changed colors with her mood. Sometimes I thought of her looking like a lioness, while Raven looked like a panther. They made an interesting pair if they stood next to each other.

"Happy esbat," Robbie said, raising his glass.

"Happy esbat," Bree said. I knew from my reading that *esbat* was just another word for a gathering where magick was done.

Matt was sitting on a low velvet settee, with Jenna curled on his lap. They were talking to Sharon Goodfine, who was sitting stiffly on the floor, her arms around her knees. Was she here just for Cal, or had Wicca spoken to her somehow?

I had always thought of her as having it easy, with her ortho-
dontist father smoothing her path through life. She was full
figured and pretty and looked older than she was.

"Here." Cal handed Bree and me wineglasses of grape
juice. I took a sip.

A patchouli-scented breeze washed into the room, and
Raven arrived, followed by Ethan. Tonight Raven looked like a
hooker who specialized in S and M. A black leather dog collar circled her neck. It was connected by leather straps to a
black leather corset. Her pants looked like someone had
dipped her in a vat of shiny black spandex, and this was the
dried result. She wouldn't have stood out in New York City,
but here in Widow's Vale, I would have given money to see
her walk into the grocery store. Did Cal find this attractive?

Ethan looked like he always did: scruffy, with long, curly
hair, and stoned. It hadn't seemed odd to me that people
would have stayed the first time we did a circle—lots of kids
will try anything once. But it was interesting that everyone
except Todd, Alessandra, and Suzanne had come back, and it
made me look at them more closely, as if I were seeing all of
them for the first time.

This group had hung out a few times at school in a new,
multiclique assemblage, but here we separated into our old
patterns: Robbie and I together; Jenna, Matt, and Sharon together, with Bree going between me and them; Beth, Raven,
and Ethan together by the drinks.

"Good, I think everyone's here," Cal said. "Last week we
celebrated Mabon and did a banishing circle. This week I
thought we'd just have an informal circle and get to know
each other better. So, let's begin."

Cal picked up a piece of white chalk and drew a large

circle that almost filled this end of the attic. Jenna and Matt got up and pushed the sofa out of the way.

"This circle can be made out of anything," Cal said conversationally as he drew. On the floor were the smudged and faded outlines of other circles. I noticed that although he was drawing freehand, the end result was almost perfectly round and symmetrical, as it had been in the woods when he had drawn a circle in the dirt with a stick. "It can be a piece of rope, a circle of objects, like shells or tarot cards, even flowers. It represents the boundary of our magick energy."

We all stepped inside the chalk circle. Cal drew the circle closed, as he had done last week. What would happen if one of us stepped outside it?

Cal picked up a small brass bowl filled with something white. For a worried moment I thought it was cocaine or something, but he picked some up in his fingers and sprinkled it all around the circle.

"With this salt, I purify our circle," he said. I remembered he had sprinkled salt last time. Cal placed the bowl on the circle's line. "Placing this bowl here, in the north position, signifies one of the four elements: earth. Earth is feminine and nourishing."

In the last several days I had gone online and done some research. I had found out that there were lots of different sects of Wicca, as there are different sects of almost every religion. I had focused on the one that Cal had said he was a part of and had found more than a thousand Web sites.

Next Cal put an identical small brass bowl, filled with sand and a burning stick of incense, at the east side of the circle.

"This incense symbolizes air, another of the four elements," Cal said, focused but utterly relaxed. "Air is for the mind, the intellect. Communication."

In the south he stood a cream-colored pillar candle about eighteen inches high. "This candle represents fire, the third element," Cal explained, looking at me. "Fire is for transformation, success, and passion. It's a very strong element."

I felt uncomfortable under his gaze and looked down at the candle instead. Firelight, my soul is bright, I thought.

Finally, at the western side, Cal put a brass bowl filled with water. "Water is the last of the four elements," he said. "Water is for emotions. For love, beauty, and healing. Each of the four elements corresponds to astrological signs," Cal explained. "Gemini, Libra, and Aquarius are the air signs. The water signs are Cancer, Scorpio, and Pisces. Earth signs are Taurus, Virgo, and Capricorn. Aries, Leo, and Sagittarius are fire signs." Cal looked at me again.

Could he tell I was a fire sign—a Sagittarius?

"Now, let's join hands," he said.

I was closest to Robbie and Matt, so I took their hands. Robbie's hand was warm and comforting. It felt strange to be holding Matt's hand, smooth and cool. I remembered how Cal's had felt and wished I was standing next to him again. Instead he was sandwiched between Bree and Raven. I sighed.

"Let's close our eyes and focus our thoughts," said Cal, bowing his head. "Breathe in and out slowly, to the count of four. Let every thought still, every worry fade. There is no past, no future, only the here and now and we ten standing together." His voice was even and calm. I bowed my head and closed my eyes. I breathed in and out, thinking about candlelight and incense. It was very relaxing. Part of me was aware of everyone else in the room, their quiet breathing and the occasional shifting of their feet, and part of me felt very pure and removed, as if I were floating over this circle, watching it from above.

"Tonight we're going to do a purifying and focusing ritual," Cal explained. "Samhain, our new year, is coming up, and most witches do a lot of spiritual work to get ready."

Once again we moved in a circle together, holding hands, but this time we moved slowly in a clockwise direction— deasil, Cal called it, as opposed to widdershins, which is counterclockwise.

For a moment I felt nervous about the end of the ritual. The last time I had done this, I had felt like someone had buried an ax in my chest, then felt like crap for two days afterward. Would that happen again? I decided it didn't matter, that I wanted to try this. Then Cal began the chant.

"Water, cleanse us,
Air, purify us.
Fire, make us whole and pure.
Earth, center us."

We began to repeat his words. For several minutes or maybe longer we moved in a circle, chanting. Glancing around the circle, I saw people starting to relax, as if they felt lighthearted and happy. Even Ethan and Raven seemed lighter, younger, and less dark. Bree was watching Cal. Robbie had his eyes closed.

We began moving faster and chanting louder. It was right after this that I became aware of palpable energy building up around me, within the circle. I looked around quickly, startled. Cal, across the circle, met my eyes and smiled. Raven's eyes were closed now as she chanted and moved unerringly in our line. The others looked intense but not alarmed.

I felt pressed in upon somehow. As if a big, soft bubble were pressing in on me, all around me. My hair felt alive and crackling with energy, and when I next looked up at Cal, I gasped because I could see Cal's aura, glowing faintly around his head.

I was awestruck. A fuzzy band of pale red light was glowing around him, shimmering in the candlelight. When I glanced around the circle, I saw that everyone had one. Jenna's was silver. Matt's was green. Raven's was orange, and Robbie was surrounded by white. Bree had a pale orange light, Beth had a black one, Ethan's was brown, and Sharon's was pink, like her flushed cheeks. Did I have an aura? What color was it? What did this mean? I stared, marveling, feeling joyful and amazed.

As before, at some unseen signal the circle stopped abruptly and we all threw our hands into the air, our arms outstretched. My heart throbbed, and so did my head, but I didn't stumble or lose my balance. I just pulled in a fast breath and grimaced, rubbing my temples and hoping that no one noticed.

"Send the cleansing energy into yourselves!" Cal said firmly, making a fist and thumping it against his chest. Everyone did the same, and when I did, I felt a great warmth rush in and settle in my abdomen. I felt calm, peaceful, and alert. Immediately after that I became nauseated and sick. Oh, help, I thought.

Cal instantly crossed the circle and came over to me. I was swallowing hard, my eyes big, hoping I wouldn't be sick right there. I just wanted to cry.

"Sit down," Cal said softly, pushing on my shoulders. "Sit down right now."

I sat on the wooden floor, feeling motion sick and awful.

"What is it *this* time?" Raven said, and no one answered.

"Lean over," Cal said. I was sitting cross-legged, and he gently pushed on the back of my neck. "Touch your forehead to the floor," he instructed, and I did, rounding my back and flattening my hands, palms down. Instantly I felt better. As soon as my forehead touched the cool wood, with my hands braced on both sides of me, the waves of sickness passed, and I quit gasping.

"Are you okay?" Bree knelt next to me, rubbing my back. I felt Cal brush her hand away.

"Wait," he said. "Wait until she's grounded."

"What's wrong?" Jenna asked, concerned.

"She channeled too much energy," Cal said, keeping his hand on the base of my neck. "Like at Mabon. She's very, very sensitive; a real energy conduit."

After a minute or so he asked, "Better now?"

"Uh-huh," I said, slowly raising my head. I looked around, feeling embarrassed and vulnerable. But physically I was fine, no longer queasy or disoriented.

"Do you want to tell us what happened?" Cal asked gently. "What you saw?"

The idea of describing everyone's auras seemed intimidating—too personal. Besides, hadn't they seen them, too? I wasn't sure. "No," I said.

"Okay," he said, standing up. He smiled. "That was amazing, you-all. Thanks. Now, let's go swimming."

11

Water

>< "Nights of a full moon or the new moon are especially powerful for working magick."

—PRACTICAL LUNAR RITUALS,
Marek Hawksight, 1978 ><

"Oh, yeah," Bree said enthusiastically. "Swimming!"

"There's a pool out back," Cal said, crossing the room. He opened a wooden door set back into an alcove. Brisk night air swirled into the room, making some flames go out and others dance.

"Okay," Jenna said. "That sounds great."

Ethan looked hot, his forehead damp beneath the tightly curled ringlets on his head. He wiped his face on the sleeve of his army-surplus shirt. "Swimming would be cool."

Raven and Beth smiled at each other like the Siamese cats in *Lady and the Tramp*, then headed to the door. Robbie nodded at me and followed them. Bree was already through the door.

"Um, is this an outdoor pool?" I asked.

Cal smiled at me. "The water's heated. It'll be okay."

Of course, the huge thing going through my mind was that I hadn't brought a bathing suit, but somehow I felt if I mentioned this, everyone would laugh at me. I went through the door after Sharon, followed by Cal. Outside was a spiral staircase, and its steps led all the way down to the first floor, to the patio. I gripped the banister tightly and went down, hoping not to lose my balance.

Behind me I felt Cal's hand on my shoulder. "Okay?" he asked.

I nodded. "Uh-huh."

A cut-stone patio, pale in the moonlight, met the edge of the staircase. Outdoor furniture, covered with water-proof covers, looked like blocky ghosts. On the far side a bank of tall shrubs pruned into neat rectangular shapes sep-arated the patio from the yard beyond. A doorway was cut into the shrubs, and Cal pointed to it.

I looked up at the sky, shivering without my jacket or shoes. The waxing moon looked like a bitten sugar cookie in the sky. Its light shone down, illuminating our path.

Through the hedge doorway was a pristine lawn of smooth, soft grass, not yet brown. It felt like velvet moss be-neath my bare feet.

Beyond the lawn was the pool. It was classical in design, almost Greek looking. It was a simple rectangular shape, with no diving board, no metal handrail anywhere. At each end was a series of tall stone columns, grown over with vines that were starting to lose their summer leaves. To one side was a cabana with several doors, and I began to hope that maybe his family kept all kinds of bathing suits there for people to borrow.

Then I saw that Jenna and Matt were already shimmying out of their clothes, and my eyes opened wide. Oh, no, I thought. No way. I whirled to find Bree, only to see that she was behind me, in her bra and underwear, dropping her clothes neatly onto a chaise longue.

"Bree!" I hissed as she undid her bra. She pushed off her undies, looking like a beautiful, moonlit marble statue. Raven and Beth were undoing hooks and buttons for each other, laughing, their teeth white in the moonlight. Naked, they ran to the pool and jumped in, their jewelry jangling cheerfully.

Next Jenna and Matt slipped into the water, Matt following Jenna as she moved across the dark expanse. Jenna laughed and went under, then surfaced, sleeking back her hair. She looked timeless, almost pagan. Sweat broke out on my forehead. Please don't let this turn into an orgy or anything, I begged whoever was listening to my thoughts. I am so not ready for this.

"Relax," Cal said behind me. I heard the rustling of his clothes and willed myself not to faint. In another minute I would see him naked. Cal, naked. All of him. Oh my God. I wanted to see him but was also writhing inside with uncertainty. He put his hand on my shoulder, and I jumped about a foot in the air.

"Relax," he said again, turning me to face him. He had taken off his shirt but was still wearing his jeans. "It's not going to turn into an orgy."

I was startled by how accurately he had read my thoughts.

"I wasn't worried about that," I said, appalled to hear a faint tremble in my voice. "It's just ... I catch cold easily."

He laughed and started undoing his jeans. My breath got stuck in my throat. "You won't catch cold," he said.

He pushed down his jeans, and I spun to face the swimming pool. I was rewarded by the sight of a naked Robbie walking down the broad steps into the water. What next?

Ethan was sitting on a chaise, peeling off his socks. His shirt was off, a lit cigarette dangled from his mouth, and his fatigue pants were unbuttoned and partially unzipped. He took a last drag on his cigarette and stubbed it out on the ground. Then he stood and dropped his pants as Bree and Sharon walked past him to the pool. His eyes narrowed and locked on their bodies, then he kicked off his pants and followed them. At the deep end he jumped in cleanly, and I prayed he knew how to swim and wasn't so stoned he would drown.

Raven and Beth were splashing each other, then Beth squealed and jumped, her dark body sleek and sparkling with water drops. Ethan surfaced close by, grinning like a fox. With his hair wet and off his face and out of his sloppy clothes, he was cuter than usual, and Sharon looked at him in surprise, as if wondering who he was.

Cal walked past me. "Come on, Morgan," he said, holding out his hand. He was completely starkers, and my cheeks turned to fire as I tried not to look down.

"I can't," I whispered, hoping no one else could hear me. I felt like such a sissy. I glanced over to the pool and saw Bree watching us. I gave her a weak smile, and she smiled back, her eyes on Cal.

He waited. If he and I had been alone, I might have gotten over myself. Maybe I could have taken off my clothes and prayed he wasn't a boob man. But every girl here was prettier than I was and had a better body. Every one of them had bigger breasts than me. Sharon's were humongous.

I needed an out. I was overwhelmed to begin with, and this was just too much.

"Please come swimming," Cal said. "No one will attack you. I promise."

"It isn't that," I muttered. I wanted to look at him, but I couldn't look at him with him looking at me. A storm of self-consciousness raged inside me.

"There are a lot of special aspects to water," Cal said patiently. "Being surrounded by water, especially under the moon, can be very magickal, a very special kind of energy. I want you to feel that. Just wear your bra and underwear."

"I don't wear a bra," I said, then instantly wanted to kick myself.

He grinned. "Really."

"I don't exactly need to," I mumbled unhappily.

He cocked his head, still grinning. "Really," he said.

I panicked, my breaking point reached.

"I have to get home. Thanks for the circle," I said, turning to go. I had come here in Bree's car, so I figured I had a long, chilly walk ahead of me. To go from the wonder and amazement of the circle to this painful humiliation seemed too much to bear. I couldn't wait till I was home, in my own bed.

Then Cal's hand snaked out and gripped the back of my shirt. With a gentle tug he drew me toward him. I wasn't breathing or thinking anymore. He bent over, put an arm under my knees, and picked me up. Strangely, I remember not feeling heavy or clumsy, but light and small in his arms. I stopped processing sensations in any normal way. I stopped being aware of the other people nearby.

He walked steadily down the pool steps into the shallow end. I didn't protest; I didn't say anything at all. I don't know if I could have. Then we were surrounded by water the exact temperature of my blood, and we were in the water, pressed together under the moon.

It was terrifying, strange, mysterious, thrilling, crushing.

And it was magickal.

12

What Goes Around

><"Should you be caught amidst two warring clans,
lie belly to earth and say your prayers."

—Old Scottish saying ><

When I got home from church the next day, Bree was sitting on our front steps, looking chilly and pissed.

I'd caught a ride home with Beth the night before because I had a curfew and Bree didn't. But I knew from the stony looks Bree gave me as I hurried from Cal's house that this was coming.

We went inside and up to my room.

"I thought you were my friend," she hissed as soon as the door was shut.

I didn't pretend not to know what she was talking about. "Of course I'm your friend," I said, unbuttoning the dress I had worn to church.

"Then explain last night to me," she said, her dark eyes narrowed. She crossed her arms over her chest and dropped onto the edge of my bed. "You and Cal, in the swimming pool."

I pulled a shirt over my head, then grabbed some socks out of my drawer. "I don't know *how* to explain it," I said. "I mean, I know you like Cal. I know I'm not competition for you. I didn't do anything. I mean, God, as soon as I could stand up in the water, he put me down." I tugged on my socks and slithered into my oldest, most comfortable jeans, automatically turning them up an inch on the bottoms.

"Well, what was the big coy act about before that? Were you playing hard to get? Were you hoping he would just rip your clothes off?" There was a sneer in her voice that stung, and I felt the first threads of anger rising in me.

"Of course not!" I snapped. "If he had ripped my clothes off, I would have run home screaming and called the cops. Don't be an idiot."

Bree stood up and jabbed her finger at me. "Don't *you* be an idiot!" she said. I had never seen her like this. "You know I'm in love with him!" Bree said, her face furious. "I don't just *like* him! I *love* him. And I want him. And I want *you* to leave him alone!"

"Fine!" I practically yelled. I stood and spread my arms wide. "But I wasn't doing anything, and I can't control what *he* does! Maybe he's just paying attention to me because he wants me to be a witch." As soon as I said that, Bree and I stared at each other. In my heart, I suddenly felt it was true. Bree's brow wrinkled as she thought back through the night before.

"Look," I said more calmly. "I don't know what he's doing.

For all I know, he has another girlfriend somewhere, or maybe Raven has already gotten to him. But I do know that *I* am not coming on to *him*. That's all I can tell you. And that'll have to be good enough." I pulled my hair over my shoulder and started to braid it with quick, practiced motions.

Bree glared at me for another moment, and then her face crumpled and she sank down on my bed. "Okay," she said, sounding like she was trying not to cry. "You're right. I'm sorry. You weren't doing anything. I was just jealous, that's all." She put her hands over her face and leaned down against my pillows. "When I saw him holding you, I just went crazy. I've never wanted anyone this bad before, and I've been working on him all week, and he doesn't seem to notice me."

I was still angry, but perversely, I also felt sorry for her. "Bree," I said, sitting down in my desk chair. "Cal left his coven behind when he moved, and he's hoping some of us will help him start a new coven. He knows I'm interested in Wicca, and I guess he thinks it's, I don't know, interesting or something that I have such a strong reaction to circles. Maybe he thinks I could be a good witch, and that's what he wants."

Bree looked up, her eyes filled with tears. "Do you really have a strong reaction to circles, or are you just pretending to?" she asked, her voice wobbly.

My eyes almost popped out of my head. "Bree! For God's sake! Why would I pretend that? It's embarrassing and uncomfortable." I shook my head. "It's like you don't even *know* me or something. But to answer your question," I said tersely, "no, I'm not *pretending* to have a strong reaction."

Bree covered her face with her hands and started crying. "I'm sorry," she sobbed. "I didn't mean that. I know you aren't pretending. I don't know what I'm doing." She stood up and grabbed a tissue from the box, then came over and hugged me. It was hard for me to hug her back, but in the end of course I did. "I'm sorry," she said again, crying against me. "I'm sorry, Morgan."

We stood there with her crying for a few minutes, and I felt like crying myself. Have you ever been afraid to start crying because you weren't sure if you'd be able to stop? That's how I felt. To fight with Bree about anything was horrible. To want Cal and not ever be able to have him made me feel desperate. For my best friend to want the same guy I did was a nightmare. To discover the complicated world of Wicca and feel drawn to it was confusing and almost scary.

Finally Bree's crying quieted, and she disentangled herself from me, wiping her nose and eyes. "I'm so sorry," she whispered. "Do you forgive me?"

I hesitated only a moment, then nodded. I mean, I love Bree. After my family, I love her the best in the world. I sighed, and we moved over to sit on my narrow bed.

"Look," I said. "Last night I didn't want to take off my clothes because—I'm shy. I admit it, okay? I'm a total wuss. You couldn't pay me enough money to stand naked next to you and those other girls."

Bree sniffled and turned to look at me. "What are you talking about?"

"Bree, please," I said. "I know what I look like. I have a mirror. I'm not a total woofer, but I'm not you. I'm not Jenna. I'm not even Mary K."

"You look fine," Bree said, frowning.

I rolled my eyes. "Bree. I'm pretty plain. And surely you've noticed that somehow nature has forgotten to give me any kind of bazongas."

Bree's dark eyes glanced quickly to my chest, and I crossed my arms.

"No, you're just, you know," Bree said lamely.

"I just am completely and totally flat chested," I said. "So if you think I'm going to go prancing around naked with you, Miss 36C, Jenna, Raven, Beth, and Miss January Sharon Goodfine, you are out of your mind. And in front of guys, people we go to school with! Give me a break! Like I really want Ethan Sharp to know what I look like naked. Jesus! No way!"

"Don't take the Lord's name in vain," Mary K. said, poking her head through the bathroom door. "Who were you prancing around naked with?"

"Oh, crap, Mary K.!" I said. "I didn't know you were there!"

She smirked at me. "Obviously. Now, who were you prancing around naked with? Can I go next time? I like my body."

I started laughing and threw a pillow at her. Bree was laughing, too, and I was relieved to see that our fight appeared to be over.

"You are not getting naked anywhere," I said, trying to sound stern. "You're fourteen years old, no matter what Bakker Blackburn thinks."

"Are you dating Bakker?" Bree asked. "I went out with him."

"Really?" said Mary K.

"Oh, that's right," I said. "I forgot."

"We went out a couple of times freshman year," Bree said. She sat up and stretched, arching her back.

"What happened?" Mary K. asked.

"I dumped him," said Bree without remorse. "Ranjit asked

me out, and I said yes. Ranjit has the most beautiful eyes."

"Then Ranjit dumped you to go out with Leslie Raines," I said, the whole story coming back to me. "They're still going out."

Bree shrugged. "What goes around comes around."

Which, of course, is one of the most basic Wiccan tenets.

13

Stirring

><"If you look, you will see the mark of a House on its progeny. These marks take many forms, but a trained witchfinder can always discover one."
—NOTES OF A SERVANT OF GOD,
Brother Paolo Frederico, 1693><

I don't understand my mother at all. It's not as if I've done something wrong. I hope she calms down. She has to, she just has to.

On Monday afternoon I skipped chess club and drove to Red Kill, to Practical Magick. As I drove, I soaked up my favorite signs of autumn: trees streaked with bright, vivid colors, protesting the little death of winter. Tall roadside grasses were feathery and tan. Small farmers' stands sold pumpkins, late corn, squash, apples, apple pies.

In Red Kill, I found a parking spot right in front of the store. Inside, it was again dim and full of the rich smells of herbs, oils, and incense. I breathed deeply as my eyes adjusted to the light. This time there were more customers than the last time.

I worked my way down the rows of books, looking for a general history of Wicca. Last night I had finished my book on the Seven Great Clans, and I was hungry for more information.

The first person I ran into was Paula Steen, my aunt's new girlfriend. She was crouched on the floor, examining books along the bottom shelf. Paula looked up, saw me, recognized me, and smiled. "Morgan!" she said, standing up. "Fancy meeting you here. How are you?"

"Oh, okay," I said, making myself smile back. "How are you?"

I liked Paula a lot, but this was a weird place to run into her, and I felt slightly nervous about it. She would mention it to Aunt Eileen, and Aunt Eileen would tell my mom. I wasn't keeping anything secret from my parents, exactly, but I hadn't gone out of my way to tell them about the circles or Cal or Wicca, either.

"Fine," she said. "Overworked, as usual. Today one of my surgery patients canceled, so I played hooky and came here." She looked around the store. "I love this place. They have all kinds of neat stuff."

"Yeah," I said. "Are you . . . into Wicca?"

"No, not me." Paula laughed. "I know lots of people who are, though. It's so pro-woman, it's sometimes popular with lesbians. But I'm still Jewish. I'm here looking at homeopathic books about animal medicine. I just went to a conference where they taught a course on pet massage, and I'm looking for more information."

"Really?" I grinned. "You mean, like giving your German shepherd a rubdown?"

Paula laughed again. "Kind of," she said. "Just like with people, there's a lot to be said for the healing touch."

"Cool," I said.

"Anyway, how about you? Are you into Wicca?"

"Well . . . I'm curious about it," I said in a measured tone, not wanting to blurt out all my messy feelings. "I'm Catholic and everything, like my parents," I went on in a rush. "But I do think Wicca is . . . interesting."

"Like anything else, it's what you bring to it," Paula said.

"Yes," I agreed. "That's true."

"Okay, I better run, Morgan. Good seeing you again."

"You too. Tell Aunt Eileen I said hi."

Paula took her books and checked out, and I examined the shelves again. I found a book that offered a broad general history and also explained the differences between some of the different branches of Wicca: Pecti-Wita, Caledonii, Celtic, Teutonic, Strega, and others I had learned about on the Internet. Tucking it under my arm, I looked through the stuff on the other side: the incense, the mortars and pestles, the candles separated by color. I saw one candle that was in the shape of a man and a woman joined, and it made me think first of me and Cal. Then my mind jumped to Bree and Cal. If I burned that candle, would Cal be mine? What would Bree do?

It was stupid even thinking about it.

I got in line, the scents of cinnamon and nutmeg all around me.

"Why, Morgan, dear, is that you?"

I whirled to find myself looking into the face of Mrs.

Petrie, a woman from my church. "Hi, Mrs. Petrie," I said a bit
stiffly. What a strange run of luck. Somehow I'd expected
more privacy on my little adventure this afternoon.

Mrs. Petrie was shorter than me now but hadn't changed
in looks for as long as I could remember. She always wore
tidy two-piece suits, stockings, and matching shoes. In church
she wore matching hats.

Now she read my book's title. "You must be doing research for a school project," she said, smiling.

"Yes," I said, nodding. "We're studying different religions
of the world."

"How interesting." She leaned closer to me and lowered
her voice. "This is a very unique bookstore. Some of the things
in here are awful, but the people who run it are very nice."

"Oh," I said. "Um, why are you here?"

Mrs. Petrie motioned over at the spices-and-herbs wall.
"You know I'm famous for my herb garden," she said
proudly. "I'm one of their suppliers. I also grow herbs for
some of the restaurants in town and for Nature's Way, the
health food store on Main."

"Oh, really? I didn't know that," I said blankly.

"Yes," she said. "I was just dropping off some dried thyme
and some of last summer's caraway seeds. Now I must run.
Good seeing you, dear. Tell your parents hello."

"Sure will," I said. "See you Sunday." Yes, indeed. I was relieved when she disappeared through the door.

I was so preoccupied with unexpected encounters that I
had forgotten how oddly the clerk had behaved last time.
But as I pushed my books across the counter, I felt his eyes
on me again.

Wordlessly I took out my wallet and counted money.

"I thought you'd be back," he said softly, ringing up my books.

I stood stone-faced, not looking at him.

"You have the mark of the Goddess on you," he said. "Do you know your clan?"

My eyes flew to his, startled. "I'm not from any clan," I said.

The clerk cocked his head thoughtfully. "Are you sure?"

He handed me my change, and I took it, then grabbed my book and got out of there. As I cranked Das Boot's big, V-8 engine, I thought about the Seven Great Clans. Over the last few hundred years they had been disbanded and hardly existed anymore. I shook my head. The only clan I was a part of was the Rowlands clan, no matter what the clerk thought.

I took the small roads home and let the fiery leaves blur into the background as I sank into the daydream I was indulging in more and more often: the cherished moment, under the moon, when Cal carried me into the water. Fantasy and memory ran together, and I wasn't even sure it had actually happened anymore.

That night Mary K. made dinner, and it was my turn to clean up. I stood at the sink, rinsing plates, daydreaming about Cal, wondering if Bree and Cal had gotten together today after school. Had they kissed yet? It made my chest feel tight, and I commanded my mind not to torture me anymore.

Why had Cal come into my life? I couldn't help wondering.

It felt like he was here for a purpose. I hoped it wasn't some sort of cruel karmic payback.

I shook my head, squishing suds through my fingers. Get over yourself, I thought as I started to load plates into the dishwasher.

"What clan are you?" the clerk had asked. He might as well have asked me, "What planet are you from?" Obviously I wasn't from one of the Seven Clans, though it was interesting to think about. It would be kind of like finding out your real father was a famous celebrity who wanted you back. The Seven Great Clans were the celebrities of Wicca, supposedly possessing supernatural powers and thousands of years of shared history.

I rearranged the glasses in the top tier of the dishwasher. My book had said the Seven Clans stayed apart from the rest of humanity for so long that they actually had a separate and distinct genetic makeup. My parents . . . my family. We were as normal as they came. The clerk was just messing with me.

All of a sudden I dropped the sponge I'd been holding and stood up straight. I frowned and glanced out the window. It was dark. I glanced around the room, feeling a strong sense of . . . I wasn't sure what. A storm coming? Some vague feeling of danger was stirring the air.

I'd just snapped the dishwasher door shut when the kitchen door swung open. My parents stood there, my dad looking rattled and my mom tight-lipped and upset.

"What's wrong?" I said, turning off the water, feeling my heart begin to thump.

My mom ran her hand through her straight russet hair, so

like Mary K.'s. "Are these yours?" she asked. "These books about witches?" She held up the books I had bought at Practical Magick.

"Uh-huh," I said. "So what?"

"Why do you have them?" my mom asked. She hadn't changed out of her work clothes, and she looked rumpled and tired.

"It's interesting," I said, dumbfounded by her tone.

My parents looked at each other. The overhead light glinted off my dad's balding spot.

"Are kids at school into this, or is it just you?" my mom asked.

"Mary Grace," my dad said, but she ignored him.

I felt my brow furrow. "What do you mean? This isn't a big deal or anything, is it?" I shook my head. "It's just . . . interesting. I wanted to know more about it."

"Morgan," my mom began, and I couldn't believe how upset she looked. She almost always kept her cool with me and Mary K., no matter how crazed her life got.

"What your mother's trying to say," my dad offered, "is that these books about witchcraft are not the kind of thing we want you to be reading." He cleared his throat and tugged on the vee of his sweater vest, looking incredibly uncomfortable.

My mouth dropped open. "How come?" I asked.

"How come!" my mom snapped, and I almost jumped at the tone in her voice. "Because it's witchcraft!"

I stared at her. "But it's not like . . . black magic or anything," I tried to explain. "I mean, there's really nothing harmful or scary in it. It's just people hanging out, getting in touch with nature. So what if they celebrate full moons?" I didn't mention penis candles, bolts of energy, or naked swimming.

"It's more than that," my mom insisted. Her brown eyes were wide, and she looked as taut as a piano wire. She turned to my dad. "Sean, help me here."

"Look, Morgan," my dad said, more calmly. "We're concerned about this. I think we're pretty open-minded, but we're Catholics. That's our religion. We are part of the Catholic Church. The Catholic Church does not condone witchcraft or people who study witchcraft."

"I don't believe this," I said, starting to get impatient. "You're acting like this is a huge threat or something." Memories of how sick I had felt after the two circles flashed through my mind. "I mean, this is Wicca. It's like people deciding to protest animal testing or wanting to dance around a maypole." Some of the facts about Wicca that I had read in my book came back to me. "You know, the Catholic Church has adopted a bunch of traditions that began with Wicca. Like using mistletoe at Christmas and eggs at Easter. Those were both ancient symbols from a religion that began long before Christianity or Judaism."

My mom stared at me. "Look, miss," she said, and I knew she was really angry. "I'm telling you that we will not have witchcraft in this house. I'm telling you that the Catholic Church does not condone this. I'm telling you that we believe in *one* God. Now, I want these books out of this house!"

It was like my mom had been replaced by an alien duplicate. This sounded so unlike her that I just gaped. My dad stood next to her, his hand on her shoulder, obviously trying to get her to calm down, but she just glared at me, the lines around her mouth deep, her eyes angry and cold and ... worried?

I didn't know what to say. My mom was usually incredibly reasonable.

"I thought we believed in the Father, the Son, and the Holy Ghost," I said. "That's three."

Mom looked almost apoplectic, the veins in her neck jumping out. I suddenly realized that I was taller than she was now. "Go to your room!" she shouted, and again I jumped. We're not a raised-voice kind of family.

"Mary Grace," my dad murmured.

"Go!" my mom yelled, throwing out her arm and pointing out the kitchen door. It almost looked like she wanted to hit me, and I was way shocked.

Dad reached out his hand and touched Mom's shoulder in a tentative, ineffectual gesture. His face looked drawn and his eyes concerned behind their wire-rim glasses.

"I'm going," I muttered, taking the long way around her. I stomped upstairs to my room and slammed the door. I even locked it, which I'm not supposed to do. I sat on my bed, spooked and trying not to cry.

Over and over, I had the same thought: What is Mom so scared of?

14

Deeper

><"The king and queen longed for a child for many years and finally adopted an infant girl. But to their misfortune, the child was destined to grow enormous and devour them with her steely teeth."
—from a Russian fairy tale><

"So how come you're in the dollhouse?" Mary K. asked the next morning.

I backed Das Boot out of our driveway, two strawberry Pop-Tarts clenched between my teeth.

Once when Mary K. was little, she had done something bad, and my mom had sternly told her she was "in the doghouse." She had heard "dollhouse," and of course the whole thing made no sense to her. Now it's what we always say.

"I was reading some stuff they didn't want me to read," I muttered casually, trying not to spew crumbs all over my dashboard.

Mary K.'s eyes opened wide. "Like pornography?" she asked excitedly. "Where'd you get it?"

"It wasn't pornography," I told her in exasperation. "It was no big deal. I don't know why they're so upset."

"So what was it?" she persisted.

I rolled my eyes and shifted gears. "They were some books about Wicca," I said. "Which is an ancient, woman-based religion that predates Judaism and Christianity." I sounded like a textbook.

My sister thought about it for a few moments. "Well, *that's* boring," she said finally. "Why can't you read porn or something fun that I could borrow?"

I laughed. "Maybe later."

"You're kidding," Bree said, her eyes wide. "I don't believe it. That's awful."

"It's so stupid," I said. "They said they want the books out of the house." The bench where we sat outside school was chilly, and the October sunlight seemed to grow feebler by the day.

Robbie nodded sympathetically. His parents were much stricter Catholics than mine. I doubted he'd shared his interest in Wicca with them.

"You can keep them at my house," Bree said. "My dad could care less."

I zipped my parka up around my neck and burrowed into it. There were only a few minutes before class started, and our new, hybrid clique was gathered by the east door of school. I could see Tamara and Janice walking up to the building, their heads bent as they talked. I missed them. I hadn't seen them much lately.

Cal was perched on the bench across from ours, sitting

next to Beth. He was wearing ancient cowboy boots, worn down at the heels. He was quiet, not looking at us, but I felt sure he was listening to every word of our conversation.

"Screw them," Raven said. "They can't tell you what to read. This isn't a police state."

Bree snorted. "Yeah. Let me be there when you tell Sean and Mary Grace to go screw themselves."

I couldn't help smiling.

"They're your parents," Cal said, suddenly breaking his silence. "Of course you love them and want to respect their feelings. If I were you, I'd feel miserable, too."

In that moment I fell deeper in love with Cal. On some level I guess I expected him to dismiss my parents as stupid and hysterical, the way everybody else had. Since he was the most ardent follower of Wicca, I expected my parents' reaction to annoy him the most.

Bree looked at me, and I prayed my feelings weren't written on my face. In fairy tales there's always one person who is made for one other, and they find each other and live happily ever after. Cal was my person. I couldn't imagine anyone more perfect. Yet what kind of sick fairy tale would it be if he was the one made exactly right for me and I wasn't right for him?

"It's a hard decision to make," Cal continued. Our group was starting to listen to him like he was an apostle, teaching us. "I'm lucky because Wicca is my family's religion." He considered this for a moment, his hand on his cheek. "If I told my mom I wanted to become Catholic, she would totally freak out. I don't know if I could do it." He smiled at me.

Robbie and Beth laughed.

"Anyway," Cal said, serious again, "everyone has to choose his or her own path. You need to decide what to do.

I hope you still want to explore Wicca, Morgan. I think you have a gift for it. But I'll understand if you can't."

The school door swung open with a bang, and Chris Holly walked out, followed by Trey Heywood.

"Oh," Chris said loudly. " 'Scuse me. Didn't mean to interrupt you *witches*."

"Piss off," Raven said in a bored tone.

Chris ignored her. "Are you casting spells right here? Is that allowed on school grounds?"

"Chris, please," said Bree, rubbing her temple. "Don't do this."

He turned on her. "You can't tell me what to do," he said. "You're not my girlfriend. Right?"

"Right," Bree said, looking at him angrily. "And this is one of the reasons why."

"Yeah, well—," Chris began, but was interrupted by the bell ringing and the appearance of Coach Ambrose striding up.

"Get to class, kids," he said automatically, pulling open the doors. Chris shot Bree an ugly look, then followed the coach inside.

I picked up my backpack and headed for the door, followed by Robbie. Bree lingered behind, and I glanced back quickly to see her talking to Cal, her hand on his arm. Raven was watching them with narrowed eyes.

Dazed, I found my way to homeroom like a cow returning to the barn. My life seemed very complicated.

That afternoon I put my Wicca books in a paper bag and brought them to Bree's house. She had promised I could come over and read them whenever I wanted.

"I'll keep them safe for you," she said.

"Thanks." I pushed my hair over my shoulder and rested my head against her door. "Maybe I could come over tonight after dinner? I'm halfway through the history of witchcraft book, and it's pretty fascinating."

"Of course," she said sympathetically. "Poor baby." She patted my shoulder. "Look, just lie low for a while, let it all blow over. And you know you can come over and read or just hang out anytime. Okay?"

"Okay," I said, giving her a hug. "How's the thing with Cal going?" It hurt to ask, but I knew it was what she wanted to talk about.

Bree made a face. "Two days ago he was happy to talk for almost an hour on the phone, but yesterday I asked him to drive out to Wingott's Farm with me and he turned me down. I'm going to have to start stalking him if he doesn't give in pretty soon."

"He'll give in," I predicted. "They always do."

"True," Bree agreed, her eyes wistful.

"Well, I'll call you later," I said, suddenly eager for this conversation to end.

"Hang in there, okay?" she called after me as I escaped.

The next week I made a point of hanging out more with Tamara, Janice, and Ben. I went to math club and tried really hard to care about functions, but I longed to be learning about Wicca and especially to be near Cal.

When I told my mom I had gotten rid of the books, she was faintly embarrassed but mostly relieved. For a moment I felt guilty for omitting the fact that the books were only at Bree's house and I was still reading them in the evenings, but

I chased the guilt away. I respected my parents, but I didn't agree with them.

"Thanks," she said quietly, and looked like she wanted to say more, but didn't. Several times that week I caught her watching me, and the weird thing was, it reminded me of the creepy clerk at Practical Magick. She was watching me with an air of expectation, as if I were about to sprout horns or something.

All that week autumn moved in slowly, sweeping up the Hudson River into Widow's Vale. The days were noticeably shorter, the wind brisker. There was a sense of anticipation all around me, in the leaves, the wind, the sunlight. I felt like something big was coming, but I didn't know what.

On Saturday afternoon the phone rang while I was doing homework. Cal, I thought before I grabbed the upstairs extension.

"Hey," he said, and the sound of his voice made me slightly breathless.

"Hey," I replied.

"Are you coming to the circle tonight?" he asked straight out. "It's going to be at Matt's house."

I had wrestled with this question for days. Granted, I was disobeying the spirit of my parents' orders by reading my Wicca books, but actually going to another circle seemed like a much bigger deal. Learning about Wicca was one thing; practicing it was another. "I can't," I said finally, almost wanting to cry.

Cal was quiet for a minute. "I promise you everyone will keep their clothes on." I could hear the humor in his voice, and I smiled. He paused again. "I promise I won't carry you into the water," he added so softly, I wasn't sure I'd actually heard it. I didn't know what to say. I could feel the blood racing through my arteries.

"Unless you want me to," he added just as quietly.

Bree, your best friend, is in love with him, I reminded myself, needing to break the spell. She has a chance. You do not.

"It's just that . . . I c-can't," I heard myself stammering weakly. I heard my mom moving around downstairs, and I went into my room and shut the door.

"Okay," he said simply, and let the silence, an intimate kind of silence, spread between us. I lay on my bed, looking at the flame-colored tree leaves outside my window. I realized I would have given up the rest of my life to have Cal lying there with me right then. I closed my eyes, and tears started seeping out to run sideways down my cheeks.

"Maybe another time," he said gently.

"Maybe," I said, trying to keep my voice steady. Maybe not, though, I thought in anguish.

"Morgan—"

"Yeah?"

Silence.

"Nothing. I'll see you on Monday at school. We'll miss you tonight."

We'll miss you. Not I'll miss you.

"Thanks," I said. I hung up the phone, turned my face into my pillow, and cried.

15

Killburn Abbey

><"There is power in the plants of the earth and the animals, in every living thing, in weather, in time, in motion. If you are in tune with the universe, you can tap into its power."
—To Be a Witch, Sarah Morningstar, 1982><

Samhain is coming. Last night the circle was thin and pale without her. I need her. I think she's the one.

"You know, some kids actually get pregnant when they're sixteen," I muttered to Mary K. on Sunday afternoon. I couldn't believe my life had come to this: sitting in the back of a school bus packed with a bunch of jolly, devout Catholics on our way to Killburn Abbey. "They have drug problems and total their parents' cars. They flunk out of school. All I did was bring home a couple of *books*."

I sighed and leaned my head against the bus window,

torturing myself by wondering what had happened at the circle the night before.

If you've never spent an hour on a school bus with a bunch of grown-ups from your church, you have no idea how long an hour can be. My parents were sitting a few rows up, and they looked happy as pigs in mud, talking and laughing with their friends. Melinda Johnson, age five, got carsick, and we had to keep stopping to let her hang out the door.

"Here we are!" trilled Miss Hotchkiss at last, standing up in front as the bus lurched to a wheezy halt in front of what looked like a prison. Miss Hotchkiss is Father Hotchkiss's sister and keeps house for him.

Mary K. looked suspiciously out the window. "Is this a jail?" she whispered. "Are we here to be scared straight or something?"

I groaned and followed the crowd as they tromped off the bus. Outside, the air was chill and damp, and thick gray clouds scudded across the sky. I smelled rain and realized no birds were chirping.

In front of us were tall cement walls, at least nine feet high. They were stained from years of weather and dirt and crisscrossed by clinging vines. Set into one wall was a pair of large black doors, with heavy riveted studs and massive hinges.

"Okay, everyone," called Father Hotchkiss cheerfully. He strode up to the gate and rang the bell. In moments the door was answered by a woman wearing a name tag that said Karen Breems.

"Hello! You must be the group from St. Michael's," she said enthusiastically. "Welcome to Killburn Abbey. This is one of New York State's oldest cloistered convents. No nuns live here anymore—Sister Clement died back in 1987. Now it's a museum and a retreat center."

We stepped through the gates into a plantless courtyard covered with fine gravel that crunched under our feet. I found myself smiling as I looked around but didn't know why. Killburn Abbey was lifeless, gray, and lonely. But as I walked in, a deep, pervasive sense of calm came over me. My worries melted away in the face of its thick stone walls, bare courtyard, and caged windows.

"This feels like a prison," said Mary K., wrinkling her nose. "Those poor nuns."

"No, not a prison," I said, looking at the small windows set high up on the walls. "A sanctuary."

We saw the tiny stone cells where the nuns had slept on hard wooden cots covered with straw. There was a large, primitive kitchen with a huge oak worktable and enormous, battered pots and pans. If I squinted, I could see a black-robed nun, stirring herbs into boiling water, making medicinal teas for sisters who were ailing. A witch, I thought.

"The abbey was almost completely self-sufficient," Ms. Breems said, waving us out of the kitchen through a narrow wooden door. We stepped outside into a walled garden, now overgrown, sad, and neglected.

"They grew all their own vegetables and fruit, canning what they would need to last through a New York winter," Ms. Breems went on. "When the abbey first opened, they even kept sheep and goats for milk, meat, and wool. This area is their kitchen garden, walled off to keep out rabbits and deer. As is typical in many European abbeys, the herb garden was laid out as a small, circular maze."

Like the wheel of a year, I thought, counting eight main

spokes, now decrepit and sometimes indistinct. One for Samhain, one for Yule, one for Imbolc, then Ostara, Beltane, Litha, Lammas, and Mabon.

Of course, I was sure the nuns had never intended to use the Wiccan wheel in their garden design. They would have been totally horrified by it. But that's how Wicca was: ancient and gently permeating many facets of people's lives without their being aware of it.

As we walked down the crumbling stone paths, worn smooth by hundreds of years of sandaled feet, Mrs. Petrie, the herb gardener, was practically in rapture. I walked behind her, listening as she murmured, "Dill, yes, and look at that robust chamomile. Oh, and that is tansy; goodness, I hate tansy; it takes over everything. . . ."

As I followed her, I swear a wave of magick passed over me. It lifted my spirit and made the sun shine on my face. Each bed, though no longer tended, was a revelation.

I didn't know the names of most of the plants, but I got impressions of them. A few times I bent and touched their dried brown heads, their broken seedpods, their withered leaves. As I did, shadowy images formed in my mind: boneset, feverfew, eyebright, meadowsweet, rosemary, dandelion again and again.

Here in front of me were the sparse autumn remains of plants with the power to heal, to work magick, to flavor food, to make incense and soap and dye. . . . My head swirled with their possibilities.

Kneeling, I brushed my fingers against a pale aloe, which everyone uses to help with burns and sunburn. My mom used to all the time and didn't worry about witchcraft. A shrubby bay laurel bush stood nearby, its trunk twisted with time and age. When I touched it, it felt clean, pure, strong. There were thyme bushes; a huge, dying catnip; caraway seeds, tiny and brown on brittle stems. It was a new world for me to explore, to lose myself in. Tenderly I touched a gnarled spearmint plant.

"Mint never dies," Mrs. Petrie said, seeing me. "It always comes back. It's actually very invasive—I grow mine in pots."

I smiled and nodded at her, no longer feeling the chill of the air. I explored every path, seeing empty spaces where plants had been or where their stems still stood, awaiting their rebirth in the spring. I carefully read the small metal plates, each with a plant's name handwritten in a feminine, even cursive.

My mom came and stood next to me. "This is so interesting, isn't it?" I felt she was trying to make amends.

"It's incredible," I said sincerely. "I love all these herbs. Do you think Dad would give me a little space in the yard so we could grow our own?"

My mom looked into my eyes, brown into brown. "You're that interested?" she said, glancing down at a tough, woody clump of rosemary.

"Yeah," I said. "It's so pretty here. Wouldn't it be cool if we could cook with our own parsley and rosemary?"

"Yes, it would," my mom said. "Maybe next spring. We'll talk to Dad about it." She turned away and went to stand next to Miss Hotchkiss, who was discussing the history of the abbey.

When it was time to get back on the bus, I had to tear myself away. I wanted to stay at the abbey and walk its halls and smell its scents and feel the drying leaves of plants crumble beneath my fingertips. The plants called me with the magick of their thin, reedy life forces, and there, outside the gates of the Killburn Abbey, it came to me.

In spite of my parents' objections, in spite of everything, it wasn't enough for me to learn about witches. I wanted to be one.

16
Blood Witch

><"There is no choice about being a witch. Either you are or you aren't. It's in the blood."
    —Tim McClellan, aka Feargus the Bright><

Frustration makes me want to howl. She isn't coming to me. I know I can't push her. Goddess, please give me a sign.

On Monday after school Robbie and I ditched chess club and went to Practical Magick. It was getting to be a real habit with me. I bought a book about using herbs and other plants in magick and also a beautiful blank book with a marbleized cover and heavy, cream-colored pages within. It would be my Book of Shadows. I planned to write down my feelings about Wicca, notes on our circle, everything I was thinking about.

Robbie bought a black penis candle that he thought was hysterical.

"Very amusing," I said. "That's going to make you popular with the chicks."

Robbie cackled.

We headed to Bree's house and hung out in her room. I lay on her bed and read my herb book while Robbie fiddled with Bree's stereo, checking out her latest CDs. Bree sat on the floor, painting her toenails, reading my book about the Seven Great Clans.

"This is so cool. Listen to this," she said as the doorbell rang downstairs. Moments later we heard Jenna and Matt's voices as they came upstairs.

"Hi!" Jenna said brightly, her pale blond hair swinging over her shoulder. "Gosh, it's so chilly outside. Where's Indian summer?"

"Come on in," Bree said. She glanced around her bedroom. "Maybe we should go down to the family room."

"I'm for staying here," Robbie said.

"Yeah. It's more private," I agreed, sitting up.

"Listen, guys," Bree announced. "I was just reading this book about the Seven Great Clans of Wicca."

"Ooh," Jenna said, pretending to shiver.

"'After practicing their craft for centuries, each of the Seven Great Clans came to work within a single domain of magick. At one end of the spectrum is the Woodbane clan, who became known for their dark work and their capacity for evil.'"

A real shiver went down my spine, but Matt wiggled his eyebrows and Robbie let out a diabolical laugh.

"That doesn't sound like Wicca," Jenna said, pulling off her jacket. "Remember? Everything you do comes back to you threefold. All that stuff Cal read last weekend. Bree, that color is fantastic. What's it called?"

Bree examined the polish bottle. "Celestial Blue."

"Very cool," Jenna said.

"Thanks," Bree said. "Hold on—this is really interesting. 'At the opposite end of the magickal spectrum is the Rowanwand clan. Ever good, ever peaceful, the Rowanwands became known for being the repository of much magickal knowledge. They wrote the first Book of Shadows. They gathered spells. They explored the magickal properties of the world around them.'"

"Cool," said Robbie. "What happened to them?"

Bree scanned down the page. "Um, let's see. . . ."

"They died," came Cal's rich voice, from Bree's open door.

We all jumped—none of us had heard the doorbell ring or his tread on the stairs.

After her moment of surprise, Bree gave him a brilliant smile. "Come on in," she said, clearing her nail polish stuff away.

"Hey, Cal," Jenna said with a smile.

"Hey," he said, hanging his jacket on the doorknob.

"What do you mean, they died?" Robbie asked.

Cal came and sat next to me on the bed. Bree turned around and saw us sitting there together, and her eyes flickered.

"Well, there were Seven Great Clans," Cal reiterated. "The Woodbanes, who were considered evil, and the Rowanwands, who were considered good, and five other clans in between, who were various shades of good and evil."

"Is this a true story?" Jenna asked, throwing her gum into the trash.

Cal nodded. "As far as we know. Anyway, the Woodbanes and the Rowanwands basically warred with each other for thousands of years, and the other five clans were sometimes allied with one, sometimes with another, during that time."

"Who were the other five clans?" Robbie asked.

"Wait, hold on. I just saw it," Bree said, trailing her finger down a page.

"The Woodbanes, the Rowanwands, the Vikroths, the Brightendales, the Burnhides, the Wyndenkells, and the Leapvaughns," I recited from memory. Everyone looked at me in surprise, except Cal, who smiled slightly.

"I just read that book," I said.

Bree nodded slowly. "Yeah, Morgan's right. It says here the Vikroths were warrior types. The Brightendales worked mostly with plants and were sort of doctors. The Burnhides specialized in gem, crystal, and metal magick, and the Wyndenkells were expert spell writers. The Leapvaughns were mischievous and humorous and sometimes pretty awful."

"The Vikroths were related to the Vikings," Cal said. "And the word *leprechaun* is related to *Leapvaughn*."

"Cool," Matt said. Jenna came and sat on the floor in front of him so she could lean back against his legs. His fingers absently played with her hair.

"So how did they die?" Robbie asked.

"They battled each other for thousands of years," Cal repeated. A strand of his hair shadowed one cheek. "Slowly their numbers dwindled. The Woodbanes and their allies simply killed their enemies, either by open warfare or through black spells. The Rowanwands also hurt their enemies, not so much with black magic but by hoarding knowledge, letting the other clans' lines of knowledge die out, refusing to share their wealth. Like, if members of the Vikroths became ill and the Rowanwands could cure them with a spell, they didn't. And so their enemies died."

"Those bastards," Robbie said, and Bree giggled. A tiny spark of irritation made me frown.

Cal shot Robbie a sardonic look.

"Go on, Cal," Bree said. "Don't mind him."

Outside, it had been dark for a while, and a cold, steady rain began to patter against the windowpanes. I hated the thought of having to go home to Mary K.'s hamburgers and french fries.

"Well, about three hundred years ago," Cal continued, "until the time of the Salem witch trials in this country, there was a huge cataclysm among the tribes. No one knows exactly why it happened just at that time, but all over the world, and the clans had spread a bit, witches were suddenly decimated. Over the course of a hundred years historians estimate that ninety to ninety-five percent of all witches were killed—either by each other or by the human authorities that had gotten involved in the conflict."

"Are you saying that the Salem witch trials were organized by other witches to destroy their rivals?" Bree asked incredulously.

"I'm saying that it isn't clear," Cal said. "It's a possibility."

On the outside my flesh felt warm, my senses soothed by Cal's presence and his voice. On the inside I felt cold to the bone. I hated hearing about witches dying, being persecuted.

"After that," Cal went on, "for over two hundred years witches everywhere fell into a Dark Age. The clans lost their cohesiveness; witches from different clans either intermarried and had children who belonged nowhere, or they married humans and couldn't have children."

I remembered reading that people thought the Seven Clans had kept to themselves for so long that they were different from other humans and couldn't reproduce with ordinary people.

"You know so much about all this stuff," said Jenna.

"I've been learning it for a long time," Cal explained.

Bree reached over and touched Cal's knee. "What happened then? I haven't gotten to that part yet."

"The old ways and the old resentments were forgotten," Cal said. "And human knowledge of magick was almost lost forever. Then, about a hundred years ago, a small group of witches, representing all seven clans or what remained of them, managed to emerge from the Dark Age and start a Renaissance of Wiccan culture." He shifted in place, and Bree's hand dropped. Matt was making a small braid in Jenna's hair, and Robbie was stretched on the carpet, one hand propping up his head.

"The book said they realized that the major clannishness of the tribes had helped cause the cataclysm," I put in. "So they decided to make just one big clan and not have distinctions anymore."

"Unity in diversity," Cal acknowledged. "They suggested interclan marriages and better witch-human relations. That small group of enlightened witches called themselves the High Council, and it's still around today. Nearly all of the modern-day covens exist because of them and their teach-

118 book of shadows

ings. Nowadays Wicca is growing fast, but the old clans are only memories. Most people don't take them seriously anymore."

I remembered the clerk at Practical Magick asking me what my clan was, and I remembered something else he had said. "What's a blood witch?" I asked. "As opposed to a witch witch?"

Cal looked into my eyes, and I felt a wave rise and swell within me. "People say someone's a blood witch if they can reliably trace their heritage back to one of the seven clans," he explained. "A regular witch is someone who practices Wicca and lives by its tenets. They take their magickal energy from the life forces found everywhere. A blood witch tends to be a much greater conduit for this energy and to have greater powers."

"I guess we're all going to be witch witches," Jenna said with a smile. She pulled up her knees and crossed her arms in front of them, looking catlike and feminine.

Robbie nodded at her. "And we have almost a whole year to go," he said, pushing his glasses up on his nose. His face looked raw and inflamed, as if it hurt.

"Except me," Cal said easily. "I'm a blood witch."

"You're a blood witch?" Bree asked, her eyes wide.

"Sure." Cal shrugged. "My mom is; my dad was; so I am. There are more of us around than you think. My mom knows a bunch."

"Whoa," Matt said, his hands still as he stared at Cal. "So what clan are you?"

Cal grinned. "Don't know. The family records got lost when my parents' families emigrated to America. My mom's family was from Ireland, and my dad's family was from

Scotland, so they could have been from a bunch of different clans. Maybe Woodbane," he said, and laughed.

"That is so awesome," Jenna said. "It makes it seem so much more real."

"I'm not as powerful as a lot of witches are," Cal said matter-of-factly.

In my mind I traced the edge of his profile—smooth brow, straight nose, carved lips—and the rest of the room faded from view. I thought dimly, It's six o'clock, and then I heard the muffled notes of the clock downstairs striking the hour.

"I have to get home," I heard myself say, as if from a great distance. I tucked my herb book under my sweater. Then I pulled my gaze away from Cal's face and walked out of the room, feeling like I was sinking knee-deep into a sponge with every step.

On the way downstairs I gripped the handrail tightly. Outside, the rain swept across my face. I blinked and hurried toward Das Boot. My car was freezing inside, with icy vinyl seats and a cold steering wheel. My wet, cold hands turned the key in the starter.

The words kept throbbing in my head. *Blood witch. Blood witch. Blood witch.*

17
Trapped

><"In 1217 witchfinders imprisoned a Vikraut witch.
Yet on the following morn the cell was empty. Thus
comes the saying 'Better to kill a witch three times
than to lock her up once,' for a witch cannot be
contained."

—WITCHES, MAGES, AND WARLOCKS,
Altus Polydarmus, 1618.><

October. I've put away my old journal. This is my first entry into my Book of Shadows. I don't know if I'm doing it right. I've never seen another BOS. But I wanted to document my coming alive, this autumn, this year. I'm coming alive as a witch, and it's the happiest and the scariest thing I've ever done.

"And it was just so amazing," I said, peeling the top off my yogurt. "The whole garden was laid out in eight spokes, like the sabbat wheel. All these plants for healing and cooking. And they were all nuns! Catholic nuns!" I spooned up some yogurt and looked around my lunch table.

We were in the school cafeteria, and Robbie had made the mistake of casually asking how the church trip had gone on Sunday—his family goes to my church. Now I wouldn't shut up about it.

"You gotta watch those nuns," Robbie said, drinking his milk shake.

"Gosh, it is just everywhere." Jenna shook her head. She wiped her lips with a paper napkin and pushed her hair back over her shoulders. "Now that I know about it, it seems like traces of Wicca are everywhere I look. My mom was talking about going up to Red Kill to buy a pumpkin for Halloween, and I realized where that tradition really comes from."

"Hey," said Ethan sleepily, sinking into a chair next to Sharon. "'Sup?" His eyes were red, and his long ringlets were clotted above his collar.

Sharon looked at him in disgust, edging away from him as if he would get dirt on her pristine tartan skirt and white oxford shirt. "Are you ever *not* stoned?" she asked.

"I'm not stoned *now*," Ethan said. "I have a cold."

I glanced over at him and could sense his muzzy headedness and stuffed-up sinuses.

"Ethan doesn't smoke anymore," Cal said quietly. "Right, Ethan?"

Ethan looked irritated and opened a can of cranberry juice from the school machine. "That's right, man. I get high on life," he said.

Cal laughed.

"Next you'll be telling me I have to be a damn vegetarian or something," Ethan grumbled.

"Anything but that," Robbie said sarcastically.

Sharon wiggled away from Ethan, looking prissy. Gold

bracelets clinked on her wrist, and she speared a piece of teriyaki chicken with a chopstick.

"Watch out for her cooties," Beth whispered to Ethan. Today she wore a diamond in her nose and another diamond bindi on her forehead. She looked exotic, her green eyes glowing catlike against her dark skin.

Sharon made a face at her as Ethan started laughing and choked on his juice.

Bree and I shared a look, then Bree's eyes fastened on Cal. Steadfastly I went back to eating my yogurt. We sat there, overflowing our lunch table designed to seat eight: me and Bree; Raven and Beth, with their nose rings and dyed hair and mehendi tattoos; Jenna and Matt, the perfect couple; Ethan and Robbie, scruffy and rough; Sharon Goodfine, stuck-up princess; and Cal, tying us all together, giving us something in common. He looked around the table at us, seeming happy to be here, glad to be with us. We were the privileged nine. His new coven, if we wanted to be.

I wanted to be.

"Morgan! Wait!" Jenna called as I headed to my car. It was Friday afternoon, another week gone. I waited for her to catch up and shifted my backpack to the other shoulder.

"Are you coming to the circle tomorrow night?" Jenna asked when she was close enough. "It's going to be at my house. I thought we could make sushi."

I felt like an alcoholic being offered a cold, strong drink. The thought of going to another circle, feeling the magick coiling through my veins, having that magickal intimacy with Cal, practically made me want to whimper.

"I really want to," I said hesitantly.

"Why wouldn't you come?" she asked, her eyes confused.

"You seem so interested in Wicca. And Cal said you have a gift for it."

I sighed. "My parents are totally against it," I explained. "I'm dying to come, but I just can't face the scene at home if I do."

"Tell them I'm having a party," Jenna said. "Or that you're sleeping over at my place. We missed you last week. It's more fun when you're there."

I grinned wryly. "You mean no one fell over, clutching her chest?"

She laughed. "No," she said. "But Cal said you were just extra sensitive, right?"

Matt walked up and put his hand around Jenna's waist, and she smiled up at him. I wondered if they ever fought, ever questioned their love for each other.

"That's me," I said. "Sensitive Morgan."

"Well, try to come if you can," Jenna said.

"Okay," I said. "I'll try. Thanks."

I got in my car, thinking how nice Jenna was and how I had never known it because before this we had always been in different social groups.

"We're just going to hang out. You want to come?" Mary K. asked me on Saturday night. "Jaycee's rented some cheesy movie, and we're going to eat popcorn and make fun of it."

I smiled at her. "Sounds almost irresistible. But somehow I'm managing to resist it. Bree and I may see a movie. Will Bakker be at Jaycee's?"

Mary K. shook her head. "No. He and his dad went to a Giants game in New Jersey."

"Are things okay with him?" I asked.

"Uh-huh." Mary K. brushed her hair until it was shiny and smooth, then looped it up in a ponytail in back. She looked adorable and casual, perfect for hanging out at a girlfriend's house.

Soon after Mary K. rode off into the chilly night to bike the half mile to Jaycee's house, my mom and dad came into the living room, all dressed up.

"Where's the show at?" I asked, propping my socked feet up on the couch.

"Where's the show playing," my mom corrected my grammar.

"That too," I said, and gave her a smile. She made a mock-disapproving face.

"Over in Burdocksville," she answered, fastening a pearl necklace around her neck. "At the community center. We should be back by eleven or so, and we told Mary K. we'd pick her up on the way home. Leave a note if you and Bree decide to go out."

"Okay," I said.

"Come on, Mary Grace, we're going to be late," my dad said.

"Bye, sweetie," my mom called. Then they were gone, and I was alone in the house. I ran upstairs and changed into an Indian-print top and a pair of gray pants. I brushed my hair hard and decided to leave it down. I even opened the bathroom drawer, looked at Mary K.'s huge collection of eye shadows and blushes and concealers. I had no idea what to do with most of the stuff and didn't have time to learn, so I just put on a layer of lip gloss and headed for the door.

Jenna lived in Hudson Estates, a fairly new subdivision filled with mansions. I grabbed my keys and a jacket and shoved my feet into my clogs. I was thinking, Circle, circle, circle, and my mind was spinning with excitement. As I was opening the door to leave, the phone rang.

To answer or not to answer? I lunged for the phone on the fourth ring, thinking it might be Jenna with a change of plans, but I suddenly knew even before I had the receiver to my ear that it was Ms. Fiorello, my mom's colleague. "Hello?" I said impatiently.

"Morgan? This is Betty Fiorello."

"Hi," I said, thinking, I know, I know.

"Hi, hon," she said. "Listen, I just got your mom on her cell phone, and she said you might be home."

"Uh-huh?" My heart was racing, my blood pounding. All I wanted was to see Cal, to feel the magick again flowing through me.

"Listen. I need to stop by and pick up some signs. Your mom said they were in the garage. I have two new listings, and I'm doing three open houses tomorrow, if you can believe it, and I seem to have run out of signs."

Ms. Fiorello has the most annoying voice in the world. I wanted to scream.

"Okay ...," I said politely.

"So is it all right if I come by in, say, forty-five minutes?" Ms. Fiorello asked.

I glanced at the clock frantically. "C-could you come a little earlier?" I asked. "I was, um, thinking of going to a movie."

"Oh. I'm sorry. I'll try. But I just have to wait for Mr. Fiorello to get home with the car," she said.

Crap, I thought. "I could leave the signs outside," I suggested. "In front of the garage."

"Oh, dear," said Ms. Fiorello, continuing to ruin my life.

"You know, I think I have to look through them myself. I'm not sure which ones I'll need until I see them."

My mom had about a hundred real estate signs in the garage. I couldn't pile them *all* outside. Thoughts flew through my head, but I couldn't see a way out. Dammit. "Well, I guess I don't absolutely have to go to the movie," I hinted ungraciously, hoping she'd take the hint.

She didn't. "I'm so sorry, dear. Was this a date?" she asked.

"No," I said sourly. I needed to hang up before I started screaming at her. "See you in forty-five minutes," I said curtly, and hung up the phone. I felt like crying. For a bitter minute I wondered if maybe my mom had put Ms. Fiorello up to this to check on me. No, that seemed unlikely.

While I waited for Ms. Fiorello, I cleaned the kitchen and started the dishwasher: Cinderella, getting very late for the ball. I put a load of my clothes into the washer. Then I played music really loud and sang along for a while at the top of my lungs. I put my wet clothes into the dryer and set the timer for forty-five minutes.

Finally, over an *hour* later, Ms. Fiorello showed up. I let her into the garage, and she poked around in my mom's signs for what felt like a lifetime. I sat on the garage steps glumly, my head in my hand. She picked out about eight signs, then cheerfully thanked me.

"No problem," I lied politely, letting her out. "'Bye, Ms. Fiorello."

"Good-bye, dear," she said.

By the time she left, it was almost ten o'clock. There was no point in driving twenty minutes to Jenna's house when the circle would already be under way. I couldn't just break in three-quarters of the way through.

As I collapsed on our living room sofa, my misery was compounded by the fear that I was falling too far behind the rest of the Wicca group to join in again. What if Cal gave up on me? What if they wouldn't let me come to another circle?

I felt almost desperate. I seized on an idea that had been floating around my brain for a while. If I couldn't explore Wicca with the group, I could at least work a little on my own. Then at least I could prove to Cal and the rest of them that I really was dedicated. I was going to try to do a magick spell. I even had an idea for a spell to try. The next day I would drive up to Practical Magick and buy the ingredients.

18

Consequences

><"Forget not that witches live among us as neighbors, and practice their craft in secret, even as we conduct honest, God-fearing lives."

—WITCHES, MAGES, AND WARLOCKS, Altus Polydarmus, 1618><

On Sunday my family and I went to church, then to the Widow's Diner for brunch. As soon as I got home, I called Jenna. She was out, so I left a message on her machine, explaining what happened the night before and apologizing for not making it to the circle. Then I called Bree, but she wasn't home, either. I left a message for her, too, trying not to imagine her at Cal's house, in Cal's room. After that I sat at the dining table for hours, doing homework and losing myself in complicated, tidy mathematical equations, so satisfying in their clear solutions, they seemed almost magickal themselves.

*   *   *

I stopped by Practical Magick just before it closed, at five that afternoon. I bought all the ingredients I needed, but I waited until later that night, until my parents and sister were already in bed, before I began my spell.

I left the door to my room open a crack so I could hear if my mom or dad or Mary K. suddenly stirred. I took out my book on herbal magick. Cal had said I was sensitive—that I had a gift for magick. I needed to know if that was true.

Opening the book *Herbal Rituals for the Beginner,* I flipped to "Clarifying the Skin."

I checked my list. Was it a waning moon? Check. In my reading I had learned that spells for gathering, calling, increasing, prosperity, and so on were done while the moon was waxing, or getting fuller. Spells for banishing, decreasing, limiting, and so on were done while the moon was waning. It sort of made sense if you thought about it.

The spell I chose specified catnip to increase beauty, cucumber and angelica to promote healing, chamomile and rosemary for purification.

My room is carpeted, but I found I could still make a chalk circle. Before closing the circle, I moved my book and everything else I would need into it. Three candles made enough light to read by. Next I trickled a line of salt around my circle and said, "With this salt, I purify my circle."

The rest of the spell consisted of crunching things up with a mortar and pestle, pouring boiling water (from a thermos) over the herbs in a measuring cup, and writing a person's name on a piece of paper and burning it over a candle. At exactly midnight I read the book's spell words in a whisper:

>"So beauty in is beauty out,
>This potion make your blemish nowt.
>This healing water makes you pure,
>And thus your beauty will endure."

I read this quickly while the clock downstairs was striking midnight. At the very last *bong* of the clock, I said the final word. In the next instant all the hairs on my arms stood up, the three candles went out, and a huge bolt of lightning made my room glow white. The next second brought a *boom* of thunder so loud, it reverberated in my chest.

I almost peed in my pants. I stared wildly out the window to see if the house had caught on fire, then I got to my feet and flicked on my lamp. We still had electricity.

My heart was crashing around my rib cage. On the one hand, it seemed so far-fetched and melodramatic that this would happen exactly when I was doing a spell, it was almost funny. On the other hand, I felt like God had seen what I was doing and sent a bolt of angry lightning to warn me off. You know that's crazy, I told myself, taking long, deep breaths to quiet my heart.

Quickly I cleaned up all my spell stuff. I poured my tincture into a small, clean Tupperware container and tucked it into my backpack. Within minutes I was in bed with the lights out.

Outside, it was pouring and thundering in our biggest autumn storm so far. And my heart was still pounding.

"Here, try this," I said casually to Robbie on Monday morning. I pushed the container into his hands.

"What is this?" he asked. "Salad dressing? What am I supposed to do with this?"

"It's a facial wash I got from my mom," I explained. "It works really well."

He looked at me, and I met his eyes for a few seconds before I looked away, wondering if I looked as guilty as I felt, not telling him the truth. In a sense, experimenting on him.

"Yeah, okay," he said, putting the capped container into his backpack.

"How was the circle on Saturday?" I whispered to Bree in homeroom. "I'm really sorry I missed it. I tried to call you to see how it went."

"Oh, I got your message," she said regretfully. "My dad and I went to the city yesterday, and I didn't get back till late. Sorry. Got my hair cut, though."

It looked exactly the same, maybe an eighth of an inch shorter.

"It looks great. Anyway, how are things with Cal?"

Her classic brows wrinkled a bit. "Cal is . . . elusive," she said finally. "He's playing hard to get. I've tried to be alone with him, but it's impossible."

I nodded, hoping my expression of sympathy was winning out over my feelings of relief.

"Yeah. It's starting to really annoy me," she said glumly.

I thought about telling her that I had done a spell for Robbie and that I was waiting to see what would happen. But I couldn't form the words, and it, along with my feelings for Cal, became another secret I kept from my best friend.

* * *

On Wednesday morning Bree and some of the other members of the circle were sitting on the benches as usual. When I walked up to them, Raven gave me a snide look, but Cal seemed completely sincere when he invited me to sit down.

"I really am sorry about Saturday," I said, mostly to Cal, I guess. "I was all set to drive over to Jenna's when this woman my mom works with called and insisted on dropping by to pick up some stuff. It took forever, and I was so frustrated—"

"I've heard your excuse already, and it's fairly lame," Raven interrupted.

I waited for Bree to step in and defend me in our traditional best-friend solidarity, but she was silent.

"Don't worry about it, Morgan," Cal said easily, washing away the awkwardness left hanging in the air.

At that moment Robbie appeared, and we all just stared. His skin looked better than it had since seventh grade.

Bree's dark eyes flicked to him, grazing his face and processing what she saw. "Robbie," she said. "God, you look terrific."

Robbie shrugged casually and dropped his backpack on the ground. I looked at him closely. His face was still broken out, but if his skin before had been a two on a scale of one to ten, with one being the worst, now it was up to a seven.

I saw Cal glance at him thoughtfully. Then he looked at me, as though assessing my involvement. It was like he knew everything. But he couldn't, didn't, so I kept quiet.

Keep it to yourself, I commanded Robbie silently. Don't tell anyone what I gave you. Inside, I was elated and flushed with a sense of awe. Had my spell potion really worked? What else could it be? Robbie had been seeing a dermatologist for years, with no visible improvement. Now he shows up after two days of my tincture and looks great. Did this mean I was actually a witch? No, it couldn't be that, I reminded myself. My parents weren't blood witches. I was safe from that. But maybe I did have a small gift for magick.

Jenna and Matt drifted toward us.

"Hey, guys," Jenna said. The October wind whipped her pale hair around her face, and she shivered and clutched her books tighter to her chest. "Hey, Robbie." She looked at him as if trying to figure out what was different.

"Hey, does anyone have a copy of *The Sound and the Fury?*" Matt asked, pushing his hands into the pockets of his black leather jacket. "I can't find mine, and I've got to read it for English."

"You can borrow mine," Raven said.

"Okay. Thanks," Matt said.

No one mentioned Robbie's appearance again, but Robbie kept looking at me. When at last I met his gaze squarely, he looked away.

By Friday, when Robbie's skin looked smooth and new and completely blemish free, when practically every student in school recognized that he was no longer a pizza face, when girls in his classes suddenly realized that hey, he wasn't bad-looking at all, he decided to tell everyone how it happened.

On Friday afternoon I was in my backyard, raking leaves or, rather, raking occasionally but mostly seeing stunning maple leaf after stunning leaf, picking them up, examining them, admiring the passionate blotch and smear of colors across their finely veined skin. Some were still half green, and

I imagined that they felt surprised to find themselves on the ground so soon. Some were almost completely dry and brown, yet with a defiant border of red or bloody tips as if they had raked the bark on the way down. Others were ablaze with autumn's fire of yellow, orange, and crimson, and some were very small still, too young to die, yet born too late to live.

I pressed my palm against a crisp leaf as big as my hand. Its colors felt warm against my skin, and with my eyes closed, I could feel impressions of warm summer days, the joy of being blown in the wind, the tenacious hanging on, and then the frightening, exhilarating release of autumn. Floating, finished, to the ground. The smell of earth, the joining to the earth.

Suddenly I blinked, sensing Cal.

"What is it telling you?" His voice floated toward me from the back steps. I startled like a rabbit and rocked backward on my heels. Looking up, I saw Mary K. at the back door, directing Cal, Bree, and Robbie to the backyard to find me.

I looked at them in the darkening afternoon. I glanced around for my leaf, but it was gone. I stood up, brushing off my hands and my seat.

"What's up?" I asked, looking from face to face.

"We need to talk to you," Bree said. She looked remote, even hurt, her full mouth pressed into a line.

"I told them," Robbie said bluntly. "I told them you gave me a homemade potion in a container, and it's fixed my skin. And I . . . I want to know what was in it."

My eyes opened wide in dismay. I felt like I was being judged. There was nothing to do but tell them the truth. "Catnip," I said reluctantly. "Catnip and chamomile and angelica and, um, rosemary and cucumber. Boiling water. Some other stuff."

"Eye of newt and skin of toad?" Cal teased.

"Was it a spell?" Bree asked, her forehead wrinkling.

I nodded, glancing down at my feet, kicking my clogs through the leaves. "Yeah. Just a beginner's spell. From a book." I looked up at Robbie. "I made sure it wouldn't have any harmful effects," I said. "I would never have given it to you if I thought it might harm you. Actually, I was pretty sure it wouldn't do anything at all."

He looked back at me. I realized that he had the potential to be good-looking, behind the clunky glasses and the lame haircut. His features had been obscured by his awful acne. His skin, now almost perfectly smooth, was etched very slightly with fine, white lines in a few places, as though it was still healing. I stared at it, fascinated by what I had apparently done.

"Tell us about it," Cal invited.

The screen door opened again, and my mom poked out her head. "Hey, honey. Dinner in fifteen," she called.

"Okay," I called back, and she went in, no doubt curious as to who the unfamiliar boy was.

"Morgan," Bree said.

"I don't know how to explain it," I said slowly, looking down at the leaves. "I told you about the abbey upstate with an herb garden. The garden . . . I felt like it spoke to me." My face got red at the far-fetched words. "I felt . . . like I wanted to study herbs more, know more about them."

"Know what, exactly?" Bree asked.

"I've been reading and reading about medicinal, magickal properties of herbs. Cal said I was . . . an energy conductor. I just wanted to see what would happen."

"And I was your guinea pig," Robbie said flatly.

I looked up at him, this Robbie I barely recognized. "I've been feeling really bad about missing two circles in a row. I wanted to work a little on my own. I decided to try a simple spell," I said. "I mean, I wasn't going to try to change the world. I didn't want anything huge or scary. I needed something small, something positive, something whose results I could evaluate pretty quickly."

"Like a science project," Robbie said.

"I knew it wouldn't hurt you," I insisted. "It was just ordinary herbs and water."

"And a spell," Cal said.

I nodded.

"When did you do it?" Bree asked.

"Sunday night, at midnight," I said. "I guess I was feeling pretty depressed about being stuck home Saturday night during the circle."

"Did anything happen when you did the spell?" asked Cal, looking at me with interest. I could feel Bree's anger.

I shrugged. "There was a storm." I didn't want to talk about the candles going out or the crack of thunder that had been so amazingly loud.

"So now you control the weather?" Bree said, hurt in her voice.

I winced. "I wasn't saying that."

"Obviously it's just some sort of weird coincidence," Bree said. "There's no way you could fix Robbie's skin, for God's sake. Cal, tell her. None of us could do something like that. *You* couldn't do something like that."

"No, I could," Cal contradicted mildly. "A lot of people

could, with enough training. Even if they weren't blood witches."

"But Morgan hasn't had *any* training," Bree said, her voice strained. "Have you?" she asked me.

"No, of course not," I said quietly.

"What we have here is an unusually gifted amateur," Cal said thoughtfully. "I'm actually glad this came up because we should talk about this stuff." He put his hand on my shoulder. "You're not allowed to perform a spell for someone without his or her knowledge," he said. "It's not a good idea, and it isn't safe. It isn't fair."

He looked uncharacteristically solemn, and I nodded, embarrassed.

"I'm really sorry, Robbie," I said. "I don't even know how to undo it. It was stupid."

"Jesus, I don't want you to undo it," Robbie said, alarmed. "It's just, I wish you had told me first. It kind of spooked me."

"Morgan, I really think you need to study more before you start doing spells," Cal went on. "It would be better if you saw the big picture instead of just little parts of it. It's all connected, you know, everything is connected, and everything you do affects everything else, so you've got to know what you're doing."

I nodded again, feeling horrible. I had been so impressed that my spell had worked, I hadn't even thought through all the far-reaching consequences.

"I'm not a high priest," Cal said, "but I can teach you what I know, and then you can go on to learn from someone else. If you want to."

"Yes, I want to," I said quickly. I glanced at Bree's face and wanted to take back the speed and certainty of my words.

"Samhain, Halloween, is eight days away," Cal said, dropping his hand. "Try to start coming to circles if you can. Think about it at least."

"Pretty intense, Rowlands." Robbie shook his head. "You're like the Tiger Woods of Wicca."

I couldn't help grinning. Bree's face was stiff.

My mom tapped on the window to tell me dinner was ready, and I nodded and waved.

"I'm sorry, Robbie," I said again. "I won't ever do anything like that again."

"Just ask me first," Robbie said, without anger.

We walked across the yard, and I led my three friends through the house and out the front door. "See you," I called to them as Cal met my eyes again.

Halloween was eight days away.

19

A Dream

The signs are there. She must be a blood witch. Her skin is splitting, and white light is leaking through. It's beautiful and frightening in its power. I vow on this Book of Shadows that I have found her. I was right. Blessed be.

That night Aunt Eileen showed up unexpectedly for dinner. Afterward she hung out with me in the kitchen and helped me clean up.

Out of nowhere, as I was scraping plates into the disposal, I found myself blurting out: "How did you know you were gay?"

She looked as surprised as I felt. "I'm sorry," I rushed to add. "Forget I asked. It's none of my business."

"No, it's okay," she said, thinking. "That's a fair question." She considered her answer for a few moments. "I guess when I was growing up, I always felt kind of *different* somehow. I didn't feel like a boy or anything. I knew I was a girl, and that was fine with me. But I just didn't get the whole point of boys existing." Her nose wrinkled, and I laughed.

"But I don't think I really figured out I was gay until about eighth grade," she went on, "when I got a crush on someone."

I looked up. "A girl?"

"Yes. Of course the girl didn't feel the same way about me—and I never told her about it or acted on it. I was so embarrassed. I felt like a freak. I felt there was something terribly wrong with me, that I needed counseling or help. Even medicine."

"How awful," I said.

"It wasn't until college that I came to terms with it and finally admitted to myself and everyone else that I was gay. I had been seeing a therapist, and he helped me see that there really wasn't anything wrong with me. It's just how I was made."

Aunt Eileen made a wry face. "It wasn't easy. My parents—your grammy and pop-pop—were so horrified and upset. They just couldn't deal with it. They were so disappointed in me. It's hard, you know, when the way you are, the way you were born, just totally bewilders and embarrasses your own parents."

I didn't say anything but felt a spark of recognition at what she was saying.

"Anyway, they gave me a really hard time. Not to be

mean or because they didn't love me but because they didn't know how else to react. They're a lot better now, but I'm still not at all what they want me to be. They don't ever want to talk about my being gay or people I'm involved with. Denial." She shrugged. "I can't help that. I've found that the more I accept it and accept myself, the less friction I have in the rest of my life and the less stressed and unhappy I am."

I looked at her in admiration. "You've come a long way, baby," I said, and she laughed. She put her arm around my shoulders and squeezed.

"Thank God for your mom and dad and you and Mary K.," she said with feeling. "I don't know what I would do without you guys."

For the rest of the night I sat on the carpet of my room, thinking. I knew I wasn't gay, but I understood how my aunt felt. I was beginning to feel different from my family and even my friends, strongly drawn to something they couldn't accept.

Part of me felt if I allowed myself to become a witch, I'd be more relaxed, more natural, more powerful, more confident than I'd ever felt in my life. Part of me knew that if I did, I'd cause pain to the people I loved most.

That night I had a terrifying dream.

It was nighttime. The sky was streaked with broad bands of moonlight, highlighting clouds in shades of eggplant, dove gray, and indigo. The air was cold and I felt the chilly breeze on my face and bare arms as I flew over Widow's Vale. It was beautiful up there, calm and peaceful, with the wind rushing in my ears, my long hair streaming out behind me, my dress whipping around my legs and molding to the outline of my body.

Gradually I became aware of a voice calling me, a frightened voice. I circled the town, wheeling lower like a hawk, circling and diving and floating on great strong currents of air that buoyed my body. In the woods at the north edge of town, the voice was louder. I went lower still until the tops of the trees practically grazed my skin. At a clearing in the middle of the woods I sank down, landing gracefully on one foot.

The voice belonged to Bree. I followed it into the woods until I came to a boggy area, a place where an underground spring seeped sullenly up through the earth, not flowing strongly enough to make a creek but not drying, either. It provided just enough moisture for breeding mosquitoes, for fungus, for soft green molds glowing emerald in the moonlight.

Bree was stuck in the bog, her ankle trapped by a gnarled root. Gradually she was sinking, being sucked under inch by inch. By the time the sun rose, she would drown.

I held out my hand. My arm looked smooth and strong, defined by muscles and covered with silvery, moonlit skin. I clasped her outstretched hand, slippery with foul-smelling mud, and I heard the suck of the bog around her ankle.

Bree gasped in pain as the root gripped her ankle. "I can't!" she cried. "It hurts!"

I made waving motions with my free hand, my brow furrowed with concentration. I felt the ache in my chest that signaled magickal workings. I began to breathe hard, and my sweat felt cold in the night air. Bree was crying and asking me to let her go.

I waved my hand at the bog, willing the roots to set Bree loose, to uncoil themselves, to stretch and open and relax and set her free. All the while I pulled steadily on her hand, easing her out as if I were a midwife and Bree was being born out of the bog.

Then she cried out, her face alight, and we rose gracefully, effortlessly in the air together. Her dress and legs were covered in dark slime, and through our hands' contact I felt the throbbing pain of her ankle. But she was free. I flew with her to the edge of the woods and set her down. Rising into the air, I left her there, weeping with relief, watching me as I rose higher in the sky, higher and higher, until I was just a speck and dawn began to break.

Then I was in a dark, rough room, like a barn. I was an infant. Baby Morgan. A woman was sitting on a bale of straw, holding me in her arms. It wasn't my mom, but she was rocking me and saying, "My baby," over and over. I watched her with my round baby eyes, and I loved her and felt how she loved me.

I woke up, shaking and exhausted. I felt like I was battling the flu, as if I could lie down and sleep for a hundred years.

"You feeling better?" Mary K. asked that afternoon. I had gotten up and dressed around noon and had puttered around the house, doing laundry, taking out the recycling.

I thought about Cal and Bree and everyone having a circle tonight, and I was aching to go. Cal probably expected me to go after what had happened yesterday. In fact, I really *had* to go.

"Yeah," I answered Mary K. I picked up the phone to call Bree. "I just didn't sleep well, woke up all headachy."

Mary K. mixed herself some chocolate milk and zapped it in the microwave. "Yeah? So everything's okay?"

"Sure. Why?"

She leaned against the countertop and sipped her hot chocolate. "I feel like there's something going on lately," she said.

I cradled the undialed phone on my shoulder. "Like what?"

"Well, like all of a sudden I feel like you're doing stuff that I don't know about," Mary K. said. "Not that I have to know all about your life," she added hastily. "You're older; you've always done other stuff. I just mean—" She stopped and rubbed her forehead with her hand. "You're not doing drugs, are you?" she blurted out.

I suddenly saw how things looked from her fourteen-year-old perspective. True, she was an *old* fourteen-year-old, but still. I was her big sister, she had picked up on my tension, and she was worried.

"Oh, Mary K., for God's sake," I said, hugging her. "No, I'm not doing drugs. And I'm not having sex or shoplifting or anything like that. Promise."

She pulled back. "What were those books about that Mom got so upset over?" she asked point-blank.

"I told you. Wicca. Crunchy tree-hugger stuff," I said.

"Then why was she so upset?" Mary K. pressed.

I took a deep breath, then turned to face her. "Wicca is the religion of witches," I explained.

Her beautiful brown eyes, so like Mom's, widened. "Really?"

"It's just, like, living in tune with nature. Picking up on stuff that already exists all around you. The power of nature. Life forces."

"Morgan, isn't witchcraft like Satan worshipping?" Mary K. asked, horrified.

"It really, really isn't," I said urgently, looking her in the eyes. "There's no Satan at all in Wicca. And it's completely forbidden to work black magic or to try to cause harm to anyone.

Everything you send out into the world comes back to you threefold, so everyone tries to do good, always."

Mary K. still looked worried, but she was paying close attention.

"Look, in Wicca you basically just try to be a good person and live in harmony with nature and with other people," I said.

"And dance naked," she said, her eyes narrowing.

I rolled my eyes. "Not everyone does that, and for your info, I would rather be torn apart by wild animals. Wicca is all about what you are comfortable with, how much you want to participate. There's no animal sacrifice, no Satan worshipping, no dancing naked if you don't want to. No taking drugs, no pushing pins into voodoo dolls."

"Then why is Mom so freaked?" she countered.

I thought for a moment. "I think it's partly that she just doesn't know a lot about it. Partly it's that we're Catholic already, and she doesn't want me to change my religion. Other than that, I don't know. Her reaction was a lot stronger than I could believe. It just really pushes her buttons."

"Poor Mom," Mary K. murmured.

I frowned. "Look, I've been trying to respect Mom's feelings, but the more I know about Wicca, the more I know that it's not a bad thing. It's nothing to be afraid of. Mom will just have to believe me."

"This sucks," Mary K. said. "What should I do if they ask me?"

"Whatever you need to say is all right," I said. "I won't ask you to lie."

"Crap," she said. She shook her head, then rinsed out her

mug and put it in the sink. "We're going to dinner at Aunt Margaret's, you know. She called this morning before you were up."

"Oh, no, I don't think I can," I said, thinking of tonight's circle. I couldn't miss another one.

"Hi, sweetie. How are you feeling?" my mom asked, coming into the kitchen with a basket of laundry balanced on her hip.

"Much better. Listen, Mom, I can't go to dinner at Aunt Margaret's tonight," I said. "I promised Bree I would go to her place." The lie slipped out of my mouth as easily as that.

"Oh," my mom said. "Can you call Bree and cancel it? I know Margaret loves seeing you."

"I want to see her, too," I said. "But I already told Bree I'd help her with her math." When in doubt, pull out school-work.

"Oh. Well." She looked like she was having trouble deciding whether to push it. "I guess that's all right. You're sixteen, after all. I suppose you can't go to every family thing."

Now I felt like crap.

"I just promised Bree," I said lamely. "She got a D on her last exam, and she freaked." I was very aware of Mary K. watching this exchange and wished she weren't there.

"Okay," Mom said again. "Some other time."

"Okay," I said. With Mary K.'s gaze following me out of the room, I headed upstairs and flopped onto my bed, cradling my pillow.

20

Broken

><"Men are natural warriors, but a woman in battle is truly bloodthirsty."

—Old Scottish saying><

The night surrounded Bree and me in the comfy interior of her car. Matt's house, where the circle would be, was about ten miles out of town. As soon as Bree picked me up, I sensed that she had a lot on her mind. So did I. After my dream last night I was actually relieved to see her safe and sound and, apart from her quietness, normal.

I thought about the thousands of hours we had spent in cars with each other, first with our parents or Bree's older brother, Ty, driving us, then, for the past year, driving ourselves. We'd had some of our best talks in cars, when it was just the two of us. It felt different tonight.

"Why didn't you tell me about the spell you put on Robbie?" Bree asked.

"I put a spell on the potion, not on Robbie," I clarified. "And I didn't tell anyone. I thought the whole thing was pointless. I was sure it wasn't going to work, and I didn't want to be embarrassed."

"Do you really believe that it worked?" she asked. Her dark eyes were on the road ahead, and Breezy's high beams cut through the night.

"I . . . I guess so," I said. "I mean, mostly because I can't think of what else could have done it. On Monday he had awful skin; now he looks great. I don't know what else to think."

"Do you think you're a blood witch?" she asked. I was starting to feel interrogated.

I laughed to relieve the tension. "Oh, please. Yeah, that's it. I'm a blood witch. Have you seen Sean and Mary Grace lately? They just bought a new pentacle to hang over our living room mantelpiece."

Bree was silent. I felt rough waves of tension and anger coming from her but couldn't pinpoint their source.

"What?" I said. "Bree, what are you thinking?"

"I don't know what to think," she said, and I noticed her knuckles were white on the leather-wrapped steering wheel. To my surprise, she pulled her car over onto the wide shoulder of Wheeler Road. She turned off the engine and shifted in her seat to look at me.

"I'm having trouble believing how two-faced you are."

I stared at her.

"You say you don't like Cal. It's okay for me to go after Cal. But the two of you are always talking, staring at each other intensely, like there's nobody else around."

I opened my mouth to reply, but she went on.

"He never looks at me like that," she added quietly, and the hurt in her face was plain. "I just don't get you," she went on. "You won't come to circles, but then you do spells behind everyone's back! Do you think you're better than we are? Do you think you're so special?"

Shock made me tongue-tied. "I'm coming to the circle *tonight*," I said. "And you know exactly why I didn't come for a couple of weeks—you know how freaked my parents were. That spell was just experimenting, playing. I had no idea how it would turn out."

"You experimented by doing something to Robbie?" Bree asked.

"Yes, I did! And that was wrong!" I practically shouted. "But I made him look a million times better than he did before. Why is that such a crime? Why isn't that a favor?"

We sat there in silence, Bree's anger coming off her in rays.

"Look," I said after a minute. "Even though it turned out well for him, I know I shouldn't have done the spell on Robbie. Cal said it wasn't allowed, and I understand why. It was a stupid mistake," I went on. "I've been confused and freaked out, and I just . . . I just wanted to . . . to *know*."

"Know what?" she spat.

"If I'm . . . special. If I have some special gift."

She looked out the window, silent.

"I mean, I see people's *auras*. Jesus, Bree, *I healed Robbie's skin!* Don't you think that's a big thing?"

She shook her head, clenching her teeth. "You are out of your mind," she muttered.

This was not the Bree I knew. "What is it, Bree?" I asked, trying not to burst into angry tears. "Why are you so mad at me?"

She shrugged abruptly. "I feel like you're not being honest with me," she said, looking out the window again. "It's like I don't even know you anymore."

I didn't know what to say. "Bree, I told you before. I think you and Cal would be a good couple. I'm not flirting with him. I never call him. I never sit next to him."

"You don't need to. He always does those things to you," she said. "But why?"

"Because he wants me to be a witch."

"And why is that?" Bree asked. "He could care less if Robbie or I became witches. Why is he playing guessing games with you, carrying you into pools, telling you that you have a gift for this? Why are you doing spells? You're not even an official coven student, much less a witch."

"I don't know," I answered in frustration. "It's like something seems to be . . . waking up inside me. Something I didn't know was there. And I want to understand what it is . . . what I am."

Bree was quiet for several minutes. In the dark small sounds came to me: the faint ticking of my watch, Bree's breathing, the clicks of Breezy's metal as the car cooled. There was a black shadow rolling toward me, toward the car, and instinctively I braced myself. Then it hit.

"I don't want you to come tonight," Bree said.

I felt my throat close.

Bree picked a piece of lint off her silky blue pants and examined her fingernails. "I thought I wanted us to do this together," she said. "But I was wrong. What I really want is for

Wicca to be something *I* do. I'm the one who's gone to every circle. I'm the one who found Practical Magick. I want Wicca to be for me and Cal. With you around, he gets distracted. Especially since you made it look like you can do spells. I don't know how you really did it. But it's all Cal can talk about."

"I don't believe this," I whispered. "Jesus, Bree! Are you choosing Cal over *me*? Over our friendship?" Hot tears welled up in my eyes. Angrily I dashed them away, refusing to cry in front of her.

Bree seemed less upset than I was. "You would do the same thing if you loved Cal," she informed me.

"Bullshit!" I yelled as she started the car again. "That's bullshit! I wouldn't."

Bree made a U-turn in the middle of Wheeler Road.

"You know, you're going to realize how stupid you're being," I said bitterly. "When it comes to guys, you have the attention span of a *gnat*. Cal is just another in a long line. When you get tired of him and dump him, you'll miss me. And I won't be there."

This idea seemed to make Bree pause. Then she nodded firmly. "You'll get over it," she said. "After Cal and I are really going out and everything calms down, it'll be a whole different picture."

I stared at her. "You are delusional," I said hotly. "Where are we going?"

"I'm taking you home."

"To hell with that," I said, popping open my door. Bree, startled, slammed on the brakes, and I lurched forward, almost whacking my head on the dashboard. Quickly I unsnapped my seat belt and jumped out onto the road.

"Thanks for the lift, Bree." I slammed the door as hard as I could. Bree roared off, spinning a fast doughnut twenty yards down, then whizzing past me again on her way to Matt's. I stood alone by the side of the road, shaking with anger and hurt.

In the eleven years of best friendship that Bree and I'd gone through, we'd had our ups and downs. In first grade she'd had three chocolate cookies in her lunch, and I'd had two Fig Newtons. She rejected my offer of my Fig Newtons for her chocolate cookies, so I had just reached out and snatched them, cramming them into my mouth. I don't know who had been more appalled, me or her. We hadn't spoken for a whole, agonizing week but finally made up when I presented her with six sheets of handmade stationery, each of which I had monogrammed with a *B* in colored pencils.

In sixth grade she had wanted to cheat on my math test, and I had said no. We didn't speak for two days. She cheated off of Robbie's test, and it was never mentioned again.

Last year, in tenth grade, we'd gotten into our worst fight ever, over whether photography counted as a valid art form or whether any idiot with a camera could capture a stunning image every once in a while. I won't tell who took what position, but I will say it culminated in a horrible, screaming fight in my backyard until my mom came out and shouted at us to stop.

That time we didn't speak for two and a half weeks, until we finally each signed a document saying that on this issue, we would agree to disagree. I still have my copy of our promise.

It was cold. I zipped my jacket up to my chin and pulled up the hood. I started walking toward Matt's house but then realized that it was too far away. The tears began to run down my face, and I couldn't stop them. Why was Bree doing this to me? In frustration, I turned around and started the long walk home.

The sharp-edged moon was so close, I could see its craters. I listened to the sounds of the night: insects, animals, birds. My eyes and ears became still more attuned, and I let them. I could make out insects on trees twenty feet away in the darkness. I saw birds' nests high on branches with the soft, rounded heads of sleeping birds visible at the edge. I became aware of the fast-paced fluttery thumping of the baby birds' hearts in syncopated rhythm with the much slower, heavier thud of my own.

I turned the volume of my senses down. I squeezed my eyes shut, but the tears kept coming.

I didn't see how Bree and I would ever recover from this, and I cried about that. I cried because I knew this meant she and Cal would really get together; she would make it happen. And I really cried, my stomach hurting, because I thought this meant I had to close all the doors inside me that had so recently opened.

21

The Thin Line

>< "Anytime you feel love for anything, be it stone, tree, lover, or child, you are touched by the Goddess's magick."

—SABINA FALCONWING,
in a San Francisco coffee shop, 1980 ><

Early the next morning the phone rang. It was Robbie. "What's going on?" he asked. "Last night Bree said you weren't going to come to circles anymore."

Bree's assumption that I would give in to her so easily filled me with fury. I swallowed it and said, "That isn't true. That's what she wants. It isn't what I want. Samhain is next Saturday, and I'll be there."

Robbie paused for a few seconds. "What's going on between you two? You're best friends."

"You don't want to know," I said tersely.

"You're right," he said. "I probably don't want to know. Anyway, we're meeting in the cornfields to the north of town, on the other side of the road from where Mabon was. We're going to meet at eleven-thirty, and if we decide we want to be initiated as students into a new coven, that will happen at midnight."

"Wow, okay. Are you . . . are you going to do it?"

"We're not really supposed to talk about it or decide yet," Robbie explained. "Cal said to just think about it in a completely personal way. Oh, and everyone has to bring stuff. I volunteered you for flowers and apples."

"Thanks, Robbie," I said sincerely. "Do we have to wear anything special?"

"Black or orange," he said. "See you tomorrow."

"Okay, thanks."

Church that day was much as usual. Father Hotchkiss noted that it was best to have a defensive line without gaps so that evil would have no place to gain access to your soul.

I leaned across my mom to Mary K. "Note to self," I whispered. "No gaps for evil."

She hid her grin behind her program.

That day I felt hyper—tuned in to the service, despite Father Hotchkiss. I wondered if following Wicca meant I really, truly couldn't ever come to church again. I decided it wouldn't. I knew that I would miss church if I stopped coming, and I also knew that my parents would kill me. Later on in my life, if I had to choose between one or the other, I could do it then. I thought about what Paula Steen had said, about it's what you brought to something that mattered.

Today I listened to the hymns and to the massive European organ played by Mrs. Lavender, as it had been since my mom was a child. I loved the candles and the incense and the formal procession of gold-robed priests and white-clothed altar boys and girls. I had been an altar girl for a couple of years, and so had Mary K. It was all so comforting, so familiar.

After church and brunch at the Widow's Diner, I went to the grocery store with that week's shopping list. On my way, I hopped up to Red Kill, to Practical Magick. I didn't plan to buy anything and didn't see anyone I knew, but I stood in the book section, reading up about Samhain for a while. I decided to bring a black candle next Saturday since black is the color that helps ward off negativity. Meanly I was tempted to buy Bree a roomful of black candles.

My anger at her was still white-hot. I couldn't believe her incredibly arrogant notion that she could kick me out of the circle. It only highlighted the harsh fact that in our relationship, she had always been the leader. I had always been the follower. I saw that now, and it made me angry with myself, too.

I dreaded going to school the next day.

"May I help you?" A pleasant-faced older woman, inches shorter than me, stood smiling at me as I looked at candles.

I decided to jump in headfirst. "Um, yes. I need a black candle for Samhain," I said.

"Certainly." She nodded and reached for the black candle section. "You're lucky we still have some left. People have been snapping these up all week." She held up two different black candles: one a thick pillar about a foot tall, the other a long, slim taper about fourteen inches tall.

"Both of these would be appropriate," she said. "The pillar lasts longer, but the taper is very elegant, too."

The pillar was much more expensive.

"Um, I guess I'll take the . . . pillar," I said. I had meant to say taper, but it hadn't come out that way. The woman nodded knowingly.

"I think the pillar wants to go home with you," she said, as if it was normal for a candle to choose its owner. "Will this be all for you?"

"Yes." I followed her to the checkout, thinking how uncreepy she was and how much more I liked her than the other clerk.

"If I brought flowers on Samhain, what kind should I bring?" I asked her a little self-consciously.

She smiled as she rang up my purchase. "Whichever ones want you to buy them," she said cheerfully. Then she looked closely into my eyes, as if searching for something.

"Are you—" she began. "You must be the girl David was telling me about," she said thoughtfully.

"Who's David?"

"The other clerk here," she explained. "He said a young witch comes in here who pretends not to be a witch. It's you, isn't it? You're a friend of Cal's."

I was stunned. "Um . . ."

She smiled broadly. "Yep, it's you, all right. How nice to meet you. My name's Alyce. If you ever need anything, you just let me know. You're going to walk a difficult road for a while."

"How do you know that?" I blurted out.

She looked surprised as she put my candle into a bag. "I just do," she said. "The way *you* know things. You understand what I'm talking about."

I didn't say anything. I took my bag and practically flew from the store, equally fascinated and unnerved.

On Monday morning I went defiantly to the benches where the Wicca group gathered and sat down, dropping my backpack at my feet. Beyond looking surprised to see me, Bree ignored me.

"We missed you Saturday night," Jenna said.

"Bree said you weren't coming anymore," Ethan put in.

There. It was right out in the open. I felt Cal's eyes on me.

"No, I am coming. I want to be a witch," I said clearly. "I think I'm supposed to be."

Jenna giggled nervously. Cal smiled, and I smiled back at him, aware of how Bree's jaw tightened.

"That's cool," Ethan said. "Here, push over," he said to Sharon, nudging her thigh with his knee.

With a put-upon sigh Sharon made room, and Ethan grinned. I watched them, suddenly recognizing a certain awareness between them. It blew my mind: Sharon and Ethan? Could they be interested in each other?

"Uh-oh, an outlander," Matt muttered jokingly, and Raven smirked.

Tamara walked up.

"Hi," I said, genuinely pleased to see her.

"Hi," Tamara said, looking around at the group. "Hey, Morgan, did you do all the functions homework last weekend? I really got stuck on number three."

I thought back. "Yeah, I did it. You want to go over it?"

"That'd be great," she said.

I grabbed my backpack. "No problem. See you all later," I

said to the group, and followed Tamara inside to the school library. For the next ten minutes we worked on the problem, me and Tamara, and it was so nice. I felt almost normal.

"I'm glad you're coming to Samhain," Cal said.

I looked back to see him following me out of calculus class. My locker was outside the lunchroom, and I had to switch books before Wednesday's chem lab.

I nodded and spun my locker combination. "I've been reading up on it. I'm looking forward to it."

"You think you want to be initiated as a student," he stated. "You need to think about whether you want to be part of this new coven." Tiny lines crinkled around his eyes as he smiled and leaned against the locker next to mine. "I know it's complicated for you at home."

I let myself look deeply into his eyes. There was a tide there, and it was pulling me strongly.

"Yes, I want to be a student," I said. "Even if you aren't a high priest. And yes, I want to be in your new coven. I've agonized over this. My parents are terrified of Wicca. They don't want me to do it, but I can't let them make this decision for me any longer. I'm feeling more certain every day."

"Give yourself a chance to think about it," he advised.

"I hardly think about anything else," I admitted.

He held my eyes and nodded. "See you in physics." He pushed off and left me there with a tingly, fluttery feeling in my stomach.

Bree wasn't my friend anymore, and that gave me the space to ask a simple question I'd been terrified to ask myself. Could Cal love me the way I loved him? Could we be together?

"Quick! Quick! Give me the tape!" Mary K. said, waving her hands. She was up on a ladder in our dining room. My mom was due home soon, and we were decorating for her birthday.

"Hang on," I said, twisting the two streamers together. "Here."

"Dad's picking up Thai food?" Mary K. asked, taping the streamers in place.

"Yep. And Aunt Eileen is picking up the ice-cream cake."

"Yum."

I stood back. The dining room looked pretty festive.

"What's all this?" my mom asked, standing in the doorway.

Mary K. and I both screamed.

"What are you doing home?" I cried. "We're not ready yet!"

Mary K. waved her hands. "Shoo! Go upstairs! Change! We need ten more minutes!"

My mom looked around and laughed. "You two," she said, then she went to go change.

Mom's birthday was fun, and nothing went wrong. She opened her presents, exclaiming over the Celtic-knot pin I gave her, the CD from Mary K., the earrings from my dad, and two books from Eileen. She wasn't recognizable as the person who had screamed at me just a few weeks ago. I smiled as she cut her cake, feeling a sense of doom about what was coming up on Saturday. But tonight we were all happy.

On Thursday, I was slumped in a chair in the school library during study hall, reading the Samhain chapter in one of my books. Tamara came up and tipped the book back to see its title.

"Are you still doing this stuff?" she asked softly, friendly interest in her face.

I nodded. "It's really cool," I said, the words lame and inadequate. "We've been holding circles every week, although I haven't been able to get to many."

"What's it all about?" she asked. "What is Cal trying to do?"

I hesitated. "He's trying to find people who are interested in creating a new coven," I said.

Tamara's brown eyes grew wide. "*Coven* sounds pretty scary."

"Kind of," I admitted. "But that's just because of . . . bad publicity," I guessed. "It's not scary at all. His coven will be more like a . . . study group."

Tamara nodded, not seeming to know what to say.

"Want to go to a movie tomorrow night?" I asked suddenly.

Her face broke into a wide smile. "That would be great. Can I ask Janice, too?"

"Yeah. Let's see what's playing at the Meadowlark," I suggested.

"Cool," said Tamara. "See you later. Happy reading."

I grinned, feeling lighthearted as she sat down across the room.

A moment later, with no warning, Bree dropped into the chair next to me. I tensed. "Relax," she said. "I just wanted to tell you that phase one of Bree and Cal is complete. I need a little more time, and then you can come to circles all you want."

I stared at her. "What are you talking about?"

"He's given in," she said happily. "He's mine. Give me a few more weeks to solidify it, and this will all be behind us."

"You've got to be kidding," I said, sitting up straighter. "This will *never* be behind us. Don't you get it? You chose a guy over our friendship. I don't even know why you're talking to me now." I looked into her beautiful face, once as familiar as my own.

"I'm talking to you to tell you to quit overreacting." She stuck out her booted foot and tapped my knee gently. "We both said things we didn't mean, but we'll get over it. We always do. All I need is a little more time with Cal."

I shook my head. I just wanted her to leave.

"You know what I'm talking about," she said softly, watching my face. "Cal and I finally went to bed. So we're going out. In a few weeks we'll be a solid couple. Then you can come back to circles."

A piercing pain in my chest startled me, and I swallowed and rubbed my shirt between my nearly nonexistent breasts. Twenty lightning-flash images of Cal and Bree intertwined on his bed, lit candles surrounding them, zipped through my brain, leaving it feeling raw and wounded. Oh God.

"How nice for you," I managed, pleased with the steadiness of my voice. "But I don't care if you're screwing everyone in the circle. You can't tell me what to do. I will be at Samhain." Anger fueled the words spooling out of my mouth. "You see, Bree, the difference between us is that I really am interested in becoming a witch. Not just pretending to be so I can seduce a good-looking guy."

"When did you become such a bitch?" she asked.

I shrugged. "Maybe I hung out with you too long."

She unfolded herself from the chair and moved off with such feminine grace that I felt like a rock sitting there.

It's true what they say. There's a thin line between love and hate.

22

What I Am

><"Beware the witches' new year, their night of unholy rites. It falls before All Saints' Eve. On that day, the line between this world and the next is thin, easily broken."

—WITCHES, MAGES, AND WARLOCKS,
Altus Polydarmus, 1618><

Tonight I'm going to a circle, and nothing can stop me. I'm going to declare myself to be a student of Cal's coven. I know my life will change tonight. I sense it in every sight and sound.

"Where's Bree?" my mom asked as Mary K. and I got dressed in our costumes. We were going to the school Halloween party since we had finally admitted to being too old to go trick or treating. It was barely seven o'clock, and already our front porch had been besieged by small pirates, devils, princesses, brides, monsters, and yes, witches.

"Yeah, good question," Mary K. said, drawing a fake

Frankenstein scar on her cheek. "I haven't seen her all week."

"She's busy," I said casually, brushing my hair. "She has a new boyfriend."

My mom chuckled. "Bree certainly is a social butterfly."

That's one way of putting it, I thought sarcastically.

Mary K. looked at my outfit critically. "Is that it?"

"I couldn't decide," I admitted. I was dressed up as me. Me, all in black, but me nonetheless.

"For heaven's sake, let's paint your face at least," my mom clucked.

They painted my face as a daisy. Since I was wearing black jeans and a black top, I looked like a daisy on a wilted stem. But no matter. Mary K. and I went to school and danced to a really bad local band called The Ruffians. Someone had spiked the punch, but of course the teachers found out about it right away and dumped it in the parking lot. No one from the circle was there, but I saw Tamara and Janice, and I danced with Mary K., with Bakker, and with a couple of guys from my various math and science classes. It was fun. Not thrilling, but fun.

We were home by eleven-fifteen. Mom, Dad, and Mary K. went to bed, and I arranged some pillows in the traditional columnar lump in my bed before I washed my face and sneaked out into the chilly darkness.

Bree and I had sneaked out before, to do stupid things like go to the twenty-four-hour QuikStop to get doughnuts or something. It had always seemed so lighthearted, like an acceptable rite of passage.

Tonight the moon shone down brightly like a spotlight, the cold October wind went bone deep, and I felt very alone and confused. As I crept toward the dark driveway, our jack-o'-lantern sputtered out on the front porch. Without its cheerful candlelit grin it seemed somehow sinister and garish. Pagan and ancient and more powerful than you'd think a carved pumpkin could be.

I breathed the night air for a moment, looking around for signs of people stirring. It came to me to try something—to sort of throw my senses out in a net, out into the world. As if they would pick up signals, like a TV antenna would or a satellite dish. I closed my eyes for a minute, listening. I heard—almost felt—dry, crumpled leaves floating to the ground. I heard the squirrels frantically scrambling. I felt the breeze carrying mist off the river. But my senses found no sign of parents or neighbors stirring. All was quiet on my street. For the moment I was safe.

My car weighs a ton, and it was hard to push it out of the driveway by myself, trying to steer and having to jump in and stomp on the brakes. I prayed some Halloween joyriders wouldn't come screeching around my corner and cream my car. I closed my eyes again for a moment, thinking about my house, and I sensed people sleeping calmly, breathing deeply, unaware I was gone.

Finally my car was in the street, facing forward, and easier to push and control. I moved it as far as the Herndons' house, with its new ramp for Mr. Herndon's wheelchair. I got in and started the engine, thinking about the heated seats in Breezy. In my hands Das Boot felt like a living animal, purring to life, excited to be eating up the road beneath its wheels. We drove off into the darkness.

I parked under the huge willow oak in the field across from the cornfields. Robbie's red Beetle was there, and so was Matt's pickup. I had already seen Bree's and Raven's cars on the other side of the road. Feeling nervous, I got out of Das Boot and walked around to the trunk. I looked over my shoulders constantly, as if expecting Bree—or worse—to leap out at me from the dark velvet shadows. Quickly I unpacked the flowers, fruit, and candle I had brought and set off to the cornfields across the road.

Even at this late, late date I still felt some uncertainty, despite what I had told Bree and the others about being a witch. Everything in my heart was a go for launching myself into Wicca, but my mind was still busily gathering information. And my heart was more fragile than it might have been, bruised from my fight with Bree, from thinking about her with Cal, from hiding all of this from my parents. I was truly torn, and at the edge of the cornfield I almost dropped everything, turned around, and ran back to Das Boot.

Then I heard the music, Celtic music, floating airily toward me on the breeze, a caressing ribbon of sound seeming to promise peace and calm and welcome. I plunged into the tall feed corn that had been left to dry on the stalk. It didn't occur to me to wonder where I was going or how I knew where to meet the others. I just went, and after brushing through the crackling golden sea, I found myself in a clearing, and the circle was waiting for me.

"Morgan!" Jenna said happily, holding out her hands to me. She was glowing, and her normally pretty face looked beautiful in the bright moonlight.

"Hi," I said self-consciously. The nine of us stood there, looking at one another. To me it felt like we had gathered to begin a journey together, as if we were going to climb Everest. As if some of us might not make it all the way, but we were together at the beginning. Suddenly these people seemed like total strangers. Robbie was distant and newly handsome, not the math geek I had known for so long. Bree was a cold, lovely statue of the best friend I had once had. The others I had never been close to. What was I doing?

My leg muscles tensed, ready for flight, and then Cal walked over, and I was rooted to the spot.

Helplessly I smiled at Jenna and Robbie and Matt.

"Where do I put this?" I asked, holding up my stuff.

"On the altar," Cal said, coming forward. His eyes met mine for a timeless, suspended second. "I'm glad you came."

I gazed stupidly into his face for the split second it took me to remember about him and Bree, what she had told me, then I nodded curtly. "Where's the altar?"

"This way. And happy Samhain, everyone," Cal said, motioning for us to follow him through the corn. When the moonlight caught his glossy hair, it glowed, and he did indeed look like the pagan god of the forest I had read about. Do you belong to Bree now? I asked him silently.

After we left the cornfield, there was a broad mowed meadow sloping gently downhill. In the spring it would be covered with flowers. Now it was brown and soft underfoot. At the bottom of the meadow there was a tiny, icy stream, clear as rainwater, flowing swiftly over smooth gray and green rocks. We stepped across easily, Cal going first and helping everyone else. His hand felt warm and sure around mine.

Since I had arrived, I had been watching Cal and Bree out of the corner of my eye. The knowledge that they had gone to bed together was inescapable. And yet tonight he at least seemed the same. Somewhat cool and remote, seeming to pay no special attention to Bree. They didn't look like a couple, like Jenna and Matt. Bree seemed high-strung, and even worse, she seemed more friendly toward Raven and Beth.

Past the stream the ground rose again and was swallowed into a line of thick trees. The trees were old, with gnarled bark, huge, spreading roots, and limbs as big around as barrels. Under the trees the darkness was almost impenetrable, yet I saw clearly and had no trouble picking my way through the underbrush.

Once we were through the trees, we found ourselves in an old cemetery.

I saw Robbie blinking. Raven and Beth shared amused smiles, and Jenna slipped her hand into Matt's. Ethan snorted but stepped closer to Sharon when she looked unsure. I knew Bree was feeling confused only because I can decipher almost every nuance of her expression.

"This is an old Methodist graveyard," Cal told us, resting his hand nonchalantly on a tall tombstone carved in the shape of a cross. "Graveyards are good places to celebrate Samhain. Tonight we honor those who have passed before us, and we acknowledge that one day we too shall pass into dust, only to be reborn."

Cal turned and led the way down a row of tombstones to what looked like a large, raised sarcophagus. A huge old stone, lichened and stained with hundreds of years of rain and snow and wind, covered a raised granite box. Its carved letters were impossible to make out even in the bright moonlight.

"This is our altar for tonight," Cal said, reaching down and opening a duffel bag. He handed a cloth to Sharon. "Could you spread this out, please?"

Sharon took it and spread it gingerly over the sarcophagus. Cal handed Ethan two large brass candlesticks, and Ethan set them on the altar.

"Jenna? Robbie? Can you arrange all the fruit and stuff?" Cal asked.

They gathered the offerings we had brought, and Jenna arranged it artistically on the altar in a cornucopia effect. There were apples, winter squashes, a pumpkin, and a bowl of nuts Bree had brought.

I took my flowers and Jenna's and Sharon's and put them into glass vases at either side of the altar. Beth gathered some boughs of dried autumn leaves and arranged them on the altar behind the food. Raven collected the other candles people had brought, including my black pillar, and fixed them to the sarcophagus by dripping wax and setting them on it. Matt lit all the candles in turn. There was hardly any wind here, and they barely flickered in the night. When the candles were lit, the place seemed more threatening somehow. I liked the idea of being able to hide in the darkness and felt exposed and vulnerable with the candlelight reflecting on my face.

"Now, everyone gather here in the middle," Cal instructed. "Jenna? Raven? Would you like to draw our circle and purify it?"

I was jealous he had chosen them—probably we all were. Cal watched the two girls patiently, ready to help if necessary. But they worked carefully together, and soon the circle was cast and purified with water, air, fire, and earth.

Now that I was again with a circle, I felt exultant, expectant. The only thing that marred my good mood was Bree's dark brooding and Raven's air of superiority. I tried to ignore them, to focus only on magick, my magick, and to open myself to perceptions from any source beyond my five senses.

"Our circle is now cast," Jenna said with awe in her voice. We all moved outward to stand just within its boundary. I made certain that I was between Matt and Robbie, two positive forces who wouldn't distract or upset me.

Cal took a small bottle and uncorked it. Moving deasil, clockwise, around the circle, he dipped his finger into it and drew a pentacle, a five-pointed star within a circle, on each of our foreheads.

"What is this?" I asked, the only person to speak.

Cal smiled faintly. "Salt water." He drew a pentacle on my forehead, his finger wet and gentle. Where he traced felt warm, as if it were glowing with power.

When he was finished, he took his place in the circle. "Tonight we're here to form a new coven," he said. "We gather to celebrate the Goddess and the God, to celebrate nature, to explore and create and worship magick, and to explore the magickal powers both within ourselves and without ourselves."

In the next moment of silence, I heard myself say, "Blessed be," and the others echoed it. Cal smiled.

"Anyone who wishes not to be of this coven, please break the circle now," Cal said.

No one moved.

"Welcome," Cal said. "Merry meet and blessed be. As we gather, so we'll be. The ten of us have found our haven, here within the Cirrus coven."

I thought, Cirrus? It was a nice name.

"You nine will now be inducted as novitiates, students of this coven," Cal explained. "I'll teach you what I know, then together we can seek out new teachers to take us further on our journey."

The only time I'd heard the word *novitiate* used was in relation to priests or nuns. I shifted on my feet, feeling the dense, soft ground beneath me. Overhead, the moon was high and white, huge. Every once in a while we heard the sound of a car or firecrackers. But in this place, in our circle, there was a deep, abiding silence, broken only by animals' night calls, the fluttering wings of bats and owls, the occasionally heard trickle of the stream.

Within myself I also felt a deep stillness. As if being put to bed one by one, my fears and uncertainties quieted. My senses were on full alert, and I felt incredibly alive. The candles, the breathing of the people with me, the scent of the flowers and fruit we had brought, all combined to create a wonderful, deep connection to Nature, the Goddess who is everywhere, all around us.

In the bowl of earth in the northern position, Cal lit an incense stick, and soon we were surrounded by the comforting scents of cinnamon and nutmeg. We joined hands. Unlike the other two times I had participated in a circle, tonight I was neither examining nor dreading what might happen. I kept my mind open.

Matt's and Robbie's hands were larger than mine; Matt's smooth and slender, Robbie's bulkier than Cal's had been. My eyes flicked to Robbie's face. It was smooth and unlined. I had done that, and within me I felt a recognition of and a pride in my own power.

Cal began the chant as we moved deasil around our circle.

"Tonight we bid the God farewell,
In the Underground he'll dwell.
Till his rebirth in springtime's sun,
But for now his life is done.

"We dance beneath the Blood Moon's shine,
This chant we'll sing to number nine.
We dance to let our heart's love flow,
To aid the Goddess in her sorrow."

I counted as we danced around the circle, and we chanted nine times. The more I studied Wicca, the more I realized that witches wove symbolism into just about everything: plants, numbers, days of the week, colors, times of the year, even fabrics, food, and flowers. Everything has a meaning. My job as a student would be to learn these symbols, to learn as much as I could about the nature surrounding me, and to weave myself into its pattern and magick.

As we chanted I thought about the end, when we would throw up our arms to release our energy. Once again I felt worried as I remembered the pain and nausea I had felt before. My facade of certainty began to crack, allowing in tendrils of fear. My power seemed scary.

Just as suddenly, as we whirled in our circle, singing the chant like a round, weaving our voices in and among one another, I realized that my *fear* would cause me pain if I didn't let it go right now. I breathed deeply, feeling the chant leave my throat, surrounded by the coven in our circle, and I tried to banish fear, banish limitations.

Faces were blurred. I felt out of control. I banish fear! The words of our chant slurred until it was a beautiful rhythm of pure sound, rising and falling and swirling around me. I was having trouble breathing, and my face was hot and damp with sweat. I wanted to throw off my jacket, throw off my shoes. I had to stop. I had to banish fear.

With one last burst of sound our circle stopped, and we threw our arms skyward. I felt a rush of energy whirling around me. My hand grasped the air, and I pushed my fist against my chest, seizing some energy for myself. I banish fear, I thought dreamily, and then the night exploded all around me.

I was dancing in the atmosphere, surrounded by stars, seeing motes of energy whizzing past me like microscopic comets. I could see the entire universe; all at once, every particle, every smile, every fly, every grain of sand was revealed to me and was infinitely beautiful.

When I breathed in, I breathed in the very essence of life, and I breathed out white light. It was beautiful, more than beautiful, but I didn't have the words to express it even to myself. I understood everything; I understood my place in the universe; I understood the path I had to follow.

Then I smiled and blinked and breathed out again, and I was standing in a darkened graveyard with nine high school friends, and tears were running down my face.

"Are you okay?" Robbie asked in concern, coming over to me.

At first it seemed he was speaking gibberish, but then I understood what he had said, and I nodded.

"It was so beautiful," I said lamely, my voice breaking. I felt unbearably diminished after my vision. I reached my finger out to touch Robbie's cheek. My finger left a warm pink line where it touched, and Robbie rubbed his cheek, looking confused.

The vases of flowers were on the altar, and I walked toward them, mesmerized by their beauty and also the overwhelming sadness of the flowers' deaths. I touched one bud, and it opened beneath my hand, blooming in death as it hadn't been allowed to in life. I heard Raven gasp and knew that Bree and Beth and Matt backed away from me then.

Then Cal was next to me. "Quit touching things," he said quietly, smiling. "Lie down and ground yourself."

He guided me to an open spot within our circle, and I lay down on my back, feeling the pulsing life of the earth centering me, easing the energy from me, making me feel more normal. My perceptions focused, and I saw the coven clearly, saw the candles, the stars, the fruit as themselves again and not as pulsing blobs of energy.

"What's happening to me?" I whispered. Cal sat down cross-legged behind me and lifted my head onto his lap, stroking my hair, which was strewn across his legs. Robbie knelt next to him. Ethan, Beth, and Sharon circled closer, peering over his shoulder at me as if I were a museum display. Jenna was holding Matt around his waist, as if she were afraid. Raven and Bree were the farthest back, and Bree looked wide-eyed and solemn.

"You made magick," Cal said, gazing at me with those endless dark gold eyes. "You're a blood witch."

My eyes opened wider as his face slowly blotted out the moon above me. With his eyes looking deeply into mine, he touched my mouth with his, and with a sense of shock I realized he was kissing me. My arms felt heavy as I moved them up to encircle his neck, and then I was kissing him back, and we were joined, and the magick crackled all around us.

In that moment of sheer happiness I didn't question what being a blood witch meant to me or my family or what Cal and I being together meant to Bree or Raven or anyone else. It would be my first lesson in magick, and it would be hard learned: seeing the big picture, not just a part of it.

Book Two

SWEEP
The Coven

All quoted materials in this work were created by the author.
Any resemblance to existing works is accidental.

The Coven

SPEAK
Published by the Penguin Group
Penguin Group (USA) Inc., 345 Hudson Street, New York, New York 10014, U.S.A.
Penguin Group (Canada), 90 Eglinton Avenue East, Suite 700, Toronto, Ontario, Canada M4P 2Y3
(a division of Pearson Penguin Canada Inc.)
Penguin Books Ltd, 80 Strand, London WC2R 0RL, England
Penguin Ireland, 25 St Stephen's Green, Dublin 2, Ireland (a division of Penguin Books Ltd)
Penguin Group (Australia), 250 Camberwell Road, Camberwell, Victoria 3124, Australia
(a division of Pearson Australia Group Pty Ltd)
Penguin Books India Pvt Ltd, 11 Community Centre, Panchsheel Park, New Delhi - 110 017, India
Penguin Group (NZ), 67 Apollo Drive, Rosedale, North Shore 0632, New Zealand
(a division of Pearson New Zealand Ltd)
Penguin Books (South Africa) (Pty) Ltd, 24 Sturdee Avenue, Rosebank, Johannesburg 2196, South Africa

Registered Offices: Penguin Books Ltd, 80 Strand, London WC2R 0RL, England

Published by Puffin Books, a division of Penguin Young Readers Group, 2001
Published by Speak, an imprint of Penguin Group (USA) Inc., 2007
This omnibus edition published by Speak, an imprint of Penguin Group (USA) Inc., 2010

1 3 5 7 9 10 8 6 4 2

Copyright © 2001 17th Street Productions, an Alloy company,
and Gabrielle Charbonnet
All rights reserved

CIP DATA IS AVAILABLE

Produced by 17th Street Productions,
an Alloy company
151 West 26th Street
New York, NY 10001

17th Street Productions and associated logos
are trademarks and/or registered trademarks of Alloy, Inc.

Speak ISBN 978-0-14-240987-9
This omnibus ISBN 978-0-14-241717-1
Printed in the United States of America

To N. and P.,
who have brought so much magic into my life

THE COVEN

Prologue

I was dancing in the atmosphere, surrounded by stars, seeing motes of energy whizzing past me like microscopic comets. I could see the entire universe, all at once; every particle, every smile, every fly, every grain of sand was revealed to me and was infinitely beautiful.

When I breathed in, I breathed in the very essence of life, and I breathed out white light. It was beautiful, more than beautiful, but I didn't have the words to express it even to myself. I understood everything; I understood my place in the universe; I understood the path I had to follow.

Then I smiled and blinked and breathed out again, and I was standing in a darkened graveyard with nine high school friends, and tears were running down my face.

"Are you okay?" Robbie asked in concern, coming over to me.

At first it seemed he was speaking gibberish, but then I understood what he had said, and I nodded.

"It was so beautiful," I said lamely, my voice breaking. I felt unbearably diminished after my vision. I reached my finger out to touch Robbie's cheek. My finger left a warm pink line where it touched, and Robbie rubbed his cheek, looking confused.

The vases of flowers were on the altar, and I walked toward them, mesmerized by their beauty and also the overwhelming sadness of the flowers' deaths. I touched one bud, and it opened beneath my hand, blooming in death as it hadn't been allowed to in life. I heard Raven gasp and knew that Bree and Beth and Matt backed away from me then.

Then Cal was next to me. "Quit touching things," he said quietly, smiling. "Lie down and ground yourself."

He guided me to an open spot within our circle, and I lay down on my back, feeling the pulsing life of the earth centering me, easing the energy from me, making me feel more normal. My perceptions focused, and I saw the coven clearly, saw the candles, the stars, the fruit as themselves again and not as pulsing blobs of energy.

"What's happening to me?" I whispered. Cal sat cross-legged and lifted my head onto his lap, stroking my hair strewn across his legs. Robbie knelt next to him. Ethan, Beth, and Sharon circled closer, peering over his shoulder at me as if I were a museum display. Jenna was holding Matt around his waist, as if she were afraid. Raven and Bree were the farthest back, and Bree looked wide-eyed and solemn.

"You made magick," Cal said, gazing at me with those endless golden eyes. "You're a blood witch."

My eyes opened wider as his face slowly blotted out the moon above me. With his eyes looking deeply into mine, he touched my mouth with his, and with a sense of shock I realized he was kissing me. My arms felt heavy as I moved them up to encircle his neck, and then I was kissing him back, and we were joined, and the magick crackled all around us.

In that moment of sheer happiness I didn't question what being a blood witch meant to me or my family or what Cal and I being together meant to Bree or Raven or Robbie or anyone else. It would be my first lesson in magick, and it would be hard learned: seeing the big picture, not just a part of it.

1

After Samhain

This book is given to my incandescent one, my fire fairy, Bradhadair, on her fourteenth birthday. Welcome to Belwicket. With love from Mathair.

><

This book is private. Keep out.

Imbolc, 1976

Here's an easy spell to start my Book of Shadows. I got it from Betts Towson, except I use black candles and she uses blue.

To Get Rid of a Bad Habit

1. Light altar candles.
2. Light black candle. Say: "This holds me back. No more will I do it. No more is it part of me."
3. Light white candle. Say: "This is my might and my courage and my victory. This battle is already won."

4. Picture in your mind the bad habit you want to break. Picture yourself free from it. After a few minutes of imagining victory, put out the black candle, then the white candle.
5. Repeat a week later if necessary. Best done during a waning moon.

   I did this last Thursday as part of my initiation. I haven't bitten my nails since. — Bradhadair

I woke slowly on the day after Samhain. I tried to resist the light behind my eyes, but soon I was awake, and there was nothing I could do about it.

My room was barely light. It was the first day of November, and the warmth of autumn had leached away. I stretched, then was flooded with memories and sensations so strong that I sat straight up in bed.

Shivering, I saw again Cal leaning over me, kissing me. Me, kissing Cal back, my arms around his neck, his hair soft beneath my fingers. The connection we made, our magick, the electricity, the sparks, the way the universe swirled around us . . . I am a blood witch, I thought. I am a blood witch, and Cal loves me, and I love Cal. And that's the way it is.

The night before, I'd had my first kiss, found my first love. I had also betrayed my best friend, created a rift in my new coven, and realized my parents had lied to me my whole life.

All of this happened on Samhain, October 31, the witches' New Year. My new year, my new life.

I lay back down in bed, the coziness of my flannel sheets and comforter reassuring. Last night I had seen my dreams come true. Now I knew, with a coldness in my stomach, I would pay the price for them. I felt much older than sixteen.

Blood witch, I thought. Cal says that's what I am, and after last night, after what I did, how can I doubt it? It must be true. I am a blood witch. In my veins flows blood that has been inherited from thousands of years of magick making, thousands of years of witches intermarrying. I'm one of them, from one of the Seven Great Clans: Rowanwand, Wyndenkell, Leapvaughn, Vikroth, Brightendale, Burnhide, and Woodbane.

But which one? Rowanwand, both teachers and hoarders of knowledge? Wyndenkell, the expert spell writers? Vikroth? The Vikroths were magickal warriors, later related to Vikings. I smiled. I didn't feel very warrior-like.

The Leapvaughns were mischief makers, joke players. The Burnhide clan focused on doing magick with gems, crystals, and metals, and the Brightendales were the medical clan, using the magick of plants to heal. Or . . . there was Woodbane. I shivered. There was no way I was of the dark clan, the ones who wanted power at any cost, the ones who battled and betrayed their fellow clans for control of land, of magickal power, of knowledge.

I considered it. Of the seven great clans, if I was in fact from one of them, I felt most like the Brightendales, the healers. I had discovered that I loved plants, that they spoke to me, that using their magickal powers came naturally to me. I hugged myself, smiling. A Brightendale. A real blood witch.

Which means my parents must also be blood witches, I thought. It was a stunning notion. It made me wonder why we'd been going to church every Sunday for as long as I could remember. I mean, I liked my church. I liked going to services. They seemed beautiful and traditional and comforting. But Wicca felt more natural.

I sat up in bed again. Two images kept coming at me: Cal leaning over me, his golden eyes locked on mine. And Bree, my best friend: the shock and pain on her face as she saw Cal and me together. The accusation, hurt, desire. Rage.

What have I done? I wondered.

I heard my parents downstairs in the kitchen, starting coffee, unloading the dishwasher. Flopping back down in bed, I listened to the familiar sounds: Not every single thing in my life had changed last night.

Someone opened the front door to get the paper. Today was Sunday, which meant church, followed by brunch at the Widow's Diner. Seeing Cal later? Would I talk to him? Were we going out now, a couple? He had kissed me in front of everyone—what had it meant? Was Cal Blaire, beautiful Cal Blaire, really attracted to me, Morgan Rowlands? Me, with my flat chest and my assertive nose? Me, who guys never looked at twice?

I stared up at my ceiling as if the answers were written on the cracked plaster. When the door to my room burst open, I jumped.

"Can you explain this?" my mom asked. Her brown eyes were wide, her mouth tight, with deeply carved lines around it. She held up a small stack of books, tied with string. They were the books I had left at Bree's house because I knew my parents didn't want me to have them, my books on Wicca, the Seven Great Clans, the history of witchcraft. A note attached to the books said in big letters: "Morgan—You left these at my house. Thought you might need them." Sitting up, I realized this was Bree's revenge.

"I thought we had an understanding," Mom said, her voice rising. She leaned out my bedroom door and yelled, "Sean!"

I swung my legs out of bed. The floor was cold, and I pushed my feet into my slippers.

"Well?" Mom's voice was a decibel louder, and my dad came into my room, looking alarmed.

"Mary Grace?" he said. "What's going on?"

Mom held up the books as if they were a dead rat. "These were on the front porch!" she said. "Look at the note!"

She turned back to me. "What do you think you're doing?" she demanded, incredulous. "When I said I didn't want these books in my house, that didn't mean I wanted you reading them in someone else's house! You knew what I meant, Morgan!"

"Mary Grace," my dad soothed, taking the books from her. He read their titles silently.

My younger sister, Mary K., padded into the room, still in her plaid patchwork pajamas. "What's going on?" she said, pushing her hair out of her eyes. No one answered.

I tried to think fast. "Those books aren't dangerous or illegal. And I wanted to read them. I'm not a child—I'm six- teen. Anyway, I was respecting your wishes not to have them in the house."

"Morgan," my dad said, sounding uncharacteristically stern. "It's not just having the books in the house, and you know it. We explained that as Catholics, we feel that witch- craft is wrong. It may not be illegal, but it's blasphemous."

"You are sixteen," Mom put in. "Not eighteen. That means you are still a child." Her face was flushed, her hair unbrushed. I could see silver strands among the red. It hit me that in four years she would be fifty. That suddenly seemed old.

"You live under our roof," Mom continued tightly. "We support you. When you're eighteen and you move out and get a job, you can have whatever books you want, read whatever you want. But while you're in this house, what we say goes."

I started to get angry. Why were they acting this way?

But before I said anything, a verse came into my head. Leash my anger, calm my words. Speak in love and do no hurt.

Where did that come from? I wondered vaguely. But whatever its origin, it felt right. I said it to myself three times and felt my emotions ratchet down.

"I understand," I said. Suddenly I felt powerful and confident. I looked at my parents and my sister. "But Mom, it isn't that easy," I explained gently. "And you know why; I know you do. I'm a witch. I was born a witch. And if I was, then you were, too."

2

Different

December 14, 1976.

Circle last night at the currachdag on the west cliffs. Fifteen of us in all, including me, Angus, Mannannan, the rest of Belwicket, and two students, Tara and Cliff. It was cold, and a fine rain fell. Standing around the great heap of peat, we did some healing for old Mrs. Paxham, down to the village, who's been ailing. I felt the cumhachd, the power, in my fingers, in my arms, and I was happy and danced for hours. — Bradhadair

My mother looked like she was about to have a stroke. Dad's mouth dropped open. Mary K. stared at me, her brown eyes wide.

Mom's mouth worked as if she was trying to speak but couldn't form the words. Her face was pale, and I wanted to tell her to sit down, to take it easy. But I kept silent. I knew this was a turning point for us, and I couldn't back down.

"What did you say?" Her voice was a raw whisper.

"I said I'm a witch," I repeated calmly, though inside, my nerves were stretched and taut. "I'm a blood witch, a genetic witch. And if I am, you two must be also."

"What are you talking about?" Mary K. said. "There's no such thing as a genetic witch! God, next you'll be telling us there are vampires and werewolves." She looked at me in disbelief, her plaid pajamas seeming young and innocent. Suddenly I felt guilty, as if I had brought evil into the house. But that wasn't true, was it? All I had brought into the house was me, a part of me.

I raised my hand, then let it fall, not knowing what to say.

"I can't believe you," Mary K. said. "What are you trying to do?" She gestured toward our parents.

Ignoring her, Mom said faintly, "You're not a witch."

I almost snorted. "Mom, please. That's like saying I'm not a girl or I'm not human. Of course I'm a witch, and you know it. You've always known it."

"Morgan, just stop it!" Mary K. pleaded. "You're freaking me out. You want to read witch books? Fine. Read witch books, light candles, whatever. But quit saying you're really a witch. That's bullshit!"

Mom snapped her gaze to Mary K., startled.

"'Scuse me," Mary K. muttered.

"I'm sorry, Mary K.," I said. "It's not something I wanted to happen. But it's true." A thought occurred to me. "You must be one, too," I said, finding that idea fascinating. I looked up at her, excited. "Mary K., you must be a witch, too!"

She is not a witch! my mom shrieked, and I stopped, frozen by the sound of her voice. She looked enraged, the veins in her neck standing out, her face flushed. "You leave her out of it!"

"But—," I began.

"Mary K. is not a witch, Morgan," my dad said harshly.

I shook my head. "But she has to be," I said. "I mean, it's genetic. And if I am, and you are, then ..."

"Nobody is a witch," my mom said shortly, not meeting my eyes. "Certainly not Mary Kathleen."

They were in denial. But why?

"Mom, it's okay. Really. More than okay. Being a witch is a wonderful thing," I said, thinking back to the feelings I'd had last night. "It's like being—"

"Will you stop?" Mom burst out. "Why are you doing this? Why can't you just listen to us?" She sounded on the verge of tears, and I was getting angry again.

"I can't listen to you because you're wrong!" I said loudly. "Why are you denying all of this?"

"We're not witches!" my mom screeched, practically rattling my windows.

She glared at me. My dad's mouth was open, and Mary K. looked miserable. I felt the first hint of fear.

"Oh," I snapped. "I guess I'm a witch, but you're not, right?" I snorted, furious at their stubbornness, their lies. "Then what?" I crossed my arms and looked at them. "Was I adopted?"

Silence. Long moments of the clock ticking, the thin, scratchy sound of elm twigs brushing my windowpanes. My heartbeat seemed to go into slow motion. Mom groped for my desk chair, then sank into it heavily. My dad shifted from foot to foot, looking over my left shoulder at nothing. Mary K. stared at all of us.

"What?" I tried to smile. "What? What are you saying? I'm *adopted?*"

"Of course you're not adopted!" said Mary K., looking at Mom and Dad for their agreement.

Silence.

Inside me, a wall came crashing down, and I saw what lay behind it: a whole world I had never dreamed of, a world in which I was adopted, not biologically related to my family. My throat closed and my stomach clenched, and I was afraid I was going to throw up. But I had to know.

I pushed past Mary K. into the hallway, then thundered down the steps two at a time. I tore around the corner, hearing my parents on the steps behind me. In the family office I yanked open my dad's files, where he keeps things like insurance papers, our passports, their marriage license . . . birth certificates.

Breathing hard, I flipped through files on car insurance, the house's AC system, our new water heater. My file read *Morgan.* I pulled it out just as my parents came into the office.

"Morgan! Stop it!" said Dad.

Ignoring him, I rifled through immunization records, school reports, my social security card.

There it was. My birth certificate. I picked it up and scanned it. *Birthday, November 23.* Correct. *Weight, eight pounds, ten ounces.*

My mom reached around me and snatched the birth certificate out of my hand. As if in a slapstick movie, I snatched it back. She held tight with both hands, and the paper ripped.

Dropping to my knees, I hunched over my half on the floor, protecting it till I could read it. *Age of mother: 23.* No.

That was wrong because Mom had been thirty before she had me.

Then the edges of the paper grew cloudy as my eyes locked onto four words: *Mother's name: Maeve Riordan.*

I blinked, reading it again and again at the speed of light. *Maeve Riordan. Mother's name: Maeve Riordan.*

Mechanically I read down to the bottom of my torn page, expecting to see my mom's real name, Mary Grace Rowlands, somewhere. Anywhere.

Shocked, I looked up at my mother. She seemed to have aged ten years in the last half hour. My dad, behind her, was tight-lipped and silent.

I held up the paper, my brain misfiring. "What does this mean?" I asked stupidly.

My parents didn't answer, and I stared at them. My fears came crashing down on me in hard waves. Suddenly I couldn't bear to be with them. I had to get away. Scrambling to my feet, I rushed from the room, colliding with Mary K., almost knocking her down. The torn scrap of paper fluttered from my fingers as I pushed through the kitchen door and grabbed the keys to my car. I raced outside as if the devil were chasing me.

3

Find Me

May 14, 1977

Going to school is more a bother these days than anything else. It's spring, everything's blooming, I'm out gathering luibh — plants — for my spells, and then I have to get to school and learn English. What for? I live in Ireland. Anyway, I'm fifteen now, old enough to quit. Tonight's a full moon, so I'll do a scrying spell to see the future. I hope it will tell me whether I should stay in school or no. Scrying is hard to control, though.

There's something else I want to scry for: Angus. Is he my mùirn beatha dàn? On Beltane he pulled me behind the straw man and kissed me and said he loves me. I don't know how I feel about him. I thought I liked David O'Hearn. But he's not one of us — not a blood witch — and Angus is. For each of us there's only one other they should be with: their mùirn beatha dàn. For Ma, it was Da. Who is mine? Angus says it's him. If it's him, I have no choice, do I?

To scry: I don't use water overmuch — water is the easiest but also the least reliable. You know, a shallow bowl of clear water, gaze at it under the open sky or near a window. You'll see things easily enough, but it's wrong so often, I think it's just asking for trouble.

The best way to scry is with an enchanted leug, like bloodstone or hematite, or a crystal, but these are hard to lay your hands on. They give the most truth, but brace yourself for things you might not want to see or know. Stone scrying is good for seeing things as they are happening someplace else, like checking on a loved one or an enemy in battle.

I scry with fire, usually. Fire is unpredictable. But I'm made of fire, we are one, and so she speaks to me. With fire scrying, if I see something, it can be past, present, or future. Of course the future stuff is only one possible future. But what I see in fire is true, as true as can be.

I love the fire.

— Bradhadair

I ran across the frost-stiffened grass, which crunched lightly under my slippers. The front door opened behind me, but I was already sliding onto the freezing vinyl front seat of my white '71 Valiant, Das Boot, and cranking the engine.

"Morgan!" my dad yelled as I squealed out of our driveway, the car lurching like a boat on rough waters. Then I roared forward, watching my parents on our front lawn in my rearview mirror. Mom was sinking to the ground; Dad was trying to hold her up. I burst into tears as I wheeled too fast onto Riverdale.

Sobbing, I dashed my tears away with one hand, then wiped my nose on my sleeve. I turned on Das Boot's heater, but of course it took forever for the engine to warm up.

I was turning onto Bree's street before I remembered that we were no longer friends. If she hadn't left those books on my porch, I wouldn't know I was adopted. If Cal hadn't come between us, she would never have left the books on my porch.

I cried harder, shaking with sobs, and spun into a sloppy U-turn right before I reached her driveway. Then I hit the gas and drove, my only destination to be away, away.

The next time my vision cleared, I had managed to fish a battered box of tissues from beneath the front seat. Damp, crumpled ones littered the passenger side and covered the floor. I had ended up heading north, out of town. The road followed a low valley, and early fog clung heavily to the asphalt. Das Boot plowed through it like a brick thrown through clouds. In the distance I saw a large, dark shadow off to the side of the road. It was the willow oak that we had parked under just last night, for Samhain. Where I had parked the first time I did a circle with Cal, weeks before. When magick had come into my life.

Without thinking, I swung my car off the road and bumped across the field, rolling to a stop beneath the oak's low-hanging branches. Here I was hidden by fog, by the tree. I turned off my engine, leaned against the steering wheel, and tried to stop crying.

Adopted. Every instance, every example of my being different from my family reared up in my face and mocked me. Yesterday they had been only family jokes—how the three of them are larks and I'm a night owl, how they're unnaturally cheerful and I'm grumpy. How Mom and Mary K. are curvy and cute and I'm thin and intense. Today those jokes caused waves of pain as I remembered them one by one.

"Dammit! Dammit! Dammit!" I shouted, banging my fists against the hard metal steering wheel. "Dammit!" I whacked the wheel until my hands were numb, until I had gone through every curse I knew, until my throat was raw.

Then I wept again, lying down in the front seat. I don't know how long I was there, cocooned in my car in the mist. From time to time I turned on the heater to stay warm. The windows fogged and steamed with my tears.

Gradually my sobs degenerated into shaky hiccups and the occasional shudder. Oh, Cal, I thought. I need Cal. As soon as I thought that, a rhyme came into my head: *In my mind I see you here. In my pain I need you near. Find me, trace me, where I be. Come here, come here, now to me.*

I didn't know where it came from, but by now I was getting used to the arrival of strange thoughts. I felt calmer hearing it, so I said it over and over again. I draped my arm over my eyes, praying desperately I would wake up in bed at home to find it had all been a nightmare.

Minutes later I jumped when someone tapped on the passenger's-side window. My eyes snapped open, and I sat up, then cleared a space on the glass to see Cal, looking sleepy and rumpled and amazingly beautiful.

"You called?" he said, and my heart filled with sunlight. "Let me in—it's freezing out here."

It worked, I thought in awe. I called him with my thoughts. Magick.

I opened the door and moved over. He slid onto the front seat next to me, and it was amazingly natural to reach out, to feel his arms come around me.

"What's the matter?" he said, his voice muffled against my hair. "What's going on?" He held me away from him and searched my tear-blotched face with his eyes.

"I'm adopted!" I blurted out. "This morning I told my mom that I'm a blood witch, so she must be, and my dad, and my sister. They said no, it wasn't true. So I ran downstairs to see my birth certificate, and it had another woman's name—not my mother's."

I started crying again, even though I was embarrassed to have him see me like this. He pulled me closer and held my head to his shoulder. It was so comforting that I stopped crying again almost immediately.

"That's a hard way to find out." He kissed my temple, and a tiny shiver of pleasure raced up my spine. It's a miracle, I thought: He still loves me, even today. It wasn't a dream.

He pulled back, and we looked at each other in the hazy light. I couldn't get over how beautiful he was. His skin was smooth and tan, even in November. His hair was thick beneath my fingers, dark and streaked with warm shades the color of walnuts. His eyes were surrounded by blunt, black lashes, with irises of a gold so fiery, they almost seemed to radiate heat.

I felt self-conscious as I realized he was examining me the same way I examined him. A tiny smile quirked the corner of his lips. "Left in a hurry, did you?"

That was when I realized I was still in my oversize football jersey and an ancient pair of my dad's long johns, complete with flap in front. A large pair of brown, furry bear-feet slippers were on my feet. Cal reached down and tickled their claws. I thought about the silky matching outfits that Bree wears to sleep in, and with a pang and an indrawn breath I remembered she'd told me that she and Cal had gone to bed. I searched his eyes, wondering if it was true, wondering if I could bear knowing for sure.

But he was here now. With me.

"You're the best thing I've seen all morning," Cal said softly, stroking my arm. "I'm glad you called me. I missed you last night, after I went home."

I looked down, thinking of him lying in his big, romantic bed, with curtains fluttering and candles flickering all around. He had been thinking of me as he lay there.

"Listen—how did you know how to call me? Did you read about it in a book?"

"No," I said, thinking back. "I don't think so. I was just sitting here, miserable, and I thought if you were here, I'd feel better, and then this little rhyme came into my head, so I said it."

"Huh," Cal said thoughtfully.

"Was I not supposed to?" I asked, confused. "Sometimes things just come into my head like that."

"No, it's okay," said Cal. "It just means you're strong. You have ancestral memories of spells. Not every witch does." He nodded, thinking.

"So tell me more," he said. "Your parents never told you about this before, your being adopted?" He kept his arm on the back of the seat, smoothing my hair and rubbing my neck.

"No." I shook my head. "Never. And you'd think they would have—I'm so different from them."

Cal cocked his head, looking at me. "I've never met your folks," he said. "But you don't look much like your sister; that's true. Mary K. looks sweet." He smiled. "She's pretty."

A hot jealousy started to burn in my chest.

"You don't look sweet," Cal went on. "You look serious. Deep. Like you're thinking. And you're more striking than pretty. You're the kind of girl that you don't notice is beautiful until you get real close." His voice trailed off, and he brought his head closer to mine. "And then all of a sudden it hits you," he whispered. "And you think, Goddess, make her mine."

His lips touched mine again, and my thoughts whirled. I wrapped my arms around Cal's shoulders and kissed him as deeply as I knew how, pulling him closer. All I wanted was to be with him, to never be apart.

Minutes passed in which I heard only our breathing, our lips coming together and parting, the crinkle of the vinyl seat as we moved to be closer. Soon Cal was lying on top of me, his weight pressing me into the seat. His hand was stroking up and down my side, along my ribs and curving around my hip. Then it was under the hem of my jersey, warm against my breast, and shock waves went through me.

"Stop!" I said, almost afraid. "Wait."

My voice seemed to echo in the quiet car. Instantly Cal pulled his hand away. He held himself up, looking into my eyes, then leaned back against the driver's door. He was breathing fast.

I was mortified. You idiot, I thought. He's almost eighteen! He's definitely had sex. Maybe even with Bree, a tiny voice added.

I shook my head. "Sorry," I said, trying to sound casual. "It was just a surprise."

"No, no, *I'm* sorry," he said. He reached out and took my hand, and I was mesmerized by its warmth, its strength. "You call me here, and I jump on you. I shouldn't have. I'm sorry." He raised my fingers to his mouth and kissed them. "The thing is, I've been wanting to kiss you ever since I met you." He smiled slightly.

I calmed down. "I've wanted to kiss you, too," I admitted.

He smiled. "My witch," he said, running a finger down my cheek, leaving a thin trail of heat. "Now, how did you tell your mother that you're a blood witch?"

I sighed. "This morning she found a pile of my Wicca books, magick books, on the front porch. She stormed into my room, yelling at me, saying they were blasphemous." I sounded more together than I felt, remembering that awful scene. "I thought she was being so hypocritical—I mean, if I'm a blood witch, then she and my dad would have to be, too. Right?"

"Pretty much," said Cal. "Definitely, with someone who has powers as strong as yours, both your parents would have to be."

I frowned. "What about only one parent?"

"An ordinary man and a female witch can't conceive a baby," Cal explained. "A male witch can get an ordinary woman pregnant, but it's a conscious thing. And their baby would have very weak powers at best, or possibly none at all. Not like you."

I felt like I had accomplished something: I was a powerful witch.

"Okay," Cal said. "Now, why were your books on the front porch? Were you hiding them?"

"Yes," I said bitterly. "At Bree's house. This morning she

left them on my porch. Because you and I kissed last night."

"What?" Cal asked, a dark expression crossing his face.

I shrugged. "Bree really . . . wanted you. Wants you. And when you kissed me last night, I know she felt that I had betrayed her." I swallowed and looked out the window. "I *did* betray her," I said quietly. "I knew how she felt about you."

Cal's eyes dropped. He picked up a long strand of my hair and twined it around his hand, over and over. "How do *you* feel about me?" he asked after a moment.

Last night he had told me he loved me. I looked at him, seeing past him to the thin November sunlight that was burning away the fog. I breathed deeply, trying to slow the sudden, rapid patter of my pulse. "I love you," I said. My voice came out a husky whisper.

Cal glanced up and caught my gaze. His eyes were very bright. "I love you, too. I'm sorry that Bree's hurt, but just because she has feelings for me doesn't mean we're going to be together."

Did that stop you from sleeping with her? I almost asked him, but I couldn't quite bring myself to. I wasn't sure I really wanted to know.

"And I'm sorry Bree is taking it out on you," he said. He paused. "So your mom found the books and yelled. You thought she was hiding being a witch herself, right?"

"Yes. Not just her but my father and my sister," I said. "But my parents went crazy when I said that. I've never seen them so upset. And I said, so, what? I'm *adopted*? And they got these horrible expressions on their faces. They wouldn't answer me. And suddenly I had to know. So I ran downstairs and looked at my birth certificate."

"And there was a different name."

"Yeah. Maeve Riordan."

Cal sat up straighter, alert. "Really?"

I stared at him. "What? Do you recognize that name?"

"It sounds familiar." He looked out the window, thinking, frowning, then shook his head. "No, maybe not. I can't place it."

"Oh." I swallowed my disappointment.

"What are you going to do now? Do you want to come to my house?" He smiled. "We could go swimming."

"No, thank you," I said, remembering when the circle had all gone skinny-dipping in his pool. I was the only one who had kept her clothes on.

Cal laughed. "I was disappointed that night, you know," he said, looking at me.

"No, you weren't," I replied, crossing my arms over my chest. He chuckled softly.

"Seriously, do you want to come over? Or do you want me to come to your house, help you talk to your parents?"

"Thanks," I said, touched by his offer. "But I think I should just go home by myself. With any luck, they all went to church, anyway. It's All Saints' Day."

"What's that?" Cal asked.

I remembered he wasn't Catholic—wasn't even Christian. "All Saints' Day," I said. "It's the day after Halloween. It's a special day of observance for Catholics. That's when we go tend our family graves in cemeteries. Trim the grass, put out fresh flowers."

"Cool," said Cal. "That's a nice tradition. It's funny that it's the day after Samhain. But then, it seems like a lot of Christian holidays came out of Wiccan ones, way back when."

I nodded. "I know. But do me a favor and don't mention

that to my parents," I said. "Anyway, I'd better get home."

"Okay. Can I call you later?"

"Yes," I said. I couldn't stop myself from smiling.

"I think I'll use the telephone," he said, grinning.

I thought of how he had come when I had said my rhyme. I was still amazed that it had worked.

He let himself out of Das Boot into the chilly, crisp November air. He walked to his car and took off as I waved.

My world was flooded with sunlight. Cal loved me.

4

Maeve

February 7, 1978

 Two nights ago someone sprayed "Bloody Witch" on the side of Morag Sheehan's shop. We've moved our circle to meeting out by the cliffs, down the coast a ways.

 Last night, late, Mathair and I went out to Morag's. Lucky it was a new moon — no light and a good time for spells.

Rite of Healing, Protection from Evil, Cleansing

1. Cast a circle completely around what you want to protect. (I had to include old Burdock's sweetshop since the two buildings are joined.)

2. Purify the circle with salt. We used no lights or incense but salt, water, and earth.

3. Call on the Goddess. I wore my copper bracelets and held a chunk of sulfur, a chunk of marble from the garden, a chunk of petrified wood, and a bit of shell.

Then Ma and I said (quietly): "Goddess, hear us where we stand, with your protection bless this land, Morag is a servant true, protect her from those who mischief do." Then we invoked the Goddess and the God and walked around the shop three times.

No one saw us, that I could tell. Ma and I went home, feeling strong. That should help protect Morag. — Bradhadair

I drove slowly up my street, looking ahead anxiously as if my parents might still be standing on the front lawn of our house. When I was close enough, I saw that Dad's car was gone. I figured that they must have gone to church.

Inside, the house was quiet and still, though I felt the shocked vibrations of this morning's events lingering in the air like a scent.

"Mom? Dad? Mary K.?" I called. No answer. I wandered slowly through the house, seeing breakfast untouched on the kitchen table. I turned off the coffeemaker. The newspaper was folded neatly, obviously unread. Not at all a normal Sunday morning.

Realizing this was my chance, I hurried to the office. But the torn birth certificate was gone, and my dad's files were locked for the first time that I could remember.

Moving quickly, listening for sounds of their return, I searched the rest of the office. I found nothing and sat back on my heels for a moment, thinking.

My parents' room. I ran upstairs to their cluttered room. Feeling like a thief, I opened the top drawer of their dresser. Jewelry, cuff links, pens, bookmarks, old birthday cards—nothing incriminating, nothing that told me anything I needed to know.

Tapping my lip with my finger, I looked around. Framed baby pictures of me and Mary K. stood on top of their dresser, and I examined them. In one, my parents held me proudly, fat, nine-month-old Morgan, while I smiled and clapped. In another, Mom, in a hospital bed, held newborn Mary K., who looked like a hairless monkey. It occurred to me that I had never seen a newborn picture of me. Not a single one in the hospital, or looking tiny, or learning to sit up. My pictures started when I was about, what, eight months old? Nine months? Was that how old I was when I had been adopted?

Adopted. It was still such a bizarre thought, yet I was already eerily used to it. It explained everything, in a way. But in another way, it didn't. It only raised more questions.

I looked through my baby book, compared it to Mary K.'s. Mine listed my birth weight correctly and my birth date. Under First Impressions, Mom had written: "She's so incredibly beautiful. Everything I ever hoped for and dreamed about for so long."

I closed the book. How could they have lied to me all this time? How could they have let me believe I was really their daughter? I felt unstable now, without a base. Everything I had believed now seemed like a lie. How could I ever forgive them?

They had to give me some answers. I had the right to know. I dropped my head into my hands, feeling tired, old, and emotionally empty.

It was noon. Would they all have lunch at the Widow's Diner after church? Would they go on to the cemetery afterward to put flowers around the Rowlandses' graves and the Donovans', my mom's family?

Maybe they would. They probably would. I headed back into the kitchen, thinking that I should have some lunch myself. I hadn't eaten anything. But I was too upset to face food yet. Instead I took a Diet Coke out of the fridge. Then I found myself wandering into the study, where the computer was.

I decided to run a search. I frowned at the screen. How had her name been spelled, exactly? Maive? Mave? Maeve? The last name was Riordan, I remembered that.

I typed in Maeve Riordan. Twenty-seven listings popped up. Sighing, I started to scroll through them. A horse farm in western Massachusetts. A doctor in Dublin, specializing in ear problems. One by one I flipped through them, reading a few lines and closing their windows. I didn't know when my family would be home or what I would face when they arrived. My emotions felt flayed and yet distant, as if this were all happening to someone else.

Click. Maeve Riordan. Best-selling romance author presents *My Highland Love.*

Click. "Maeve Riordan" as part of an html. Frowning, I clicked on the link. This was a genealogy site, with links to other genealogy sites. Cool. It looked like the name Maeve Riordan appeared on three sites. I clicked on the first one. A scanty family tree popped up, and after a few minutes I found the name Maeve Riordan. Unfortunately, this Maeve Riordan had died in 1874.

I backtracked, and the next Maeve link took me to a site where there were no dates anywhere, as if they were still filling it in. I gritted my teeth in frustration.

Third time lucky, I thought, and clicked on the last site. The words *Belwicket and Ballynigel* appeared at the top of the screen in fancy Irish-style lettering. This was another family tree but with many separate branches, as if it was more of a family forest or the people hadn't found the common link between these families.

Quickly I scanned for Maeve Riordan. There were lots of Riordans. Then I saw it. *Maeve Riordan. Born Imbolc, 1962, Ballynigel, Ireland. Died Litha, 1986, Meshomah Falls, New York, United States.*

My jaw dropped open as I stared at the screen. Imbolc. Litha. Those were Wiccan sabbats. This Maeve Riordan had been a witch.

A sudden wave of heat pulsed through my head, making my cheeks prickle. I shook my head and tried to think. 1986. She died the year after I was born. And she was born in 1962. Which would have made her the same age as the woman listed on my birth certificate.

It's her, I thought. It has to be.

I clicked all over the screen, trying to find links. I felt almost frantic. I needed more information. More. But instead a message popped up: *Connection timed out. URL not responding.*

Frustrated, I shut down the computer. Then I sat tapping my lower lip with a pen. Thoughts raced through my head. Meshomah Falls, New York. I knew that name. It was a little town not too far away from here, maybe two hours. I needed to see their town records. I needed to see their ... newspapers.

Two minutes later I had grabbed my jacket and was in Das Boot, heading for the library. Of Widow's Vale's three library branches, only the biggest one, downtown, was open on Sundays. I pushed through the glass door and immediately headed downstairs to the basement.

No one else was down there. The basement was empty except for rows and rows of books, out-of-date periodicals, stacks of books to be mended, and four ugly black-and-wood-grain microfiche machines.

Come on, come on, I thought, pawing through the microfiche files. It took twenty minutes to find the drawer containing past issues of the *Meshomah Falls Herald*. Another tedious fifteen minutes trying to figure dates, counting forward from my birthday to about eight months after it. Finally I pulled out an envelope, turned on a microfiche machine, and sat down.

I slid the tiny film card under the light and began to turn the knob.

Forty-five minutes later I rubbed the back of my neck. I now knew more about Meshomah Falls, New York, than anyone could possibly want to know. It was a farming community, smaller and even more boring than Widow's Vale.

I hadn't found anything about Maeve Riordan. No obituary, nothing. Well, that wasn't really surprising. I should probably get used to the idea that I would never know about my past.

There were two more film cards to look at. With a sigh I sat down again, hating the machine.

This time I found the article almost immediately. The little hairs on the back of my neck prickled, and there it was: Maeve Riordan. Stiffening in my chair, I scrolled back to center the page and peered into the viewer. *A body burned almost beyond recognition has been identified as that of Maeve Riordan, formerly of Ballynigel, Ireland. . . .*

My breath caught in my throat, and I stared at the screen. Was this her? I wondered again. My birth mother? I'd never been to Meshomah Falls. I'd never heard my parents talk about it. But Maeve Riordan had lived there. And somehow, in Meshomah Falls, Maeve Riordan had died in a fire.

I surprised myself by shaking uncontrollably as I gazed blankly at the screen. Quickly I scanned the short news clipping.

On June 21, 1986, the body of an unidentified young woman had been found in the ruins of a charred and smoldering barn on an abandoned farm in Meshomah Falls. After an examination of dental X-rays, the body had been identified as belonging to one Maeve Riordan, who had been renting a small house in Meshomah Falls and working at the local café downtown. Maeve Riordan, twenty-three years old, formerly of Ballynigel, Ireland, was not well known in the town. Another body found in the fire had been identified as Angus Bramson, twenty-five years old, also of Ballynigel. It was unknown why they were in the barn. The cause of the fire seemed unclear.

June 21 might have been Litha in that year—it varied according to exactly when the equinox was. But what about a baby? It didn't say anything about a baby.

My heart was thudding painfully inside my chest. Images of a recent dream I'd had, of being in a rough sort of room while a woman held me and called me her baby, flashed through my head. What did this all mean?

Abruptly I shut off the machine. I stood up so fast, I felt dizzy and had to clutch the back of my chair.

I was almost certain that this Maeve Riordan had given birth to me. Why had she given me up for adoption? Or was I only adopted after she died? Was Angus Bramson my father? How had that barn caught on fire?

Moving slowly, I put all the microfiche files where I had found them. Then, my hands to my temples, I went upstairs and walked out of the library. Outside it was gray and overcast, and the library's lawn was covered with bright yellow maple leaves. It was autumn, and winter was on the way.

The seasons changed with such a gradual grace, easing you gently from one to the next. But my life, my whole life, had changed in a bare moment.

5

Reasons

Samhain, October 31, 1978

Ma and Da just went over this Book of Shadows and said it was a poor one indeed. I need to write more often; I need to explain spells more; I need to explain the workings of the moon, the sun, the tides, the stars. I said, Why? Everybody knows that stuff. Ma said it's for my children, the witches who come after me. Like how she and Da show me their books — they've got five of them now, those big thick black books by the fireplace. When I was little, I thought they were photo albums. It makes me laugh now — photos of witches.

But you know, my spells and stuff are in my head. There's time to put them down later. Plenty of time. Mostly I want to write about my feelings and thoughts. But then, I don't want my folks to read that — when they got to the parts when I was kissing Angus, they blew up! But they know Angus, and they like him. They see him often enough, know that I've settled on him. Angus is good, and who else is there for me here? It's not like I can be with just anyone, not if I want to live my life and have kids and all. Lucky for me Angus is as sweet as he is.

Here's a good spell for making love fade: During a waning moon, gather four hairs from a black cat, a cat that has no white anywhere on her. Take a white candle, the dried petals of three red roses, and a piece of string. Write your name and the name of the person you want to push away on two pieces of paper, and tie one to each end of the string.

Go outside. (This works best under a new moon or a moon the day before the new moon.) Set up your altar; purify your circle; invoke the Goddess. Set up your white candle. Sprinkle the rose petals around the candle. Take each of the cat's hairs and set them at the four points of the compass: N, S, E, and W. (Hold them down with rocks if the night's windy.) Light the candle and hold the middle of the string taut over the candle, about five inches up. Then say:

As the moon wanes, so wanes your love;
I am an eagle, no more your dove.
Another face, more fair than mine,
Will surely win your love in time.

Say that over and over until the string burns through and the two names are separated forever. Don't do this in anger because your love really will no more be yours. You have to want to truly get rid of someone forever.

P.S. The cat hairs don't do anything. I just put them in to sound mysterious.

— Bradhadair

I was in the kitchen, eating some warmed-up lasagna, when my parents and Mary K. came home late that afternoon. They all stared at me as if they had come home to find a stranger in their kitchen.

"Morgan," said my dad, clearing his throat. His eyes looked red-rimmed, his face drawn and older than this morning. His thinning black hair was brushed tightly against his scalp, too long on the ends. His thick, wire-rimmed glasses gave him an owlish look.

"Yes?" I said, marveling at the cold steadiness of my voice. I took a sip of soda.

"Are you all right?"

It was such a ludicrous question, but it was so like my dad to ask.

"Well, let's see," I said coolly, not looking at him. "I just found out I was adopted. I've been sitting here realizing you've both been lying to me my whole life." I shrugged. "Other than that, I'm fine."

Mary K. looked like she was about to burst into tears. In fact, she looked like she had been crying all morning.

"Morgan," said my mom. "Maybe we made the wrong decision in not telling you. But we had our reasons. We love you, and we're still your parents."

I couldn't stay cool any longer. "Your reasons?" I exclaimed. "You had good reasons for not telling me the most important fact of my life? There are no good reasons for that!"

"Morgan, stop," Mary K. said, her voice wobbling. "We're a family. I just want you to be my sister." She started crying, and I felt my own throat tighten.

"I want you to be my sister, too," I said, standing up. "But I don't know what's going on anymore—what's real and what's not."

Mary K. burst into real sobs and threw herself on Dad's shoulder.

Mom tried to come over to me, to take me in her arms, but I backed away. I couldn't stand her touch right at that second. She looked stricken.

"Look, let's not say anything right now," Dad said. "We need some time. We've all had a shock. Please, Morgan, just hear me on one thing: Your mother and I have two daughters whom we love more than anything in the world. Two daughters."

"Mary K. is your daughter," I said, hating hearing my voice crack. "Biologically. But I'm nobody!"

"Don't say that!" Mom said, looking devastated.

"You're both our daughters," said my dad. "And you always will be."

It was about the most comforting thing he could have said, and it made me burst into tears. I was so exhausted, physically and emotionally, that I stumbled upstairs to my room, lay on my bed, and began to drift toward sleep.

While I was half dreaming, half awake, my mom came into my room and sat on the bed next to me. She stroked my hair, her fingers gently working through the tangles. It reminded me of my dream, my other mother. Maybe it wasn't a dream, I thought. Maybe it was a memory.

"Mom," I said.

"Shhh, sweetie, sleep," she whispered. "I just wanted to say I love you, and I'm your mother, and you've been my daughter since the first second I laid eyes on you."

I shook my head, wanting to protest that it wasn't true, but I was already too close to sleep. As I drifted off into a deep, blessed numbness I was aware of warm tears soaking my pillow. I don't know if they were hers or mine.

The next morning was bizarre in how ordinary it seemed. As usual, Mom and Dad got up and went to work early, before I was even awake. As usual, Mary K. yelled for me to hurry as I drifted through my shower, trying to brace myself for the day.

Mary K. looked pale and pinch-faced and was unusually quiet as I gulped down a Diet Coke and threw books into my backpack.

"I want you to stop what you're doing," she said so softly, I could barely hear her. "I want us to go back to being how we were."

I sighed. I had never felt jealous or competitive when it came to Mary K. I'd always wanted to take care of her. I wondered if it would be different now. I had no idea. But I knew that I still hated seeing her hurt.

"It's too late for that," I said quietly. "And I need to know the truth. There have been too many secrets for too long."

Mary K. raised her hands, and they fluttered for a moment in midair as she tried to think of something to say. But there wasn't anything to say, and in the end we just got our backpacks and headed outside to Das Boot.

Cal was waiting for me at school. He walked over to my

car as I parked and met me as I opened the door. Mary K. looked at him, as if to measure his involvement in all of this. He met her gaze calmly, sympathetically.

"I'm Cal," he said, holding out his hand. "Cal Blaire. I don't think we've really met."

Mary K. looked at him. "I know who you are," she said, not taking his hand. "Are you doing witchcraft with Morgan?"

"Mary K.!" I started, but Cal held up his hand.

"It's okay," he said. "Yes, I'm doing witchcraft with Morgan. But we're not doing anything wrong."

"Wrong for who?" Mary K. sounded older than fourteen. She slid past Cal and got out of the car. She was immediately surrounded by her friends, but she looked unhappy and withdrawn. I wondered what she would tell them. Then Bakker Blackburn, her boyfriend, came up. They walked off together.

"How are you?" Cal asked, and kissed my forehead. "I've been thinking about you. I called last night, but your mom said you were asleep."

I saw people looking at us, Alessandra Spotford, Nell Norton, Justin Bartlett. Of course they were surprised to see Cal Blaire, human god, with Morgan Rowlands, Girl Most Likely to Remain Dateless Forever.

"Yeah—I think my brain just shut down. Thanks for calling. I'll tell you about everything later." He squeezed my shoulder, and together we walked up to where the coven—we were a coven now and not just a group of friends—hung out, on the cement benches by the east side of the school. The redbrick building looked reassuringly familiar and unchanged, but that was about the only thing in my life that was the same today.

Seven pairs of eyes were on us as we came up the crumbling brick walkway. I sought out Bree's face. She was studiously examining her brown suede boots. She looked beautiful and remote, cool and aloof. Two weeks ago she had been my best friend in the world, the person I loved most besides my family, the person who knew me the best.

Something in me still cared about her, still wanted to confide in her, as impossible as that was. I thought about telling my problems to one of my other friends, like Tamara Pritchett or Janice Yutoh, but I knew I couldn't.

"Hi, Morgan, Cal," said Jenna Ruiz, her face as open and friendly as ever. She gave me a sincere smile, and I smiled back. Matt Adler was sitting next to her, his arm around her shoulders. Jenna coughed, covering her mouth, and for a moment Matt looked at her in concern. She shook her head and smiled at him.

"Hi, Jenna. Everyone," I said.

Raven Meltzer was looking at me with open dislike. Her dark eyes, heavily rimmed with kohl and sprinkled with glitter, glowed with an inner anger. She had wanted Cal for herself, like Bree. Like me.

"Samhain was amazing," said Sharon Goodfine, crossing her arms over her ample chest as if she were cold. She gave the word its proper pronunciation: Sowen. "I feel so different. I felt different all weekend." Her carefully made-up face looked thoughtful rather than snobbish.

Without thinking about what I was doing, I cast my senses out, gently, carefully, feeling for the emotions of the

people surrounding me. It was like what I'd experienced during the circle in the cemetery, but this time I directed it. This
time I did it on purpose.

It occurred to me only in passing that perhaps my
friends' emotions should be private, belonging only to them.

Jenna was just as she appeared; open, good-natured. Matt
seemed the same, but deep within him I sensed a dark space
he kept to himself. Cal . . . Cal glanced at me in quick surprise as my sense net touched his mind. As I scanned him I
felt a sudden, hot rush of desire from him, and I blushed and
pulled back quickly. He gave me a look, as if to say, Well, you
asked. . . .

Ethan Sharp was interesting—a colorful mosaic of
thoughts and feelings, tightly held distrust, poetry, and disappointment. Sharon had a stillness to her, a calm center that
seemed new. There was also a hesitant, half-embarrassed
tenderness—for whom? Ethan?

Beth Nielson, Raven's best friend, mainly seemed bored
and wanted to be somewhere else. My best friend after
Bree, Robbie Gurevitch, was startling: a mixture of anger, desire, and repressed emotion that didn't show at all on his
face. Who was it directed at? I couldn't tell.

But it was Bree and Raven who almost blew me off the
bench. Deep, intense waves of fury and jealousy came from
both of them, aimed at me and, to a lesser extent, Cal. With
Raven it was all jagged, snaggletoothed edges of anger and
frustration and hunger. For all her reputation of being easy,
she hadn't actually ever been linked seriously to anyone.
Maybe she had wanted Cal to be the one.

If Raven's feelings were barbed wire, Bree's were smoldering coals. Instantly I knew that as much as she had loved me two weeks ago, she now hated me to the same extent. She had been desperate for Cal. Maybe it wasn't real love, but it was a powerful desire, that was certain. And she had never before wanted a guy without his wanting her back. Cal had deeply wounded her when he had chosen me over her.

All these impressions had taken only a moment. A heartbeat and the knowledge was within me.

It struck me that none of these people, the people in my coven, knew about my adoption, except Cal. It was such a huge, momentous thing, so life changing, so frightening, yet it had all happened in one day, yesterday. And yesterday had been just another Sunday for them. It made me feel disoriented and strange.

"So," Bree said, breaking the silence. She didn't look at me. "Did your parents enjoy their new reading material?"

I blinked. If only she knew what her revenge had begun. All I could do was shake my head and sit down. I didn't trust myself to talk.

Bree smirked, still gazing at her boots.

Cal took my hand in his, and I held it tightly.

"What are you talking about, Bree?" Robbie asked. He took off his thick glasses and rubbed his eyes. Without his glasses he looked like a different person. The spell I had performed two weeks before had worked better than I could have possibly imagined. His skin, once pitted with acne scars, now was smooth and fine textured, showing a dim outline of dark beard. His nose was straight and classical, where it had been swollen and red. Even his lips seemed firmer, more attractive, though I couldn't remember how they had been before.

"Nothing," Bree said lightly. "It's not important."

No, it was just the destruction of my life, I thought.

"Whatever," Robbie muttered, rubbing his eyes. "Damn. Anyone have some Tylenol? I have an incredible headache."

"I've got some," said Sharon, reaching for her purse.

"Always prepared," said Ethan with a smile. "Like a Girl Scout." Sharon shot him a look, then gave Robbie two pills, which he took dry.

Our coven had united cool kids with losers, brains and geeks and stoners and princesses. It was interesting to watch people who were so different from one another interact.

"I had a good time on Saturday night," Cal said after a pause. "I'm glad you all came. It was a good way to celebrate the most important Wiccan holiday."

"It was so cool," said Jenna. "And Morgan was amazing!"

I felt self-conscious and gave my knees a tiny smile.

"It was really awesome," said Matt. "I spent most of the day yesterday on the Web, looking up Wiccan sites. There's a million of them, and some of them are pretty intense."

Jenna laughed. "And some of them are so lame! Some of those people are so weird! And they have the cheesiest music."

"I like the ones with chat rooms," said Ethan. "If you get one where people know what they're talking about, it's really interesting. Sometimes they have spells and stuff to download."

"There's a lot about Yule coming up in a couple of months," said Sharon.

"Maybe we could have a Yule party," I said, caught up in their talk. Then I saw the looks that Raven and Bree were giving me: superior, snide looks as if I were an annoying little sister instead of the most talented student in our coven. My jaw set, and at that instant I saw a large, curled maple leaf that was drifting lazily earthward. Without thinking, I caught it with my mind and sent it floating over Raven's head.

I kept my gaze on it, holding it in place while it hovered over her shiny black hair. Then it rested, ever so lightly, on her head, and it became a ludicrous, laughable hat.

I laughed openly, pleased with myself, and Raven's eyes narrowed, not understanding. She couldn't feel the large leaf perching there like a flat brown pancake, but it looked absurd.

Jenna saw it next, then our whole coven was looking at Raven and grinning, except Cal.

"What?" Raven snapped. "What are you looking at?"

Even Bree had to bite back a smile as she swept the leaf off Raven's head. "It was just a leaf," she said.

Flustered, Raven picked up her black bag just as the homeroom bell rang.

We all got up to go to class. I was still smiling when Cal leaned over me and whispered, "Remember the threefold law." He touched my cheek softly and then left, heading toward the other school entrance for his first class.

I swallowed. The Wiccan threefold law was one of the most important tenets of the craft. Basically it stated that anything you sowed, good or evil, would come back to you threefold, so always put good out there. Don't put bad. Cal was telling me (1) he knew I had controlled the leaf, and (2) he knew I was being mean when I did it. And it wasn't cool.

Taking a deep breath, I pulled my backpack strap over my shoulder.

As soon as Cal was out of earshot, Raven said nastily, "Okay, so he's yours—for now. But how long do you think that's going to last?"

"Yeah," Bree murmured. "Wait till he finds out you're a virgin. He'll find that pretty amusing."

My cheeks flamed. I had a sudden image of his hand under my shirt yesterday morning and how I had jumped.

Raven raised her eyebrows. "Don't tell me she's a virgin?"

"Oh, Raven, leave it," Beth said, brushing past her. Raven watched her for a second in surprise, then turned her attention back to me.

Bree and Raven laughed together, and I stared at Bree. How could she reveal such a personal thing about me? I kept my mouth stonily shut and kept walking to home-room—which I shared with Bree, of course.

"Come on, Raven," said Bree, behind me. "Anyone looking at her can tell *that* isn't why he wants her."

I couldn't believe it. Bree, who had always told me I was too negative about my looks, who insisted my flat chest didn't matter, who had worked for years to get me to see myself as attractive. She was turning on me so completely.

"You know what it is, don't you?" Raven sniped on. Did either of them have any clue that I was ready to kill them both? I wondered. "Cal saw her, and it was witch at first sight."

I ran to class, hearing the echoes of their laughter floating behind me. Those *bitches,* I snarled to myself. In class I sat for ten minutes, trying to calm my breathing, trying to release my anger.

For just a moment I was glad I had been mean to Raven. I should have been ten times as mean. I couldn't help it. I wanted to wipe Bree and Raven out. I wanted to see them miserable.

6

Searching

January 9, 1980

They found Morag Sheehan's body last evening. Down at the bottom of the cliffs, by old Towson's farm. The tide would have taken her away and none of us the wiser, but it was a low tide because of the moon. And so she was found by young Billy Martin and Hugh Beecham. At first they thought she was the charred, rotted mast of a ship. But she wasn't. She was only a burned witch.

Of course Belwicket met before dawn. We hung blankets over the shutters inside and gathered around my folks' kitchen table. The thing is, Ma and I had put that powerful protection on Morag last year, and since then nothing had gone amiss with her. All was right as rain.

"You know what this means," said Paddy McTavish. "No human could have got close to her, not with that spell on her and all the ward-evil spells she was doing herself."

"What are you saying?" Ma asked.

"I'm saying she was killed by a witch," Paddy answered.

When he said that, of course it seemed obvious. Morag was killed by a witch. One of us? Surely not. Then is there someone in the neighborhood, someone we don't know about? Someone from a different coven?

It makes me cold to think of such evil.

Next circle we're going to scry. Until then I'm keeping a weather eye on everybody and everything. — Bradhadair

The first chance I had to tell Cal about my research was after school. He walked with me to Das Boot, and we stood by my car and talked. "I found out about Maeve Riordan," I said bluntly. "A little bit, anyway."

"Tell me about it," he said, but I saw him glance at his watch.

"Do you need to go?" I asked.

"In a minute," he said apologetically. "My mom needs me to help her this afternoon. One of her coven members is sick, and we're going to do some healing."

"You can do that?" It seemed every day I learned of new magickal possibilities.

"Sure," Cal said. "I'm not saying we'll definitely cure him, but he'll do a lot better than if we weren't working for him. But tell me what you found out."

"I ran a search on the computer," I said. "I hit a lot of dead ends. But I found her name on a genealogy site, which led me to a small article from the *Meshomah Falls Herald*. So I looked it up at the library."

"Where's Meshomah Falls?" asked Cal.

"Just a few hours from here. Anyway, the article said that a burned body had been identified as Maeve Riordan, formerly of Ballynigel, Ireland. She was twenty-three."

Cal wrinkled his brow. "Do you think that's her?" he asked.

I nodded. "I think it must be. I mean, there were other Maeve Riordans. But this one was close to here, and the timing's right. . . . When she died, I would have been about seven months old."

"Did the article mention a baby?" asked Cal.

I shook my head.

"Huh." He stroked my hair. "I wonder if there's somewhere else we could get more information. Let me think about it. Will you be okay? I don't want to leave, but I kind of have to."

"I'm okay," I said, looking up into his face, relishing the fact that he cared about me. And it wasn't just because I was a blood witch like him. Raven and Bree were just jealous— they didn't know what they were talking about.

We kissed gently, then Cal headed toward his car. I watched him drive off.

Motion caught my eye, and I glanced over to see Tamara and Janice about to get into Tamara's car. They grinned at me and raised their eyebrows suggestively. Tamara gave me a thumbs-up. I grinned back, embarrassed but pleased. As they drove off, it occurred to me that the three of us should try to see a movie soon.

"Skipping chess club?" came Robbie's voice.

I blinked and looked around to see Robbie loping toward me, sunlight flashing from his glasses. His choppy brown hair that only last month had looked so awful now seemed to have a rakish trendiness.

I considered for a moment. "Yeah, I am," I said. "I don't know—chess seems kind of pointless now."

"Not chess itself," Robbie said, his blue-gray eyes serious behind his ugly glasses. "Chess itself is still really awesome. It's beautiful, like a crystal."

I braced myself for one of Robbie's chess rants. He's almost in love with the game. But he just said, "It's just the club thing that's pointless now. The school thing." He looked at me. "After you've seen a friend of yours make a flower bloom, school and clubs and all of that seem kind of ... silly."

I felt proud and self-conscious at the same time. I loved the idea that I was gifted, that my heritage was showing in my ability. But I was also so used to blending in with the woodwork, not making waves, standing happily in Bree's shadow. It was hard to get used to being noticed so much.

"Are you going home?" Robbie asked.

"I don't know. I don't really feel like it," I said. In fact, the thought of facing my parents made my stomach knot up. Then I had a better idea. "Hey, do you want to go to Practical Magick?" I felt a mixture of guilt and pleasure as I suggested it. My mom definitely wouldn't approve of my going to a Wicca store. But so what? It wasn't my problem.

"Cool," said Robbie. "Then we'll hit Baskin-Robbins. Leave your car here, and I'll bring you back to it."

"Let's do it." As I was walking up the street to Robbie's car, I caught a flash of Mary K.'s straight auburn hair. Glancing over, my eyes locked on Mary K. and Bakker plastered together against the side of the life sciences building. My eyes narrowed. It was the most bizarre feeling, seeing my four-teen-year-old sister making out with someone.

"Go, Bakker," Robbie murmured, and I punched his arm.

I couldn't help looking at them as we approached Robbie's dark red VW Beetle. I saw Mary K., laughing, squirming out of Bakker's arms. He followed her and caught her again.

"Bakker!" Mary K. squealed, her hair flying.

"Mary K.!" I called suddenly, without knowing why.

She looked up, still caught in his arms. "Hey."

"I'm getting a ride with Robbie," I said, gesturing to him.

Nodding, she motioned toward Bakker. "Bakker will take me home. Right?" she asked him.

He nuzzled her neck. "Whatever you say."

Suppressing a feeling of unease, I got into Robbie's car.

The drive north to Red Kill took only about twenty-five minutes. After Das Boot, Robbie's car felt small and intimate. I noticed Robbie squinting and rubbing his eyes.

"You've been doing that a lot lately," I said.

"My eyes are killing me. I need new glasses," he said. "My mom made an appointment for tomorrow."

"Good."

"What was Bree talking about this morning?" he asked. "About your parents' new reading material?"

I wrinkled my nose and sighed. "Well, Bree is really angry at me," I said, stating the obvious. "It's all about Cal—she wanted to go out with him, and he wanted to go out with me. So now she hates me, I guess. Anyway—you know I was keeping my Wicca books at her house?"

Robbie nodded, his eyes on the road.

"She dumped them all on my porch yesterday morning," I explained. "My mom went ballistic. It's all a big mess," I summed up inadequately.

"Oh," said Robbie.

"Yeah."

"I knew Bree liked Cal," said Robbie. "I didn't think they would be a good couple."

I smiled at him, amused. "Bree would make anyone into a good couple. Anyway, let's not talk about it. Things have been kind of . . . awful. The only good thing is that Cal and I got together, and it's really great."

Robbie glanced over at me and nodded. "Hmmm," he said.

"Hmmm, what?" I asked. "Do you mean, hmmm, that's great? Or hmmm, I'm not so sure?"

"More like—hmmm, it's complicated, I guess," Robbie told me. "You know, because of Bree and everything."

I stared at him, but he was watching the road again, and I couldn't read his profile.

I looked out the window. I wanted to talk about something that we hadn't really hashed out. "Robbie, I really am sorry about that spell. You know. The one about your skin."

He shifted gears without saying anything.

"I won't ever do it again," I promised once more.

"Don't say that. Just promise you won't do it without telling me," he said as he parked his Beetle in a tiny space. He turned to me. "I was mad that you did it without telling me," he said. "But I mean, Jesus, look at me." He gestured to his newly smooth face. "I never thought I'd look like this. Thought I'd be a pizza face forever. Then have awful scars my whole life." He glanced out over the steering wheel. "Now I look in the mirror and I'm happy. Girls look at me—girls who used to ignore me or feel sorry for me." He shrugged. "How could I be upset about that?"

I reached out and touched his arm. "Thanks."

He grinned at me and swung open his door. "Let's go get in touch with our inner witches."

As usual, Practical Magick was dim and scented with herbs, oils, and incense. After the chilly November sunshine, the store felt warm and welcoming. Inside, it was divided in two, one half floor-to-ceiling bookshelves and the other half shelves covered with candles, herbs, essential oils, altar items and magical symbols, ritual daggers called athames, robes, posters, even Wiccan fridge magnets.

I left Robbie looking at books and went over to the herb section. Learning about working with them could take my whole life and then some, I thought. The idea was daunting but also thrilling. I had used herbs in the spell that had cured Robbie's acne, and I had felt almost transported in the herb garden of the Killburn Abbey, when I'd gone there on a church trip.

I was looking through a guide to magickal plants of the northeast when I felt a tingling sensation. Glancing up, I saw David, one of the store's clerks. I tensed. He always put me on edge, and I could never pinpoint why.

I remembered how he had asked me what clan I was in and how he had told Alyce, the other clerk, that I was a witch who pretended not to be a witch.

Now I watched him warily as he walked toward me, his short, gray hair looking silver in the store's fluorescent lights.

"Something about you has changed," he said in his soft voice, his brown eyes on me.

I thought about Samhain, when the night had exploded

around me, and about Sunday, when my family had blown apart. I didn't say anything.

"You're a blood witch," he stated, nodding as if he were simply confirming something I'd said. "And now you know it."

How can he tell? I wondered with a tinge of fear.

"Were you really surprised?" he asked me.

I looked around for Robbie. He was still over by the books.

"Yes, I was kind of surprised," I admitted.

"Do you have your BOS?" he asked. "Book of Shadows?"

"I've started one," I said, thinking of the beautiful blank book with marbled paper that I had bought a couple of weeks before. In it I had written down the spell I had done for Robbie and also about my experiences on Samhain. But why did David want to know?

"Do you have your clan's, your coven's?" he asked. "Your mother's?"

"No," I said shortly. "No chance of that."

"I'm sorry," he said, after a pause. Then a bell tinkled, and he moved off to help another customer choose some jewelry.

Glancing down the aisle, I saw that the other clerk, Alyce, was on the floor way at the end, arranging some candleholders on a low shelf. She was older than David, a round, motherly woman with beautiful gray hair in a loose bun on top of her head. I had liked her the first moment I had seen her. Still holding my herb book, I wandered down the aisle closer to her.

She looked up and smiled briefly, as if she had been waiting for me. "How are you, dear?" There was a world of meaning in her words, and for a moment I felt like she knew about everything that had happened since she had helped me pick out a candle, a week before Samhain.

I didn't know what to say. "Awful," I blurted out. "I just found out I'm a blood witch. My parents have lied to me all my life."

Alyce nodded knowingly. "So David was right," she said, her voice reaching me alone. "I thought you were, too."

"How did you know?"

"We can recognize them," she said matter-of-factly. "We're blood witches ourselves, though we don't know our clans."

I stared at her.

"David in particular is quite powerful," Alyce went on. Her plump hands made neat rows of candleholders shaped like stars, like moons, like pentacles.

"Do you have a coven?" I whispered.

"Starlocket," said Alyce. "With Selene Belltower."

Cal's mother.

Robbie appeared at the end of the aisle, thirty feet away. He was talking to a young woman, who was smiling at him flirtatiously. Robbie pushed his glasses aside, rubbed his eyes, then answered her. She laughed, and they drifted back over to the book aisle. I heard the murmur of their voices. For a moment curiosity made me want to concentrate on hearing their words, but then I realized that just because I could didn't mean I should.

A sudden idea sparked in my head. "Alyce, do you know anything about Meshomah Falls?" I asked.

It was as if a snake had bitten her. She literally drew back, anguish crossing her round face. Frowning, she got slowly to her feet, as if troubled by a great weight.

She looked into my eyes. "Why do you ask?" she said.

"I wanted to know more about . . . a woman named Maeve Riordan," I said. "I need to know more."

For long moments Alyce's gaze held mine.

"I know that name," she said.

7

Burned

May 8, 1980

Angus asked me to marry him at Beltane. I told him no. I'm only eighteen and have hardly ever been out of Ballynigel. I was thinking of doing one of those tours, you know, with a bus and going through Europe for a month. I do love Angus. And I know he's good. He might even be my mùirn beatha dàn, my soul mate, but who knows? He might not! Sometimes I feel like he is, sometimes I don't. The thing is: How would I know? I've met precious few witches in my life that I'm not related to. I need to be sure. I need to know more before I can decide to stay with him forever.

"Where will you go?" he asks me. "Who will you be with? Someone not your kind, like David O'Hearn? A human?"

Of course not. If I want children, I can't be with a human. But maybe I don't want children. I don't know. There aren't that many of our clan. To go outside our clan to another would be disloyal. But to seal my fate at eighteen seems disloyal, too — disloyal to me.

And after all that's been happening — Morag's murder, the bad-luck spells, the bespelled runes (Mathair calls them sigils) we've found — I just don't know. I want to get away. Only three more weeks and I'll take my A levels and be done with school. I can't wait.

Now it's late, and I have to do a warding spell before I sleep, to keep away evil. We all do, nowadays. — Bradhadair

I waited while Alyce cast back her mind. There was a tall stool nearby, battered and blotched with multicolored paint spills. I perched on it, my eyes on Alyce's face.

"I never knew Maeve Riordan," Alyce said at last. "I never met her. I was living in Manhattan at the time all of this happened. I really only learned of it years later, when I moved here. But it was big news in the Wiccan community, and most witches around here know about it."

It was shocking to me that many people knew the story of what had happened to my mother while I knew virtually nothing. I waited, not wanting to disturb Alyce's thoughts.

"The way I heard the story is this," Alyce said, and it was as if her voice were coming to me from a distance. "Maeve Riordan was a blood witch, from one of the Seven Great Clans, but we aren't sure which one. Her local coven was called Belwicket, and she was from Ballynigel, Ireland."

I nodded. I had seen the words Belwicket and Ballynigel on Maeve's genealogy site, the one that had shut down.

"Belwicket was very insular and didn't interact with other clans or covens much," Alyce continued. "They were quite secretive, and maybe they had cause to be. Anyway, back in the late seventies, early eighties, as I understand it, Belwicket was persecuted. The members were taunted in the streets by the townspeople; their children were ostracized at school. Ballynigel was a small town, mind you, small and close to the coast of western Ireland. The people there were mainly farmers or fishermen. Not worldly, not overly educated. Very conservative," Alyce explained. She paused, thinking.

In my mind I saw rolling hills as deep a green as a peridot. Salt air seemed to kiss my skin. I smelled tangy, brackish seaweed, fish, and an almost unpleasant yet comfortable odor my brain identified as peat, whatever that was.

"The villagers had probably always lived among witches in peace, but for some reason, every so often, a town gets stirred up; people get scared. After months of persecution a local witch was murdered, burned to death and thrown from a cliff."

I swallowed hard. I knew from my reading that burning was the traditional method of killing witches.

"There was some talk that it had been another witch, not a human, who had done it," continued Alyce.

"What about Maeve Riordan?" I asked.

"She was the daughter of the local high priestess, a woman named Mackenna Riordan. At fourteen Maeve joined Belwicket under the name Bradhadair: fire starter. Apparently she was very powerful, very, very powerful."

My mother.

"Anyway, things in Ballynigel grew more and more intolerable for the witches. They had to shop in other towns, leases expired and weren't renewed, but they could deal with all that somehow."

"Why didn't they leave?" I asked.

"Ballynigel was a place of power," Alyce explained. "At least it was for that coven. There was something about that area, perhaps just because magick had been worked there for centuries—but it was a very good place to be for a witch. Most of Belwicket had roots in the land going back more generations than they could count. Their people had always lived there. I imagine it was hard to fathom living anywhere else."

It was hard for an American, with family roots going back only a hundred years or so, to comprehend. Taking a deep breath, I looked around for Robbie. I could hear him still talking to the girl on the other side of the store. I glanced at my watch. Five-thirty. I had to get home soon. But I was finally learning about my past, my history, and I couldn't pull myself away.

"How do you know all this?" I asked.

"People have talked of it over the years," Alyce said. "You see, it could so easily happen to any of us."

A chill went through me, and I stared at her. To me, magick was beautiful and joyful. She was reminding me that countless women and men had died because of it.

"Maeve Riordan finally did leave," Alyce went on, her face sad. "One night there was a huge . . . decimation, for want of a better word."

I shivered, feeling an icy breeze float over me, settling at my feet.

"The Belwicket coven was virtually destroyed," Alyce continued, sounding like the words were hard to say. "It's unclear whether it was the townspeople or a dark, powerful, magickal source that swept through the coven, but that night homes were burned to the ground, cars were set on fire, fields of crops were laid to waste, boats were sunk . . . and twenty-three men, women, and children were killed."

I realized I was panting, my stomach in knots. I felt ill and dizzy and panicky. I couldn't bear hearing about this.

"But not Maeve," Alyce whispered, looking off at some far-away sight. "Maeve escaped that night, and so did young Angus Bramson, her lover. Maeve was twenty, Angus twenty-two, and together they fled, caught a bus to Dublin and a plane to England. From there they landed in New York, and from New York City they made their way to Meshomah Falls."

"Did they get married?" I said hoarsely.

"There's no record of it," Alyce replied. "They settled in Meshomah Falls, got jobs, and renounced witchcraft entirely. Apparently for two years they practiced no Wicca, called upon no power, created no magick." She shook her head sadly. "It must have been like living in a straitjacket. Like smothering inside a box. And then they had a baby in the local hospital. We think the persecution began right after that."

My throat felt like it was closing. I pulled my sweater away from my neck because it was choking me.

"It was little things at first—finding runes of danger and threat painted on the side of their little house. Evil sigils, runes bespelled for some magickal purpose, scratched into their car doors. One day a dead cat hanging from their porch. If they had come to the local coven, they could have been helped. But they wanted nothing to do with witchcraft. After Belwicket had been destroyed, Maeve wanted nothing more to do with it. Though, of course, it was in her blood. There's no point in denying what you are."

Terror threatened to overwhelm me. I wanted to run screaming from the store.

Alyce looked at me. "Maeve's Book of Shadows was found after the fire. People read it and passed on the stories of what was written there."

"Where is it now?" I demanded, and Alyce shook her head.

"I don't know," she said gently. "Maeve's story ends with her and Angus burned in a barn."

Tears ran slowly down my cheeks.

"What happened to the baby?" I choked out.

Alyce gazed at me sympathetically, years of wisdom written on her face. She reached up one soft, flower-scented hand and touched my cheek. "I don't know that, either, my dear," she said so quietly, I could barely hear her. "What did happen to the baby?"

A mist swam over my eyes, and I needed to lie down or fall over or run screaming down the street.

"Hey, Morgan!" Robbie's voice broke in. "Are you ready? I should get home."

"Good-bye," I whispered. I turned and raced out the door, with Robbie following me, concern radiating from him in waves.

Behind me I felt rather than heard Alyce's words: "Not good-bye, my dear. You'll be back."

8

Anger

November 1, 1980

What a glorious Samhain we had last night! After a powerful circle that Ma let me lead, we danced, played music, watched the stars, and hoped for better times ahead. It was a night full of cider, laughter, and hope. Things have been so quiet lately — has the evil moved on? Has it found another home? Goddess, I pray not, for I don't wish others to suffer as we have. But I'm thankful that we no longer have to jump at every noise.

Angus gave me a darling kitten—a tiny white tom I've named Dagda. He has a lot to live up to with that name! He's a wee thing and sweet. I love him, and it was just like Angus to come up with the idea. Today my world is blessed and full of peace.

Praise be to the Goddess for keeping us safe another year.

Praise be to Mother Earth for sharing her bounty far and near.

Praise be to magick, from which all blessings flow.

Praise be to my heart; I will follow where it goes.

Blessed be.

— Bradhadair

Now Dagda is mewing to go out!

"What's wrong?" Robbie demanded in the car.

I sniffled and wiped my hand over my face. "Oh, Alyce was telling me a sad story about some witches who died."

His eyes narrowed. "And you're crying because . . . ," he prompted.

"It just got to me," I said, trying to sound light. "I'm so tenderhearted."

"Okay, don't tell me," he said, sounding irritated. He started the car and began the drive back to Widow's Vale.

"It's just . . . I can't talk about it yet, okay, Robbie?" I almost whispered.

He was quiet for a few moments, then nodded. "Okay. But if you ever need a shoulder, I'm here."

It was so sweet of him that a wave of warmth rushed over me. I reached out to pat his shoulder. "Thanks. That helps. Really."

Darkness fell as we drove, and by the time we got back to school, streetlights were on. My thoughts had been churning around my birth mother's fate, and I was surprised to recognize the school building when Robbie stopped and I saw my car sitting by itself on the street.

"Thanks for the ride," I said. It was dark, and leaves were blowing off trees, flitting through the air. One brushed against me, and I flinched.

"You okay?" he asked.

"I think so. Thanks again. I'll see you tomorrow," I said, and got in Das Boot.

I felt like I had lived through my birth mother's story. She had to be the same Maeve Riordan on my birth certificate. She had to be. I tried to remember if I had seen the place of birth—if it had been Meshomah Falls or Widow's Vale. I couldn't remember. Did my parents know any of this story? How had they found me? How had I been adopted? The same old questions.

I started my car, feeling anger come over me again. They had the answers, and they were going to tell me. Tonight. I couldn't go through another day without knowing.

At home I parked and stormed up the front walk, already forming the words I was going to say, the questions I would ask. I pushed through the front door—

And found Aunt Eileen and her girlfriend, Paula Steen, sitting on the couch.

"Morgan!" said Aunt Eileen, holding out her arms. "How's my favorite niece?"

I hugged her as Mary K. said, "She said the exact same thing to me."

Aunt Eileen laughed. "You're both my favorite nieces."

I smiled, trying to mentally switch gears. A confrontation with my parents was out for now. And then—it was only then that I realized that Aunt Eileen knew I was adopted. Of course she did. She's my mom's sister. In fact, all of my parents' friends must know. They had always lived here in Widow's Vale, and unless my mom had faked a pregnancy, which I couldn't see her doing, they would all know that I had just turned up out of nowhere. And then two years later she really had had a baby: Mary K. Oh my God, I thought, appalled. I was utterly, utterly humiliated and embarrassed.

"Listen, we brought Chinese food," said Aunt Eileen, standing up.

"It's ready!" Mom called from the dining room. I would have given anything not to have to go in, but there was no way to get out of it. We all swarmed in. White cartons and plastic foam containers filled the center of the table.

"Hi," Mom said to me, scanning my face. "You got back in time."

"Uh-huh," I said, not meeting her gaze. "I was with Robbie."

"Robbie looks amazing lately," said Mary K., helping herself to some orange beef. "Has he been seeing a new dermatologist?"

"Um, I don't know," I said vaguely. "His skin has gotten a lot better."

"Maybe he's just grown out of it," suggested my mom. I couldn't believe she was making polite chitchat. Frustration started to boil in me as I tried to choke down my dinner.

"Can you pass the pork?" my dad asked.

For a while we all ate. If Aunt Eileen and Paula noticed that things were a bit weird, if we were stilted and less talkative, they didn't show it. But even Mary K., as naturally perky as she is, was holding back.

"Oh, Morgan, Janice called," said my dad. I could tell he was striving for a normal tone. "She wants you to call her back. I said you would, after dinner."

"Okay, thanks," I said. I stuffed a big bite of scallion pancake in my mouth so it wouldn't seem weird that I was being so quiet.

After dinner Aunt Eileen stood up and went into the kitchen, returning with a bottle of sparkling cider and a tray of glasses.

"What's all this?" my mom asked with a surprised smile.

"Well," Aunt Eileen said shyly as Paula got up to stand next to her. "We have some very exciting news."

Mary K. and I exchanged glances.

"We're moving in together," Eileen announced, her face full of happiness. She smiled at Paula, and Paula gave her a hug.

"I've already put my apartment on the market, and we're looking for a house," said Paula.

"Oh, awesome," said Mary K., getting up to hug Aunt Eileen and Paula. They beamed. I stood up and hugged them, too, and so did Mom. Dad hugged Eileen and shook Paula's hand.

"Well, this is lovely news," said Mom, although something in her face said that she thought it would be better if they had known each other longer.

Eileen popped the cork on the sparkling cider and poured it. Paula handed glasses around, and Mary K. and I immediately gulped down sips.

"Are you going to buy a house together or rent?" Mom asked.

"We're looking to buy," said Eileen. "We both have apartments now, but I want to get a dog, so we need a yard."

"And I need room for a garden," said Paula.

"A dog and a garden might be mutually exclusive," said my dad, and they laughed. I smiled, too, but it all felt so unreal: as if I were watching someone else's family on television.

"I was hoping you could help us with the house hunting," Eileen said to my mom.

Mom smiled, for the first time since yesterday, I realized. "I was already running through possibilities in my head," she admitted. "Can you come by the office soon, and we can set up some appointments?"

"That would be great," said Eileen. Paula reached over and squeezed her shoulder. They looked at each other as if no one else was in the room.

"Moving is going to be insane," said Paula. "I have stuff scattered everywhere: my mom's, my dad's, my sister's. My apartment was just too small to hold everything."

"Fortunately, I have a niece who's not only strong but has a huge car," Aunt Eileen offered brightly, looking over at me.

I stared at her. I wasn't really her niece, though, was I? Even Eileen had been playing into this whole fantasy that was my life. Even she, my favorite aunt, had been lying and keeping secrets from me for sixteen years.

"Aunt Eileen, do you know why Mom and Dad never told me I was adopted?" I just put it out there, and it was as if I had mentioned I had the bubonic plague.

Everyone stared at me, except Mary K., who was staring at her plate miserably, and Paula, who was watching Aunt Eileen with a concerned expression.

Aunt Eileen looked like she had swallowed a frog. Her eyes wide, she said, "What?" and shot quick glances at my mom and dad.

"I mean, don't you think somebody should have told me? Maybe just mentioned it? You could have said something. Or maybe you just didn't think it was that important," I pressed on. Part of me knew I wasn't being fair. But somehow I couldn't stop myself. "No one else seems to. After all, it's just my life we're talking about."

Mom said, "Morgan," in a defeated tone of voice.

"Uh ...," said Aunt Eileen, for once at a loss for words.

Everyone was as embarrassed as I was, and the festive air had gone out of dinner.

"Never mind," I said abruptly, standing up. "We can talk about it later. Why not? After sixteen years what's a few days more?"

"Morgan, I always felt your parents should be the ones to tell you—," Aunt Eileen said, sounding distressed.

"Yeah, right," I said rudely. "When was that going to happen?"

Mary K. gasped, and I pushed my chair back roughly. I couldn't stand being here one more second. I couldn't take their hypocrisy anymore. I would explode.

This time I remembered to grab my jacket before I ran out to my car and peeled off into the darkness.

9

Healing Light

St. Patrick's Day, 1981

Oh, Jesus, Mary, and Joseph, I'm so drunk, I can hardly write. Ballynigel just put on a St. Paddy's party to end all parties. All the townspeople, everyone, gathered together to have a good time in the village. Human or witch, we all agree on St. Paddy's Day, the wearing of the green.

Pat O'Hearn dyed all his beer green, and it was sloshing into mugs, into pails, into shoes, anything. Old Towson gave some to his donkey, and that donkey has never been so tame or good-natured! I laughed until I had to hold my sides in.

The Irish Cowboys played their music all afternoon right in the town green, and we all danced and pinched one another, and the kids were throwing cabbages and potatoes. We had a good day, and our dark time seems to be well and truly over.

Now I'm home, and I lit three green candles to the Goddess

for prosperity and happiness. There's a full moon tonight, so I have to sober up, dress warm, and go gather my luibh. The dock root down at the pond is ready for taking in, and there's early violets, dandelions, and cattails, too, ready. I can't drink any more beer until then, or they'll find me facedown in the marsh, too drunk to pick myself up! What a day!

— Bradhadair

As I drove it occurred to me that there was nowhere to go at eight o'clock on a Monday night in Widow's Vale, New York. I pictured myself showing up at Schweikhardt's soda shop, on Main Street, with tears streaming down my cheeks. I pictured myself showing up at Janice's the same way. No—Janice had no idea how complicated my life had gotten. Robbie? I considered for a second but shook my head. I hated going to his house, with his dad drinking beer in front of the TV and his mom all tight-lipped and angry. And of course Bree didn't even enter into it—God, what a bitch she'd been today.

Cal? I turned and headed toward his neighborhood, feeling desperate and daring, brave and terrified. Was I being presumptuous by going to his house uninvited? There was so much going on in my mind: my birth parents' story, my other parents' refusal to tell me the truth about my past, Bree—it was all too much to think about. I felt like I couldn't make any kind of decision about anything—even about whether it was okay for me to show up at Cal's house unannounced.

By the time I pulled into the long, cobblestone driveway of Cal's big stone house, I felt completely incoherent. What was I doing? I just wanted to drive off into the night forever, far away from everyone I knew. Be a different person. I couldn't believe this was my life.

I cut the lights and the engine and hunched over my steering wheel, literally frozen with uncertainty. I couldn't even start the car again to get out of there.

Who knows how long I huddled in the darkness outside Cal's home. I finally looked up when strong headlights flooded the interior of my car, reflecting off my rearview mirror and shining into my eyes. An expensive-looking SUV pulled around my car and parked neatly, close to the house. Its door opened, and a tall, slender woman stepped out, her hair barely visible in the darkness. The house's outdoor floodlights came on, bathing the driveway in warm yellow light. The woman walked to my car.

Feeling like an idiot, I rolled down my window as Selene Belltower approached. For long moments she gazed at my face, as if evaluating me. We neither smiled nor spoke to each other.

Finally she said, "Why don't you come inside, Morgan? You must be chilled through. I'll make some cocoa." As if it was normal to find a girl in a car sitting in the dark outside her house.

I got out of Das Boot and slammed the door. We walked up the broad stone steps together, Cal's mom and I, and through the massive wooden front door. She led me across the foyer, down a hall, into a huge French country–style kitchen I hadn't seen on my other visit here.

"Sit down, Morgan," she said, gesturing to a tall stool by the kitchen island.

I sat, hoping Cal was here. I hadn't seen his car outside, but maybe it was in the garage.

I cast my senses out, but I couldn't feel his presence close by. Selene Belltower's head snapped up as she poured milk into a pan. Her brows came together, and she looked at me assessingly.

"You're very strong," she commented. "I didn't learn how to cast my senses until I was in my twenties. Cal isn't here, by the way."

"I'm sorry," I said awkwardly. "I should go. I don't want to bother you...."

"You're not bothering me," she said. She spooned some cocoa powder into the milk and whisked it smooth on the cooktop across from me. "I've been curious. Cal has told me some very interesting things about you."

Cal talked to his mother about me?

She laughed, a warm, earthy laugh, when she saw the expression on my face. "Cal and I are pretty close," she said. "For a long time it's been just the two of us. His father left us when Cal was about four."

"I'm sorry," I said again. She was speaking to me as if I were an adult, and for some reason this made me feel younger than sixteen.

Selene Belltower shrugged. "I was sorry, too. Cal missed his father very much, but he lives in Europe now, and they don't see each other often. At any rate—you shouldn't be startled that my son confides in me. It would be silly for him to try to hide anything, after all."

I breathed in, trying to relax. So this was life in a blood-witch household. No secrets.

Cal's mother poured the cocoa into two brightly colored hand-painted mugs and handed one to me. It was too hot to drink, so I set it down and waited. Selene waved her hand over her mug twice, then took a sip.

"Try this," she suggested, looking up at me. "Take your left hand and circle it widdershins over your mug. Say, 'Cool the fire.'"

I did, wondering. I felt warmth go into my left hand.

"Try the cocoa now," she said, watching me.

I took a sip. It was noticeably cooler, perfect to drink. I grinned, delighted.

"Left hand takes away," she explained. "Right hand gives. Deasil for increasing, widdershins for decreasing. And simple words are best."

I nodded and drank my cocoa. This one small thing was so fascinating to me. The idea that I could speak words, make movements that cooled a hot drink to the right temperature!

Selene smiled, and then her eyes focused on mine sympathetically. "You look like you've had a rough time."

This was an understatement, but I nodded. "Has Cal . . . told you about . . . anything?"

She put her mug down. "He's told me you recently found out you were adopted," she said. "That your biological parents must be blood witches. And this afternoon he told me you thought you were probably the daughter of two Irish witches who died here sixteen years ago."

I nodded again. "Not exactly here—Meshomah Falls. About two hours away. I think my mother's name was Maeve Riordan."

Selene's face became grave. "I've heard that story," she said. "I remember when it happened. I was forty years old;

Cal wasn't quite two. I remember thinking that such a thing could never happen to me, my husband, our child." Her long fingers played with the rim of her mug. "I know better now." She looked up at me again. "I'm very sorry this has happened to you. It's always somewhat difficult to be different, even if you have a lot of support. One is still set apart. But I know you must be having an especially hard time."

My throat felt like it was closing again, and I drank my cocoa. I didn't trust myself to agree. I distracted myself with pointless details: If she had been forty sixteen years ago, she would be about fifty-six now. She looked like she was about thirty-five.

"If you want," said Selene, sounding hesitant, "I can help you feel better."

"What do you mean?" I asked. For a wild moment I wondered, Is she offering me drugs?

"Well, I'm picking up waves of upset, discord, unhappiness, anger," she said. "We could make a small, two-person circle and try to get you to a better place."

I caught my breath. I had only ever made a circle with Cal and our coven. What would it be like with someone who was even more powerful than he was? I found myself saying, "Yes, please, if you don't mind."

Selene smiled, looking very much like Cal. "Come on, then."

The house was shaped like a U, with a middle part and two wings. She led me to the back of the left wing, through a very large room that I figured she must use for her coven's circles. She opened a door that set into the wall paneling, so you could barely see it. I felt a thrill of pure, childlike delight. Secret doors!

We stepped into a much smaller, cozier room furnished only with a narrow table, some bookshelves, and candelabras on the walls. Selene lit the candles.

"This is my private sanctuary," she said, brushing her fingers over the doorjamb. For a fleeting moment I saw sigils glimmering there. They must be for privacy or protection. But I had no idea how to read them. There was so much I needed to learn. I was a complete novice.

Selene had already drawn a small circle on the wooden floor, using a reddish powder that gave off a strong, spicy scent. She motioned me into the circle with her and then closed it behind us.

"Let's sit down," she said. With us facing each other, sitting cross-legged on the floor, there was very little room inside the circle.

We each sprinkled salt around our half of the circle, saying, "With this salt, I purify my circle."

Then Selene closed her eyes and let her head droop, her hands on her knees as if doing yoga. "With every breath out, release a negative emotion. With every breath in, take in white light, healing light, soothing and calming light. Feel it enter your fingers, your toes, settle in your stomach, reach up through the crown of your head."

As she spoke her voice became slower, deeper, more mesmerizing. My eyes were closed, my chin practically resting on my chest. I breathed out, forcing air completely out of my lungs. Then I breathed in, listening to her soothing words.

"I release tension," she murmured, and I repeated it after her without hesitation.

"I release fear and anger," she said, her words floating to me on a sea of calm. I repeated it and literally felt the knots in my stomach begin to uncoil, the tightness in my arms and calves unravel.

"I release uncertainty," she said, and I followed her.

We breathed deeply, silently for several minutes. My headache dissolved, my temples ceased throbbing, my chest expanded, and I could breathe more easily.

"I feel calm," Selene said.

"Me too," I agreed dreamily. I sensed rather than saw her smile.

"No, say it," she prompted, humor in her voice.

"Oh. I feel calm," I said.

"Open your eyes. Make this symbol with your right hand," she prompted, drawing in the air with two fingers. "It's the rune for comfort."

I watched her, then carefully drew in the air one straight line down, then a small triangle attached to the top, like a little flag.

"I feel at peace," she said, drawing the same rune on my forehead.

"I feel at peace," I said, feeling her finger trace heat on my skin. The memory of what had happened to my birth parents receded into the distance. I was aware of it, but it had less power to hurt me.

"I am love. I am peace. I am strength."

I said the words, feeling a delicious warmth flow over me.

"I call on the strength of the Goddess and the God. I call on the power of the Earth Mother," said Selene, tracing another rune onto my forehead. This one felt like half of a lopsided rectangle, and as it sank into my skin I thought, Strength.

Selene and I were joined. I could feel her strength inside

my head, feel her smoothing every wrinkle in my emotions, searching out every knot of fear, every snarl of anger. She probed deeper and deeper, and languidly I let her. She soothed away the pain until I was almost in a trance.

Ages later, I seemed to come awake again. Unbidden, I opened my eyes in time to see her raising her head and opening hers. I felt a little groggy and so much better, I couldn't help smiling. She smiled back.

"All right now?" she said softly.

"Oh, yes," I said, unable to put my feelings into words.

"Here's one more for you," she said, and she traced two triangles, touching, onto the backs of my hands. "That's for new beginnings."

"Thank you," I said, awed by her power. "I feel much better."

"Good." We stood, and she dissolved the circle and blew out the candles mounted around the small room. As we passed through the larger coven's room I saw a reflection of Selene's face in a huge, gilt-frame wall mirror. She was smiling. Her face was bright, almost triumphant as she led the way back to the foyer. Then the image was gone, and I thought I must have imagined it.

At the front door she patted my arm, and I thanked her again. Then I practically floated to my car, not feeling the slightest bit of November wind, November chill. I felt absolutely perfect all the way home. I didn't even wonder where Cal had been.

10

Split

August 14, 1981

The coven over at Much Bencham has three new students, they tell us. We have none. Tara and Cliff were the last to join Belwicket as students, and that was three years ago. Until Lizzie Sims turns fourteen in four years, we have no one. Of course, at Much Bencham they take almost anyone who wants to study.

I say we should do the same — if we could even convince anyone to join us. Belwicket chose its own path long ago, and it is not for everyone. But we must expand. If we stick to only blood-born, clan-born witches, we will surely die out. We must seek out others of our kind, mingle clans. But Ma and the elders have shot me down time and again. They want us to remain pure. They refuse to let outsiders in.

Maybe some in Belwicket would rather die.

— Bradhadair

When I got home that night, my parents' light was already out, and if my car's rumbling engine woke them up, they didn't show it. Mary K. had waited up for me, listening to music in her room. She looked up and took off her headphones when I poked my head in.

"Hi," I said, feeling a deep love for her. After all, she'd always been my sister, if not by blood, then by circumstance. I regretted hurting her.

"Where did you go?" she asked.

"To Cal's. He wasn't there, but I talked to his mom."

Mary K. paused. "It was awful after you left. I thought Mom was going to burst into tears. Everyone was really embarrassed."

"I'm sorry," I said sincerely. "It's just that I can't believe Mom and Dad kept this to themselves my whole life. They lied to me." I shook my head. "Tonight I realized that Aunt Eileen, and our other relatives, and Mom and Dad's friends *all* know I'm adopted. I just felt so stupid for not knowing myself. I was just ... furious that they never told me when all these other people know."

"Yeah, I hadn't thought of that," said Mary K., frowning slightly. "But you're right. They would all know." She looked at me. "*I* didn't know. You believe that, don't you?"

I nodded. "There's no way *you'd* be able to keep a secret like that." I smiled as Mary K. aimed her pillow at me.

The blanket of peace, forgiveness, and love that Selene Belltower had wrapped around over me was still cocooning me in its comfortable embrace. "Look, it's going to be pretty awful for a while. Mom and Dad have to tell me about my past and how I was adopted. I can't stop till I know. But it doesn't mean I don't love you or them. We'll get through it somehow," I said.

Uncertainty played across Mary K.'s pretty face. "Okay," she said, accepting my word.

"I'm happy about Aunt Eileen and Paula," I said, changing the subject.

"Me too. I didn't want Aunt Eileen to be alone anymore," said Mary K. "Do you think they'll have kids?"

I laughed. "First things first. They need to live together for a while."

"Yeah. Oh, well. I'm tired." Mary K. took off her headphones and dropped them on the floor.

"Here, let me do this." Reaching over, I gently traced the rune for comfort on her forehead, the way Selene had showed me. I felt the warmth leave my fingertips and stood back to see Mary K. looking at me unhappily.

"Please don't do that to me," she whispered. "I don't want to be part of it."

Stung, I blinked, then nodded. "Yeah, sure," I mumbled. I turned and fled to my own room, feeling dismayed. Something that had given me joy was only upsetting to my sister. It was a clear sign of the differences between us, the growing space that pushed her in one direction and me in another.

That night I slept deeply, without dreams, and woke up feeling wonderful. I put my hands together as if I could still see the sigil traced there: Daeg. A new dawn. An awakening.

"Morgan?" Mary K. called from the hallway. "Come on. School."

I was already shoving my feet into my slippers. No doubt I was running late, as usual. I rushed through my shower, threw on some clothes, and pounded downstairs, my wet hair practically strangling me. In the kitchen I grabbed a breakfast bar, ready to dash out the door. Mary K. looked up calmly from her orange juice.

"No hurry," she said. "I got you up early for once. I've been late twice in the last month."

Mouth open, I looked at the clock. School didn't start for almost forty-five minutes! I sank into a chair and waved incoherently at the fridge.

Taking pity on me, my sister reached in and handed me a Diet Coke. I gulped it down, then stomped back upstairs to untangle my hair.

Somehow, we were late anyway. At school I parallel parked my car with practiced efficiency. Then I spotted Bakker, coming toward the car to meet Mary K. My mood soured.

"Look, there he is," I said. "Lying in wait like a spider."

Mary K. punched my leg. "Stop it," she said. "I thought you liked him."

"He's okay," I said. I've got to chill, I thought. I'd be so peeved if anyone tried to pull the big-sister routine on me. But I couldn't help asking, "Does he know you're only fourteen?"

Mary K. rolled her eyes. "No, he thinks I'm a junior," she said sarcastically. "Don't let the cat out of the bag." She got out of the car. As she and Bakker kissed, I slammed my car door shut and hitched my backpack onto my shoulder. Then I headed toward the east door.

"Oh, Morgan, wait!" someone called. I turned and spotted Janice Yutoh, her hair bouncing as she hurried toward me. Whoops—I'd totally forgotten to return her call the night before.

"Sorry I spaced on calling you," I said as she caught up to me.

She waved a hand in the air. "No biggie. I just wanted to say hi," she said, panting slightly. "I haven't seen you at all lately, except in class."

"I know," I said apologetically. "A lot of stuff's been going on." This was such a lame representation of the truth that I almost laughed. "My aunt Eileen is moving in with her girl-friend," I said, thinking of one bright spot.

"That's great! Tell her I'm happy for her," said Janice.

"Will do," I said. "What'd you get on Fishman's essay test?"

"I somehow pulled an A out of my hat," she said as we walked toward the main building.

"Cool. I got a B-plus. I hate essay tests. Too many words," I complained. Janice laughed. Then we saw Tamara and Ben Reggio heading into the main door just as the bell rang.

"Gotta catch Ben," said Janice, moving off. "He's got my Latin notes."

"See you in class." I went in through the east door, where the coven had started to meet in the mornings, but the cement benches were empty. Cal must have gone inside already. My disappointment at not seeing him was almost equaled by my relief at not having to face Bree.

By lunchtime it was drizzling outside, with sullen rivulets tracing lines on the windows. I filed into the lunchroom, for once grateful for its warm, steamy atmosphere. By the time I collected a tray and looked around, most of the coven was sitting at a table closest to the windows. Raven and Bree weren't there, I saw with a lift of relief. Neither was Beth Nielson.

I made my way over and sat down next to Cal. When he smiled, it was like the sun coming out.

"Hi," he said, making space for me on the table. "Did you get here late this morning?"

I nodded, opening my soda. "Just as the bell rang."

"Can I have a fry?" he asked, taking one without waiting for my answer. I felt a warm glow at his easy familiarity.

"Mom told me you dropped by last night," he said. "I'm sorry I missed you." He squeezed my knee under the table. "You okay?" he asked softly.

"Yeah, your mom was really nice. She showed me some rune magick," I said, dropping my voice.

"Cool," Jenna said, leaning over the table. "Like what?"

"A few different runes for different things," I said. "Like runes for happiness, starting over, peace and calm."

"Did they work?" asked Ethan.

"Yes!" I said, laughing. As if a spell by Selene Belltower wouldn't work. "It would be great if we could start learning about runes, everything about them."

Cal nodded. "Runes are really powerful," he said. "They've been used for thousands of years. I have some books on them if you want to borrow them."

"I'd like to read them, too," said Sharon, stirring her straw around in her milk carton.

"Here's a rune for you guys," said Cal. He cleared a space in the center of the table and traced an image with his finger. It looked like two parallel lines with two other lines crossed between them, joining them. He drew it several times until we could all picture it.

"What does that mean?" asked Matt.

"Basically it means interdependence," Cal explained. "Community. Feeling goodwill toward your kinsmen and kinswomen. It's how we all feel about each other, our circle. Cirrus."

We all looked at each other for a minute, letting this sink in.

"God, there's so much to learn," said Sharon. "I feel like I'll never be able to put it all together—herbs, spells, runes, potions."

"Can I talk to you?" Beth Nielson had walked up and now stood in front of Cal, a multicolored crocheted cap covering her short hair.

"Sure," said Cal. He looked more closely at her. She was frowning. "Do you want to go somewhere private?"

"No." Beth shook her head, not looking at him. "It doesn't matter. They can hear it."

"What's wrong, Beth?" Cal asked quietly. Somehow we all heard him, even over the din of the lunchroom.

Beth shrugged and looked away. Glittery aqua eye shadow glowed above her eyes and contrasted sharply with her coffee-colored skin. She sniffed, as if she had a cold.

Across the table I looked at Jenna. She raised her eyebrows at me.

"It's just—the whole thing doesn't feel right to me," Beth said. "I thought it would be cool, you know? But it's all too weird. Doing circles. Morgan making flowers bloom," she said, gesturing to me. "It's too strange." She raised her shoulders beneath her brown leather jacket and let them fall. "I don't want anything more to do with it. I don't like it. It feels wrong." Her nose ring twinkled under the fluorescent lights.

"That's too bad," said Cal. "Wicca isn't intended to make anyone uncomfortable. It's meant to make you celebrate the beauty and power of the earth."

Beth gave him a blank look, as if to say, Come on.

"So you want to quit the coven. Are you sure about this?" Cal asked. "Maybe you just need more time to get used to it."

Beth shook her head. "No. I don't want to do it anymore."

"Well, if Wicca isn't for you, then that's your choice. Thanks for being honest," Cal said.

"Uh-huh," said Beth, shifting her weight from one Doc Marten to the other.

"Beth, one thing," Cal said. "Please respect our privacy." There was a serious note in his voice that made Beth look up.

"You've come to our circles; you've felt magick's power," Cal went on. "Keep those experiences to yourself, okay? They're no one's business but ours."

"Yeah, okay," Beth said, looking at Cal.

"Well," Cal said. "It's your decision to go. But just remember that the circle won't be open to you again if you change your mind. Sorry, but that's how it works."

"I'm not changing my mind," said Beth. She moved off without looking back.

For a few moments we all looked around at each other.

"What was that about?" I asked.

Jenna coughed. "Yeah, that was pretty weird."

"Don't know," said Cal. A shadow crossed his face. Then he

seemed to shrug it off. "But like I said, Wicca isn't for every-one." He leaned forward. "I thought at our next circle, I could show you guys some more runes and maybe a small spell."

"All right," Ethan said. "Cool." He leaned across to Sharon. "Are you gonna eat that brownie?"

She made a pained face, but I could tell she was kidding. "Yes."

"Halfies?" he asked. Ethan, former pothead, now merely scruffy underdog, grinned coyly at Sharon. It was like watching a street mongrel trying to flirt with a well-groomed poodle.

"I'll give you a tiny bite," Sharon said, breaking off a piece. Her cheeks were slightly pink.

Ethan grinned more broadly and popped the brownie morsel into his mouth.

Around us hundreds of students filed to and from tables, eating, talking to one another, busing their trays. We were a small, private microcosm of the school. To me it felt like we were the only ones talking about things that really mat-tered—things that were far more important and interesting than the latest pep squad rally or prom theme contest. I couldn't wait to be finished with high school, to move on with the rest of my life. I saw myself devoted to Wicca, still with Cal, living a life full of meaning and joy and magick.

Robbie's elbow knocking into me jolted me out of my daydream.

"Sorry," he said, rubbing his temples. "Do you have any Tylenol?"

"Nope, sorry. Your doctor's appointment is today, right?" I asked him, then took a bite of hamburger.

"Yeah."

"Here, take this." Jenna rummaged in her purse and took out two tablets.

Robbie squinted at them, then tossed them down with the rest of his soda. "What was that?"

"Cyanide," said Sharon, and we laughed.

"Actually, it was Midol," Jenna said, turning away to give another cough. I wondered if she was getting sick.

Matt whooped with laughter as Robbie gaped at her in dismay.

"It'll really help," Jenna insisted. "It's what I take for my headaches."

"Oh, man." Robbie shook his head. I was almost doubled over with laughter.

"Look at it this way," said Cal brightly. "You won't get that awful bloated feeling."

"You'll feel pretty all day," suggested Matt, laughing so hard, he had to wipe his eyes.

"Oh, man," said Robbie again as we cackled.

"Well, this is nice," came Raven's snide voice. "Everyone all happy and laughing together. Cozy, huh, Bree?"

"Very cozy," said Bree.

I stopped laughing and looked up at them, standing by our lunch table. People streamed by in back of them, making Bree edge closer to me. I still felt profoundly relaxed, thanks to Selene, and as I gazed at my former best friend, I couldn't help missing her powerfully. She was so familiar to me—I had known her before she was beautiful, when she was just a pretty little girl. She'd never gone through an awful awkward stage, like most kids, but when she was twelve, she'd had braces and a bad haircut. I had known her before she liked boys, while her mother and brother still lived at home.

So much had changed.

"Hi, Raven, Bree," Cal said, still smiling. "Grab some chairs—we'll make room."

Raven took out one of her foul-smelling Gauloises and tapped it against her wrist. "No, thanks. Did Beth tell you she was ditching the coven?" she asked, her voice seeming harsh and unfriendly. I glanced at Bree, who was keeping her eyes on Raven.

"Yes, she did," Cal replied, shrugging. "Why?"

Raven and Bree looked at each other. A month ago, Bree and I were making fun of Raven together. Now they acted like best friends. I tried hard to hold on to my feelings of calm and peace.

Bree gave Raven a tiny nod, and Raven's lips thinned in what could pass for a smile.

"We're leaving, too," she announced.

I know my surprise showed on my face, and when I quickly surveyed the table, there was no mistaking that it was shared. Next to me Cal was suddenly alert, frowning as he looked at them.

"No," said Robbie. "Come on."

"Why?" Jenna asked. "I thought you were both so into it."

"We are into it," Raven said pointedly. "We're just not into you." She tapped her cigarette harder, and I could practically feel how much she wanted to light it up.

"We've joined a different coven," Bree announced. The expression on her face made me think of a kid I had babysat once. He had once thrown a live lizard onto the dining room table, during a meal, just to see what would happen.

"A different coven!" exclaimed Sharon. She twitched her short suede skirt down, bracelets jangling. "What different coven?"

"A different one," said Raven in a bored tone. She raised one shoulder and let it drop.

"Bree, don't be stupid," said Robbie, and his words seemed to hurt her.

"We've started our own group," Bree told Robbie, and Raven glanced at her sharply. I wondered if Bree had been supposed to keep that secret.

"Started your own?" Cal said, rubbing his chin. "What is wrong with Cirrus?"

"To tell you the truth, Cal," Bree said coldly, "I don't want to be in a coven with backstabbers and betrayers. I need to be able to trust the people I do magick with."

This was aimed at me, and possibly at Cal, and I felt heat rise in my cheeks.

Cal raised his eyebrows. "Yes, trust is really important," he said slowly. "I agree with you there. Are you sure you can trust the people in your new coven?"

"Yes," said Raven, a bit too loudly. "It's not like you're the only witch in town, you know."

"No, no, I'm not," Cal agreed. I heard a hint of annoyance in his voice. He put his arm around my shoulders. "For example, there's Morgan here. Does your new coven have any blood witches?"

All eyes turned to me.

"Blood witch?" asked Bree, derision in her voice.

"You said that on Samhain," remembered Raven. "You were just yanking our chains."

"I wasn't," Cal said. I swallowed and looked down, hoping

this conversation would stop before people followed it to its logical conclusion.

"If she's a blood witch," Bree all but snarled, "then so are her parents, right? Isn't that what you told us? I mean, am I supposed to believe that Sean and Mary Grace Rowlands are blood witches?"

Cal went silent, as if he just at that moment realized what this could lead to. "Whatever," he said, and I leaned against him, knowing he was trying to protect me.

"Anyway," said Cal. "Let's not get off the subject. So you really want out of the coven?"

"Out and about, baby," said Raven, putting her unlit cigarette in her mouth.

"Bree, think about what you're doing," Robbie urged her, and I was glad he was trying to talk her out of it since I couldn't.

"I have thought," said Bree. "I want out."

"Well, be careful," said Cal, standing up. I stood up, too, grabbing my purse and my lunch tray. "Remember, most witches are good, but not all of them. Make sure you haven't left the frying pan for the fire."

Raven gave a short bark of a laugh. "How pithy. Thanks for the advice."

Cal gave them a last, considering look, then nodded at me. We walked away from the group. I dumped my tray at the bus bin, and we left the lunchroom, heading for the main building.

Cal walked with me to my locker. I spun the combination and opened the door while he waited.

"If they make a new coven, will it affect us somehow?" I asked, my voice low.

Cal brushed back his dark hair and shrugged. "I don't think so," he said. "It's just . . ." He pinched his lip with two fingers, thinking.

"What?"

"Well, I wonder who they're working with," he said. "They're obviously not doing this by themselves. I hope they're being careful. Not every witch is . . . benign."

I felt tension weave its way into my short-held peace and looked at Cal. He kissed me, warmth in his golden eyes.

"See you later." A flashing grin, and he was gone.

11

Connected

January 3, 1982

Old Towson lost three more sheep last night. This is after all the ward-evil spells we've been doing for the past month. Now most of his flock is gone, and he's not the only one. He said today in the Eagle and Hare that he's wiped out — doesn't have enough ewes left to start over. There's nothing for him to do except sell out.

I feel like all I do is go around doing warding spells. We're all paranoid and living under a dark shadow. For the past week I've been spelling Ma's leg after she broke it, bicycling to the village. But even with my spells she says it's hurting, not healing properly.

I want to get out of here. Being a witch is doing no one good nowadays and is doing a bushel of harm. It's like a film is over us, lessening our powers. I don't know what to do. Angus doesn't, either. He's worried, too, but he tries not to show it.

Damnation! I thought the evil was behind us! Now it looks like it was only sleeping, sleeping among us, in our beds. Winter has awoken it. — Bradhadair

On Wednesday morning, when I was toasting two Pop-Tarts for breakfast, I heard footsteps overhead.

"Mary K.!" I said. "Who's upstairs?"

Mary K. blinked. "Mom," she said, turning back to the comics. "She's staying home sick today."

I looked at the top of my sister's head. Mom never stayed home from work. She had been known to show houses in a snowstorm when she had the flu.

"What's wrong with her?" I asked. "She was fine last night, wasn't she?" She and my dad had had dinner out alone, something they almost never did. I had figured they were avoiding me, and I had waited up for them, but at eleven-thirty I had given up and gone to bed.

"I don't know. Maybe she just wanted a day off."

"Huh." Maybe this was my chance: I could go upstairs right now and get her to answer all my questions.

On the other hand, I would be late for school. And Cal was at school. Besides, if she wanted to tell me anything, she'd have told me by now. Right?

I sighed. Or maybe the truth was, now that the chance was staring me in the face, as it were, I was afraid to seize it. Scared of what I might learn.

My Pop-Tarts leaped energetically out of the toaster and broke on the kitchen counter. I gathered up the pieces in a paper towel and gave my sister a gentle kick.

"Let's go," I said. "Education awaits us." Mom would be

home when I got out of school. I could talk to her then.

Mary K. nodded and got into her coat.

As it turned out, my big confrontation didn't work out the way I'd planned. When I got home from school, I'd worked myself up for a real scene. I went up to Mom's room, threw open the door ... and found her sound asleep. Her red hair lay across her pillow, and once again I noticed the silver strands in it. Was it my imagination, or were there more of them than even a couple of days before?

She looked so tired. I didn't have the heart to wake her.

I crept out like a mouse. Then Tamara called and asked if I could come over and study with her for a calc test. So I went. Anything to get out of the house.

I had dinner at Tamara's, and when I got home, Mom and Dad had both gone to bed.

I went into the study and switched on the computer. I wanted to go to one of the online Wicca sites and see if I could find out the meaning of the runes on Selene Belltower's door frame. I could still picture at least five of them in my mind. I also wanted to look up Maeve Riordan's family tree again. Maybe there was some link I hadn't noticed or some other information I'd missed.

While the computer booted up, I sat there, biting my thumbnail and thinking. Part of me was getting more and more wound up, the longer my parents avoided answering my questions. But I also had to admit that part of me was almost happy about these delays. I was honestly afraid of how painful and ugly the whole scene might be.

I logged on and entered in the html address that I remembered from before. But instead of Maeve's family tree a message popped onto the screen:

The page cannot be displayed. The page you are looking for is currently unavailable. The Web site might be experiencing technical difficulties, or you may need to adjust your browser settings.

I frowned. Had I entered the address wrong? I typed in *Maeve Riordan* and ran a search. Twenty-six matches popped up.

Last time there had been twenty-seven.

I scrolled rapidly down the list. No html. Was the genealogy site gone?

I tried running a search for *Ballynigel*. That took me to a map site and opened a window with a map of Ireland. Ballynigel was a dot on the west coast. I couldn't zoom in on it.

I typed in *Belwicket* and clicked the search button. I got no hits.

I slapped the keyboard in frustration. The site was gone. Just gone. As if it had never been there.

I told myself not to get too worked up. Maybe it was being upgraded or updated or something. If I just tried it again in a couple of days, it might well be back.

Closing my eyes for a moment, I tipped back my head and breathed deeply. Then, feeling calmer, I entered a Web address I'd gotten from Ethan—an address for a site about rune magick.

In a moment the home page opened, and mysterious symbols glowed before my eyes. I leaned closer, my worries fading to the back of my mind as I began to read.

It was nearly an hour later when I finally logged off and shut down the computer. When I closed my eyes, runes still danced across the insides of my lids. I'd learned a lot tonight.

I picked up a pen and traced my new favorite rune on a scrap of paper that sat by the keyboard. Ken: It looked like a V turned on its side. It stood for fire, including inspiration and passion of spirit. It was so simple, yet so strong.

Underneath it I traced my other new favorite rune, Ur, strength.

I sighed. I needed a lot of that right now.

On Thursday afternoon I was startled when Mom came into the family room. I was watching Oprah and doing my American history homework.

"Hi, Morgan," she said, sounding tentative. Her hair was brushed and held back from her face by two combs. She wore no makeup, but she had on a sweat suit embroidered with leaves. "Where's Mary K.?"

"I dropped her at Jaycee's," I said.

"Oh, all right." Mom wandered over to the far wall and picked up a clay pot that I'd made in third grade, then set it back down on its shelf. "Hey, how come I haven't seen Bree around this week?"

I swallowed hard, replaying the scene yesterday in the cafeteria, when Bree and Raven had announced they were starting their own coven. I didn't think Bree would be spending a whole lot of time with me anymore.

But I didn't have the strength to get into it with Mom right now. So I just said, "I guess she's been pretty busy."

"Mmmm." To my surprise, Mom let it go at that. She prowled around the room some more, picking things up and putting them down. Then she said abruptly, "Mary K. says you have a boyfriend."

"Huh? Oh, yeah," I said in surprise, realizing she wasn't up on the whole Cal thing. Of course. How could she have been? Cal and my discovery about my birth happened at almost the same time.

"His name is Cal Blaire," I explained, feeling awkward. First of all, we'd never talked about boys before. There had never been anything to discuss. Second, why was I obligated to tell her anything? She obviously had no problem keeping secrets from me.

But still, I'd had sixteen years of thinking of her as my mom. That habit was hard to break. "He and his mom moved here in September," I added.

Mom leaned against the doorjamb. "What does he think of witchcraft?"

I blinked and flicked off the TV. "Um, he likes it," I said stiffly.

Mom nodded.

"Why didn't you ever tell me that I was adopted?" I said, the words rushing out now that I had my chance.

I saw her swallow as she searched for an answer. "There were some very good reasons at the time," she said finally. The silence of the house seemed to underscore her words.

"Everyone says you're supposed to be open about it," I said. Already I could feel my throat getting tight, and suddenly my nerves felt like thorns.

"I know," Mom said quietly. "I know you want—need— some answers."

"I deserve some answers!" I said, raising my voice. "You and Dad lied to me for sixteen years! You lied to Mary K.! And everyone else knew the truth!"

She shook her head, an odd look on her face. "No one

knows the whole truth," she said. "Not even your father and me."

"What does that mean?" I crossed my arms over my chest. I tried to hold on to my anger so I wouldn't cry.

"Your dad and I have been talking," she said. "We know you want to know. And we're going to tell you. Soon."

"When?" I snapped.

Mom gave an odd smile, as if at a private joke. She was being so calm and yet looked so fragile that it was hard for me to stay angry. There was nothing here to fight against, and that pissed me off even more.

"It's been sixteen years," she said gently. "Give us a few more days. I need time to think."

I stared at her in disbelief, but with that same odd smile she brushed her hand lightly against my cheek, then left the room.

For some reason, the memory of my sneaking into my parents' bed at night, when I was little, came into my mind. I used to worm my way in between them and go right to sleep. Nothing had ever felt so secure or so safe. Now it seemed strange. My childhood memories were being revised every day.

The phone rang, and I seized it like a lifeline. I knew it was Cal.

"Hi," said Cal, before I could speak, and a warm sense of comfort passed over me. "I miss you. Can I come over?"

I went from utter despair to pure joy in one second. "Actually, could I come over there?" I asked.

"You don't mind?"

"Oh, God, no. I'll be right there, okay?"

"Great," he said.

I flew from the house, rushing toward happiness.

Cal met me at the front door of his house. It was already almost dark, and the air felt heavy and damp, as if it might snow early this year.

"I can only stay a little while," I said, my breath puffing slightly.

"Thanks for coming," he said, leading me inside. "I could have come to your house."

I shook my head, taking off my coat. "You have more privacy here," I said. "Is your mom home?"

"No," said Cal as we started up the stairs to his room. "She's at the hospital with someone from her coven. I have to go over later and help her." It occurred to me that the two of us were alone in his house. A little shiver of anticipation went through me.

"I forgot to ask Robbie today," Cal said, opening the attic door to his room. "Is he getting new glasses?"

"I don't know. They're going to do more tests." I rubbed my arms as we walked into Cal's room, even though it was toasty warm. I felt comfortable here, with Cal. The rest of my life might be in turmoil, but here I knew I had power. And I knew Cal understood. It gave me a wonderful feeling of relief.

Looking around Cal's room, I remembered the night we had done a circle here and I had seen everyone's auras. It had been so seductive, being touched by magick. How could anyone not want to pursue it?

Behind me Cal touched my arm, and I turned to him. He

smiled at me. "I like having you here," he said. "And I'm glad you came. I wanted to give you something."

I looked up at him questioningly.

"Here." Reaching up, he untied the knot in the leather string around his neck. Its silver pentacle dangled, catching the lamplight and shining. This necklace had been one of the first things I'd noticed about him, and I remembered thinking how much I'd liked it. I stepped closer, and Cal fastened it around my neck. It fell to a point above my breastbone, and he traced around it on my shirt.

"Thank you," I whispered. "It's beautiful." Reaching up my hand, I curled it around his neck and pulled him to me. He met my kiss halfway.

"How are things at home?" Cal asked a moment later, still holding me.

I felt like I could tell him anything. "Strange," I said. I pulled myself out of his arms and walked around his room. "I've hardly seen my parents. Today Mom was home, and I asked her about being adopted, and she said she needed more time." I shook my head, looking at Cal's tall bookcase, its rows of books on witchcraft, spell making, herbs, runes. . . . I wanted to sit down and start reading and not get up for a long time.

"Every time I think about how they lied to me, I feel furious," I told Cal, my hands clenching into fists. I let out a breath. "But today my mom looked—I don't know. Older. Fragile, somehow."

I stopped next to Cal's bed. He walked over to me and rubbed my back. I took his hand and brought it to my cheek.

"Part of me feels like they're not my real family," I said.

"And another part of me thinks, of course they're my real family. They feel like my real family."

He nodded, his hand stroking up and down my arm. "It's strange when people you think you know really well feel suddenly different somehow."

He sounded like he was speaking from experience, and I looked up at him.

"Like my father," he said. "He was the high priest of my mom's coven when they were married. And he met another woman, another witch, in the coven. Mom and I used to make mean jokes about how she had put a love spell on him, but really, in the end, I think maybe he just . . . loved her more."

I heard the hurt in his voice and rested my head against his chest, my arms going around his waist.

"They live in northern England now," Cal went on. His chest vibrated against my ear as he spoke. "She had a son, my age, from her first marriage, and they've had, I think, two more kids together."

"That's awful," I said.

He breathed in and out slowly. "I don't know. Maybe I'm just used to it now. But I just think that's how it goes. Nothing is static; things always change. The best you can do is change along with them and work with what you have."

I was silent, thinking about my own situation.

"I think the important thing is to get through the anger and negative feelings because they get in the way of magick," Cal said. "It's hard, but sometimes you just have to decide to let those feelings go."

His voice trailed off, and we stood there comfortably for a while. Finally, reluctantly, I glanced at my watch.

"Speaking of going, I have to go," I said.

"Already?" Cal said, leaning down to kiss me. He murmured something against my lips.

Smiling, I wriggled out of his grasp. "What did you say?"

"Nothing." He shook his head. "I shouldn't have said anything."

"What?" I asked again, concerned now. "What's wrong?"

"Nothing's wrong," he said. "It's just . . . suddenly I thought of *mùirn beatha dàn*. You know."

I looked at him. "What? What are you talking about?"

"You know," he said again, sounding almost shy. "*Mùirn beatha dàn*. You've read about it, right?"

I shook my head. "What is it?"

"Um, soul mate," said Cal. "Life partner. Predestined mate."

My heart almost stopped beating, and my breath froze in my throat. I couldn't speak.

"In the form of Wicca that I practice," Cal explained, "we believe that for every witch, there's one true soul mate who's also a full-blooded witch; male or female, it doesn't matter. They're connected to that person, and belong together, and basically will only be truly happy with that person." He shrugged. "It sort of . . . came into my head just now, when we were kissing."

"I never heard of it," I whispered. "How do you know if it happens?"

Cal laughed wryly. "That's the tricky part. Sometimes it isn't that easy. And of course, people have strong wills: They can choose to be with people, insist on believing that this person is their *mùirn beatha dàn* when they're wrong and just won't admit it."

I wondered if he was talking about his mother and father.

"Is there any surefire way to tell?" I asked.

"I've heard of spells you can do: complicated ones. But mostly witches just rely on their feelings, their dreams, and their instincts. They just feel this person is the one, and they go with it."

I felt exhilarated, like I was about to take off and fly. "And do you think . . . maybe we're connected that way?" I asked breathlessly.

He touched my cheek. "I think we might be, yes," he said, his voice husky.

My eyes felt huge. "So what now?" I blurted out, and he laughed.

"We wait; we stay together. Finish growing up together."

This was such an amazing, wonderful, seductive idea that I wanted to shout, I love you! And we will always be together! I'm the one for you, and you're the one for me!

"How do you say it again?" I asked.

"*Mùirn beatha dàn*," he said slowly, the words sounding ancient and lovely and mysterious.

I repeated them softly. "Yes," I said, and we met again in a kiss.

Long minutes later I pulled away from him. "Oh, no, I've really got to go! I'm going to be late!"

"Okay," he said, and we headed out of his room. It felt so hard to leave this place where everything felt so right. Especially when I knew I had to go home.

Again I thought about the first time I'd been in Cal's room, when the coven had met there. "Are you upset that Beth and Raven and Bree have quit?" I asked as we headed down the stairs.

He thought for a moment. "Yes and no," he said. "No because I don't think you should try to keep someone in a coven against their will or even if they're not very sure. It just makes negative energy. And yes because they were all kind of challenging personalities, and they added something to the mix. Which was good for the coven." He shrugged. "I guess we'll just have to wait and see what happens."

I put on my coat, wishing I didn't have to go out into the cold. Outside the trees were almost bare, and the leftover leaves were a faded brown everywhere I looked.

"Ugh," I said, glancing out at Das Boot.

"Fall is trying to turn into winter," said Cal, breathing steam in the chilly air.

I watched his chest rise and fall, and a bolt of desire ripped through me. I wanted so badly to touch him, to run my hands through his hair, down his back, to kiss his throat and chest. I wanted to be close to him. To be his _mùirn beatha dàn_.

Instead I tore myself away, fumbling in my coat pocket for my keys, leaving Cal standing in the light from his door. My heart was full and aching, and I felt heavy with magick.

12

Beauty Out

Imbolc, 1982

Oh, Goddess, Goddess, please help me. Please help me. Mathair, her hand rising up black from the smoking ashes. My little Dagda. My own da.

Oh, Goddess, I'm going to be ill; my soul is breaking. I cannot bear this pain.

— Bradhadair

That night my parents tried to act normal at dinner, but I kept looking at them with questions in my eyes, and by dessert we were all staring at our plates. Mary K. was obviously upset by the silence, and as soon as dinner was over she went up to her room and started playing loud music. Ceiling-shaking thumps told us she was dancing out some of her stress.

I couldn't stand being there. If only Cal wasn't helping his mom. Impulsively I called Janice and joined her, Ben Reggio, and Tamara at the dollar movies up in Red Kill. We saw some stupid action movie that involved a lot of motorcycle chases. The whole time I sat there in the dark theater, I kept thinking, *mùirn beatha dàn*, over and over.

On Saturday morning Dad went outside to rake leaves and cut back the shrubs and trees so they wouldn't be broken in a winter ice storm. Mom took off after breakfast to go to her church women's club.

I put on my jacket and crunched my way outside to my dad.

"When are you guys going to tell me?" I said flatly. "Are you just going to pretend nothing happened?"

He paused and leaned on the rake for a moment. "No, Morgan," he said at last. "We couldn't do that, no matter how much we wanted to." His voice was mild, and again I felt some of my anger deflate. I was determined not to let it go and kicked at a small pile of leaves.

"Well?" I demanded. "Where did you get me? Who were my parents? Did you know them? What happened to them?"

Dad flinched as if my words were physically hurting him.

"I know we have to talk about it," he said, his voice thin and raspy. "But . . . I need more time."

"Why?" I exploded, throwing my arms wide. "What are you waiting for?"

"I'm sorry, sweetheart," he said, looking down at the ground. "I know we've made a lot of mistakes in the past sixteen years. We tried to do our best. But Morgan." He looked at me. "We've buried this for sixteen years. It isn't easy to dredge it up. I know you want answers, and I hope we can give them to you. But it isn't easy.

And in the end, it might be that you wish you didn't know."

I gaped at him, then shook my head in disbelief and stalked back to the house. What was I going to do?

On Saturday night I dropped Mary K. off at her friend Jaycee's house. They were going to meet Bakker and a bunch of other people at the movies. I was going on to meet with our coven at Matt's house.

"Where's Bakker's car?" I asked as I pulled up in front of Jaycee's house.

Mary K. made a face. "His folks took it away for a week after he flunked a history exam."

"Oh, too bad," I said. "Well, have a good time. Don't do anything I wouldn't do."

Mary K. rolled her eyes. "Oh, okay," she said dryly. "Note to self: Try not to dance around naked, doing witchcraft. Thanks for the ride." She got out and slammed the car door, and I watched her go into Jaycee's house.

Sighing, I drove on to Matt's house, following his directions to the very outskirts of town. Ten minutes later I parked in front of a low-slung brick modern house, and Jenna let me in.

"Hey!" she said brightly. "Come on in. We're in the living room. I can't remember—have you ever been here before?"

"No," I said, leaving my coat on a metal hook. "Are Matt's parents here?"

Jenna shook her head. "His dad had a medical convention in Florida, and his mom went, too. We have the whole place to ourselves."

"Sweet," I said, following her. We took a right into a large living room, a white rectangle with one whole wall made of glass. I guess it must have looked out onto the backyard, but right now it was dark outside, and all I could see was our own reflections.

"Hi, Morgan," said Matt. He was wearing an old rugby shirt and jeans. "Welcome to Adler Hall."

We both laughed as Sharon came into the room. "Hi, Morgan," she said. "Matt, what's with all the bizarre furniture?"

"My mom is into sixties stuff," Matt explained.

Ethan poked his head up from a red plush couch. It was so deep, it looked like it was about to swallow him. A white floor lamp shaped like a globe with one flat side curved over his head. "I feel like I've gone back in time," he said. "All we need is a conversation pit."

"There's one in the study," said Matt, grinning.

The doorbell rang, and I felt a warm thrill of recognition even before Jenna went to answer it. Cal, I thought happily, a tingle going down my spine. *Mùirn beatha dàn.* Moments later I heard his voice as he greeted Jenna. All my nerve cells came alive at the sound and at the memory of yesterday, in his room.

"Does anyone want tea, or water, or a soda?" Matt offered as Cal came into the room, holding a big, beat-up leather satchel. "We don't keep alcohol in the house 'cause my dad's in AA."

This frank admission startled me. "Water sounds great." I crossed to Cal and gave him a quick kiss, marveling at my own boldness.

The doorbell rang again. A moment later Matt came back

into the room, carrying some bottles of seltzer. Robbie was right behind him. "Hey," he said.

I stared. I guess I should have been used to it by now, but I wasn't. It was as if Robbie's personality and lame social skills had been transferred into the body of a teen star. "Where are your glasses?" I asked.

Robbie took a bottle of seltzer from Matt and popped the cap. "That's the funny thing," he said slowly. "I don't need them anymore."

"How could you not need glasses?" I demanded. "Did you have laser surgery without telling me?"

"Nope," Robbie said. "That's what all the tests this week were about. Apparently my eyesight has just gotten better. I was having headaches because I didn't need to wear glasses anymore, and the lenses were straining my eyes."

He didn't sound happy, and it took me a few moments to realize that slowly, everyone's attention had turned to me.

"No!" I said strongly. "I absolutely did not do another spell! Honestly—I swear! I promised Robbie, and everyone else, that I wouldn't do another spell, and I haven't! I haven't done any spells at all!"

Robbie looked at me with his clear, gray-blue eyes, no longer hidden by thick, distorting lenses. "Morgan," he said.

"I swear! I absolutely promise you," I said, holding up my right hand. Robbie looked unconvinced. "Robbie! Believe me."

Conflict showed in his face. "What could it be, then?" he asked. "Eyes don't just get better. I mean, the actual shape of my eyeballs has changed. They were giving me MRIs to see if I had a tumor pressing on my brain."

"Jesus," Matt muttered.

"I don't know," I said helplessly. "But it wasn't me."

"This is incredible," said Jenna, sounding short of breath. "Could someone else have put a spell on him?"

"I could have," Cal said thoughtfully. "But I didn't. Morgan, do you remember the actual words of your spell?"

"Yes," I said. "But I put the spell on the potion I gave him, not on him."

"That's true," Cal mused. "Though if the potion was supposed to act on him in some way . . . what were the words?"

I swallowed, thinking back. "Um, 'So beauty in is beauty out," I recited softly. "This potion make your blemish nowt. This healing water makes you pure, and thus your beauty will endure."

"That was it?" Sharon asked. "God, why didn't you do it sooner?"

"Sharon," Robbie said in irritation.

"Okay, okay," said Cal. "We have a couple of possibilities here. One is that Robbie's eyes have spontaneously healed themselves due to some unfathomable miracle."

Ethan snorted, and Sharon shot him a glance.

"The second possibility," Cal went on, "is that Morgan's spell wasn't specific enough, wasn't limited only to Robbie's skin. It was a spell to eliminate blemishes, imperfections. His eyes were imperfect; now they're perfect. Like his skin."

The enormity of that thought was just sinking in when Ethan said brightly, "Great! I can't wait to see what it does for his personality!"

Jenna couldn't help snickering. I sank weakly into a chair shaped like a giant cupped hand.

"The third possibility," said Cal, "is that someone we

don't know has put a spell on Robbie. That doesn't seem likely—why would a stranger want to do that? No, I think it's more likely that Morgan's spell has just continued to fix things."

"That's kind of frightening," I said, chilled. Did I really have that kind of power?

"It's pretty unusual. That's why you're not supposed to be doing spells until you know more," Cal said. I felt terrible. "When we start learning spells, I'll show you how to limit them. Limitations are just about the most important things to know, along with how to channel power. When you work a spell, you need to limit it in time, effect, purpose, duration, and target."

"Oh, no." I dropped my head into my hands. "I didn't do any of that."

"And actually, now that I think about it, you banished limitations at the very first circle. Remember?" Cal asked. "That might have something to do with this also."

"So what now?" Robbie demanded. "What else is going to change?"

"Probably not much more," Cal said. "For one thing, even though Morgan's really powerful, she's still just a beginner. She's not in touch with her full powers."

I was glad he hadn't referred to me again as a blood witch. I wanted people to forget about it for now.

"Also," Cal said, "this kind of spell is usually self-limiting. I mean, the potion was for your face, and you put it only on your face, right? You didn't drink it or anything?"

"God, no," Robbie said.

Cal shrugged. "So it's just fixing that general area, including your eyes. It's unusual, but I guess it's not impossible."

"I don't believe this." I moaned, hiding my face. "I'm such an idiot. I can't believe I did this. I am so, so sorry, Robbie."

"What are you sorry about?" Ethan asked. "Now he can be an airline pilot."

Sharon giggled, then stifled it.

"So you don't think it's going to do anything else?" Robbie asked Cal.

"I don't know," Cal said. He grinned. "Have you been feeling especially smart lately? It could be working on your brain."

I moaned again.

Cal nudged me. "I'm only kidding. It's probably over. Stop worrying."

He clapped once. "Well. I think it's time to start talking about spells and limitations!"

I couldn't laugh, though some of the others did.

"This is our first circle without Bree, Raven, and Beth," said Cal.

"I'm going to miss them," said Jenna softly. Her eyes flicked to me, and I wondered if she thought it was my fault that they had left.

Cal nodded. "Yeah. Me too. But maybe without them we'll be more tightly focused. We'll find out."

We sat in a ring on the floor around Cal. "First, let's go over clans," he said. "You know how they all have qualities associated with them. The Brightendales were healers. The Woodbanes—the 'dark clan'—supposedly fought for power at any cost."

"Ooh," Robbie said. He gave me a mock-fearful look. But

I just shivered. The very idea of the Woodbanes made me cold. I didn't think it was something to laugh at.

"The Burnhides were known for their magick with crystals and gems," Cal went on. "The Leapvaughns were mischief makers. The Vikroths were warriors. And so on." He looked around the circle. "Well, just as each clan had qualities associated with it, so each clan also had certain runes that it tended to use. So—I think it's time we took a look at some runes."

Cal opened his large leather satchel and pulled out a sheaf of what looked like index cards. He held them up, and I saw that each one had a rune drawn on it, very large.

"Rune flash cards!" I said, and Cal nodded.

"Basically, yes," he said. "Using runes is a quick way to get in touch with a deep, old source of power. Tonight I just want to show them to you and have you concentrate on each one. Each symbol has many meanings. They're all there for you, if you open yourself up to them."

We all watched, fascinated, as he held up the white cards one by one, reading the runes' names and telling us what they traditionally stood for.

"There are different names for each symbol. The names depend on whether you're working within a Norse tradition, or German, or Gaelic," Cal explained. "Later on, we'll talk about which runes are associated with which clans."

"This is so beautiful," said Sharon. "I love that people have used these for thousands of years."

Ethan turned to her, nodding his agreement. I watched as their eyes met and held.

Who would have known that Sharon Goodfine would

find Wicca beautiful? Or that Ethan would dare to like her? Witchcraft was revealing us not only to ourselves but to each other.

"Let's make a circle," said Cal.

13

Starlight

March 17, 1982

St. Paddy's day in New York City. Below, the city is celebrating a holiday they imported from my home, but I cannot join in. Angus is out looking for work. I sit here by the window, crying, though the Goddess knows I have no more tears left.

Everything I knew and loved is gone. My village is burned to the ground. My ma and da are dead, though it's still hard for me to believe it. My little cat Dagda. My friends. Belwicket has been wiped out, our cauldrons broken, our brooms burned, our herbs turned to smoke above our heads.

How did this happen? Why didn't I fall victim as so many others did? Why did Angus and I alone survive?

I hate New York, hate everything about it. The noise blunts my ears. I can't smell any living thing. I can't smell the sea or hear it in the background like a lullaby. There are people everywhere, packed in tight, like sardines. The city is filthy; the people are rude and common. I ache for my home.

There is no magick in this place.

And yet if there is no magick, surely there is no true evil, either? — M. R.

We purified our circle with salt and then invoked earth, air, water, and fire with a bowl of salt, a stick of incense, a bowl of water, and a candle. Cal showed us the rune symbols for these elements, and we worked to memorize them.

"Let's try to raise some energy and focus it," said Cal. "We'll try to focus it in ourselves, and we'll limit its effects to a good night's sleep and general well-being. And does anyone have any particular problem they'd like help with?" He met my eyes, and I could tell we were both thinking of my parents. But Cal left it up to me to ask for help in front of everyone, and I said nothing.

"Like, help my stepsister quit being such a pain?" Sharon asked. I hadn't known she had a stepsister. I was between Jenna and Sharon, and their hands felt small and smooth in mine.

Cal laughed. "You can't ask to change others. But you *could* ask to make it easier for *you* to get along with *her*."

"My asthma's been acting up since it got colder," Jenna said. I remembered her coughing but hadn't known she had asthma. People like Jenna, Sharon, Bree—they ruled our school. I had never really considered that they might have problems and difficulties. Not until Wicca came into all our lives.

"Okay, Jenna's asthma," agreed Cal. "Anything else?"

None of us said anything.

Cal lowered his head and closed his eyes, and we did the same. The room was filled with our deep, even breathing, and little by little, as the minutes passed, I felt our breathing tune in to one another, becoming aligned so that we inhaled and exhaled together.

Then Cal's voice, rich and slightly rough, said:

"Blessed be the animals, the plants, and all living things.
Blessed be the earth, the sky, the clouds, the rain.
Blessed be all people,
those within Wicca and those without.
Blessed be the Goddess and the God,
and all the spirits who help us.
Blessed be. We raise our hearts,
our voices, our spirits to the Goddess and the God."

As we began to move deasil, the words rose and fell in a pattern so that it became a song. We half skipped, half danced in our circle, and the chant became a joyous cry that filled the room, filled all the air around us. I was laughing, breathless, feeling happy and weightless and safe in this circle. Ethan was smiling but intent, his face flushed and his corkscrew curls bouncing around his head. Sharon's silky black hair was flying, and she looked pretty and carefree. Jenna looked like a blond fairy queen, and Matt was dark and purposeful. Robbie moved with new grace and coordination as we spun faster and faster. The only thing I missed was Bree's face in the circle.

I felt the energy rise. It coiled around us, building and

thickening and swirling in our circle. The living room floor was warm and smooth beneath my socked feet, and I felt like if I let go of Jenna's and Sharon's hands, I would fly off through the ceiling into the sky. As I looked above me, still chanting the words, I saw the white ceiling waver and dissolve to show me the deep indigo night and the white and yellow stars popping out of the sky so brightly. Awestruck, I gazed upward, seeing the infinite possibilities of the universe where before there had been only a ceiling. I wanted to reach out and touch the stars, and without hesitating, I unclasped my hands and stretched my arms overhead.

At the same instant everyone else let go and threw their arms overhead, and the circle stopped where it was while the swirling energy continued to coil around us, stronger and stronger. I reached for the stars, feeling the energy pressing against my backbone.

"Take the energy into you!" Cal called, and automatically I pressed my clasped fist against my chest. I breathed in warmth and white light and felt my worries melt away. I swayed on my feet and once again tried to touch the stars. Reaching overhead, I felt myself brush a tiny, prickly firelight that was hot and sharp against my fingers. It felt like a star, and I brought down my hand.

With the light in my hand I gazed at the others, wondering if they could see it. Then Cal was at my side because I always channeled too much energy and had to ground myself afterward. But this time I felt fine—not too dizzy, not too sick, just happy and lighthearted and full of wonder.

"Whoa," Ethan whispered, his eyes on me.

"What is that?" asked Sharon.

"Morgan!" Jenna said in awe. Her breath sounded tight and strained, and she was breathing fast and shallowly. I turned to her. I felt like I could do anything.

Reaching out, I pressed the light against her chest. She gasped with a small "Ah!" and I traced a line from one side to the other beneath her collarbones. Closing my eyes, I flattened my hand on her breastbone and felt the starlight dissolve into her. She gasped again and staggered on her feet, and Cal put out his hand but didn't touch me. Under my fingers I felt Jenna's lungs swell as she sucked in air. I felt the microscopic alveoli opening to admit oxygen, tiny capillaries absorbing the oxygen; I felt it as, from the smallest veins to the thick, ridged muscles of her bronchial tubes, each one expanded in a domino effect, loosening, relaxing, absorbing oxygen.

Jenna panted.

My eyes opened, and I smiled.

"I can breathe," Jenna said slowly, touching her chest. "I was starting to tighten up. I knew I'd need my inhaler after the circle, and I didn't want to use it in front of everyone." Jenna's eyes sought Matt, and he came to put his arm around her. "She opened up my lungs and put air in with that light," Jenna said, sounding dazed.

"Okay, stop," Cal said, gently taking my hands. "Quit touching things. Like on Samhain, maybe you should lie down and ground yourself."

I shook off his hands. "I don't want to ground myself," I said clearly. "I want to keep it." I flexed my fingers, wanting to touch something else, see what happened.

Cal looked at me. Something flickered in his eyes.

"I just want to keep this feeling," I explained.

"It can't stay forever," he said. "Energy doesn't linger—it needs to go somewhere. You don't want to go around zapping things."

I laughed. "I don't?"

"No," he assured me. Then he led me to a clear place on the polished wood floor, and I lay down, feeling the strength of the earth beneath my back, feeling the energy cease its whizzing around inside me, being absorbed by the earth's ancient embrace. In a few minutes I felt much more normal, less light-headed and . . . I guess, less drunk. Or at least, that's what I imagined feeling drunk was like. I didn't have much practice with it.

"Why can she do this?" Matt asked, his arm still protectively around Jenna. Jenna was taking deep, experimental breaths. "It's so easy," she marveled. "I feel so . . . so unconstricted."

Cal gave a wry chuckle. "It freaks me out, too, sometimes. Morgan does things that would be amazing for a high priestess to do—someone with years and years of training and experience. She just has a lot of power, that's all."

"You called her a blood witch," Ethan remembered. "She's a blood witch, like you. But how is that?"

"I don't want to talk about it," I said, sitting up. "I'm sorry if I did something I shouldn't have—again. But I didn't mean to do anything wrong. I just wanted to fix Jenna's breathing. I don't want to talk about being a blood witch. Okay?"

Six pairs of eyes looked at me. The members of my coven nodded or said okay. Only in Cal's face did I read the message that we would definitely have to talk about it later.

"I'm hungry," complained Ethan. "Got any munchies?"

"Sure," said Matt, heading toward the kitchen.

"Too bad we can't go swimming again," Jenna said regretfully.

"We can't?" Cal asked with a wicked smile at me. "Why not? My house isn't that far away."

Cringing, I crossed my arms over my chest.

"No way," Sharon scoffed, to my relief. "Even if the water is heated, the air's way too cold. I don't want to freeze."

"Oh, well," Cal said. Matt came in with a bowl of popcorn, and he helped himself to a big fistful. "Maybe some other time."

When no one could see me, I made a face at him, and he laughed silently.

I leaned against him, feeling warm and happy. It had been an amazing, exhilarating circle, even without Bree.

My smile faded as I wondered where she and Raven were tonight and who they were with.

14

Lesson

May 7, 1982

We're leaving this soulless place. I've been working as a cashier in a diner, and Angus has been down in the meat district, unloading huge American cows and putting their carcasses on hooks. I feel my soul dying, and so does Angus. We're saving every penny so we can leave, go anywhere else.

Not much news from home. None of Belwicket is left to tell us what happened, and what little bits and pieces we get aren't enough to figure out anything. I don't even know why I write in this book anymore, except as a diary. It is no longer a Book of Shadows. It hasn't been since my birthday, when my world was destroyed. I haven't done any magick since being here, nor has Angus. No more will I. It has done nothing but wreak destruction.

I am only twenty, and yet I feel ready for death's embrace.

—M. R.

The next morning during church I suddenly had an idea. I glanced over at the dark confessionals. After the service was over, I told my parents that I wanted to make confession. They looked a little surprised, but what could they say?

"I don't want to go to the diner today," I added. "I'll just see you at home later."

Mom and Dad looked at each other, then Dad nodded.

Mom put her hand on my shoulder. "Morgan—," she began, then shook her head. "Nothing. I'll see you later, at home."

Mary K. looked at me but didn't say anything. Her face was troubled as she left with my parents.

I waited impatiently in line as parishioners went in to confess their sins. I realized I could probably tune in to what they were talking about, but I didn't want to try. It would be wrong. Father Hotchkiss heard some pretty steamy stuff sometimes, I'd guess. And probably some really boring, petty things, too.

Finally it was my turn. I knelt inside the cubicle and waited for the small grated window to slide open. When it did, I crossed myself and said, "Forgive me, Father, for I have sinned. It's been, um . . ." I thought back quickly. "Four months since my last confession."

"Go ahead, my child," said Father Hotchkiss, as he had all my life, every time I had confessed.

"Um . . ." I hadn't thought ahead this far and didn't have a list of sins ready. I really didn't want to go into some of the things I'd been doing, and I didn't consider them sins, anyway. "Well, lately I've been feeling very angry at my parents," I stated baldly. "I mean, I love my parents, and I try to honor them, but I recently . . . found out I was adopted." There. I had said it, and on the other side of the screen I saw Father Hotchkiss's head come up a bit as he took in my words. "I'm upset and angry that they didn't tell me before and that they won't talk to me about it now," I went on. "I want to know more about my birth parents. I want to know where I came from."

There was a long pause as Father Hotchkiss digested what I had said. "Your parents have done as they thought best," he said at last. He didn't deny that I was adopted, and I still felt humiliated that practically everyone had known but me.

"My birth mother is dead," I said, pushing on. I swallowed, feeling uncomfortable, even nervous talking about this. "I want to know more about her."

"My child," Father Hotchkiss said gently. "I understand your wishes. I can't say that I would not feel the same, were I in your place. But I tell you, and I speak with years of experience, that sometimes it really is best to leave the past alone."

Tears stung my eyes, but I hadn't really expected anything else. "I see," I whispered, trying not to cry.

"My dear, the Lord works in mysterious ways," said the priest, and I couldn't believe he was saying something so clichéd. He went on. "For some reason, God brought you to your parents, and I know they couldn't love you more. He chose them for you, and He chose you for them. It would be wise to respect His decision."

I sat and pondered this, wondering how true it was. Then I became aware that other people were waiting after me and it was time to go. "Thank you, Father," I said.

"Pray for guidance, my dear. And I will pray for you."

"Okay." I slipped out of the confessional, put on my coat, and headed out the huge double doors into bright November sunshine. I had to think.

After so many gray days it was nice to be walking in sunlight, kicking through the damp, brown leaves underfoot. Every now and then a golden leaf floated down around me, and each one that fell was like another second ticking off on the clock that turned autumn to winter.

I passed through downtown Widow's Vale, glancing in the shop windows. Our town is old, with the town hall dating back to 1692. Every once in a while I notice again how charming it is, how picturesque. A cool breeze lifted my hair, and I caught a scent of the Hudson River, bordering the town.

By the time I got home, I'd thought about what Father Hotchkiss had said. I could see some wisdom in his words, but that didn't mean I could accept not knowing the whole truth. I didn't know what to do. Maybe I would ask for guidance at the next circle.

Walking two miles had warmed me up nicely, and I tossed my jacket over a chair in the kitchen. I glanced at the clock. If I assumed my family followed their usual routine at the diner, they wouldn't be home for another hour or so. It would be nice to have the house to myself for a while.

A thump overhead made me freeze. Weirdly, the first thought I had was that Bree was in my house, possibly with Raven, and they were casting a spell on my bedroom or something. I don't know why I didn't think of burglars or a stray squirrel that had somehow gotten in—I just immediately thought of Bree.

I heard scuffling sounds and the loud scraping noise of a piece of furniture being jolted out of place. I quietly opened the mudroom door and picked up my baseball bat. Then I kicked off my shoes and headed upstairs in my stocking feet.

By the time I reached the top of the landing, I could tell the sounds were coming from Mary K.'s room. Then I heard her voice, saying, "Ow! Stop it! Dammit, Bakker!"

I stopped, unsure of what to do.

"Get off me," Mary K. said angrily.

"Oh, come on, Mary K.," was Bakker's response. "You said you loved me! I thought that meant—"

"I told you I didn't want to do that!" Mary K. cried.

I flung open the door to find Bakker Blackburn entangled with my sister on her single bed. Her legs were kicking.

"Hey!" I said loudly, making them both jump. Their heads turned to stare at me, and I saw relief in Mary K.'s eyes. "You heard her," I said loudly. "Get off!"

"We're just talking," said Bakker.

Mary K.'s hands pushed against his chest, and he resisted it. Fury roiled inside me, and I raised the bat.

Whap! I gave Bakker a smart rap on his shoulder to get his attention. I hadn't been this furious since Bree and I'd had our last fight.

"Ow!" Bakker yelled. "What are you doing? Are you nuts?"

"Bakker, get off!" Mary K. said again, pushing at him.

I thrust my face close to Bakker's, and with my teeth clenched, I spoke as menacingly as I could. "Get the hell off her!"

Bakker's face went stiff, and he quickly moved away from the bed. He looked embarrassed and angry, his eyes dark.

Then he snapped out his hand and knocked the bat out of my grip. My jaw dropped in surprise as the wood went flying across the room.

"Stay out of this, Morgan," he said. "You don't know what's going on. Mary K. and I are just talking."

"Ha!" said Mary K., jumping up from the bed and yanking down her shirt. "You're being an ass! Now get out!"

"Not until you tell me what's going on," Bakker said. "You said come over!" He was almost yelling, his voice filling the room. "You said come up here! What was I supposed to think? We've been going out almost two months!"

Mary K. was crying now. "I didn't mean that," she said, holding her pillow to her stomach. "I just wanted to be alone with you."

"What did you think being alone with me was all about?" he asked, his arms wide. He took a step closer to her.

"Watch it, Bakker," I warned, but he ignored me.

"I didn't mean that," Mary K. repeated, crying.

"Jesus!" he said, leaning over her. My teeth clenched, and I started edging over toward the bat. "You don't know what you want."

"Shut up, Bakker," I snapped. "For God's sake, she's fourteen."

Mary K. cried into her pillow.

"She's my girlfriend!" Bakker shouted. "I love her, and she loves me, so stay out of this! It's none of your business!"

"None of my business?" I couldn't believe what I was hearing. "That's my little sister you're talking about!"

Without planning it, I snapped out my arm, finger pointed at Bakker. Before my eyes a small ball of spitting, crackly blue light shot out of my finger and streaked toward him, hitting him in the side. It was like the light I had given to Jenna last night, but different. Bakker yelped and stumbled, clutching his side and clawing at the bedspread. I stared at him, horrified, and he stared back at me as if I had suddenly sprouted wings and claws.

"What the hell—" he gasped, clasping his side. I was praying blood wouldn't start running out through his fingers. When he took his hand away, there were no marks on his shirt, no blood. I breathed out in relief.

"I'm out of here," he said in a strangled voice, lurching to his feet. He turned back to look at Mary K. one last time. She had her face buried in her pillow, and she didn't look up. With a last glare at me Bakker stormed through the bedroom door and pounded down the steps. The front door slammed moments later, and I peeked out down the stairwell to make sure he was gone. Through the front door sidelight I saw him striding fast down the street, rubbing his side. His lips were moving as if he was swearing to himself.

Back in Mary K.'s room, she was holding a tissue to her eyes and sniffling.

"Jesus, Mary K.," I said, sitting next to her on the bed. "What was that about? Why aren't you at the diner?"

She started crying again and leaned forward into me. I put my arms around her and held her, so thankful she hadn't been hurt, that I had come home when I had. For the first time in a week it felt like the two of us again, the way we used to be. Close. Comfortable. Trusting each other. I had missed that so much.

"Don't tell Mom and Dad," she said, tears wetting her cheeks. "I just wanted to see Bakker alone, so I told them I needed to study, and I had them drop me off here while they went to lunch. It's just—we're always with other people. I didn't know he would think—"

"Oh, Mary K.," I said, trying to soothe her. "It was a huge misunderstanding, but it wasn't your fault. Just because you said you wanted to see him alone doesn't mean that you're obligated to go to bed with him. You meant one thing; he understood another. What's awful is what an ass he was being. I should have called the cops."

Mary K. sniffled and drew back. "I don't really think he was going to . . . hurt me," she said. "I think it kind of looked worse than it was."

"I can't believe you're defending him!"

"I'm not," said my sister. "I'm not defending him, and I'm definitely breaking up with him."

"Good," I said strongly.

"But I have to say, it really wasn't like him," Mary K. went on. "He's never pushed me too far, always listened when I said no. I'm sure he'll be really sorry tomorrow."

My eyes narrowed as I looked at her. "Mary Kathleen Rowlands, that's not good enough. Don't you dare make excuses for him. When I walked in here, he was pinning you down!"

Her brows creased. "Yeah," she said.

"And he knocked the bat out of my hands," I said. "And he was yelling at us."

"I know," said Mary K., looking angry. "I can't believe him."

"That's more like it," I said, standing up. "Tell me you're breaking up with him."

"I'm breaking up with him," my sister repeated.

"Okay. Now I'm going to go change. You better wash

your face and straighten your room before Mom and Dad come home."

"Okay," said Mary K., standing up. She gave me a watery smile. "Thanks for rescuing me." She reached out to hug me.

"You're welcome," I said, and turned to go.

"How did you stop him, anyway? He said, 'Ow!' and then fell against the bed. What did you do?"

I thought fast. "I kicked his knee and made it buckle," I said. "Made him lose his balance."

Mary K. laughed. "I bet he was surprised."

"I think we both were," I said honestly. Then, feeling a little shaky, I went downstairs. I had shot a bolt of light at someone. Surely that was strange, even for a witch.

15

Who I Am

September 1, 1982

Today we're moving out of this hellhole, to a town about three hours north of here. It's called Meshomah Falls. I think Meshomah is an Indian word. They have Indian words all over the place around here. The town is small and very pretty, kind of like home.

We already have jobs — I'm going to waitress at the little café in town, and Angus will be helping a local carpenter. We saw people dressed in queer old-fashioned clothes there last week. I asked a local man about them, and he said they were Amish.

Last week Angus got back from Ireland. I didn't want him to go, and I couldn't write about it until now. He went to Ireland, and he went to Ballynigel. Not much of the town is left. Every house where a witch lived was burned to the ground and now has been razed flat for rebuilding. He said none of our kind are left there, none he could find. Over in Much Bencham he got a story that people have been telling about a huge dark wave that wiped out the town, a wave without water. I don't know what could cause or create something so big, so powerful. Maybe many covens working together.

I was terrified for him to go, thought I'd never see him again. He wanted to get married before he left, and I said no. I can't marry anyone. Nothing is permanent, and I don't want to fool myself. Anyway, he took the money, went home, and found a bunch of charred, empty fields.

Now he's here, and we're moving, and in this new town, I'm hoping a new life can begin. —M. R.

Late that afternoon I decided to hunt down my Wicca books. I lay on my bed and cast out my senses, sort of feeling my way through the whole house. For a long time I got nothing, and I started to think I was wasting my time. But then, after about forty-five minutes, I realized I felt the books in my mom's closet, inside a suitcase at the very back. I looked, and sure enough, there they were. I took them back to my room and put them on my desk. If Mom or Dad wanted to make something of it, let them. I was through with silence.

On Sunday night I was sitting at my desk, working my way through math homework, when my parents knocked on my door.

"Come in," I said.

The door opened, and I heard Mary K.'s music playing louder from inside her room. I winced. Our musical tastes are completely different.

I saw my parents standing in the doorway. "Yes?" I said coolly.

"May we come in?" Mom asked.

I shrugged.

Mom and Dad came in and sat down on my bed. I tried not to glance at the Wicca books on my desk.

Dad cleared his throat, and Mom took his hand.

"This past week has been very . . . difficult for all of us," Mom said, looking reluctant and uncomfortable. "You've had questions, and we weren't ready to answer them."

I waited.

She sighed. "If you hadn't found out on your own, I probably never would have wanted to tell you about the adoption," she said, her voice ending on a whisper. "I know that's not what people recommend. They say everyone should be open, honest." She shook her head. "But telling you didn't seem like a good idea." She raised her eyes to my dad's, and he nodded at her.

"Now you know about it," Mom said. "Part of it, anyway. Maybe it's best for you to know as much as we know. I'm not sure. I'm not sure what the best thing is anymore. But we don't seem to have a choice."

"I have a right to know," I said. "It's my life. It's all I can think about. It's there, every day."

Mom nodded. "Yes, I see that. So." She drew in a long breath and looked down at her lap for a moment. "You know Daddy and I got married when I was twenty-two and he was twenty-four."

"Uh-huh."

"We wanted to start a family right away," said my mom. "We tried for eight years, with no luck. The doctors found one thing wrong with me after another. Hormonal imbalances, endometriosis . . . it got to where every month I would get my period and cry for three days because I wasn't pregnant."

My dad kept his gaze on her. He freed his hand from hers and wrapped his arm around her shoulders instead.

"I was praying to God to send me a baby," said Mom. "I lit candles, said novenas. Finally we applied at an adoption agency, and they told us it might be three or four years. But we applied anyway. Then . . ."

"Then an acquaintance of ours, a lawyer, called us one night," said my dad.

"It was raining," my mom put in as I thought about their friends, trying to remember a lawyer.

"He said he had a baby," my dad said. He shifted and tucked his hands under his knees. "A baby girl who needed adopting, a private adoption."

"We didn't even think about it," Mom said. "We just said yes! And he came over that night with a baby and handed her to me. And I took one look and knew this was *my* baby, the one I'd prayed for for so long." Mom's voice broke, and she rubbed her eyes.

"That was you," Dad said unnecessarily. He smiled at the memory. "You were seven months old and just so—"

"So perfect," Mom interrupted, her face lighting up. "You were plump and healthy, with curly hair and big eyes, and you looked up at me . . . and I knew you were the one. In that moment you became my child, and I would have killed anyone who tried to take you away from me. The lawyer said that your birth parents were too young to raise a baby and had asked him to find you a good home." She shook her head, remembering. "We didn't even think about it, didn't ask for more information. All I knew was, I had my baby, and frankly, I didn't care where you had come from or why."

I clenched my jaw, feeling my throat start aching. Had my birth parents given me to someone to keep me safe, knowing they were in danger somehow? Had the lawyer been telling the truth? Or had I just been found somewhere, after they were dead?

"You were everything we wanted," said Dad. "That night you slept between us in our bed, and the next day we went out and bought every kind of baby thing we'd ever heard of. It was like a thousand Christmases, all of our dreams coming true, in you."

"A week later," Mom said, sniffling, "we read about a fire in Meshomah Falls. How two bodies had been found in a barn that had burned to the ground. When the bodies were identified, they matched the names on your birth certificate."

"We wanted to know more, but we also didn't want to do anything to hurt the adoption," said my dad. He shook his head. "I'm ashamed to say, we just wanted to keep you, no matter what."

"But months later, after the adoption was final—it went through really fast, and finally it was all legal and no one could take you away—then we tried to find out more," Mom continued.

"How?" I asked.

"We tried calling the lawyer, but he had taken a job in another state. We left messages, but he never returned any of our calls. It was kind of odd," Dad added. "It almost seemed like he was avoiding us. Finally we gave up on him.

"I went through the newspapers," Dad went on. "I talked to the reporter who had covered the fire story, and he put me in touch with the Meshomah police. And after that I did research in Ireland, when I was there on a business trip. That was when you were about two years old and your mom was expecting Mary K."

"What did you find out?" I asked in a small voice.

"Are you sure you want to know?"

I nodded, gripping my desk chair. "I do want to know," I said, my voice stronger. I knew what Alyce had told me and what I had found out at the library. I needed to know more. I needed to know it all.

"Maeve Riordan and Angus Bramson died in that barn fire," my dad said, looking down as if he were reading the words off his shoes. "It was arson—murder," he clarified. "The barn doors had been locked from the outside, and gasoline had been poured around the building."

I trembled, my eyes huge and fastened on my dad. I hadn't read anywhere that it had definitely been murder.

"They found symbols on some of the charred pieces of wood," said Mom. "They were identified as runes, but no one knew why they were written there or why Maeve and Angus had been killed. They had kept to themselves, had no debts, went to church on Sundays. The crime was never solved."

"What about in Ireland?"

Dad nodded and shifted his weight. "Like I said, I went there on business, and I didn't have a lot of time. I didn't even know what to look for. But I took a day trip to the town where the Meshomah police had said Maeve Riordan was from: Ballynigel. When I got there, there wasn't much of a town to see. A couple of shops on a main street and one or two ugly new apartment buildings. My guidebook had said it was a quaint old fishing village, but there was hardly any sign of it or what it had used to be."

"Did you find out what happened?"

"Not really," Dad said, holding his hands wide. "There was a newsstand there, a little shop. When I asked about it, the old lady kicked me out and slammed the door."

"Kicked you out?" I asked in amazement.

Dad gave a dry chuckle. "Yes. Finally, after walking around and finding nothing, I went to the next town—I think its name was Much Bencham—and had lunch in the pub. There were a couple of old guys sitting at the bar, and they struck up a conversation with me, asking where I was from. I started talking, but as soon as I mentioned Ballynigel they went quiet. 'Why do ye want to know?' they asked suspiciously. I said I was investigating a story for my hometown newspaper about small Irish towns. For the travel section."

I stared at my dad, unable to picture him blithely lying to strangers, going on this quest to find out my heritage. He'd known all of this, both of them had, almost all of my life. And they'd never breathed a word to me.

"To make a long story short," Dad went on, "it finally came out that until four years earlier, Ballynigel had been a small, prosperous town. But in 1982 it had suddenly been destroyed. Destroyed by evil, they said."

I could hardly breathe. This was similar to what Alyce had said. My mom was chewing her bottom lip nervously, not looking at me.

"They said that Ballynigel had been a town of witches, with most of the people there being descendants of witches for thousands of years. They called them the old clans. They said evil had risen up and destroyed the witches, and they didn't know why, but they knew you should never take a chance with a witch." Dad coughed and cleared his throat. "I laughed and said I didn't believe in witches. And they said, 'More fool you.' They said that witches were real and there had been a powerful coven at Ballynigel until the night they had been destroyed, and the whole town with them. Then I had an idea, and I asked, Did anyone escape? They said a few humans. Humans, they called them, as if there was a difference. I said, What about witches? And they shook their heads and said if any witches had escaped, they would never be safe, no matter where they went. That they would be hunted down and killed, if not sooner, then later."

But two witches had escaped and had come to America. Where they were killed three years later.

Mom had quit sniffling and now watched my dad as if she hadn't heard this story for many years.

"I came home and told your mom about it, and to tell you the truth, we were both pretty frightened. We thought about how your birth parents had been killed. Frankly, it scared us. We thought there was a psycho out there, hunting these people down, and if he knew about you, you wouldn't be safe. So we decided to go on with our business, and we never spoke of your past again."

I sat there, interlacing this story with the one Alyce had told me. For the first time I could almost understand why my parents had kept all this to themselves. They had been trying to protect me. Protect me from what had killed my birth parents.

"We wanted to change your first name," Mom said. "But

you were legally Morgan. So we gave you a nickname."

"Molly," I said, light dawning. I had been Molly until fourth grade, when I decided I hated it and wanted to be called Morgan.

"Yes. And by then, when you wanted to be Morgan again, well, we felt safe," Mom said. "So much had changed. We'd never heard anything more about Meshomah Falls or Ballynigel or witches. We thought all of that was behind us."

"Then we found your Wicca books," said Dad. "And it brought everything back, all the memories, the awful stories, the fear. I thought someone had found you, had given you those books for a reason."

I shook my head. "I bought them myself."

"Maybe we've been unreasonable," Mom said slowly. "But you don't know what it's like to worry that your child might be taken from you or might be harmed. Maybe what you're doing is innocent and the people you're doing it with don't mean any harm."

"Of course they don't," I said, thinking of Cal, and his mother, and my friends.

"But we can't help feeling afraid," said my dad. "I saw a whole town that had been wiped out. I read about the burned barn. I talked to those men in Ireland. If that's what witchcraft entails, we don't want you to have any part of it."

We sat there in silence for a few minutes while I tried to absorb this story. I felt overwhelmed with emotion, but most of my anger toward them had melted away.

"I don't know what to say." I took a deep breath. "I'm glad you told me all this. And maybe I wouldn't have understood it when I was younger. But I still think you should have told me about the adoption part earlier. I should have known."

My parents nodded, and my mom sighed heavily.

"But I can't help feeling that Wicca is not connected to that—disaster in Ireland. It's just—a weird coincidence. I mean, Wicca is a part of me. And I know I'm a witch. But the kind of stuff we do couldn't cause anything like what you described."

Mom looked like she wanted to ask more but didn't want to hear the answers. She kept silent.

"How come you were able to have Mary K.?" I asked.

"I don't know," Mom said in a low voice. "It just happened. And after Mary K., I've never gotten pregnant again. God wanted me to have two daughters, and you've both brought untold joy into our lives. I care about you both so much that I can't stand to think of any danger coming to you. Which is why I want you to leave witchcraft alone. I'm *begging* you to leave witchcraft alone."

She started crying, so of course I did, too. It was all too much to take in.

"But I can't!" I wailed, blowing my nose. "It's a part of me. It's natural. It's like having brown hair or big feet. It's just—me."

"You don't have big feet," my dad objected.

I couldn't help laughing through my tears.

"I know you love me and want what's best for me," I said, wiping my eyes. "And I love you and don't want to hurt you or disappoint you. But it's like you're asking me not to be Morgan anymore." I looked up.

"We want you to be safe!" my mom said strongly, meeting my eyes. "We want you to be happy."

"I'm happy," I said. "And I try to be safe all the time."

The music went off across the hall, and we heard Mary K. enter the bathroom that connected her room to mine. The water ran, and we heard her brushing her teeth. Then the door shut again and it was quiet.

I looked at my parents. "Thank you for telling me," I said. "I know it was hard, but I'm glad that you did. I needed to know. And I'll think about what you said, I promise."

Mom sighed, and she and my dad looked at each other. They stood, and we all hugged each other for the first time in a week.

"We love you," said Mom into my hair.

"I love you, too," I said.

16

Hostile

December 15, 1982

We're getting ready to celebrate Christmas for the first time ever. We're going to the Catholic church in town. The people are very nice. It's funny, all the Christmas stuff—it's so close to Yule. The Yule log, the colors red and green, the mistletoe. Those things have always been a part of my life. It feels strange to be practicing Catholics instead of what we were.

This town is nice, much greener than New York City. I can see nature here; I can smell rain. It's not a bunch of ugly gray boxes full of unhappy people racing around.

Over and over I find myself wanting to say a little spell for this or that—to get rid of slugs in the garden, to bring more sunshine, to help my bread rise. But I don't. My whole life is in black and white, and that's the way it has to be now. No spells, no magick, no rituals, no rhymes. Not here. Not ever.

Anyway, I love our wee house. It's lovely and easy for me to keep clean. We're saving up to buy our own washing machine. Imagine! Everyone in America has their own.

I can't forget the horror of this year. It is seared on my soul forever. But I am glad to be in this new place, safe, with Angus.
—M. R.

"Are you going to the game on Friday?" Tamara asked me.

I kicked off my clogs and stowed them in the bottom of my gym locker. As usual, the air in the girls' locker room smelled like a mixture of sweat, baby powder, and shampoo. Tamara pulled on her gym shorts and sat down to put on her socks.

"I don't know," I answered, pulling my shirt over my head. Quickly I wriggled into my gym clothes and saw Tamara's eyes glance at the small silver pentacle around my neck. She looked away, and I wasn't sure if she got the significance: that it was a symbol of my commitment to Wicca and to Cal. I bent down to tie my sneakers and didn't say anything about it.

Across the room Bree stood next to her own locker, changing. Since Raven was a senior, she was in a different class. It was unusual to see Bree alone.

Bree's eyes met mine for a moment, and their coldness shocked me. It was hard to believe that I hadn't been able to share my huge news with her: finding out I was adopted, the story of my birth parents. We had always promised to tell each other everything, and until this school year we had. She'd told me about when she'd lost her virginity and tried pot for the first time and how she'd found out about her mom's affair. My own confidences had been much more banal.

"Guess who asked me out," said Tamara, pulling her tight curls into a puffy ponytail.

"Who?" I asked, quickly braiding my hair in two long braids so I looked like an Irish Pocahontas.

Tamara lowered her voice. "Chris Holly."

My eyes got wide. "Get out! What did you say?" I whispered.

"I said no! Number one, I'm sure he only asked because he's flunking trig and needs help, and number two, I saw what a jerk he was with Bree." Her dark brown eyes looked at me. "Are you two talking yet?"

I shook my head.

So did Tamara. I shoved my feet into my sneakers and tied them.

"So did you go after Cal?" she asked.

"No," I said honestly. "I mean, I was crazy about him, but I knew Bree liked him. I just assumed they'd end up together. But then . . . he picked me." Shrugging, I stuck my braids down the back of my T-shirt so they wouldn't whip anyone in the face. Then Ms. Lew, our PE teacher, blew her whistle. Ms. Lew loved that whistle.

"It's raining out, girls!" she called in her clear voice. "So give me five laps around the gym!"

We all groaned, as expected, then started to jog out of the locker room. Tamara and I quickly passed Bree, who was going as slowly as she possibly could.

"Witch," I heard Bree mutter as I jogged past. My cheeks burned, and I pretended not to hear her.

"She called you a bitch," Tamara whispered angrily, jogging next to me. "I can't believe she's being such a bad sport about this. I mean, they didn't even go out. Besides, she can get any *other* guy she wants. Does she really have to have them all?"

Hooting and whistling assaulted our ears as all the junior boys ran out of their locker room and started jogging in the opposite direction. I could hear the rain as it hit the small windows set high in the gym walls.

"Hey, baby!"

"Looking good!"

I rolled my eyes as the boys jogged past. Robbie made a face at me as he passed, and I laughed.

"Bree says they did go out once," I said, starting to pant. Actually, she had said that she and Cal had sex. It wasn't exactly the same thing.

Tamara shrugged. "Maybe they did, but I never heard about it. It couldn't have meant much, anyway. Oh, guess who asked Janice out? You've been out of the whole gossip loop."

"Who?"

"Ben Reggio," announced Tamara. "They've had two study dates."

"Oh, that's great," I said. "They seem like they'd be perfect together. I hope it works out."

I felt so normal, talking about regular high school stuff with Tamara. As exciting and fantastic and empowering as my Wicca experiences were, they made me feel kind of isolated. They were also exhausting. It was nice, not having to think about anything deep or life changing for a few minutes.

After our laps we split into teams for volleyball. The girls were on one side of the gym with Ms. Lew, and the boys were on the other with Coach.

Bree and I ended up on opposite teams.

"God, look at Robbie," a girl whispered behind me. I

turned around and saw Bettina Kretts talking to Paula Arroyo. "He is so hot."

I looked at Robbie. With great skin and no glasses, he was moving around the volleyball court with new confidence.

"I heard that senior, Anu Radtha, asked when he had transferred here," Paula said in a low voice.

I raised an eyebrow. Anu was the older sister of one of Bree's old boyfriends, Ranjit. So Anu actually thought Robbie was a new student and one worthy of a senior's attention.

"Is he going out with anyone?" Bettina asked.

"Don't think so," Paula answered. Their conversation was interrupted when the ball came into our quarter for a minute. We bounced it around, and I knocked it across the net, anxious to hear the rest of what they were saying.

"He hangs out with the witches," Bettina shocked me by saying. She was several people away and speaking in a low tone. Only by concentrating could I hear what she was saying. I'd had no idea that people around school thought of our group as "the witches."

"Yeah, I've seen him with Cal and the rest of them," said Paula. "Hey, if he isn't going out with anyone, why don't you ask him to the game?"

Bettina giggled. "Maybe I will."

Well, well, well, I thought, popping the ball over to Sarah Fields. She hit it over the net to Janice, and Janice returned with a quick, neat pop that went right between Bettina and Alessandra Spotford, costing us a point and giving our opponents the serve.

Bree was in the server's position on the other team, and while she was holding the ball, someone gave a wolf whistle from the other side of the gym. She looked up, her eyes flitting from boy to boy until she found Seth Moore giving her a big, lecherous grin. Seth was good-looking in a punky kind of way. His hair was cut in a buzzed flattop, he wore two silver earrings in his left ear, and he had pretty hazel eyes.

Bree grinned back and wiggled her shoulders at him.

Automatically I looked for Chris Holly, Bree's most recent ex. He was watching it all with a kind of frozen animosity, but he said nothing and made no move.

"Come on, Miss Warren," ordered Ms. Lew.

"You and me, baby!" Seth shouted.

Bree laughed, and then our glances met. She gave me this snarky, superior smile, as if to say, See? Boys would never do that for *you*. I tried to look bored, but of course it was true. Cal was the only guy who had ever paid me any attention. Bree's showing off hurt me, as she intended.

"Anytime!" Bree called to Seth, getting ready to serve. Several of his teammates made a big show of holding him back. Everyone was laughing now, everyone but me, Chris Holly—and one other person. When I saw the look on Robbie's face, my jaw almost dropped open. Good old Robbie, my pal Robbie, was watching Bree and Seth with a barely concealed jealousy. His hands were clenching at his sides, and his whole body was tense.

Huh, I thought in wonder. He had never said a word about liking Bree.

Then I felt a stab of guilt. Of course, I hadn't asked.

"Come on, Bree," said Ms. Lew, sounding irritated.

Bree gave me another superior smile, as if this whole show was for my benefit, to show me how hot she was and how nothing I was. A spark of anger ignited in me. Looking at her, I impulsively hooked my finger in the neck of my T-shirt and tugged it down, revealing the silver pentacle that Cal had once worn and that was now mine.

Bree paled visibly and drew in a quick breath. Then she pulled back her arm, made a fist, and smashed the volleyball right at me with all her strength. Automatically I threw my hand in front of my face a split second before the powerful serve came right at me. It knocked me down, and the entire junior class saw me whack my head on the wooden floor. A tangy, coppery smell alerted me one second before my nose and mouth filled with blood. Putting my hands over my face, I tried to sit up before I drowned, and my blood ran out through my fingers and down my shirt.

Everyone was gasping, talking fast, and Ms. Lew's voice, urgent and in control, said, "Let me see, honey." Her hands pried my fingers away from my face, and when she did, I saw Bree, standing over her, peering at me in alarm, a horrified expression on her face.

I looked at her, trying not to swallow blood. Her mouth opened, and silently she said, "I'm sorry." She looked so much like her old self for a minute that I almost felt happy. Then all of a sudden the shock subsided, and my face was filled with pain.

"Are you all right?" someone asked.

"Unh," I mumbled, putting my hands up to my nose. "Hurts."

"Okay, Morgan," said Ms. Lew. "Can you stand up? Let's get you to my office so we can put some ice on it. I think we'd better call your mom." She helped me up and called, "Get back to the game, girls. Bettina, get some paper towels and wipe that blood up so someone doesn't slip on it. Ms. Warren, see me in my office after class."

I cast a last look at Bree as I left. Bree looked back at me, but suddenly every remnant of friendship or emotion was gone, replaced by calculation. It made my heart sink, and tears filled my eyes.

When Mom came to get me, she was still in her work clothes. Clucking with worry, she took me to the emergency room, where they X-rayed my face. My nose was broken, and my lip needed one tiny stitch. Everything was swollen, and I looked like a Halloween mask.

It had come to this, between me and Bree.

17

The New Coven

April 14, 1983

My peas are coming up nicely — I thought I might have put them in too early. They're a symbol of my new life: I can't believe they're growing on their own so strongly, without magickal help. Sometimes the urge to get in touch with the Goddess is so strong, I ache with it — it's like a pain, something trying to get out. But that part of my life is over, and all I have from that time is my name. And Angus.

We have a new addition to our household: a gray-and-white kitten. I've named her Bridget. She's a funny little thing, with extra toes on each paw and the biggest purr you ever heard. I'm glad to have her.

— M. R.

That afternoon, as I lay in bed with an ice pack on my face, the doorbell rang.

I immediately sensed that it was Cal. My heart thumped painfully. I listened as he spoke to my mom. I focused my attention, but I could still barely make out their words.

"Well, I don't know," I heard Mom say.

"For Pete's sake, Mom. I'll stay the whole time and chaperon them," said Mary K., much louder. She must have been standing right at the bottom of the steps. Then footsteps sounded on the stairs. I watched nervously as my door opened.

Mom came in first, presumably to make sure I was properly dressed and not, say, wearing a sexy, see-through negligee. In fact, I was wearing stretched-out gray sweatpants, an undershirt of my dad's, and a white sweatshirt. Mom had helped me wash the blood out of my hair, but I hadn't dried it or anything like that. It hung loose in long damp ropes. Basically, I looked as awful as I had ever looked in my life.

Cal came into my room, and his presence made it seem small and young. Note to self: Redecorate.

He gave me a big smile and said, "Darling!"

I couldn't help laughing, though it hurt, and I put my hand to my face and said, "Ungh—doan make me laugh."

As soon as Mom saw I was decent, she left, even though she was obviously uncomfortable about my having a boy in my room.

"Doesn't she look great?" Mary K. said. "Too bad Halloween's over. I bet by Thursday everything will be yellow and green." I noticed she was holding a white teddy bear wearing a heart-shaped bib.

"For me?" I asked.

Mary K. shook her head, looking embarrassed. "It's from Bakker."

I nodded. Bakker had been sending flowers and leaving notes on our porch all day. He'd called several times, and when I had answered the phone, he had apologized to me. I knew Mary K. was weakening.

She perched in my desk chair, and I gave her a look. "Don't you have homework?"

"I promised to chaperon," she objected. Then, seeing my expression, she held up her hands. "Okay, okay, I'm going."

As the door closed behind her I looked at Cal. "I didn't want you to see me like this." Because of the swelling in my nose, my voice sounded clogged and distant.

His face grew solemn. "Tamara told me about what happened. Do you think she did it on purpose?"

I thought of Bree's face, of the fright in her eyes when she saw what she'd done to me.

"It was an accident," I said, and he nodded.

"I brought you some stuff." He held up a small bag.

"What?" I asked eagerly.

"This, for starters," Cal said, taking out a small potted plant. It was silvery gray, with cut, feathery leaves.

"Artemesia," I said, recognizing it from one of my herb books. "It's pretty."

Cal nodded. "Mugwort. A useful plant. Also this." He handed me a small vial.

I read the label. *"Arnica montana."*

"It's a homeopathic medicine," Cal explained. "I got it at the health-food store. It's for when you've had a traumatic injury. It's good for bruises, stuff like that." He leaned closer. "I spelled it to help you heal faster," he whispered. "It's just what the doctor ordered."

I sank back gratefully on my pillows. "Cool."

"One more thing," Cal said, taking out a bottle of Yoo-Hoo. "I bet you can't eat much, but a Yoo-Hoo can be sucked down with a straw. And it's got all the major food groups—dairy, fat, chocolate. You could say it's the perfect food."

I laughed, trying not to move my face. "Thanks. You thought of everything."

Mom called upstairs: "Dinner will be ready in five minutes."

I rolled my eyes, and Cal smiled. "I can take a hint," he said. He sat carefully on the edge of my bed and took my hand in both of his. I swallowed, feeling lost, wanting to hold him to me. *Mùirn beatha dàn*, I thought.

"Is there anything you want me to do for you?" he asked with quiet meaning. I knew he meant, Do you want me to get back at Bree?

I shook my head, feeling my face ache. "I don't think so," I whispered. "Let it go."

He regarded me evenly. "I'll let it go so far and no further," he warned. "This sucks."

I nodded, feeling very tired.

"Okay, I'll get going. Call me later if you want to talk."

He stood up. Then he very gently put his hands on my face, barely touching me with his fingertips. He closed his eyes and muttered words I didn't understand. Closing my eyes, I felt the heat from his fingers warm my face. As I breathed in, some of the pain dissipated.

It took less than a minute, then he opened his eyes and stepped back. I felt much better.

"Thanks," I said. "Thanks for coming."

"I'll talk to you later," he said. Then he turned and left my room.

As I sank back down in bed my face felt lighter, less

swollen. My head hurt less. I opened the arnica and popped four of the tiny sugar pills under my tongue. Then I lay quietly, feeling the pain wash out of me.

That night before I went to sleep, both my black eyes were almost gone, the swelling had gone way down, and I felt like I could breathe through my nose.

I stayed home from school the next day, although I looked tons better, except for the ugly black stitch on my lip.

At two-thirty that afternoon I called Mom at work and told her I was going over to Tamara's house to pick up some homework assignments.

"Are you sure you feel up to it?" she asked.

"Yeah, I feel almost fine," I said. "I'll be back before dinner."

"Okay, then. Drive carefully."

"I will."

I hung up the phone, got my keys and my coat, put on my clogs, and set off toward school. It's pretty much impossible to hide a huge white whale like Das Boot, but I parked on a side street two blocks away, where I thought I could see Bree's car pass as she left school. I could have waited for her at home, but I wasn't sure she'd go straight there.

It wasn't like I had a totally fleshed-out plan. Basically I was hoping to confront Bree, to hash everything out. In the best of all possible worlds, it would have a positive result. I felt like I had reached a breakthrough with my parents, and Mary K. and I had bonded again after the Bakker incident: Now I wanted to get things straight with Bree. The habits of a lifetime aren't easy to erase, and I still thought of her as my best friend. Hating her was too much to bear. The scene in gym showed how desperately we needed to work things out.

But it wasn't only that. I had other reasons for wanting to

mend things between us, too. Magick was clarity. According to my books, to work the best magick was to see the most clearly. If I lived with an ongoing feud in my life, it could seriously hamper my ability to do magick.

I almost missed Bree's car as it passed the corner at the end of the block. Quickly I started up mine and crept slowly behind her, as far back as I could.

Luckily Bree headed straight home. I knew the way well enough that I could hang back at a great distance, staying behind other cars. Once she had pulled into her driveway and parked, I pulled over myself at the very end of her block, behind a big maroon minivan, and shut off my engine.

Just as I was about to get out, though, Raven pulled up in her battered black Peugeot. Bree ran back out of her house.

I waited. The two girls talked for a while on the sidewalk, then headed to Raven's car and got in. Raven roared off, leaving a trail of foul exhaust behind her.

I was nonplussed. This hadn't been in my plan. Right now I was supposed to be talking to Bree, possibly arguing with her. Raven hadn't figured into it. Where were they going?

A sudden fierce curiosity took hold of me, and I started my car again. After four blocks I caught sight of them once more.

They headed north, out of town on Westwood. I followed, already suspecting where they were headed.

When they reached the cornfields at the north of town, where our coven had had its first meeting, Raven pulled off onto the road's shoulder and parked.

Slowing, I waited until they had disappeared into the recently stripped cornfield, then drove to the other side and hid Das Boot under the huge willow oak. Though the branches were almost bare, its trunk was thick and the ground dipped slightly so that no one casually glancing over would spot my car.

Then I hurried across the road and began to pick my way through the crumpled, messy remains of what had been a tall field of golden feed corn.

I couldn't see Raven and Bree ahead of me, but I knew where they were going: to the old Methodist cemetery where we had celebrated Samhain just ten days ago. Ten days ago, when Cal had kissed me in front of the coven and Bree and I had become true enemies.

It felt like much longer ago than that.

I stepped across the trickling stream and headed uphill into a stand of old hardwood trees. I went more slowly, casting my senses, listening for their voices. I didn't really know what I was doing and felt kind of like a stalker. But I had been wondering about their new coven. I couldn't resist finding out what they were up to.

When I reached the edge of the graveyard, I saw them ahead, standing by the stone sarcophagus that had served as our altar on Samhain. The two of them stood there, not talking, and it came to me: They were waiting for someone.

I sank down on the damp, cold earth beside an ancient tombstone. My face ached a little, and the stitch in my lip was itching. I wished I had remembered to take more arnica or Tylenol before I left the house.

Bree rubbed her hands up and down her arms. Raven kept pushing back her dyed black hair. They both looked nervous and excited.

Then Bree turned and peered into the shadows. Raven grew very still, and my heart beat loudly in the silence.

The person meeting them was a woman, or rather a girl, maybe a couple of years older than Raven. Maybe just a year. The more I looked at her, the younger she became.

She was beautiful in an unusual, otherworldly kind of way. Fine blond hair shone starkly against her black leather motorcycle jacket, and she had very short, almost white bangs. Her cheekbones were high and Nordic, her mouth full and too wide for her face. But it was her eyes that seemed so compelling, even from far away. They were large and deep set and so black that they looked like holes, drawing light in and not letting it out again.

She greeted Bree and Raven so quietly, I couldn't hear the murmur of her voice. She seemed to ask them a question, and her dark eyes darted here and there like negative spotlights raking the area.

"No, no one followed us," I heard Bree say.

"No way." Raven laughed. "No one comes out here."

Still the girl looked around, her eyes flicking again and again to the tombstone I hid behind. If she was a witch, she might pick up on my presence. Quickly I closed my eyes, trying to shut everything down, focusing on becoming invisible, on trying to wrinkle the fabric of reality as little as possible. I am not here, I sent out into the world. I am not here. There is nothing here. You see nothing, you hear nothing, you feel nothing. I repeated this smoothly again and again, and finally the three girls started talking again.

Moving a centimeter at a time, I turned and faced them again.

"Revenge?" the girl said, her voice rich and musical.

"Yes," said Raven. "You see, there's . . ."

A breeze rustled the trees just then, and her words were

lost. They were speaking so quietly that it was only by using my strongest concentration that I could hear them at all.

"Dark magic," Raven said, and Bree looked at her with troubled eyes.

". . . to wither love," were the next words to float to me on the breeze. That was from the girl. I looked at her aura. Next to Bree's and Raven's darkness, she was made of pure light, shining like a sword in the increasing shadows of the graveyard.

"Their circle . . . our new coven . . . a girl with power . . . Cal . . . Saturday nights, at different places . . ."

They talked on, and my frustration grew at not being able to hear more. The sun went down quickly, as if a lamp had been dimmed, and I started to feel seriously chilly.

I leaned against the tombstone. What did this mean? They had mentioned Cal's name. I figured the "girl with power" was me. What were they planning? I had to tell Cal.

But there was no way to leave without their seeing me, so I was stuck on that damp ground, feeling my butt and legs go to sleep while my bruised face ached more and more.

At last, after about forty endless minutes, the girl left silently the way she had come, with only her light hair visible when she stepped into the darkness beneath the trees. Bree and Raven walked back through the graveyard, passing within ten feet of me, and headed back out through the cornfield. A minute later I heard Raven's car belch and peel off, and two minutes after that its exhaust drifted to me on the evening breeze.

I got up and brushed myself off, anxious to get home to take a hot, hot shower. The cornfields were now totally dark, and I felt weirded out by the creepy scene I had just witnessed. At one point I was sure I felt someone's concentrated stare on the back of my head, but when I whirled, nothing was there. Running back to my car, I jumped in, slamming and locking my door after me.

My hands were so cold and stiff, it took me a second to get the key in the ignition, and then I popped on my headlights and did a fast U-turn on Westwood. I was scared and irritated, and my earlier thoughts of clearing things up with Bree now seemed naive, laughable.

What were they planning? Were they really so angry with Cal and me that they would turn to dark magick? They were putting themselves in danger, making choices that were stupid and shortsighted.

I swung into my own driveway, shaken and chilled to the bone. Inside, I hurried up the stairs and stripped off my wet clothes. As the hot water dissolved my chills I thought and thought.

After dinner I called Cal and asked him to meet me by the willow oak the next day after school.

18

Desire

September 20, 1983

Angus and I sat home glumly tonight, thinking about what we would be doing if we were at home and everything was as it had been. I can't believe no one here celebrates the harvest, the richness of the autumn. The closest thing they have is Thanksgiving in November, but that seems to be more about pilgrims and Indians and turkey.

The summer was blessed: hot, quiet, full of long slow days and nights filled with the sound of frogs and crickets. My garden grew magnificently, and I was so proud. The sun and earth and rain worked their magick without my helping or asking.

Bridget is fine and fat. She's a champion mouser and can even catch crickets.

My job is dull but fine. Angus is learning some beautiful woodworking. We have little money, but we're safe here.

—M. R.

"I guess you're wondering why I asked you to meet me," I said as Cal slid into the front seat of my car on Wednesday afternoon.

"Because you wanted my body?" he guessed, and then I was laughing and holding him tightly and he was trying to find a part of me to kiss that wouldn't hurt. I was ninety percent better, but my face was still sensitive.

"Try here," I said, tapping my lips gently.

Slowly, carefully, he lowered his mouth to mine and applied just the slightest pressure.

"Mmmm," I said. Cal pulled back and looked at me.

"Let's get in the backseat," he said.

This seemed like a fine idea. The backseat of the Valiant was huge and roomy, and we felt comfortable and private as the November wind blew against the windows and whistled beneath the car.

"How are you feeling?" he asked, once we were cozily settled. "Did that arnica help?"

I nodded. "I think it did. The bruises seem to have gone away really fast."

He smiled and gently touched my temple. "Almost."

I had planned to tell him about what I'd seen yesterday, but now that we were together, the words flew out of my head. Contentedly I lay against him, feeling his hands smooth my skin, and I didn't want to think about following Bree or spying on her.

"Does this feel good?" Cal asked, sounding sleepy as he stroked my back. His eyes were closed, his knees were bent, his feet propped on the side door handle.

"Uh-huh," I said. I let my hand roam up and down his firm

chest. After a second I undid the top of his shirt. I slid my hand inside.

"Ummm," Cal whispered, and he turned a little so that we were facing each other, chest to chest. He kissed me so gently and so softly that it didn't hurt a bit.

Then I felt the shocking, hot sensation of my skin against his and realized our shirts had somehow edged up so that our stomachs were touching. It felt amazing, and I wrapped my leg around his hips, feeling the tiny ribs of his brown corduroy jeans pressing against my thigh through my leggings.

As I pressed myself closer to him I kept thinking, He's the one, the one, the one. My only one. My *mùirn beatha dàn*. The one meant for me. This was all supposed to happen.

Cal pulled back a little bit, then spoke against my cheek. "Am I the first person you've been close to?"

"Yes," I whispered. I felt his lips smile against my skin, and he held me tighter.

"I'm not your first person." I stated the obvious.

"No," he said after a moment. "Does that bother you?"

"Did you sleep with Bree?" I blurted out, then winced, wanting to erase the words.

Cal looked surprised. "Bree? Why . . ." He shook his head. "Where did that come from?"

"She told me you did," I said, trying to prepare myself for the answer, to act like it didn't matter. Gazing at my fingers resting against his chest, I waited to see what he would say.

"Bree told you that she slept with me?" he asked.

I nodded.

"Did you believe her?"

I shrugged, trying to suppress the panicky feeling that was

building inside me. "I didn't know. Bree is gorgeous, and she usually gets what she wants. I guess it wouldn't surprise me."

"I don't kiss and tell," Cal said, considering his words. "I think that stuff should be private."

My heart threatened to explode.

"But I'll tell you this much because I don't want it between us. Yes, Bree made it clear she was into the idea. But I wasn't available at the time, so it didn't happen."

I frowned. "Why weren't you available?"

He laughed, brushing back my hair. "I had already seen you."

"And it was witch at first sight." The words just slipped out. I winced, wishing I could take them back.

Cal shook his head, bemused. "What do you mean?"

"Raven and Bree said . . . that you're only with me because I'm a witch, a strong witch."

"Is that what you believe?" Cal asked, his voice cooler.

"I don't know," I said, starting to feel awful. Why did I ever begin this conversation?

Cal was silent for a couple of minutes and very still. "I don't know what the right answer is. Sure, your powers as a witch are really exciting to me. The idea of us working together, of helping you learn what I know, is . . . tantalizing. And as for the rest, I just . . . think you're beautiful. You're pretty and sexy, and I'm drawn to you. I don't even understand why we're having this conversation, after I told you about the *mùirn beatha dàn*." He shook his head.

I was silent, feeling like I had dug myself into a hole.

"Could you do me a favor?" he asked.

"What?" I asked, afraid of what he was about to say.

"Could you ignore what other people say?"

"I'll try," I said quietly.

"Could you do me another favor?"

I looked at him.

"Could you kiss me again? Things were just starting to get interesting."

Laughing, wanting to cry, I leaned down and kissed him. He held me to him strongly, pressing me against his body from chest to knees. His hands swept over my back, my sides, and explored my skin underneath my shirt. I felt his fingers smooth over the small birthmark I have under my right arm, feeling its raised edges.

"I've always had that," I whispered. He hadn't seen it, but it was a rose pink mark about an inch and a half long. I had always thought it looked like a small dagger. It made me smile to think of it now: I could say it looked like an athame.

"I love it," Cal murmured, feeling it again. "It's part of you." Then he kissed me again, sweeping me away on a tide of emotion.

"Think about magick," Cal whispered, and my scattered thoughts couldn't comprehend his meaning. He continued touching me, and he said, "Magick is a strong feeling, and this is a strong feeling. Put them together."

If I had tried talking just then, it would have come out as gibberish. But inside my mind, his words strung together and made some sort of dim sense. I thought about how I felt when I made magick or gathered magick: that feeling of power, of completion, of being connected to things, being part of the world. With Cal's hands on me I felt a similar and yet very different sensation: it, too, was power and a kind of gathering, but it was also like a door leading somewhere else.

And then I got it. It all came together. Our mouths together, our breaths wreathing themselves together, our minds in tune with each other, my hands on his skin, his hands on mine, and it felt almost like we were in a circle, when the energy is all around, there for the taking.

There was energy surrounding us, wrapping us together, and my shirt was pushed up, my breasts against the warm skin of his chest, and we were holding each other tightly and kissing, and magick sparked. Any words I said then would be a spell. Any thought I had would be a magickal directive. Anything I called to me would come.

It went way beyond exhilarating.

When we stopped and I opened my eyes, it was dark outside. I had no idea of what time it was and glanced at my watch to see I was late for dinner.

Groaning, I pulled down my shirt.

"What time is it?" Cal murmured, his fingers already reaching for his buttons.

"Six-thirty," I said. "I have to go."

"Okay."

As I reached for the door, he pulled me back against him so I sat in his lap.

"That was incredible," he whispered, kissing my cheek. He gave me a big grin. "I mean, that was incredible!"

I laughed, still feeling powerful as he opened the car door. "I'll see you tomorrow," he said. "And I'll think about you tonight."

He headed back to his own car. As I climbed into the

front seat of Das Boot and started the engine, emotion almost overwhelmed me.

It was only late that night, when I was lying in bed, that I remembered that I'd never told him about the blond witch.

On Thursday morning the only parking spot was right behind Breezy, Bree's sleek BMW. I thought about how easy it would be for my car to crush hers, then I smiled wryly at having such a mean, unmagickal thought.

"You look different," Mary K. said as I carefully maneuvered my car into the spot. She peered into the passenger's-side makeup mirror and reapplied her lip gloss.

I glanced at her, startled. Had she seen me in the car with Cal yesterday? "What do you mean?"

"Your bruises are a lot better," said Mary K. She looked out her car window. "Oh God, there he is."

My eyes narrowed at the sight of Bakker Blackburn skulking around the life sciences building, obviously waiting for Mary K.

"Mary K., he tried to hurt you," I reminded her.

She bit her lip, looking at him. "He's so sorry," she muttered.

"You can't trust him." I gathered up my backpack, and we opened our doors.

"I know," my sister said, looking at him. "I know." She moved off to see some of her girlfriends, and I headed for the coven hangout.

"Morgan." Raven's voice reached me from a few feet away. I looked over to see her and Bree striding along beside me.

I didn't say anything.

"Your face is looking more normal," said Raven snidely. "Did you do a magick spell to fix it? Oh, wait, you're not supposed to, right?"

I just kept on walking. So did they. I realized Raven and Bree were going to follow me all the way to the east door.

Jenna and Matt saw us first. Then Cal met my eyes and gave me an intimate smile, which I returned. His gaze grew cold when he saw Bree and Raven behind me.

"Hi, guys," said Jenna, with her usual friendliness. "Bree, how's it going?"

"Peachy keen," Bree said sarcastically. "Everything's great. How about you?"

"Fine," said Jenna. "I haven't had an asthma attack all week." Her eyes flicked to me, and I looked down.

"Really?" said Raven.

"Hey, Bree," called Seth Moore. He loped up to us, his baggy pants long around his ankles.

"Hi," said Bree, making that one word sound like a promise. "Why didn't you call me last night?"

"Didn't know I was supposed to," he said. "Tell you what—I'll call you twice tonight." He looked jubilant at this clear sign of approval and shifted his feet, looking at Bree.

"It's a date," she said in a smarmy, come-hither voice that anyone with two brain cells to rub together would see right through.

"Knock it off, Bree," Robbie said suddenly. Everyone else seemed surprised, but I remembered the look I'd seen on his face that day in the gym.

"Whaaat?" Bree looked at him with wide eyes.

"Knock it off," he said, sounding bored and angry. "It's not a date. Seth, take a hike. You won't be calling her."

We were all staring at Robbie, whose face was set and stiff with dislike.

Seth met his stare. "Who the hell are you?" he asked belligerently. "Her dad?"

Robbie shrugged, and I realized how tall he was, how heavy. He looked pretty formidable and made Seth seem slim and young. "Whatever," he said. "Forget about her."

"Robbie!" Bree snapped, her hands on her hips. "Who do you think you are? I can go out with anyone I want! God, you're worse than Chris!"

Robbie looked down at her. "Stop it, Bree," he said more quietly. "You don't want him." He held her gaze for a long time. I glanced at Jenna, and she raised an eyebrow.

Bree opened her mouth as if to speak, but no words came out. She seemed almost mesmerized.

"Hey!" said Seth. "You don't own her! You can't tell her who she wants!"

Slowly Robbie raised his eyes and looked at Seth like he was an insect. "Whatever," he said again, then he turned and walked into the school building as the bell rang.

For one startled moment Bree watched him leave, then she quickly looked at me, and it was like old times when we could pass a wealth of information in one second. Then she turned, and Raven snickered, and the two of them walked away. Seth stood there, looking dumb, and finally turned and headed off, muttering under his breath.

"She sure can pick 'em," Sharon said brightly.

Cal took my hand.

"Yeah," I said, wondering exactly what we had just witnessed. "And they can pick her, too."

19

Sky and Hunter

March 11, 1984

We have conceived a child. We were not trying to, but it happened, anyway. For the last two weeks I have been trying to find the strength to have an abortion so this child will never know the pain that we have seen in this life. But I cannot. I am not strong enough. So the child rests in my womb, and I will give birth sometime in November.

It will be a girl, and she will be a witch, but I will not teach her the craft. It is no longer a part of my life, nor will it be a part of my child's. We will name her Morgan, for Angus's mother. It is a strong name.

— M. R.

On Friday night Cal and I had a date. We were going to a movie with Jenna, Matt, Sharon, and Ethan.

Sharon picked me up—we were meeting Cal at his

house. At seven o'clock she pulled her Mercedes into my driveway and honked the horn.

" 'Bye!" I yelled, slamming the door behind me.

When I got to the car, I saw that Ethan was in the front seat, so I climbed into the back. Sharon roared out of my driveway and hung a fast left onto Riverdale.

"Do you have to drive like a crazy person?" Ethan said, lighting a cigarette.

"Don't you dare make my car smell like an ashtray!" Sharon said, spinning the wheel and stepping on the gas.

Ethan cracked the window and expertly blew out smoke.

"Um, Ethan?" I said. "It's freezing back here."

Ethan sighed and tossed his cigarette out the window, where it hit the street with a thousand tiny orange sparks.

"Now you litter," Sharon said. "Very nice."

"Morgan's cold," Ethan said, rolling up his window. "Turn on her automatic butt warmer back there."

"Morgan?" Sharon asked, looking in the rearview mirror. "Do you want the seat warmer?"

"No, thanks," I said, trying not to laugh.

"How about the vibrator?" Ethan asked. "Hey, watch it! You were two inches away from that truck!"

"I was fine," Sharon said, rolling her eyes. "And there's no vibrator in this car."

"You left it at home?" Ethan asked innocently, and I cracked up while Sharon tried to punch Ethan as hard as she could without having an accident. I wished they would just start going out, but I wasn't sure Sharon had even realized how much she liked Ethan yet.

Amazingly, we made it to Cal's in one piece and saw

Matt's Jeep already parked in the driveway, along with at least twelve other cars.

"Cal's mom must be having a circle," Sharon said.

I hadn't seen Selene Belltower since the night she had helped calm my fears, and I wanted to thank her again. Cal let us in, kissing me hello, and took us back to the kitchen, where Matt was drinking a seltzer and Jenna was on the phone to the theater.

"What time?" she asked, making notes.

Cal leaned against the counter, pulling me against him.

Jenna hung up the phone. "Okay. It starts at eight-fifteen, so we should leave here around seven forty-five."

"Cool," said Matt.

"So we've got some time. You guys want something to drink?" asked Cal. He looked apologetic. "We have to keep the noise down because my mom's having a circle in a while."

"What time do they usually start?" I asked.

"Not till ten or so," he answered. "But people come early, hang out and talk, get caught up on their weeks."

"I wanted to tell your mom thanks again," I said.

"Oh, well, come on, then," he said, taking my hand. "You can see her. We'll be right back," he told the others.

"Did you take the last Coke?" Sharon accused Ethan as we left the kitchen.

"I'll split it with you," was his muffled reply.

Cal and I shared a grin as we walked through the foyer and then through the formal living room and the more casual great room. "There is definitely something happening there," he said, and I nodded.

"It'll be fun when they get together. Sparks will fly."

Cal gave two quick taps on the tall wooden door that led to the huge room Selene used for her circles. Then he opened it, and we walked in. It was quite different tonight than it had been the night I'd arrived here alone, shaken and upset. Now it was aglow with the light of at least a hundred candles. The air was scented with incense, and there were people, both men and women, standing around chatting.

"Morgan, dear, how nice to see you." Turning, I saw Alyce, from Practical Magick. She was wearing a long, purple, batik robe, and her silver hair was loose and hanging around her shoulders.

"Hi," I said. I'd forgotten she belonged to Starlocket. Quickly I searched for David, the clerk who made me nervous. He saw me and smiled, and I gave a tentative smile back.

"How are you?" Alyce asked, seeming to mean it as more than just a polite question.

I thought. "Up and down," I said honestly.

She nodded as if she understood.

Cal had left my side for a moment, and now he returned with his mother. She was also wearing a long, loose robe, but hers was a brilliant red and painted with gold moons and stars and suns. It was stunning.

"Hello, Morgan," she said in her rich, beautiful voice. She took both my hands in hers and kissed both of my cheeks, European style. I felt like royalty. She looked into my eyes and then placed a hand on my cheek. After a few moments she nodded. "It's been difficult," she murmured. "I'm afraid it will be more difficult still. But you're very strong. . . ."

"Yes," I surprised myself by saying clearly. "I *am* very strong."

Selene Belltower gave me an assessing glance, then smiled at me and at Cal as if in approval. He grinned back at his mother and took my hand.

Her eyes swept the room then, and she focused on someone.

"Cal, I want you to meet someone," she said, and there was an undercurrent of something I didn't understand in her voice.

I followed her gaze and almost jumped a foot in the air when I saw the same pale-haired girl that Bree and Raven had met with in the cemetery. My mouth opened to say something, but a tension in Cal's hand made me look up at him.

He had the most extraordinary look on his face. As best as I can describe it, it was . . . predatory. I barely controlled a shiver. Suddenly I felt like I didn't know him at all.

I found myself following him as he crossed the room.

"Sky, this is my son, Cal Blaire," said Selene, introducing them. "Cal, this is Sky Eventide."

Wordlessly Cal pulled his hand free from mine and held it out to her. Sky shook it, her night dark eyes never leaving his face. I hated her. My stomach clenched as I saw the appraising way they looked at each other. I wanted to scratch her, tear at her, and I drew in a shuddering breath.

Then Cal looked at me. "This is my girlfriend, Morgan Rowlands," he said. He called me his girlfriend, which was mildly reassuring. Then her dark eyes were on me, like two pieces of coal, and I shook her hand, feeling its strength.

"Morgan," said Sky. She was English, and she had an incredibly musical, lilting voice, a voice that made me instantly want to hear her chanting, spelling, singing rituals. Which made me hate her more.

"Selene has mentioned you to me," said Sky. "I'm looking forward to getting to know you."

Over my dead body, I thought, but forced my mouth to stretch into something resembling a smile. I could feel Cal's tension, feel his body next to mine as he looked at her and practically drank her in with his eyes. Sky Eventide regarded Cal calmly, as if she saw his challenge and would meet it.

"I believe you know Hunter," she said, gesturing to someone behind her, who had his back to us.

The person behind Sky turned, and I almost gasped. If Sky was daytime, Hunter was sunlight. His hair was a pale gold, and he had fine, pale skin, with some freckles on his cheeks and nose. His eyes were a wide, clear green, with no traces of blue or brown or gray in them. He was stunningly good-looking, and he made my stomach turn. Like Sky, I hated him on sight, in a primitive, inexplicable way.

"Yes. I know Hunter," Cal said flatly, not extending his hand.

"Cal," said Hunter. He met Cal's gaze, then turned to me. I didn't smile. "And you are?"

I said nothing.

"Morgan Rowlands," Sky supplied. "Cal's girlfriend. Morgan, this is Hunter Niall."

Still I said nothing, and Hunter looked at me hard, as if trying to see through to my skeleton. It reminded me of the way Selene Belltower had first looked at me, but it caused no pain. Only a strong urge to be away from these people. My insides felt hollow and shaky, and I suddenly wanted desperately to go back to the kitchen, to be just a girl waiting to go to the movies with my friends.

"Hello, Morgan," Hunter said finally. I noticed that he was English, too.

"Cal," I said, trying not to choke, "we have to go. The movie." It wasn't true—we had nearly half an hour before we had to go—but I couldn't stand another minute of this.

"Yes," he said, looking down at me. "Yes." He looked at Sky again. "Have a good circle."

"We will," she said.

I wanted to run out of there. In my mind I wildly pictured Sky and Cal kissing, twining together, wrestling on his bed. I hated the jealousy I felt about him: I knew all too well how destructive jealousy could be. But I couldn't help it.

"Cal?" asked Selene as we were almost at the door. "Do you have a minute?"

He nodded, then squeezed my hand. "I'll be back in a sec," he said, and walked over to his mom. I kept walking, out the door, through the great room, through the living room and into the foyer. Feeling hot and clammy, I couldn't face Jenna, Matt, Sharon, and Ethan just yet. There was a powder room down the hall from the foyer, and I locked myself in. Again and again I splashed cold water on my face and cupped my hands and drank some.

What was the matter with me? Slowly my breathing calmed, and my face, despite its lingering, faint bruises, looked pretty normal. In all of my life I had never had such a strong reaction to anyone. Ever since Cal had first come to

Widow's Vale, my life had changed with huge, sweeping movements.

Finally I felt capable of seeing the others. Opening the door, I headed down the hall to the kitchen.

But then my skin prickled. In another moment I heard voices in the hall, low, murmuring. They were unmistakable: Sky and Hunter. And they were coming toward me.

I shrank against the wall, trying to fade into the woodwork, and suddenly I heard a click and fell backward. Catching myself, I didn't fall, but gaped in surprise as I realized there was a door hidden in the hallway.

Without thinking, hearing the voices grow closer, I slipped farther into the room and closed the door with a tiny snick. I leaned against it, my heart hammering, and listened as the voices moved past, down the hall. I strained to concentrate but couldn't make out any words. Why were Sky and Hunter affecting me this way? Why did they fill me with dread?

Then they passed, their voices faded, and silence filled my ears.

I blinked and looked at my surroundings. Although I hadn't even noticed the door in the hallway, in here it was clearly outlined, and a small inset catch showed me I could get out again.

It was a study, Selene's study, I realized quickly. A large library table in front of a window was draped with a tapestry and held a display of various mortars, pestles, and pint-size cauldrons. There was a sturdy leather couch, an antique desk with a computer and printer, and tall, oak bookcases filled with thousands of volumes.

The desk lamp was on, providing an intimate light, and I found myself drifting toward the bookcases. For the moment I forgot that my friends were waiting for me, that Cal had probably returned, that we had to leave for the movie soon. It all went out of my head as I started reading titles.

20

Knowledge

September 9, 1984

The child moves inside me all the time now. It is the most magickal thing. I can feel her quicken and grow, and it is unlike any
other feeling. I sense that her powers will be strong.

Angus is after me to get married so the child will bear his name, but
something in me is reluctant. I love Angus, but I feel separate from him.
The people here think we are married already, and that is fine with me.
— M. R.

Angus just came in. He found a sigil on the fence post by our
driveway. Goddess, what evil has followed us here?

Selene Belltower had the most amazing library, and I felt I
would be content to be locked in it for the rest of my life,
just reading, reading everything. The top shelves were so
high that there were two small ladders on tracks, library ladders, that ran around the room on brass rungs.

In the dim light from the desk lamp I peered at the book spines. Some books had no titles at all, others were worn down, some were stamped in silver or gold, and some had titles that were simply written on the spine with a marker. Once or twice I saw a book whose title appeared only when I was very close: It glowed softly, like a hologram, and then disappeared when I looked again.

I knew I should go. This was obviously Selene's private place; I shouldn't be in here without her permission. But couldn't I just sneak a quick peek at a book or two first?

Did I even have time? I glanced at my watch, which read seven-twenty. We weren't leaving for the movies for almost a half hour. Surely no one would miss me in the next five minutes. I could always say I'd been in the bathroom. . . .

The room was heavy and full with magick. It was everywhere; I breathed it in as I inhaled, and it vibrated beneath my feet as I walked.

Shaking, I read book titles. One whole bookcase held what appeared to be recipe books: recipes for spells, for foods that enhance magick, for foods appropriate for various holidays. In the next case were books about spell making and rituals. Some of the books looked ancient, with thin, disintegrating covers that I was afraid to touch. Yet I longed to read their yellowed pages.

Looking around at the wealth of magick contained in the room, I thought of the Rowanwands, who were famous for hoarding their knowledge and their secrets. Could Selene Belltower be a Rowanwand? Cal had said he and his mother didn't know which clan they were from, but maybe this library was a clue. I wondered how I could get my hands on these books. Would Selene lend them to me? Could Cal bor-row them?

The books in the next case were labeled *Black Arts, Uses of Black Magick, Dark Spells,* even one called *Summoning Spirits*. It seemed dangerous to even have such books in the house, and I wondered why Selene had them. I felt a chill, and suddenly I was even less sure that I should be in the study. I turned to leave, but then I saw a narrow display case, with glass shelves lit from below. Small marble cups held handfuls of crystals and rocks of all kinds and color. I saw bloodstone, tigereye, lapis lazuli, turquoise. There were gems also, polished and cut.

It was incredible to me to have such materials at one's disposal: The idea that Selene could walk into this room and have in front of her everything she would need for almost any kind of spell—it was just amazing.

This knowledge was what I hungered for, what I knew I had to work for. My parents' dreams of my future, my old, half-formed plans to become a scientist—those thoughts seemed like smoke screens that would only hamper me in my real work: becoming as powerful a witch as I could be.

I knew I had to leave, but I couldn't tear myself away. I'll stay just five more minutes, I told myself as I moved across the room to the other bank of bookcases. Oh, the covens were here, I saw. Shelf after shelf of Books of Shadows. I took one down and opened it, feeling like a lightning bolt might strike me down at any second.

The book was heavy. I put it on the edge of Selene's desk. Inside, the pages were yellowed and tattered, almost crum-bling at my touch. It was an ancient book—one entry was dated 1502! But it was either in code or another language, and there was no way for me to decipher it. I put the book back.

I knew that I really had to get out of there and head back to the others. I started thinking of what excuse I would use for my disappearance. Would it be realistic if I said I got lost?

I moved sideways toward the door and bumped into a library ladder. Without knowing why, I climbed it. Up high, the scent of dust and old leather and decaying paper was stronger. Holding the ladder, I leaned close to the books, trying to read in the faint light. *Covens in Ancient Rome. Theories of Stonehenge. Rowanwand and Woodbane: From Prehistoric Times Till Now.*

I knew there wasn't enough time to read everything, to linger and savor and devour as I ached to. I felt tormented by the knowledge that these books were here and yet weren't mine. A raging hunger had awoken in me, a craving for information, for learning, for enlightenment.

My fingertips skimmed the book spines, lingering on ones that were harder to read. On one of the upper shelves I found a dark red unmarked book tucked between two taller, thicker books on early Scottish history. As I passed its spine my fingers tingled. I brushed them over it again, forward and back. Tingle. Grinning, I pulled it out. It was too dark to make out its title, so I climbed down the ladder and took the book closer to Selene's desk.

Under the desk lamp I carefully opened the book to its title page. *Belwicket* was written there in a beautiful, flowing script. I paused, the blood hammering in my ears. Belwicket. That was my birth mother's coven.

Turning the page, I saw on the overleaf an inscription:

This book is given to my incandescent one, my fire fairy, Bradhadair, on her fourteenth birthday. Welcome to Belwicket. With love from Mathair.

My heart stopped, and my breath turned to ice inside my lungs. Bradhadair. My mother's Wiccan name. Alyce had told me. This was her Book of Shadows. But how could it be? It had been lost after the fire, hadn't it? Could there be some other Bradhadair, some other Belwicket?

Hands shaking, I started skimming the entries. About twenty pages in, "The whole town of Ballynigel turned out for Beltane," I read silently. "I was too old to dance around the maypole, but the younger girls did it and looked lovely. I saw that Angus Bramson lurking by the bicycles, watching me like he does. I pretended not to see him. I'm only four-teen, and he's sixteen!

"Anyway, we had a lovely Beltane feast, and then Ma led us in a gorgeous circle, out by the stone cliffs. —Bradhadair."

I tried to swallow but felt I was choking. I flipped through more pages toward the end. Instead of being signed Bradhadair, these entries were signed M. R.

Those were my initials. They also stood for Maeve Riordan. My mother.

Stunned, feeling dizzy, I sank down into Selene's desk chair, which squeaked. I had tunnel vision, and my head felt too heavy for my neck. Remembering long-ago Girl Scout training, I scooted the desk chair back and put my head between my knees, trying to take deep, calming breaths.

While I hung upside down in this graceless position, trying not to faint, my mind whirled with thoughts that bombarded me so fast, I couldn't make sense of them. Maeve Riordan. This was Maeve Riordan's Book of Shadows. This book before me, the one that had spoken to me even before I touched it, had belonged to my birth mother. The birth mother who had been burned to death only sixteen years ago, in a town two hours from here.

Selene Belltower had her Book of Shadows. Why?

I straightened up. Rapidly I read passages here and there, reading the entries as my mother changed from being a girlish fourteen-year-old, newly initiated, to a teenager experiencing love, to a woman who'd lived through hell by the age of twenty-two, as she found herself pregnant with an unplanned child. Me.

My gaze blurred with hot tears, and I flipped back to the front of the book, where the entries were light, girlish, full of wonder and the joy of magick.

Of course this book was mine. Of course I would take it with me tonight. There was no doubt about that. But how had Selene Belltower come to have it in her library? And why, knowing what she knew about me, had she never mentioned it or offered it to me? Was it possible that she'd forgotten she had it?

I rubbed the tears out of my eyes and flipped through the pages, watching as my birth mother's spells became more ambitious and far-reaching, her love deeper and more compassionate.

This was my history, my background, my origin. It was all here in these handwritten pages. In this book I would discover everything there was to know about who I was and where I had come from.

I looked at my watch. It was seven forty-five. Oh my God. I'd been in here for more than twenty minutes already. And now it was time to go. The others were surely looking for me.

As hard as it was, I started to close the book. How was I going to get it out of the house?

Then the secret study door opened. A shaft of light from the hall dropped into the room, and I looked up to see Cal and Selene standing there, staring at me sitting at Selene's desk, an open book before me.

And I knew I had trespassed unforgivably.

BOOK THREE

SWEEP
Blood Witch

Blood Witch

SPEAK
Published by the Penguin Group
Penguin Group (USA) Inc., 345 Hudson Street, New York, New York 10014, U.S.A.
Penguin Group (Canada), 90 Eglinton Avenue East, Suite 700, Toronto, Ontario, Canada M4P 2Y3
(a division of Pearson Penguin Canada Inc.)
Penguin Books Ltd, 80 Strand, London WC2R 0RL, England
Penguin Ireland, 25 St Stephen's Green, Dublin 2, Ireland (a division of Penguin Books Ltd)
Penguin Group (Australia), 250 Camberwell Road, Camberwell, Victoria 3124, Australia
(a division of Pearson Australia Group Pty Ltd)
Penguin Books India Pvt Ltd, 11 Community Centre, Panchsheel Park, New Delhi - 110 017, India
Penguin Group (NZ), 67 Apollo Drive, Rosedale, North Shore 0632, New Zealand
(a division of Pearson New Zealand Ltd)
Penguin Books (South Africa) (Pty) Ltd, 24 Sturdee Avenue, Rosebank, Johannesburg 2196, South Africa

Registered Offices: Penguin Books Ltd, 80 Strand, London WC2R 0RL, England

Published by Puffin Books, a division of Penguin Young Readers Group, 2001
Published by Speak, an imprint of Penguin Group (USA) Inc., 2007
This omnibus edition published by Speak, an imprint of Penguin Group (USA) Inc., 2010

1 3 5 7 9 10 8 6 4 2

CIP DATA IS AVAILABLE

Produced by 17th Street Productions,
an Alloy company
151 West 26th Street
New York, NY 10001

17th Street Productions and associated logos
are trademarks and/or registered trademarks of Alloy, Inc.

Speak ISBN 978-0-14-240988-6
This omnibus ISBN 978-0-14-241717-1
Printed in the United States of America

With love to my circle

BLOOD WITCH

1

Secrets

May 4, 1978

Today for the first time I helped Ma cast a circle for Belwicket. In time I'll be high priestess. Then I'll be leading the circles as she does now. Already people come to me for charms and potions, and me only seventeen! Ma says it's because I have the Riordan sight, the Riordan power, like my grandma. My own ma is a very powerful witch, stronger than anyone in Belwicket. She says I'll be stronger than that yet.

And then what, I wonder. What will I do? Make our sheep healthy? Make our fields more fertile? Heal our ponies when they go lame?

I have so many questions. Why would I have such power, the power to shake mountains? My granny's Book of Shadows says that our magick is just to be used here, in this village, this place in the country, so far away from other towns and cities. Is that so? Maybe the Goddess has a purpose for me, but I cannot see it.

— Bradhadair

For a moment the name hung in the air before me, wavering like a black insect in front of my eyes. Bradhadair! Also known as my birth mother, Maeve Riordan. I was holding her Book of Shadows, started when she first joined her mother's coven, when she was fourteen. Her Wiccan name, Bradhadair, was Gaelic for "fire starter." And I was reading words she had written in her very own hand—

"Morgan?"

I glanced up, startled. And then I felt a jolt of alarm.

My boyfriend, Cal Blaire, and his mother, Selene Belltower, stood at the entrance of the secret library. Their bodies were backlit by a shaft of light from the hall. Their faces were blank masks, hidden in shadow.

My breath caught in my throat. I had entered this room without permission. Not only had I kept Cal and our other friends waiting, I had trespassed in a private area of Selene's house. I had no business being in this room, reading these books. This I knew. A hot flush of shame made my face burn.

But I couldn't help myself. I was desperate for more knowledge—about Wicca, about my birth mother. After all, I'd only recently uncovered extraordinary secrets: that I'd been adopted; that my birth mother, a powerful witch, had been murdered, burned to death in a barn. But so many questions still remained unanswered. And now I had found Maeve Riordan's Book of Shadows: her private book of spells, thoughts, and dreams. The key to her innermost life. If the answers I sought were anywhere, they were in this book. Subconsciously—in spite of my guilt—my hands tightened around it.

"Morgan?" Cal repeated. "What are you doing in here? I've been looking all over for you."

"I'm sorry," I said, the words rushing out. I looked around, wondering how I could explain being in this place. "Uh—"

"The others went on to the movie," Cal interrupted. His voice hardened. "I told them we'd try to catch up with them, but it's too late now."

I glanced at my watch. Eight o'clock. The movie theater was at least a twenty-minute drive from here, and the movie started at eight-fifteen. I swallowed. "I'm really sorry," I said. "I just—"

"Morgan," Selene said. She stepped farther into the room. For the first time I saw tense lines on her youthful face, so like Cal's. "This is my private retreat. No one is allowed in here except me."

Now I was nervous. Her voice was calm, but I sensed the leashed anger underneath. Was I in real trouble? I stood up at her desk and closed the book. "I—I know I shouldn't be in here, and I didn't mean to intrude. But I was walking along the hall, and then suddenly I just fell against this door, and it opened. Once I was inside, I couldn't stop looking at everything. It's the most amazing library. . . ." My voice trailed off.

Selene and Cal gazed at me. I couldn't read their eyes, nor could I get any sense of what was going through their minds, and that made me even more nervous. I wasn't lying, but I hadn't told them the whole story, either. I had also been trying to avoid Sky Eventide and Hunter Niall, two English witches who were here tonight to take part in one of Selene's circles. For some reason, these two guests of Selene's filled me with inexplicable dread. When I'd heard them coming along the hall, I had tried to avoid them—and had ended up stumbling into this secret library. It had been an accident.

That's right, I thought. It *had* been an accident. Nothing to be ashamed of. Besides, I wasn't the only one who had some explaining to do. I had a few questions for Selene.

"This is Maeve Riordan's Book of Shadows," I found myself saying. My voice sounded loud, harsh in my ears. "Why do you have it? And why didn't you tell me you had it? You both know I've been trying to find out about her. I mean . . . don't you think I'd want to see something that belonged to her?"

Cal seemed surprised. He glanced at his mother.

Selene reached behind her and shut the door, closing us all inside the secret room. No one walking down the hall would ever notice the door's almost invisible line. Her beautiful eyebrows arched as she came closer to me.

"I know you've been trying to find out about your mother," she said. In the golden halo of the lamplight her expression seemed to soften. She glanced at the book. "How much have you read?"

"Not a lot." I chewed my lip anxiously.

"Have you come across anything surprising?"

"Not really," I said, watching her.

"Well, a Book of Shadows is a very personal thing," Selene said. "Secrets are revealed there, unexpected things. I was waiting to tell you about it because I know what it contains, and I wasn't sure you were ready to read it." Her voice fell to a whisper. "I'm not sure you're ready now, but it's too late."

My face tightened. Maybe I had been violating a private area of her house, but I had a right to know about my mother. "But it's not really your decision to make," I argued. "I mean, she was *my* mother. Her Book of Shadows should be mine. That's what you're supposed to do with Books of Shadows, pass them down to your children. It *is* mine."

Selene blinked at my strong words. She glanced at Cal again, but he was looking at me. Once more my fingers tingled as they traced the book's worn leather cover.

"So why do you have it?" I repeated.

"I got it by accident," Selene said. A fleeting smile crossed her face. "Though of course most witches don't believe in accidents. My hobby is collecting Books of Shadows—really, I collect almost any book having to do with witchcraft, as you can see." She waved an elegant hand at the shelves in the room. "I work with several dealers, mostly in Europe, who have standing orders to send me whatever books they have of interest—any Book of Shadows, no matter what its condition. I find them fascinating. I take them with me wherever we go and set them up in a private study, as I did here when we moved in this past summer. To me, they're a window into the human side of the craft. They're diaries, records of experiments; they're people's histories. I have over two hundred Books of Shadows, and Maeve Riordan's is just one of them."

I waited for her to elaborate, but she didn't. Her response sounded strangely voyeuristic—especially from a high priestess, someone who was otherwise so in touch with people's feelings. Why couldn't she see that Maeve Riordan's book wasn't just another Book of Shadows? At least not to me.

My initial guilt and nervousness were giving way to anger. Selene had read my mother's private words. But right then Cal stepped across the room and put his hand on my shoulder, rubbing gently. He seemed to be saying he was on my side, that he understood. So why couldn't his mother? Did she think I was too much of a child to handle my mother's secrets?

"Where did you get *this* Book of Shadows?" I asked insistently.

"From a dealer in Manhattan," Selene said. Once again her tone was impossible to read. "He had acquired it from someone else—someone who had no credentials, who may have stolen it or found it in a secondhand store somewhere." She shrugged. "I bought it about ten or eleven years ago, sight unseen. When I opened it, I realized it was by the same young witch who I'd read about dying in a fire, not far from here. It's a special Book of Shadows, and not just because it's Maeve's."

"I'm going to take it home," I said boldly, surprising myself again.

For a long moment silence hung thick in the air. Again my heart started to race. I'd never challenged Cal's mother before; I hardly ever challenged adults at all . . . and she was a powerful witch. Cal's eyes flashed between the two of us.

"Of course, my dear," Selene finally said. "It's yours."

I let my breath out silently. Selene added, "After Cal told me your story, I knew one day I would give it to you. If, after you read it, you have any questions or concerns, I hope you'll come and talk to me."

I nodded. "Thanks," I mumbled. I turned to Cal. "You know, I really just want to go home now." My voice was shaky.

"Okay," Cal said. "I'll drive you. Let's get our coats."

Selene stepped aside to let us pass. She remained in the study, probably to look around at what else I had touched or examined. Not that I could blame her. I didn't know what to feel. I hadn't meant to abuse her trust, but there was no denying the reward: I now possessed an intimate record of my birth mother's life, written in her hand. No matter what mysteries lay inside, I knew I could handle them. I *had* to handle them.

Cal squeezed my shoulder as we walked down the hall, reassuring me.

Outside, the November wind whipped through my hair, and I brushed it out of my face. Cal opened his car and I climbed in, shivering against the cold leather seats and pushing my hands deep inside my pockets. The Book of Shadows was zipped up inside my jacket, next to my chest.

"The heater will warm things up in a minute," Cal said. He turned the key and punched buttons on the dash. His handsome face was just a silhouette in the dark of night. Then he turned to me and brushed his hand, surprisingly warm, against my cheek. "Are you okay?" he asked.

I nodded, but I wasn't sure. I was grateful for his concern, yet I was all wrapped up in the mystery of the book and still uneasy about what had just happened with Selene.

"I wasn't trying to spy or sneak around," I told him. The words were true, but they sounded even less convincing the second time around.

He glanced at me again as he turned the Explorer onto the main road. "That door is spelled shut," he said thoughtfully. "I still have to get Mom's permission to go in—I've never been able to open the door by myself. And believe me, I've tried." His grin was a white flash in the darkness.

"But that's weird," I said, frowning. "I mean, I didn't even try to open the door—it just popped open, and I almost fell down."

Cal didn't respond. He concentrated on the road. Maybe

he was trying to figure out how I had gotten in there, wondering if I'd used magick. But I hadn't, at least not consciously. Maybe I had been destined to find my way into that study, to find my mother's book.

Snow had started to fall, and now it brushed against the windshield, not sticking anywhere. It would be gone by morning. I couldn't wait to get home, to run upstairs to my room and start reading. For some reason, my thoughts turned to Sky Eventide and Hunter Niall. I had instantly disliked both of them: their piercing gazes, their snotty English accents, the way they looked at Cal and at me.

But why? Who were they? Why did they seem so important? I'd seen Sky only once before, in the cemetery a few days ago. And Hunter—Hunter upset me in a way I couldn't explain. I was still thinking about it when Cal pulled into my driveway and switched off the engine.

"Are your folks home?" he asked.

I nodded.

"Are you okay? Do you want me to come in?"

"That's all right," I said, appreciating his offer. "I think I'll just hole up and read."

"Okay. Listen, I'll be home all night. Just call me if you want to talk."

"Thanks," I said, reaching for him.

He came into my arms, and we kissed for a few moments. The sweetness momentarily washed away any confusion and uncertainty I was feeling about my encounter with Selene. Finally, reluctantly, I untangled myself and opened the car door.

"Thanks," I said again. "I'll call you."

"Okay. Take care." He gave me a smile and didn't leave until I was inside.

"Hi!" I called. "I'm home."

My parents were watching a movie in the family room. "You're early," said Mom, looking at the clock.

I shrugged. "We missed the movie," I explained. "And I just decided to come home. Well, I'll be upstairs." I fled up to my room, ditched my coat, and flopped down on my bed. Then I pulled out a *Scientific American* magazine and got it ready in case I suddenly needed to cover the Book of Shadows. My parents and I had reached an uneasy truce—about Wicca, about my birth mother, about all the deception. It was best not to disturb that. I didn't want to have to explain anything painful to them.

Maeve Riordan's own words, I thought.

My hands trembling, I opened my mother's Book of Shadows and began to read.

2

Picketts Road

What to write? The pressure inside me is building until my head pounds. Until recently I've always wanted to do what I needed to do. Now for the first time these two paths are diverging. She is blooming like an orchid: transforming from a plain plant into something crushingly beautiful, a blossom that cries out to be picked.

But now, somehow, the thought bothers me. I know it's right, it's necessary, it's expected. And I know I'll do it, but they keep hounding me. Nothing is turning out the way I had envisioned. I need more time to tie her to me, to join with her mentally, emotionally, so she'll see through my eyes. I even find myself liking the idea of joining with her. I'll bet the Goddess is laughing at me.

As to craft, I've found a variant reading of Hellorus that describes how sitting beneath an oak can bend the will of Eolh. I want to try it soon.

—Sgàth

Saturday morning I didn't exactly leap out of bed. I'd been up until the wee hours, reading Maeve's Book of Shadows. She'd started it when she was fourteen years old. So far, I couldn't figure out what Selene meant about finding out something upsetting. Aside from unpronounceable Gaelic words and lots of spells and recipes, I hadn't found anything really disturbing or strange. I knew that Maeve Riordan and Angus Bramson, my birth parents, were burned to death after they came to America. I just didn't know why. Maybe this book would explain it somehow. But I was reading slowly. I wanted to savor every word.

When I finally woke up and groped my way downstairs, my eyes were slits. I stumbled toward the refrigerator for a Diet Coke.

I was working on a couple of Pop-Tarts when Mom and Mary K. breezed in, having taken a brisk mother-daughter walk in the chill November air.

"Wow!" said Mom, her nose pink. She clapped her gloved hands. "It's nippy outside!" She came over and gave me a kiss, and I flinched as her icy hair brushed against my face.

"It's pretty, though," Mary K. added. "The snow is just starting to melt, and all the squirrels and birds are on the ground, looking for something to eat."

I rolled my eyes. Some people are just too cheerful in the morning. It isn't natural.

"Speaking of something to eat," Mom said, taking off her gloves and sitting down across from me, "can you two hit the grocery store this morning? I'm showing a house at ten-thirty, and we're out of almost everything."

Mentally I reviewed my blank calendar. "Sure," I said. "Got a list?"

Mom plucked it off the fridge and started adding items to it. Mary K. put the last bagel in the toaster. The phone rang, and she whirled to get it.

Cal, I thought, my heart picking up a beat. Happiness washed over me.

"Hello?" answered Mary K., sounding perky and breathless at the same time. "Oh, hi. Yeah, she's here. Just a sec."

She handed the phone to me, mouthing, "Cal."

I knew it. Ever since I'd discovered Wicca, since I'd discovered Cal, I'd always been able to tell who was calling. "Hi," I said into the phone.

"How are you?" he asked. "Did you stay up all night, reading?"

He knew me. "Yes . . . I want to talk to you about it," I said. I was very aware of my mother and Mary K. sitting right there, especially since Mary K. was patting her heart and making swooning gestures at me. I frowned.

"Good—I'd like that," Cal said. "Want to drive up to Practical Magick this afternoon?"

Practical Magick was a Wicca store in the nearby town of Red Kill, and one of my favorite places to spend a spare hour or two. "I'd love to," I said. My frown melted into a smile. All my senses were waking up.

"I'll come get you. Say, one-thirty?"

"Okay. See you then."

I hung up the phone. My mom lowered the newspaper and looked at me over her reading glasses.

"What?" I said self-consciously, a big grin on my face.

"Everything going all right with Cal?" she asked.

"Uh-huh," I said. I could feel my cheeks reddening. It felt weird to talk to my parents about my boyfriend—especially since he was the one who had introduced me to Wicca. I'd always been able to discuss my life with Mom and Dad, but Wicca was a part of it they wanted gone, forever. It had created a wall between us.

"Cal seems nice," Mom said brightly, trying to put me at ease and fish for information at the same time. "He's certainly good-looking."

"Um . . . yeah, he's really nice. Let me go take a shower," I mumbled, standing up. "Then we'll go to the store."

I fled.

"Okay, first stop, coffee shop," Mary K. directed a half hour later. She folded Mom's grocery list and stuck it in her coat pocket.

I wheeled Das Boot—my massive, submarine-like old car—into the parking lot of the small strip mall that boasted Widow's Vale's one and only coffee emporium. We dashed from the car to the café, where it smelled like coffee and pastry. I looked at the board and tried to decide between a grande latte or a grande today's special. Mary K. leaned over the glass case, gazing longingly at the bear claws. I checked my cash.

"Get one if you want," I said. "My treat. Get me one, too."

My sister flashed me a smile, and I thought again that she looked so much older than fourteen. Some fourteen-year-olds are so gawky: half formed, childlike. Mary K. wasn't. She was savvy and mature. For the first time in a long while, it occurred to me that I was lucky to have her as my sister, even if we didn't share the same blood.

The door swung open, bells jangling. Bakker Blackburn came in, followed by his older brother, Roger, who had been a senior at Widow's Vale High last year and was now at Vassar. My insides clenched. Mary K. glanced up, eyes wide. She looked away quickly.

"Hey, Mary K., Morgan," Bakker mumbled, avoiding my gaze. He probably hated me. About a week earlier, I'd kicked him out of our house in no uncertain terms when I'd found him pinning Mary K. down on her bed, practically raping her. He also probably thought I was an alien, since those terms had included hitting him with a ball of crackly blue witch fire—without even meaning to. I still didn't know how I'd done it. My own power constantly surprised me.

Mary K. nodded at Bakker. She clearly didn't know what to say.

"Hey, Roger," I said. He was two years older than me, but Widow's Vale is a small town, and we all pretty much know each other. "How's it going?"

Roger shrugged. "Not bad."

Bakker's eyes remained glued to Mary K.

"We'd better go," I stated, heading toward the exit.

Mary K. nodded, but she took her time following me out the door. Maybe she secretly wanted to see if Bakker would say anything. Sure enough, he approached her.

"Mary K.," he began pleadingly.

She looked at him but turned and caught up to me without a word. I was relieved. I knew he'd been groveling hard since the Incident, and I could tell that Mary K. was weakening. I was afraid that if I spoke too harshly, it might drive her back to him. So I kept my mouth shut. But I had promised myself that if I got the slightest inkling of his forcing himself on her again, I would tell my parents, his parents, and everyone I knew.

And Mary K. would probably never forgive me, I thought as we got into the car.

I started Das Boot's engine and pulled out onto the street. Thinking about Mary K.'s love life made me think about my own. I started to smile and couldn't stop. Was Cal my *mùirn beatha dàn*—the Wiccan term for soul mate, life partner? He seemed to believe so. The possibility sent a shiver down my spine.

At the grocery store we stocked up on Pop-Tarts and other necessities. In the snacks aisle I lifted twelve-packs of Diet Coke into the cart while Mary K. piled bags of pretzels and chips on top. Farther down the shelf were boxes of Fudge Therapy, Bree's favorite junk food.

Bree. My former best friend.

I swallowed. How many times had Bree and I smuggled boxes of Fudge Therapy into a movie theater? How many boxes had we consumed during sleepovers as we lay in the dark, spilling our secrets to each other? It still seemed bizarre that we were enemies, that our friendship had broken up because she had wanted Cal and he had wanted me. In the past few weeks I had wished again and again that I could talk to her about all that I'd learned. Bree didn't even know I was adopted. She still thought I was a Rowlands by birth, like Mary K. But Bree was being such a bitch to me now, and I was being cold to her. Oh, well. For now, there was nothing I could do about it. It seemed best not to dwell on what I couldn't change.

Mary K. and I checked out and loaded up the car. I stifled a yawn as we climbed back in. The gray, cheerless weather seemed to sap my energy. I wanted to go home and nap before Cal came over.

"Let's go down Picketts Road," said Mary K., adjusting the car's heater vents to blow right on her. "It's so pretty, even if it takes longer."

"Picketts Road it is," I said, taking the turn. I preferred this route, too: it was hilly and winding, and there weren't many houses. People kept horses back here, and though most of the trees were now bare, colorful leaves still littered the ground, like the patterns on an Oriental carpet.

Up ahead were two cars parked by the side of the road. My eyes narrowed. I recognized them as Matt Adler's white jeep and Raven Meltzer's beat-up black Peugeot . . . parked right next to each other on a road few people used. That was odd. I hadn't even realized that they spoke to each other. I looked around but didn't see either one of them.

"Interesting," I muttered.

"What?" said my sister, fiddling with the radio dial.

"That was Matt Adler's jeep and Raven Meltzer's Peugeot," I said.

"So?"

"They're not even friends," I said, shrugging. "What are their cars doing out here?"

Mary K. pursed her lips. "Gosh, maybe they killed someone and are burying the body," she said sarcastically.

I smirked at her. "It's just kind of unusual, that's all. I mean, Matt is Jenna's boyfriend, and Raven . . ." *Raven doesn't care if a guy is someone's boyfriend,* I finished silently. *Raven just liked to get guys, chew them up, and spit them out.*

"Yeah, but they both do this Wicca stuff with you, right?" said Mary K., flipping down the sun visor mirror to check her appearance. It was pretty obvious that she didn't want to look me in the eye. She'd made it very clear that she disapproved of "this Wicca stuff," as she liked to call it.

"But Raven's not in our coven," I said. "She and Bree started their own coven."

"Because you and Bree aren't talking anymore?" she asked pointedly, still looking in the mirror.

I bit my lip. I still hadn't explained very much about Bree and Cal to my family. They had noticed, of course, that Bree and I weren't hanging out and that Bree wasn't calling the house nine times a day. But I'd mumbled something about Bree being busy with a new boyfriend, and no one had called me on it till now.

"That's part of it," I said with a sigh. "She thought she was in love with Cal. But he wanted to be with me. So Bree decided the hell with me." It hurt to say it out loud.

"And you chose Cal," my sister said, but her tone was forgiving.

I shook my head. "It's not like I chose Cal *over* her. Actually, she chose him over me first. Besides, I didn't tell Bree she had to get out of my life or anything. I still wanted to be friends."

Mary K. flipped the visor back up. "Even though she loved your boyfriend."

"She *thought* she loved him," I said, getting prickly. "She didn't even know him, though. She still doesn't. Anyway, you know how she is about guys. She likes the thrill of the chase and the conquest much more than any long-term thing. Use them and lose them. And Cal didn't want to be with her." I sighed again. "It's complicated."

Mary K. shrugged.

"You think I shouldn't go out with Cal just because Bree

wanted him?" I asked. My knuckles whitened on the steering wheel.

"No, not exactly," said Mary K. "It's just, I feel kind of sorry for Bree. She lost you *and* Cal."

I sniffed. "Well, she's being a total bitch to me now," I muttered, forgetting how much I had been missing Bree just minutes ago. "So she obviously isn't all broken up about it."

Mary K. stared out the window. "Maybe being a bitch is just how Bree acts sad," she murmured absently, watching the barren trees pass. "If you were my best friend for about twelve years and you left me for a guy you just met, maybe I would be a bitch, too."

I didn't answer. Just stay out of it, I thought. Like my fourteen-year-old sister knew anything. She'd allowed herself to get involved with a sleazebag like Bakker, after all.

But deep down, I wondered if I was irritated because Mary K. was right.

3

Woodbane

Litha, 1998

This is the time of year when I am most sad. Sad and angry. One of the last circles that I did with my mum and dad was for Beltane, eight years ago. I was eight, Linden was six, and Alwyn was only four. I remember the three of us sitting with the other kids, sons and daughters of the coven's members. The warmth of May was trying to steal in and banish April's cold, dreary wetness. Around our maypole the grown-ups were laughing and drinking wine. We kids danced, weaving our ribbons in and out of one another, gathering magick to us in a pastel net.

I felt the magick inside me, inside everything. I was so impatient. I didn't know how I'd ever make it till I was fourteen, when I could be initiated as a full witch. I remember the sunset glowing on Mum's hair, and she and Dad held each other, kissing, while the others laughed. The other kids and I groaned and covered our faces. But we were only pretending to be embarrassed. Inside, our spirits were dancing. The air was full of life, and everything was glowing and swelling with light and wonder and happiness.

And before Litha, seven weeks later, Mum was gone, Dad was gone—vanished, without a trace, without a word to us, their children. And my life changed forever. My spirit shriveled, shrank, twisted.

Now I'm a witch and almost full-grown. Yet inside, my spirit is still a mean, twisted thing. And even though I have since learned the truth, I am still angry—in some ways, more than I have ever been. Will it always be that way? Maybe only the Goddess knows.
—Giomanach

After lunch I was in my room, twisting my long hair into a braid, when I felt Cal's presence. A smile spread across my face. I focused my senses and felt my parents in the living room, my sister in the bathroom—and then Cal, coming closer, tickling my nerves as he approached. By the time I snapped an elastic around my braid, he was ringing the doorbell. I dashed from my room and down the stairs.

Mom answered the door.

"Hello, Cal," she said. She'd met him once before, when he'd come to visit after Bree had practically broken my nose with a volleyball during gym. I could feel her giving him the standard maternal up-and-down as he stood there.

"Hi, Mrs. Rowlands," Cal replied easily, smiling. "Is Morgan—oh, there she is." Our eyes met, and we grinned foolishly at each other. I couldn't hide the pleasure that I took in seeing him, not even from my mom.

"Will you be back for dinner?" Mom asked, unable to resist giving me a quick kiss.

"Yes," I said. "And then I'm going to Jenna's tonight."

"Okay." Mom took a deep breath, then smiled at Cal again. "Have a good time."

I knew that she was trying hard not to ask Cal to drive safely, and to her credit, she managed it. I waved good-bye and hurried out to Cal's car.

He climbed in and started the engine. "Still want to go to Practical Magick?" he asked.

"Yes." I settled back in my seat. My thoughts instantly turned to the night before, to finding Maeve's Book of Shadows.

As soon as we were out of eyesight of my house, Cal pulled the car over and reached across to kiss me. I moved as close to him as I could in the bucket seats and held him tightly. It was so strange: I had always counted on Bree and my family for grounding, for support. But now Bree was out of my life, and my family and I were still coming to terms with the fact that I was adopted. If it weren't for Cal . . . well, it seemed best not to think of that.

"Are you okay?" he asked, pulling back to kiss my face again. "No worries with the BOS?"

"Not yet," I told him, shaking my head. "It's really amaz- ing, though. I'm learning so much." I paused. "Your mom isn't mad I took it, is she?"

"No. She knows it's yours. She should have told you about it." He smiled ruefully. "It's just—I don't know. Mom is used to being in charge, you know? She leads her coven. She's a high priestess. She's always helping people solve problems, helping them with stuff. So sometimes she acts like she's got to protect the whole world. Whether they want her to or not."

I nodded, trying to understand. "Yeah. I can see that. I guess I just felt that it wasn't really her business, you know? Or maybe it could be, but it should be my business first."

There was a flash of faint surprise in Cal's eyes, and he gave a dry laugh. "You're funny," he said. "Usually people are swarming all over my mom. Everyone is so impressed with her power, her strength. They blurt out all their problems and tell her everything, and they want to be as close to her as possible. She's not used to people challenging her."

"But I like her a lot," I said, worried that I'd sounded too harsh. "I mean, I—"

"No, it's okay," he interrupted, nodding. "It's refreshing. You want to stand on your own two feet, do things yourself. You're your own person. It makes you interesting."

I didn't know what to say. I blushed slightly.

Cal pulled my braid out from underneath my coat. "I love your hair," he murmured, watching the braid run through his fingers. "Witch hair." Then he gave me a lopsided grin and shifted the car into gear.

Now I knew my face must be bright red. But I sat back, feeling happy and strong and unsure all at once. My eyes wandered out the window as we drove. The clouds had darkened, moving sluggishly across the sky as if trying to decide when to start dumping snow. By the time we reached Red Kill, they let loose with big, wet flakes that stuck to everything in clumps.

"Here we go," said Cal, turning on his windshield wipers. "Welcome to winter."

I smiled. Somehow the falling snow and thumping wipers

made the silence inside the car even more peaceful. I was so glad to be here right now, in this moment, with Cal. I felt like I could tackle anything.

"You know, there's something I meant to tell you before," I said. "The other day I followed Bree because I wanted to have it out with her once and for all."

Cal glanced over at me. "Really?"

I nodded. "Yeah—but it didn't end up that way. Instead I saw her and Raven meeting Sky Eventide."

His hand darted away, and he shot another quick glance at me. His brow was furrowed. "Sky?"

"Yeah, the blond witch I met last night at your mom's." The really good-looking one, I thought with an odd pang of jealousy. Even though I knew Cal loved me, that he had *chosen* me, I still felt insecure, especially when we were around pretty girls. It was just that he was so handsome, with his golden eyes and tall frame and perfect body. And I . . . well, I wasn't so perfect. A flat-chested girl with a big nose could hardly be called perfect.

"Anyway, I saw Sky with Bree and Raven," I continued, shoving my insecurities aside. "I bet she's the blood witch they have in their coven."

"Hmmm," said Cal. He gazed forward at the road, as if thinking intently. "Really. Yeah, I guess it's possible."

"Is she . . . bad?" I asked, for lack of a better term. "I mean, I feel like you dislike her and Hunter, too. Are they, I don't know, from the dark side?" I stumbled over the words. They sounded so melodramatic.

Cal laughed, startled. "Dark side? You've been watching too many movies. There's no dark side to Wicca. It's just a big circle. Everything magickal is part of that circle. You, me, the world, Hunter, Sky, everything. We're all connected."

I frowned. It seemed a strange thing to say, considering the way he'd glared at Hunter and Sky. "Last night you guys seemed not to like each other," I persisted.

Cal shrugged. He turned onto Red Kill's main street and cruised slowly, looking for a parking spot. After a few moments' silence he finally said, "Sometimes you just meet people who rub you the wrong way. I met Hunter a couple of years ago, and . . . we just can't stand each other." He laughed as if it were no big deal. "Everything about him pisses me off, and it's mutual. That doesn't sound very witchy, I know. But I don't trust him."

"What do you mean? Trust him as a person or a witch?"

Cal parked the car at an angle and turned off the engine. "There isn't a difference," he muttered. His expression was distant.

"What about the big circle?" I asked, unable to help myself. "If you're connected, then how can he piss you off so much?"

"It's just . . . ," he began, then shook his head. "Forget it. Let's talk about something else." He opened his door and stepped out into snowfall.

I opened my mouth, then closed it. Pursuing the conversation seemed important. After all, Hunter and Sky had both had a profound effect on me, and I couldn't figure out why. But if Cal wanted to leave it alone, I could respect that. There were things I didn't want to talk about with him, either. I hopped out of the car and slammed the door behind me, then ran to catch up with him.

"It's too bad you don't have anything else of your mom's," Cal remarked as we walked toward the cozy little shop. We both buried our faces in our coats to protect ourselves from the cold. "Like the coven's tools, its athame, or wand, or maybe your mom's robe. Those things would be great to have."

"Yeah," I agreed. "But I guess all that stuff's long gone by now."

Cal swung open Practical Magick's heavy glass door, and I ducked inside. Warm air wafted over us, rich with the scent of herbs. We stamped the snow off our shoes, and I took off my gloves. I smiled. Automatically I started scanning book titles on the shelves. I loved this store. I could stay here and read all day. I glanced at Cal. He was already reading book spines, too.

Alyce and David, the two store clerks, were both in the back, talking quietly to customers. My eyes immediately flashed from David—with his short gray hair, his unusually youthful face, and his piercing dark eyes—to Alyce. I'd felt a connection with Alyce the first time I had met her. It was Alyce who had told me the story of my birth mother, how her coven had been completely destroyed. From Alyce, I'd learned that Maeve and my father had fled for America and settled in Meshomah Falls, a town about two hours from here. In America they had renounced magick and witchcraft and lived quietly by themselves. Then, about seven months after I was born, they gave me up for adoption. Soon after that they had been locked in a barn, and the barn was set on fire.

"Have you read this?" Cal asked, breaking into my thoughts. He reached for a book on a shelf near the register. Its title was *Gardens of the Craft.* "My mom has a copy of it. She uses it a lot."

"Really?" I took it from him, intrigued. I hadn't remembered seeing it in Selene's library. Then again, there had been hundreds of books. "Oh, this is incredible," I murmured, flipping through the pages. It was all about laying out an herb garden to maximize its potential, to get the most out of healing plants and plants for spells. "This is exactly what I want to do—"

I broke off. At the very back of the book there was a chapter titled "Spells to Cross Foes." An unpleasant tingling sensation crept across my neck. What did that mean, exactly? Could the plants' magick be used to harm people? It didn't seem right somehow. On the other hand, maybe a witch needed to know about the negative possibilities of herbal magick—in order to guard against them. Yes. Maybe that knowledge was a crucial part of the big circle of Wicca that Cal had mentioned only moments ago.

Gently Cal took the book from me and tucked it under his arm. "I'll get it for you," he said, kissing me. "As a pre-birthday present."

I nodded, feeling my concerns evaporate in a wash of pleasure. My seventeenth birthday was still eight days away. I was surprised and thrilled that Cal was thinking about it already.

We started walking through the store. I'd never been here with Cal, and he showed me hidden treasures I'd never noticed before. First we looked at candles. Each color of candle had different properties, and Cal told me about which ones were used in which rituals. My mind whirled with all of the names. There was so much to learn. Next we examined sets of small bowls. Wiccans used them to hold salt or other ritual substances, like water or incense. Cal told me that when he lived in California, he and Selene had spent a whole summer gathering ocean water and evaporating it for the salt. They saved the salt and used it to purify their circles for almost a year afterward.

After that we saw brass bells that helped charge energy fields during a circle, and Cal pointed out magickally charged twine and thread and ink. These were everyday objects, but they had been transformed. Like me, I thought. I almost laughed aloud with pleasure. Magick was in everything, and a truly knowledgeable witch could use literally anything to imbue spells with power. I'd had glimpses of this knowledge before, but with Cal here—really showing it to me—it seemed more real, more accessible, and infinitely more exciting than it ever had before.

And everywhere there were books: on runes, on how the positions of the stars affected one's spells, on the healing uses of magic, on how to increase one's power. Cal pointed out several he thought I should read but said he had copies and would lend them to me.

"Do you have a magickal robe yet?" he suddenly asked. He gestured to one on a rack near the rear of the store. It was made of deep blue silk that flowed like water.

I shook my head.

"I think that by Imbolc we should start using robes in our circles," he said. "I'll speak to the others about it. Robes are usually better than street clothes for making magick: you wear them only when you're doing magick, so they don't get contaminated with the jangled vibrations of the rest of your life. And they're comfortable, practical."

I nodded, brushing my hand against the fabric of the different robes. The variety was astounding. Some were plain; some were painted or sewn with magickal symbols and runes. But I didn't see any that I felt I absolutely had to have, though they were all beautiful. That was okay, though; Imbolc wasn't until the end of January. I had plenty of time to find one.

"Do you wear a robe?" I asked.

"Uh-huh," he said. "Whenever I do a circle with my mom or by myself. Mine is white, a really heavy linen. I've had it a couple of years. I sort of wish I could wear it all the time," he added with a grin. "But I don't think the people of Widow's Vale are ready for that."

I laughed, picturing him casually walking into Schweik-hardt's drugstore in a long, white robe.

"Sometimes robes are passed down from generation to generation," Cal continued. "Like tools. Or sometimes people weave the cloth and sew them themselves. It's like anything else—the more thought and energy you put into something, the more it stores up magickal energy and the more it can help you focus when you do spells."

I was beginning to understand that, although I knew I would spend a lot of time meditating on how I could start applying it to my own magickal doings.

Cal stepped across the aisle and reached for something on an upper shelf. It was an athame: a ceremonial dagger, about ten inches long. The blade was made of silver, so brightly polished, it looked like a mirror. Its handle was carved with silver roses. There was a skull joining the handle and the blade together.

"It's beautiful, isn't it?" Cal murmured.

"Why does it have a skull on it?" I asked.

"To remind us that in life, there is always death," he said

quietly, turning it in his fingers. "There is darkness in light, there is pain in joy, and there are thorns on the rose." He sounded solemn and thoughtful, and I shivered.

Then he glanced up at me. "Maybe a certain lucky some-one will get it for her birthday."

I wiggled my eyebrows, looking hopeful, and he laughed.

It was getting late, and I had to get home. Cal checked out, buying some green candles, some incense, and the book on gardening for me. I felt Alyce's eyes on me.

"Nothing for you?" she asked in her gentle way.

I shook my head.

She hesitated, then cast a quick glance at Cal. "I have something I think you should read," she said to me. Moving with surprising grace for a short, round person, she left the counter and walked down the aisle of books. I shrugged at Cal—and then Alyce was back, her lavender skirts swishing. She handed me a plain, dark brown book.

"*Woodbane, Fact and Fiction,*" I read aloud. A chill shot through my body. The Woodbanes were the darkest of the seven ancient Wiccan clans, notorious for their quest for power at any cost. The evil ones. I looked at her, baffled. "Why should I read this?" I asked.

Alyce met my gaze squarely. "It's an interesting book that debunks many of the myths surrounding the Woodbanes," she said, ringing it up. "It's useful for any student of the craft."

I didn't know what to say, but I pulled out my wallet and counted out money, pushing the bills across the counter. I trusted Alyce. If she thought I should read this, I would. But at the same time I was aware of tension tightening Cal's body. He wasn't angry, but he seemed hyperalert, watching

Alyce, watching me, measuring everything. I put my arm around his waist and gave him a reassuring squeeze.

He smiled.

"Good-bye, Alyce," I said. "Thanks."

"My pleasure," she replied. "Good-bye, Morgan. Good-bye, Cal."

I held my two new books under my arm as we walked to the door—one book I wanted to read, one I didn't. Yet I would read them both. Although I had been studying witch-craft for barely two months, I had already learned a valuable lesson: Everything had two sides. I had to take the good with the bad, the fun with the discomfort, the excitement with the fear. The thorns with the rose.

Cal pushed open the door, and the bells jingled.

He stopped so suddenly that I walked right into his back.

"Oof," I said, steadying myself. I peeked around him.

That was when I saw what had made him pause.

It was Hunter Niall, crouched in the street, looking under Cal's car.

4

Spell

Litha, 1990

I'm frightened. I woke up this morning to the sound of weeping. Alwyn and Linden were in my room. They were crying because they could not find Mum and Dad. I was angry and told them that they weren't babies anymore. I said Mum and Dad would be back soon. I thought they must have run to town for something we needed.

But night has fallen and we are still alone. I've heard no word from our neighbors, none from Mum and Dad's coven. I went to Siobhan's house, and to Caradog Owens's house over in Grasmere, to ask if they knew where Mum and Dad were. But there was no one home.

And there's something else. When I was making my bed I found Dad's lueg under my pillow—the stone he uses to scry with. How did it get there? He always keeps it safe with the rest of his magickal tools. He never even let me touch it before. So how did it get under my pillow? I have a bad feeling....

Dad has often told me that when he and Mum are on their errands, I am master of the house. It is my job to watch over my brother and sister. But I am not a man like him. I am only eight years old. I won't be a witch for many years yet. What can I do if there is trouble?

What if something happened to them? They have never left us alone like this. Did someone take them away? Are they being held prisoner somewhere?

I must sleep, but I can't. Alwyn and Linden can sleep for me. I must be strong for them.

Mum and Dad will come back to us soon. They will. I know it.

Goddess, bring them home.

—Giomanach

As if he sensed our approach, Hunter stood quickly. His green eyes were puffy and bloodshot. His face was pale from the cold, and snowflakes had settled on his hat. But aside from the redness of his eyes, he looked like he was carved of marble—still and somehow dangerous. Why was he looking under the car? More important, why did I find him so threatening? I didn't know the answers, but I knew that as a blood witch, I should trust my instincts. I shuddered inside my coat.

"What are you doing, Niall?" Cal demanded. His voice was so low and steady that I hardly recognized it. I looked at him and saw that his jaw was tight. His hands were clenched at his sides.

"Just admiring your big American car," Hunter said. He sniffed, then pulled a handkerchief from his pocket. He must have a cold, I thought. I wondered how long he'd been out here in the snow.

Cal flicked his gaze to the Explorer, sweeping it from

bumper to bumper, as if scanning for something out of place.

"Hello, Morgan," Hunter murmured. With his sickly nasal voice the greeting sounded like an insult. "Interesting company you keep."

The falling snowflakes were cold against my hot skin.

I shifted my books to my other arm and gazed at Hunter, confused. Why should he care?

Hunter stepped onto the sidewalk. Cal turned to face him, placing himself between me and Hunter. My hero, I thought. But a part of me still felt a palpable fear as well. Hunter scowled, his cheekbones so sharp that snowflakes seemed to glance off them.

"So Cal is teaching you the secrets of Wicca, is he?" he asked. He leaned nonchalantly against the hood of the car, and Cal didn't take his eyes off him for a second. "Of course, he has quite a few secrets of his own, eh?"

"You can leave now, Niall," Cal spat.

"No, I think not," Hunter replied evenly. "I think I'll be around for a while. Who knows, I might have to teach Morgan a thing or two myself."

"What is that supposed to mean?" I asked.

Hunter just shrugged.

"Get away from me," Cal commanded.

Hunter stood back with a slight smile, his hands in the air as if to show he was unarmed. Cal glanced from him to the car. I'd never seen Cal so angry, so on the verge of losing control. It frightened me. He was like a tiger, waiting to pounce.

"There is one thing you should learn, Morgan," Hunter remarked. "Cal isn't the only blood witch around. He'd like to think he's a big man, but he's really just small fry. One day you'll realize that. And I want to be there to see it."

"Go to hell," Cal spat.

"Look, you don't *know* me," I told Hunter loudly. "You don't know anything about me. So shut up and leave us alone!" I stomped angrily to the car. But as I pushed past Hunter, barely brushing against him, a sickening rush of energy hit me in my stomach—so hard that I gasped. He's put a spell on me, I thought in a panic, groping for the door handle. But he'd said nothing; he'd done nothing that I could see. I blinked hard.

"Please, Cal," I whispered, my voice shaking. "Let's go."

Cal was still staring at Hunter as if he'd like to rip him apart. His eyes blazed, and his skin seemed to whiten.

Hunter stared back, but I felt his concentration break: he was shaken for a moment. Then he steeled himself again.

"Please, Cal," I repeated. I knew something had happened to me; I felt hot and strange and desperate to be gone, to be at home. My voice must have alerted Cal to my distress because he took his eyes off Hunter for a second. I stared at him pleadingly. Finally he pulled his keys from his pocket, slid into the car, and opened my door.

I collapsed inside and put my hands over my face.

"Good-bye, Morgan!" Hunter called.

Cal gunned the engine and sped backward, shooting snow and ice toward Hunter. I peeked through my fingers and saw Hunter standing there with an indecipherable expression on his face. Was it . . . anger? No. Snow swirled around him as he watched us leave.

It wasn't until we were almost at my house that it suddenly hit me.

The look on his face had been hunger.

5

Dagda

Beltane, 1992

I feel like punching everyone and everything. I hate my life, hate living with Uncle Beck and Aunt Shelagh. Nothing has been the same, not since Mum and Dad disappeared that day two years ago, and it never will be.

Today Linden fell off Uncle Beck's ladder and bloodied his knee. I had to clean him up and bandage the wound, and all the while he wept. And I cursed Mum and Dad while I did it, I cursed them for leaving us and leaving me to do their job. Why did they go? Where did they go? Uncle Beck knows, but he won't tell me. He says I am not ready. Aunt Shelagh says he's only thinking of my good. But how can it be good not to know the truth? I hate Uncle Beck.

In the end, when I was finished with Linden, I made a face, and he laughed through his tears. That made me feel better. But

only for a while. No happiness lasts very long. That's what I've learned. Linden would do well to learn it, too.
 —Giomanach

Mom came into my room that night as I was getting dressed to go to Jenna Ruiz's for the circle. "Are you guys going to a movie?" she asked. She automatically began straightening the pile of rejected clothes on my bed.

"No," I said, and left it at that. When it came to Wicca, silence was the best policy. I turned in front of the mirror, frowning. As usual, I looked hopeless. I pulled open the bathroom door and yelled, "Mary K.!" Having an endlessly trendy sister had its perks.

She appeared at once.

I held out my arms. "Help."

Her warm brown eyes skimmed me critically, then she shook her head. "Take it all off," she ordered.

I obeyed meekly. Mom grinned at us.

While Mary K. pawed through my closet, Mom tried to wheedle more information from me. "You said you were going to Jenna's? Will Bree be there?"

I paused for a moment. Both Mary K. and Mom had mentioned Bree today. I wasn't really surprised; she had been a virtual fixture at our house for years—but talking about her was painful. "I don't think so," I finally said. "It's just going to be our regular group, getting together. You know, I've never been to Jenna's house before." A lame attempt to change the subject, I knew. Mary K. threw a pair of skinny jeans at me, and I obediently shimmied into them.

"We never see Bree anymore," Mom commented as Mary K. disappeared into her room.

I nodded, aware of Mom's eyes on me.

"Did you guys have a fight?" Mom asked straight out.

Mary K. returned, holding an embroidered cotton sweater.

"Kind of," I said with a sigh. I really didn't want to get into this, not now. I pulled off my sweatshirt and tugged on the sweater. It fit smoothly, to my surprise. I'm taller and thinner than Mary K., but she inherited my mom's curvy chest. My adoptive mom, that is. I wondered fleetingly if Maeve Riordan had been built like me.

"Did you fight over Wicca?" Mom pried with the subtlety of an ax. "Does Bree not like Wicca?"

"No," I said, pulling my hair out of the sweater and examining my new look. It was a big improvement, which lifted my mood a little. "Bree does Wicca, too." I sighed again, finally giving in to Mom's interrogation. "Actually, we fought over Cal. She wanted to go out with him, but he wanted to go out with me. Now she pretty much hates me."

Mom was quiet for a moment. Mary K. stared at the floor.

"That's too bad," Mom said after a moment. "It's sad when friends fight over a boy." She laughed gently, reassuringly. "Usually the boys aren't worth it."

I nodded. A lump had formed in my throat. I didn't want to talk about Bree anymore; it hurt too much. I checked the clock. "I wish it didn't have to be like this. Anyway, I'm late; I better go." My voice was strained. "Thanks, Mary K." I kissed the air beside Mom's cheek—then I was down the stairs and out the door, pulling on my coat and shivering in the cold.

In a few moments, though, the sadness over Bree began to melt away. I felt a tingle of anticipation. It was circle night.

Jenna lived not far from me in a small, Victorian-style house. It was charmingly run-down, with an overgrown yard. The paint was peeling, and one shutter was missing a hinge.

As soon as I walked up the steps to the porch, a cat greeted me. It meowed and rubbed its head against my legs.

"What are you doing out here?" I whispered as I rang the doorbell.

Jenna opened the door right away, her cheeks flushed, blond hair pulled back, a big smile on her face.

"Hi, Morgan!" she said, then looked down at the cat squeezing its way inside. "Hugo, I told you it was freezing out there! I called you! You ignored me. Now your paws are cold."

I laughed and glanced around to see who was here. No Cal, not yet. Of course, I knew that already; I hadn't seen his car outside, hadn't felt his presence. Robbie was examining Jenna's stereo system, which had a real turntable. A stack of old vinyl records was piled haphazardly next to the fireplace.

"Hey," he said.

"Hi," I answered. I was amazed that this was Jenna's home. Jenna was by far one of the most popular girls in school and thoroughly up-to-date, like Mary K.—but her house looked like a throwback to the 1970s. The furniture was comfortably shabby, with plants hung in front of every window, some needing water. There seemed to be dust and cat hair everywhere. And dog hair, I amended, seeing two basset hounds snoring on a dog bed in a corner of the dining room. No wonder Jenna has asthma, I found myself thinking. She'd have to live in a plastic bubble in this house to breathe clean air.

"Want some cider?" Jenna asked, handing me a cup. It was warm and smelled deliciously spicy. I took a sip as the doorbell rang again.

"Hey!" It was Sharon Goodfine. She shrugged off her thick black leather coat and hung it on the stairs' newel post. "Hugo! Don't even think about it!" she cried as the cat reached up to pat her coat with his fat white paws. Obviously she had been here before.

Ethan Sharp came right after Sharon, looking underdressed in a thin fatigue jacket.

Sharon handed him a cup of cider. "Apparently you lack the gene that allows you to dress for the weather," she teased.

He grinned at her, looking vaguely stoned, even though I knew he didn't smoke pot anymore. She smiled back. I tried not to roll my eyes. When would they realize that they liked each other? Right now they sort of sniped at each other childishly.

Cal arrived next, and my heart lifted as he walked through the door. I was still upset about what had happened with Hunter at Practical Magick; Cal and I had hardly said two words to each other on the way home. But seeing him now made me feel much better, and when he met my eyes, I could tell he had missed me in the hours we had been apart.

"Morgan, can I talk to you for a second?" he asked, hesitating near the door. He didn't have to add "alone." I could see it in his face.

I nodded, surprised, and stepped toward him.

"What's up?" I asked.

Turning his back on the living room, he pulled a small stone from his pocket. It was smooth, round, and gray—about the size of a Ping-Pong ball. Inscribed on it in black ink was a rune. I had been reading about runes, so I recognized it instantly: it was Peorth, the rune for hidden things revealed.

"I found this stuck into the suspension of my car," Cal whispered.

My head jerked up in alarm. "Did Hunter . . . ?" I didn't finish.

Cal nodded.

"What does it mean?" I asked.

"It means that he's using dirty tricks to spy on us," he muttered, shoving the stone back into his pocket. "It's nothing to worry about, though. If anything, it proves that he doesn't have much power."

"But—"

"Don't worry," Cal said. He flashed me a reassuring smile. "You know, I don't even know why I bothered showing this to you. It's not a big deal. Really."

I watched him as he headed to the living room to say hi to the others. He wasn't being completely honest with me; I could feel that even without using my heightened witch senses. Hunter's little trick did concern him, at least to some degree.

What is Hunter up to? I wondered again. What does he want with us?

It was already nine o'clock, when we usually got started. We drank cider. Robbie played music. I tried to forget about the stone. Looking at the pets soothed me: the dogs snored and twitched in their sleep, and the cats rubbed our legs in quiet demands for attention. I realized that the only one of us missing was Jenna's boyfriend, Matt. Jenna kept glancing at the tall grandfather clock in the foyer. As the minutes went by, she seemed increasingly ill at ease.

Her parents wandered in, met us, totally unconcerned with the fact that we were here to perform a Wiccan circle. It must be nice not to worry about making your parents mad, I thought. They headed upstairs to watch TV and told us to have a good time.

"Well, I'll get started with the circles," Cal said finally, opening his bag and settling down on the floor. "We'll give Matt ten more minutes."

"It's not like him to be late," Jenna murmured. "I called his cell phone, but it went straight to voice mail."

I suddenly remembered seeing Matt's car, parked next to Raven's. Was that only this morning? It had been a long day. I stifled a yawn as I sat on the worn green couch in the living room, watching Cal work.

"What are you doing?" I asked. Usually he drew a simple, perfect circle in salt. When we stepped in, he closed it and purified it with earth, air, fire, and water. But tonight's circle was different.

"This is more complicated," Cal explained.

Slowly the others drifted over to watch him. He was drawing circles within circles, leaving an opening in each one. There were three geometrically perfect circles now, the largest one taking up every inch of available space in Jenna's living room.

At the four compass points of the circles Cal drew a

rune in chalk and also in the air: Mann, the rune for community and interdependence; Daeg, symbolizing dawn, awakening, clarity; Ur, for strength; Tyr, for victory in battle. Cal named them as he drew them but didn't offer any explanation. Before we could ask, the front door blew open and Matt breezed in, looking uncharacteristically disheveled and scattered.

"Hi, everyone. Sorry I'm late. Car trouble." He kept his head down, not meeting anyone's eye. Jenna looked at him, first in concern, then in confusion as he threw off his coat and came to watch Cal. For a moment Jenna hesitated. Then she walked up to him and took his hand. He gave her a brief smile but ignored her otherwise.

"Okay, everyone, step inside, and I'll close the circles," Cal instructed.

We did. I stood between Matt and Sharon. I tried never to stand next to Cal at a circle—I knew from experience that it would be too much to handle or control. Sharon and Matt were safe.

"Tonight we're working on personal goals," Cal continued, standing up. He handed Ethan a small bowl of salt and told him to purify the circle. Next he asked Jenna to light the incense, symbolizing air, and Sharon to touch each of our foreheads with a drop of water from its matching bowl. There was a fire in the living room fireplace—and we used it for fire, naturally. My tiredness started to fade as I glanced around at everyone united for the same purpose. This circle felt special somehow, more important, more focused.

"During our breathing exercises," Cal said, "I want you each to concentrate on your own personal goals. Think about what you want out of Wicca and what you can offer to Wicca. Try to make it as simple and pure as possible. Stuff like 'I want a new car' isn't it."

We laughed.

"It's more like, I want to be more patient, or I want to be more honest, or I want to be braver. Think about what that means to you and how Wicca can help you achieve it. Any questions?"

I shook my head. There were so many things about myself I wanted to improve. I pictured myself as a smiling, confident person—open and honest and giving: a poster girl for Wicca. Feeling no anger, no envy, no greed. I sighed. Yeah, right. Accomplishing all that was a pretty ambitious project. Maybe too ambitious.

"Everyone take hands, and let's begin our breathing exercises," said Cal.

I reached for my neighbors. Matt's hand was still cool from being outside. Sharon's bracelets jingled against my wrist. I began to breathe slowly and deeply, trying to let all the day's negativity and tensions drain from my body, trying to draw in all the positive energies I could. I consciously relaxed every muscle, starting at the top of my head and working my way down. Within a few minutes I felt calm and focused, in a meditative state where I was only semi-aware of my surroundings. This was good.

"Now think about your goals." Cal's voice seemed to float from everywhere at once. Unbidden, we began to move in a circle, first slowly, then more quickly and smoothly. My eyes opened, and I saw Jenna's living room as a series of dark smudges, a wild blur as we spun around and around. The fireplace marked our turns, and I looked into the fire, feeling its warmth and light and power.

"I want to be more open," I heard Sharon murmur, as if on a breeze.

"I want to be happy," said Ethan.

There was a moment of silence while I thought about what I wanted, and then Jenna said, "I want to be more lovable."

I felt Matt's hand clench mine for an instant, and then he said, "I want to be more honest." The words sounded reluctant and pained.

"I want to be strong," Cal whispered.

"I want to be a good person," said Robbie—and I thought, But you are.

I was last. I could feel the seconds ticking by. I still didn't know what I needed to work on the most. Yet words seemed to explode from my mouth, as if by their own accord. They hung on the air like smoke from a bog fire.

"I want to realize my power."

As soon as I said it, a current ran through the circle, like a wind whipping a rope. It was electric: it charged me, so that I felt I could fly or dance above the earth.

A chant came to my lips, one I didn't remember ever hearing or reading. I had no idea what it meant, but I let it flow from me, as my wish had flowed from me.

> "An di allaigh an di aigh
> An di allaigh an di ne ullah
> An di ullah be nith rah
> Cair di na ulla nith rah
> Cair feal ti theo nith rah
> An di allaigh an di aigh."

I chanted it by myself, very softly at first—then more loudly, hearing my voice weaving a beautiful pattern in the air. The words sounded Gaelic and ancient. Someone was speaking through me. I lost myself, but I wasn't frightened. I was exhilarated. I threw my arms up in the air and swirled in circles within our circle. Together the coven spun in orbit; they were planets around a shining star—and the shining star was me. Silver rain was sprinkling down on my head, making me a goddess. My hair came undone from its tidy braid and whirled in a stream, catching the firelight. I was all-powerful, all-knowing, all-seeing—a goddess indeed. It came to me that the words must have been a spell, an ancient spell, one that called power.

It had called power to me tonight.

"Let's take it down."

The voice belonged to Cal. Again his words seemed to come from everywhere and nowhere at once. In answer to his bidding I slowed my whirling and let myself come to a wavering stop. I was as old as time itself; I was every woman who had ever danced for magick under the moon, every goddess who had celebrated life and death and the joy and sorrow in between.

Hunter Niall's face suddenly flashed into my mind, his superior, contemptuous smirk. Look at me, Hunter! I wanted to shout. Look at my power! I am a match for you or any witch!

Then, all at once, with no warning, I felt frightened, no longer in control. Without Cal telling me, I immediately lay facedown on Jenna's wooden floor—with my hands flat by my shoulders to ground my energy. The wood was warm and smooth beneath my cheek, and energy flowed over and around me like water.

Slowly, very slowly, my breathing returned to normal. The fear fluttered, weakening. I became aware that someone was taking my right hand.

I blinked and glanced up. It was Jenna.

"Please," she said, placing my hand on her breastbone. I knew that she wanted me to help her. A week ago I had sent energy into her and eased her asthma. But I didn't think I had the power left now to do anything. Still, I closed my eyes and concentrated on light . . . white, healing light. I gathered it within me and sent it coursing down my arm, through my hand, into Jenna's constricted lungs. She breathed deeply, exclaiming slightly at the warmth.

"Thank you," she murmured.

I was lying on my side now. Suddenly I noticed that everyone was staring at me. Once again I was the center of attention. Self-consciously I pulled my hand away, wondering why a minute ago it was so natural to dance alone in front of everyone while now I felt embarrassed and shy. Why couldn't I hold on to those wonderful feelings of strength?

Matt put his hands on Jenna's shoulders, the most attention he'd shown her since he'd arrived. He was panting slightly from the effort of the dance.

"Did Morgan help your breathing?" he asked.

Jenna nodded, a blissful smile on her lips.

Cal crouched by my side, his hand on my hip.

"Everything all right?" he asked. He sounded excited, breathless.

"Uh . . . yeah," I murmured.

"Where did the chant come from?" he asked, gently brushing my hair off my shoulder. "What did it do?"

"I don't know where it came from, but it seemed to call power to me," I said.

"It was so beautiful," said Jenna.

"Pretty witchy," said Sharon.

"It was really cool," said Ethan.

I looked at Robbie, and he gazed calmly back at me, warm satisfaction on his face. I smiled at him. At that moment I was perfectly content—but the mood was abruptly broken when I felt nails on the back of my legs.

"Ow!" I muttered.

Half sitting up, I looked over to see the fuzzy, triangular head of a tiny gray kitten.

It mewed in greeting, and I laughed.

Jenna grinned. "Oh, sorry. One of our cats had kittens two months ago. We're trying to get rid of them. Anyone want a cat?" she joked.

I picked him up. He looked back at me intently, a world of feline wisdom in his baby blue eyes. He was solid gray, shorthaired, with a fat baby's belly and a short spiky tail that stuck straight up like an exclamation mark. He mewed in my face again and reached out a paw to pat my cheek.

"Hello," I said, remembering Maeve's kitten from her Book of Shadows. His name had been Dagda. I gazed at Jenna's cat in wonder, suddenly knowing that he was meant for me, that this was a perfect way to end the evening.

"Hi," I said softly. "Your name is Dagda, and you're going to come home and live with me. All right?"

He mewed once more, and I fell in love.

6

Communion

Imbolc, 1993

A Seeker is here. He came two days ago and took a room above the pub on Goose Lane. He talked with Uncle Beck a good while yesterday. Uncle Beck says he'll talk with everyone and that we all have to be honest. But I don't like the man. His skin is white and he doesn't smile, and when he looks at me, his eyes are like two black holes. He makes me feel cold as frost.

—Giomanach

"A rat!" Mary K. screeched the next morning, right in my face. Not the best way to wake up. "Oh God, Morgan, there's a rat! Don't move!"

Of course by now I was stirring in my bed, and little Dagda was, too. He huddled next to me, small ears flat, body hunkered down. But he summoned enough courage to give Mary K. a good hiss. I wrapped my hand around him protectively.

Mom and Dad ran into my room, wide-eyed.

"It isn't a rat," I croaked, clearing sleep out of my throat.

"It isn't?" Dad asked.

I sat up. "It's a kitten," I said, stating the obvious. "Jenna's cat had kittens, and they were trying to get rid of them, so I took one. Can I keep him? I'll pay for his food and litter and everything," I added.

Dagda rose up on his little legs and eyed my family curiously. Then, as if to prove how cute he really was, he opened his mouth and mewed. They all melted at once. I hid a smile.

Mary K. sat on my bed and gently extended her hand. Dagda cautiously made his way across my comforter and licked her finger. Mary K. giggled.

"He's very sweet," said my mom. "How old is he?"

"Eight weeks," I said. "Old enough to leave his mom. So—is it okay?"

Mom and Dad exchanged a glance.

"Morgan, cats cost more than just food and litter," my dad said. "They need shots, checkups. . . ."

"He'll need to be neutered," my mom added.

I grinned. "Fortunately, we have a vet in the family," I said, referring to my aunt Eileen's girlfriend. "Besides, I have money saved from working last summer. I can pay for all that."

Mom and Dad both shrugged, then smiled.

"I guess it's okay, then," said Mom. "Maybe after church we can go to the store and get the stuff he needs."

"He's hungry," Mary K. announced, holding him to her

chest. She immediately hopped up and dashed from the room, cradling him like a baby. "There's chicken left over from last night. I'll get him some."

"Don't give him milk," I called after her. "It'll upset his tummy. . . ."

I leaned back against my pillow, happy. Dagda was an official member of our family.

It was the second-to-last Sunday before Thanksgiving, so our church was decorated with dried leaves, pyracantha branches with bright red berries, pinecones, and rust-colored mums in pots. The atmosphere was beautiful, warm, and inviting. I decided it would be nice to find natural decorations like that for our own house at Thanksgiving.

In some way, I guess because I still wasn't sure about how coming to church fit in with Wicca, I felt strangely detached from everything going on around me. I stood when I was supposed to and knelt at the right time; I even followed along in the prayers and sang the hymns. But I did it without being a part of the congregation. My thoughts roamed freely, without restraint.

A thin, wintry sunlight had broken through the clouds. Yesterday's snow had mostly melted, and the church's stained-glass windows glowed with fiery reds, deep blues, pure greens, and crystalline yellows. There was a faint aroma of incense, and as I sank deeper within myself, I felt the weight of the people all around me. Their thoughts began to intrude, their hearts beating incessantly. I took a deep breath and shut my eyes, closing myself off to them.

Only when I had walled them out of my senses did I

open my eyes again. I felt peaceful and full of gladness. The music was lovely, the ecclesiastical words moving. It all seemed timeless and traditional. It wasn't the bark and earth and salt of Wicca, nor was it the grounding of energy and the working of spells. But it was beautiful, in its own way.

I rose automatically when it was time to take communion. I followed my parents and sister up to the railing in front of the altar. The tall altar candles burned brightly, reflecting off the brass fixtures and dark polished wood. I knelt on the flat needlework pillow that had been embroidered by the women's guild. My mom had made one of these pillows a couple of years ago.

My hands clasped, I waited as Father Hotchkiss said the wine blessing for every person in the row. I felt at peace. Already I was looking forward to going home to see Dagda, read Maeve's Book of Shadows, and do some more rune research. Last night when Cal had drawn runes in the air around our circle, it seemed to focus our energy in a whole new way. I liked runes and wanted to find out more about them.

Next to me Mary K. took a sip of wine. I caught a whiff of the fruity scent. A moment later it was my turn. Father Hotchkiss stood in front of me, wiping the large silver chalice with a linen cloth.

"This is the blood of Christ our Lord," he murmured. "Drink this in his name, that you may be saved."

I tilted my head forward to sip.

With an unexpected stumble Father Hotchkiss lurched toward me. The chalice slipped from his hands. It dropped to the white marble floor with a metallic clang, and Father Hotchkiss gripped the wooden rail that separated us.

I put my hand on his, searching his face. "Are you okay, Father?" I asked.

He nodded. "I'm sorry, my dear. I slipped. Did I splash you?"

"No, no." I looked down, and sure enough, my dress was wine free. Deacon Carlson was hurrying to get another blessed chalice, and Father Hotchkiss stepped away to help him.

Mary K. was waiting for me, looking uncertain. I stayed kneeling, watching the dark red wine flow across the white marble floor. The contrast of color was mesmerizing.

"What happened?" Mary K. whispered. "Are you okay?"

That was when the thought came to me: What if I was the one who had made Father Hotchkiss stumble? I almost gasped, with my hand over my mouth. What if, in the middle of all my Wicca thoughts, a force had decreed that my taking communion was not a good idea? Quickly I stood, my eyes large. Mary K. headed back to our pew and our parents, and I followed her.

No, I thought. It was just a coincidence. It didn't mean anything.

But inside me a witchy voice said sweetly: There are no coincidences. And everything means something.

So what did it mean, exactly? That I should stop taking communion? That I should stop coming to church altogether? I glanced at my mother, who smiled at me with no awareness of the confusion that was raging inside me. I was thankful for that.

I couldn't imagine cutting church out of my life completely. Catholicism was part of the glue that held our family together; it was a part of me. But maybe I should hold off on taking communion for a while, at least until I figured out what it all meant. I could still come to church. I could still participate. Couldn't I?

I sighed as I sat back down beside Mary K. She looked at me but didn't say anything.

With every door that Wicca opened, I thought, another door seemed to shut. Somehow I had to find balance.

After lunch at the Widow's Diner we stopped at the grocery store. I bought a litter box and a scoop, a box of cat litter, and a bag of kitten food. Mom and Dad pitched in for a couple of cat toys, and Mary K. bought some kitty treats.

I was really touched, and I hugged them all, right in the pet aisle.

Of course, when we got home, we found that Dagda had peed on my down comforter. He had also eaten part of Mom's maidenhair fern and barfed it up on the carpet. Then he had apparently worked himself into a frenzy sharpening his tiny but amazingly effective claws on the armrest of my dad's favorite chair.

Now he was asleep on a pillow, curled up like a fuzzy little snail.

"God, he's so *cute,*" I said, shaking my head.

7

Symbols

I had to draw a spell of protection tonight. I invoked the Goddess and drew the runes at the four points of the compass: Ur, Sigel, Eolh, and Tyr. I took iron nails and buried them at the four corners, wearing a gold ring. And from now on, I will carry a piece of malachite for protection.

A Seeker is here.

But I am not afraid. The first blow has already been struck, and the Seeker is weakened by it. And as the Seeker weakens, my love grows stronger and stronger.

—Sgàth

On Monday, Mary K. and I were late for school. I had stayed up late reading Maeve's BOS, and Mary K. had stayed up late having a heartfelt, tortured talk with Bakker—and so we both overslept. We signed ourselves in at the office and got our tardy slips: the New York Public School System's version of the Scarlet Letter.

The halls were empty as we split up for our lockers and headed toward our respective homerooms. My mind swam with what I had been reading. Maeve had loved the herbal side of Wicca. Her BOS was filled with several long passages about magickal uses for plants—and how they're affected by time of year, amount of recent rainfall, position of stars, and phases of the moon. I wondered if I was a descendant of the Brightendale clan, the clan that farmed the earth for healing powers.

In homeroom I slithered into my desk chair. Out of habit I glanced at Bree, but she ignored me, and I felt irritated that it still caused me grief. Forget her, I thought. I'd once read somewhere that it takes about half as long to recover from a deep relationship as the relationship lasted. So in Bree's case, I would still be upset about her a good six years from now. Great.

I thought about Dagda and how Bree would adore him: she'd loved her cat Smokey and had been devastated when he died, two days after her fourteenth birthday. I'd helped her bury him in her backyard.

"Hey. Slept late?" my friend Tamara Pritchett called softly from the next desk. It seemed as if I barely saw her any-more, now that Wicca was taking up so much of my time.

I nodded and started organizing my books and note-books for my morning classes.

"Well, you missed the big news," Tamara went on. I looked up. "Ben and Janice are officially going out. Boyfriend and girlfriend."

"Really? Oh, cool," I said. I glanced across the room at

the lovebirds in question. They were sitting next to each other, talking quietly, smiling at each other. I felt happy for them. But I also felt removed—they, too, were friends I'd hardly seen in recent weeks.

My senses prickled, and I glanced across to see Bree's dark eyes on me. I was startled by their intense expression, and then we both blinked and it was gone. She turned away, and I was unsure if I had imagined it or not. I felt unsettled. Cal had said there was no dark side to Wicca. But aren't two sides of a circle opposite each other? And if one side was good, what was the other? I had disliked Sky as soon as I had met her. What was Bree doing with her?

The bell rang for first period. I felt sour, as if I shouldn't be there—and thought enviously of Dagda at home, wreaking feline havoc.

During American lit it started to drizzle outside: a depressing, steady stream that was trying hard to turn into sleet but not quite making it. My eyelids felt heavy. I hadn't even had time for a Diet Coke yet. I pictured my bed at home and for just a moment considered getting Cal, skipping out, and going home to be alone with him. We could lie in my bed, reading Maeve's BOS and talking about magick. . . .

Major temptation. By lunchtime I was really torn, even though I never skipped school. Only the knowledge that my mom sometimes popped home in the middle of the day prevented me from bringing up the idea to Cal when I saw him.

"You bought lunch?" he asked, eyeing my tray as I slid it onto our lunch table. He met my eyes. As clear as the rainfall, I heard the words *I missed you this morning* inside my head.

I smiled and nodded, sitting down across from him, next

to Sharon. "I overslept, so I didn't have time to make anything at home."

"Hey, Morgan," Jenna said, brushing her wheat-colored hair over her shoulder. "You know what I've been thinking about? Those words you said the other night. They were so amazing. I still can't get them out of my mind."

I shrugged. "Yeah, it's funny. I don't know where they came from," I said, popping the top off my soda. "I haven't had time to research it, either. At the time I thought it felt like a spell, calling power to me. But I don't know. The words sounded really old."

Sharon smiled tentatively. "It was kind of creepy, to tell you the truth," she murmured. She opened her container of soup and took out a crusty roll. "I mean, it was beautiful, but it's weird to have words you don't even know coming out of your mouth."

I looked up at Cal. "Did you recognize them?"

He shook his head. "Uh-uh. But later I thought about it, and I felt like I had heard them before. I wish I had taped our circle. I could play it for Mom and see if she knew what it was."

"Cool, you're speaking in tongues," Ethan joked. "Like that girl in *The Exorcist.*"

I pursed my lips. "Great," I said, and Robbie laughed.

Cal shot me an amused glance. "Want some?" he asked, handing me a slice of his apple.

Without thinking, I took a bite. It was astonishingly delicious. I looked at it: it was just an apple slice. But it was tart and sweet, bursting with juice.

"This is a *great* apple," I said, amazed. "It's perfect. It's the *über*-apple."

"Apples are very symbolic," said Cal. "Especially of the Goddess. Look." He took his pocketknife and cut his apple again—but across the middle instead of top to bottom. He held up a piece. "A pentacle," he said pointing to the pattern made from the seeds. It was a five-pointed star within the circle of the apple's skin.

"Whoa," I said.

"Awesome," said Matt. Jenna glanced at him, but he didn't meet her eye.

"Everything means something," said Cal lightly, taking a bite of the apple. I looked up at him sharply, reminded of what had happened yesterday in church.

Across the lunchroom I saw Bree sitting with Raven, Lin Green, Chip Newton, and Beth Nielson. I wondered if Bree was enjoying hanging out with her new crowd . . . people she had once referred to as stoners, wastoids. Her old crowd—Nell Norton, Alessandra Spotford, Justin Bartlett, and Suzanne Herbert—were sitting at a table near the windows. They probably thought Bree was crazy.

"I wonder how their coven's circle went on Saturday," I mumbled, half to myself. "Bree and Raven's. Robbie, do you know? Did you talk to Bree?"

Robbie shrugged and finished his piece of pizza.

"It went really well," said Matt absently. Then he blinked and frowned a tiny bit, as if he hadn't expected to say anything.

Jenna looked at him. "How do you know?" she asked.

Matt's face turned slightly pink. He shrugged, his attention on his lunch. "Uh, I talked to Raven during English," he said finally. "She said it was cool."

Jenna regarded Matt steadily. She started to gather up her tray. Once again I remembered seeing Matt's car and

Raven's car on the side of the road. As I wondered what it could mean, I heard Mary K.'s laughter, a few tables away. She was sitting next to Bakker with her friend Jaycee, Jaycee's older sister, Brenda, and a bunch of their friends. Mary K. and Bakker were looking into each other's eyes. I shook my head. He had won her over. But he'd better watch his step.

"What are you doing this afternoon?" Cal asked in the parking lot after school. The rain had all but stopped, and an icy wind was blowing.

I glanced at my watch. "Besides waiting for my sister? Nothing. I have to get dinner together."

Robbie snaked his way through a few cars, heading toward us. "Hey, what's going on with Matt?" he called. "He's acting all squirrelly."

"Yeah, I thought so, too, " I said. "Almost like he wants to break up with Jenna but doesn't want to at the same time. If that makes any sense."

Cal smiled. "I don't know them as well as you guys do," he said, putting his arm around me. "Is Matt acting that different?"

Robbie nodded. "Yeah. Not that we're bosom buddies or anything, but he seems kind of off to me. Usually he's really straightforward. He's always just right there." He gestured with his hands.

"I know," I agreed. "Now he seems to have something else going on." I wanted to mention the Matt-Raven car thing but thought it would be too gossipy. I wasn't even sure if it meant anything. I suddenly wished Bree and I were still close. She would have appreciated the significance.

"Morgan!" called Jaycee. "Mary K. asked me to tell you that she was catching a ride with Bakker." Jaycee waved and trotted off, her blond ponytail bouncing.

"Damn!" I said, disengaging myself from Cal. "I have to get home."

"What's the matter? Do you want me to come with you?" Cal asked.

"I would love it," I said gratefully. It would be nice to have an ally in case Bakker needed to be kicked out of the house again.

"See you, Robbie," I called, hurrying off to my car. Damnation, Mary K., I thought. How stupid can you be?

8

Mùirn Beatha
Dàn

Ostara, 1993

Aunt Shelagh told me she saw someone under a braigh before, when she was a girl, visiting her granny in Scotland. A local witch had been selling potions and charms and spells to cause harm. When Aunt Shelagh was there one summer, the Seeker came.

Shelagh says she woke in the night to screams and howls. The whole village turned out to see the Seeker take away the herbwife. In the moonlight, Shelagh saw the glint of the silver braigh around the herbwife's wrists, saw how the flesh was burned. The Seeker took her away, and no one saw her again, though they whispered she was living on the streets in Edinburgh.

Shelagh doesn't think the woman was ever able to do magick again, good or bad, so I don't know how long she would have wanted to live like that. But Shelagh also said that one sight of that herbwife under the braigh was enough to make her promise to never ever misuse her power. It was a terrible thing, she said. Terrible to see. She told me this story last month, when the Seeker was here. But he took no one away with him, and our coven is placid once more.

I am glad he's gone.

—Giomanach

I drove home as quickly as I could, considering that the streets were basically one big ice slick. The temperature kept dropping, and the air was miserable with the kind of bone-drenching chill that Widow's Vale seems to specialize in.

"I thought Mary K. broke up with Bakker after what happened," said Cal.

"She did," I grumbled. "But he's been begging her to take him back, it was all a mistake, he's so sorry, it'll never happen again, blah blah blah." Anger made my voice shrill.

My tires skidded a bit as I turned into our driveway. Bakker's car was parked out front. I slammed the car door and crunched up our walk—only to find Mary K. and Bakker huddled together on the front steps, shaking and practically blue with cold.

"What are you doing?" I exclaimed, relief washing over me.

"I wanted to wait for you," Mary K. muttered, and I silently applauded her good sense.

"Come on, then," I said, pushing open the front door. "But you guys stay downstairs."

"Okay," Bakker mumbled, sounding half frozen. "As long as it's warm."

Cal started making hot cider for us all while I stayed outside and salted the front walk and the driveway so my parents wouldn't have a hard time when they got home. It was nice to get back inside, and I cranked up the thermostat, then headed to the kitchen. It was my night to make dinner. I washed four potatoes, stabbed them with a fork, and put them in the oven to bake.

"Hey, Morgan, can we just run upstairs for a sec?" Mary K. asked tentatively, clutching her mug. Since I'd met Cal, I'd begun drinking a ton of cider. It was incredibly warming on cold days. "All my CDs are in my room."

I shook my head. "Tough," I said shortly. I blew on my cider to cool it. "You guys stay downstairs, or Mom will have my ass."

Mary K. sighed. Then she and Bakker brought their stuff to the dining room table and self-righteously started to do their homework. Or at least they pretended to do their homework.

As soon as my sister was gone, I waved my left hand in a circle, deasil, over my cider, and whispered, "Cool the fire." The next time I took a sip, it was just right, and I beamed. I loved being a witch!

Cal grinned and said, "Now what? Do we have to stay downstairs, too?"

I let my mind wander tantalizingly over the possibilities if I didn't practice what I preached but finally sighed and said, "I guess so. Mom would go insane if I was upstairs with an evil boy while she wasn't home. I mean, you've probably got only one thing on your mind and all."

"Yeah." Cal raised his eyebrows and laughed. "But it's one good thing, let me tell you."

Dagda padded into the kitchen and mewed.

"Hey, little guy," I crooned. I put my cider down on the

counter and scooped him up. He began to purr hard, his small body trembling.

"He gets to go upstairs," Cal pointed out, "and he's a boy."

I grinned. "They don't care if *he* sleeps with me," I said.

Cal let out a good-natured groan as I carried Dagda into the family room and sat on the couch. Cal sat next to me, and I felt the warmth of his leg against mine. I smiled at him, but his face turned solemn. He stroked my hair and traced the line of my chin with his fingers.

"What's wrong?" I asked.

"You surprise me all the time," he said out of the blue.

"How?" I was stroking Dagda's soft triangular head, and he was purring and kneading my knees.

"You're just—different than I thought you would be," he said. He put his arm across the back of the couch and leaned toward me as if trying to memorize my face, my eyes. He seemed so serious.

I didn't know what to think. "What did you expect me to be like?" I asked. I could smell the clean laundry scent of his shirt. In my mind I pictured us stretched on the couch, kissing. We could do it. I knew that Mary K. and Bakker were in the other room, that they wouldn't bother us. But suddenly I felt insecure, remembering again that I was almost seventeen and he was the first boy who'd ever asked me out, ever kissed me. "Boring?" I asked. "Kind of vanilla?"

His golden eyes crinkled at the edges, and he tapped my lips gently with one finger. "No, of course not," he said. "But you're so strong. So interesting." His forehead creased momentarily, as if he regretted what he'd said. "I mean, right when I met you, I thought you were interesting and good-looking and the rest of it, and I could tell right away you had a gift for the craft. I wanted to get close to you. But you've turned out to be so much more than that. The more I know you, the more you feel equal to me, like a real partner. Like I said, my *mùirn beatha dàn*. It's kind of a huge idea." He shook his head. "I've never felt this way before."

I didn't know what to say. I looked at his face, still amazed by how beautiful I found it, still awed by the feelings he awoke in me. "Kiss me," I heard myself breathe. He leaned closer and pressed his lips to mine.

After several moments Dagda shifted impatiently in my lap. Cal laughed and shook his head, then drew away from me as if deciding to exercise better judgment. He reached down and pulled a pad of paper and pen out of his book bag and handed them to me.

"Let's see you write your runes," he said.

I nodded. It wasn't kissing, but it was magick—a close second. I began to draw, from memory, the twenty-four runes. There were others, I knew, that dated from later times, but these twenty-four were considered the basics.

"Feoh," I said softly, drawing a vertical line, then two lines that slanted up and to the right from it. "For wealth."

"What else is it for?" asked Cal.

"Prosperity, increase, success." I thought. "Things turning out well. And this is Eolh, for protection," I said, drawing the shape that was like an upside-down Mercedes logo. "It's very positive. This is Geofu, which stands for gift or partnership. Generosity. Strengthening friendships or other relationships. The joining of the God and Goddess."

"Very good," said Cal, nodding.

I kept on until I had drawn all of them, as well as a blank space for the Wyrd rune, the undrawn one, the symbol that

signified something you ought not know: dangerous or hurt-
ful knowledge, a path you should not take. In rune sets it
was represented by a blank tile.

"That's great, Morgan," Cal whispered. "Now close your
eyes and think about these runes. Let your fingers drift over
the page, and stop when you feel you should stop. Then
look at what rune you've stopped on."

I loved this kind of thing. I closed my eyes and let my fingers
skim the paper. At first I felt nothing, but then I focused my
concentration, trying to shut out everything except what I was
doing. I tuned out the murmur of Mary K. and Bakker's voices
from the dining room, the ticking of the cuckoo clock my dad
had built from a kit, the gentle hum of the furnace kicking in.

I don't know how long it was before I realized that my
fingertips were picking up impressions. I felt feathery softness, a cool stone, a warm prickle . . . were these the
images of the runes? I let myself go deeper into the magick,
losing myself in its power. *There.* Yes, there was one place
where I felt a stronger sensation. Each time my fingers
passed it, it called to me. I let my hand drift downward to
rest on the paper and opened my eyes.

My fingers were on the rune called Yr. The symbol for
death.

I frowned. "What does this mean?"

"Hmmm," said Cal, looking at the paper, his hand on his
chin. "Well, you know, Yr can be interpreted many different
ways. It doesn't mean that you or someone you know is
going to die. It may simply mean the ending of something
and the beginning of something new. Some sort of big
change, not necessarily a bad one."

The double-fishhook symbol of Yr shone darkly on the

white paper. Death. The importance of endings. It seemed like an omen. A scary omen. A jet of adrenaline surged through me, making my heart thud.

All at once I heard the back door open.

"Hello?" came my mom's voice. "Morgan? Mary K.?" There were footsteps in the dining room. My concentration evaporated.

"Hey, sweetie," she said to Mary K. She paused. "Hello, Bakker. Mary K., is your sister here?" I knew she meant: For God's sake, you're not here alone with a boy, are you?

"I'm in here," I said, tucking the paper of runes into my pocket. Cal and I walked out of the family room. Mom's eyes flashed over us, and I could immediately see the thoughts going through her mind. *My girls, alone in the house with two boys.* But we were all downstairs, we had our clothes on, and Mary K. and Bakker were at least sitting at the dining room table. I could see Mom consciously decide not to worry about it.

"Are you baking potatoes?" she asked, sniffing.

"Yep," I said.

"Do you think we could mash them instead?" she asked. "I've asked Eileen and Paula to dinner." She held up a folder. "I've got some hot prospects for them housewise."

"Cool," I said. "Yeah, we can mash them, and then there'll be enough. I'm making hamburgers, too, but there's plenty."

"Great. Thanks, sweetie." Mom headed upstairs to change out of her work clothes.

"I'd better go," I heard Bakker say reluctantly. Good, I thought.

"Me too," said Cal. "Bakker, do you think you could

give me a lift back to school? That's where I left my car."

"No prob," said Bakker.

I walked Cal outside, and we hugged on the front porch. He kissed my neck and whispered, "I'll call you later. Don't get all bent about the Yr thing. It was just an exercise."

"Okay," I whispered back, although I still wasn't sure how I felt. "Thanks for coming over."

Aunt Eileen arrived first. "Hi!" she said, coming in and taking off her coat. "Paula called and said she was running a few minutes late—something about a Chihuahua having a difficult labor."

I smiled awkwardly in the front hall. I hadn't seen her since I had demanded to know why she hadn't told me I was adopted, at a family dinner two weeks ago. I felt a little embarrassed to see her again, but I was sure Mom had been talking to her, keeping her up-to-date with everything.

"Hi, Aunt Eileen," I said. "I . . . uh, I'm sorry about making a scene last time. You know."

As if to answer, she swept me up in a tight hug. "It's okay, sweetie," she whispered. "I understand. I don't blame you a bit."

We pulled back and smiled at each other for a moment. I knew Aunt Eileen would make everything okay again. Then she glanced down and gasped, pointing urgently to my dad's La-Z-Boy, where a small gray butt and tail were sticking out from under the skirt.

I laughed and scooped Dagda out.

"This is Dagda," I said, rubbing him behind his ears. "He's my new cat."

"Oh, my goodness," said Eileen, stroking his head. "I'm sorry. I thought he was a rat."

"You should know better," I joked, putting him back on the chair. "You *date* a vet."

Aunt Eileen laughed, too. "I know, I know."

Soon afterward Paula arrived, her sandy hair windblown, her nose pink with cold.

"Hey," I greeted her. "Is the Chihuahua okay?"

"Fine, and the proud mom of two pups," she said, giving me a hug. "Oh! What a beautiful kitten!" she said, spotting Dagda on Dad's chair.

I beamed. *Finally!* Somebody who knew what a treasure Dagda was. I'd always liked Aunt Eileen's new girlfriend, but now it struck me that they were a perfect match. Maybe Paula was even Eileen's *mùirn beatha dàn*.

Thinking about it brought a smile to my face. Everybody deserved somebody. Not everyone was as lucky as I was, of course. I had Cal.

9

Trust

The magick is working, as I knew it would. The Seeker no longer frightens me as much. I believe I am the stronger of us two, especially with the power of the others behind me.

Soon I will join with my love. I do understand the urgency, though I wish they would trust me to do it my way, at my pace. More and more, lately, I want to do this for my own sake. But the timing must be perfect. I dare not frighten her; there is too much at stake.

I have been reading the ancient texts, the ones about love and union. I have even copied down my favorite passage from Song of the Goddess: "To give pleasure to yourself and to others, that is my ritual. To love yourself and others, that is my ritual. Celebrate your body and spirit with joy and passion, and as you do so, you worship me."

—Sgàth

"I hope you know that you can't trust Bakker," I said to Mary K. the next morning. I tried not to sound snotty, but it came out that way anyhow.

Mary K. didn't answer. She just looked out her car window. Frost covered everything in lacy, powdered-sugar patterns.

I drove slowly, trying to avoid the hard patches of black ice where the newly plowed roads had puddled and frozen. My breath came out in a mist inside Das Boot.

"I know he's really sorry," I went on, in spite of my sister's stiff face. "And I believe he really cares about you. But I just don't trust his temper."

"Then don't go out with him," Mary K. muttered.

Alarm bells went off in my brain. I was criticizing him, and she was defending him. I was doing what I feared: pushing them closer together. I took a deep breath. Goddess, guide me, I said silently.

"You know," I said finally, several blocks from school. "I bet you're right. I bet it was just a onetime thing. But you guys have talked, right?" I didn't wait for an answer. "And he *is* really sorry. I guess it will never happen again."

Mary K. looked over at me suspiciously, but I kept my face neutral and my eyes on the road.

"He *is* sorry," my sister said. "He feels terrible about it. He never meant to hurt me. And now he knows he has to listen to me."

I nodded. "I know he cares about you."

"He does," said Mary K.

She looked transparently self-assured. Inside, my heart throbbed. I hated this. Maybe everything I had just said was true. But I couldn't help fearing that Bakker would try again to force Mary K. into doing something she didn't want to do.

If he did, I would make him pay.

I got to school early enough to see Cal before the bell rang. He was waiting for me by the east entrance, where our coven gathered during better weather.

"Hey," he said, kissing me. "Come on, we found a new place to hang out. It's warmer."

Inside, we passed the steps leading to the second floor and turned a corner. There another set of steps led down to the building's cellar. No one was supposed to go down here except the janitors. But Robbie, Ethan, Sharon, and Jenna were sitting on the steps, talking and laughing.

"Morganita," Robbie said, using a nickname he had given me in fifth grade. I hadn't heard it for years, and I smiled.

"We were just talking about your birthday," said Jenna.

"Oh!" I said in surprise. "How did you know about it?"

"I told them," said Robbie, drinking from a carton of orange juice. "Let the cat out of the bag."

"Speaking of cats, how's Dagda?" Jenna asked.

Matt's long, black-jean-clad legs obscured my view for a moment as he came and sat on the step above Jenna. She gave him a faint smile but didn't respond when he rubbed her shoulder.

"He's great," I said enthusiastically. "And he's growing really fast!"

"So your birthday's this weekend?" Sharon asked.

"Sunday," I said.

"Let's have a special birthday circle on Saturday, then," said Jenna. "With a cake and all."

Sharon nodded. "That sounds good," she said.

"Um, I can't make it Saturday night," Matt mumbled. He ran a hand through his thick black hair, lowering his eyes.

We all looked at him.

"I've got family stuff to do," he added, but the words were empty.

He is the worst liar in the world, I thought, seeing Jenna staring at him.

"Actually, could we do the birthday thing some other time?" Robbie asked. "I'm thinking I wouldn't mind skipping Saturday night's circle, too."

"Why?" I asked.

"Bree's been after me to come to one of their circles," Robbie admitted. I was surprised by his honesty, not in a bad way—but I felt a renewed rush of anger toward Bree. Robbie shrugged. "I don't want to join their coven, but it wouldn't be a bad idea for me to go to one of their circles, see what they're doing, scope it out."

"Like spying?" Jenna asked, but her tone was soft.

Robbie shrugged again, his hair falling onto his forehead. "I'm curious," he said. "I care about Bree. I want to know what she's doing."

I swallowed and forced myself to nod. "I think that's a good idea," I said. I couldn't believe that Bree would try to poach from our coven, but on the other hand, I was glad that Robbie wanted to keep an eye on her to make sure she wasn't doing anything crazy.

"I don't know," said Cal, shifting and stretching his legs out two steps below. "A lot of what's important in Wicca is continuity. It's about getting in touch with the day-in, day-out stuff, the cycle of the year, the turn of the wheel. Meeting every Saturday, being committed to that, is part of it. It's not something you should skip whenever you want to."

Matt stared at the floor. But Robbie looked back at Cal calmly.

"I hear what you're saying," Robbie said. "And I agree with it. But I'm not doing this just for me, and it isn't just because I feel lazy or I want to watch the game. I need to know what's going on with Bree and her coven, and this is how I can find out."

I was impressed with the air of quiet confidence Robbie projected. His acne and glasses had been gone ever since I'd put a healing spell on him. But something seemed to have healed inside him as well, something that didn't have anything to do with my magick. After years of being a somewhat awkward geek, he was growing into himself and finding new sources of strength. It was great to see.

Cal was silent for a while, and he and Robbie regarded each other. A month ago I would never have thought that Robbie would be a match for someone as strong as Cal, but now they didn't seem that different in a way.

Finally Cal nodded and let out a breath. "Yeah, okay. It won't kill us to take a break. Since there's only seven of us, if two of us can't make it, the circle will be kind of unbalanced. So let's all just take Saturday night off, and we'll meet again the week after."

"And *that's* when we'll have Morgan's birthday cake," said Robbie, smiling at me.

Sharon cleared her throat. "Um . . . I guess this isn't a good time to mention that next Saturday I'll be in Philadelphia for Thanksgiving."

Cal laughed. "Well, we'll just do the best we can. It's always tough around the holidays, with everyone having family stuff. How about you, Matt? Can you make it the following week?"

Matt nodded automatically, and I wondered if he'd even heard what Cal had said. The bell rang, and we all stood. Jenna put her hand in Matt's, staring into his face. He looked drawn, tense. I wished I knew what was going on.

As I headed to homeroom, the halls rapidly filled with streams of students, and Cal tugged on my coat sleeve.

"This Saturday we can have a birthday circle, just us two," he whispered into my ear. "This could be a good thing."

I shivered with delight and looked up at him. "That would be great."

He nodded. "Good. I'll plan something special."

In homeroom I noticed that Tamara was absent. Janice told me she had a cold. Everyone seemed to have colds lately.

Bree was absent, too, or so I thought before I saw her stop outside the class door. She was dressed all in black and was wearing vivid dark makeup, like Raven. It obscured her naturally beautiful face and made her seem anonymous somehow, as if she were wearing a mask. It filled me with an uneasy feeling. She stood outside, talking in a low voice to Chip Newton, and then they both came in and sat down.

I swallowed. Chip was cute and seemed like a pretty nice guy. He was brilliant in math, too—way better than me, and I'm pretty good. But Chip was also our school's biggest dealer. Last year Anita Fleming had gone to the hospital after overdosing on Seconal that she had gotten from him. Which made me wonder just how nice he really was.

What are you doing with him, Bree? I asked silently. And what's your coven up to?

*   *   *

Later that morning, while I was in the first-floor girls' bathroom, I heard Bree's voice, then Raven's, outside my stall. Quickly I pulled up my feet and braced them against my door so nobody could tell that the stall was occupied. I just didn't feel up to facing the two of them, having them sneer at me, right now.

"Where are we meeting?" Raven asked. I heard Bree rustling in her purse, and in my mind's eye I could picture her fishing out lipstick.

"At Sky's place," answered Bree. My interest perked up. They must be talking about their new coven.

"It's so cool that they have their own place," said Raven. "I mean, they're barely older than we are."

I breathed silently, intent on their voices.

"Yeah," said Bree. "What do you think of him?"

"He's hot," said Raven, and they laughed. "But it's Sky who knocks me out. She knows everything, she's so cool, and she's got awesome powers. I want to be just like that." I heard more rustling, then one of them turned on the water for a moment.

"Yeah," said Bree. "Did you think it was weird, what she was talking about on Saturday?"

"Not really," Raven said. "I mean, everything has a light side and a dark side, right? We have to be aware of it."

"Yeah." Bree sounded thoughtful, and I wondered what the hell Sky had been talking about. Was Sky pulling them toward dark magick? Or was she just showing them part of Wicca's big circle, like Cal had said? It didn't seem—

"You got the hair, didn't you?" Raven asked.

"Yeah," Bree answered. Now she sounded almost . . .

depressed. I couldn't follow the conversation at all. What hair?

"What's wrong?" Raven demanded. "Sky promised no one would get hurt."

"I know," Bree mumbled. "It's just, you know, I found the hair in this old comb—"

"Morgan will be *fine*," Raven interrupted.

"That's not what I was talking about," Bree snapped. "I'm not worried about her."

My eyes flew open wide. I bit my lip to keep from gasping as everything fell into place. Bree was talking about *my* hair. I couldn't believe it. She was turning over a strand of my hair to a strange girl—a witch—behind my back.

There could be only one reason: Sky wanted my hair to put a spell on me. So why had Bree gone through with it? Did she really believe that Sky didn't intend to harm me? Why *else* would she want the hair?

Or did Bree want me to be harmed? I wondered miserably.

"We need more people," Raven stated in the silence.

"Yeah. Well, Robbie's going to come. And we might get Matt, too."

Raven laughed. "Yeah. Matt. Oh God, I can't wait to see Thalia's face when Robbie walks in. She'll probably jump him right there."

I frowned. Who was Thalia?

"Really?" Bree asked.

"She just broke up with her boyfriend, and she's trolling," Raven said. "And Robbie's really hot now. I wouldn't mind hooking up with him myself."

"Oh, Jesus, Raven," said Bree.

Raven laughed again, and I heard a purse being zipped shut. "Just kidding. Maybe."

Silence. I held my breath.

"What?" said Raven as the door opened.

"Thalia's not his type," Bree said as sounds from the out-side hall filtered into the room.

"If she wants him, she's his type."

The bathroom door closed again, and air exploded from my lungs. I got to my feet, shaking with reaction. So Sky was manipulating Bree. They were definitely trying to get Matt and Robbie to leave our coven and join theirs. And Sky had her own place, where they were meeting. Did she live with Hunter? Was that who Raven thought was hot? Maybe. Then again, Raven thought most breathing males were hot. And they knew somebody named Thalia who was going to jump Robbie. For some reason, Bree had sounded less than thrilled by that idea—as she had about turning over my hair to Sky. But her reluctant tone was small consolation.

I hated everything that I had just overheard. But more than that, now I was afraid.

10

Magesight

Things are starting to heat up, and not just because of the Seeker. We have been having many visitors. Many I've never seen before—others I remember from all over the world: Manhattan, New Orleans, California, England, Austria. They come and go at all hours, and I keep coming across little knots of people huddled in this room or that, heads together, discussing, arguing, making magick. I don't know all of what's going on, but it's clear that our discovery here has set many things in motion. And the circles! We are having them almost every day now. They are powerful and exhilarating, but they leave me tired the next day.
        —Sgàth

After school I wanted to talk to Cal about what I had overheard, but he was already gone. He'd left a note on my locker, saying he'd had to go home and meet with one of his mother's friends. So for now I was on my own with my questions about Bree and Raven and their coven. Even Mary K. wasn't coming home with me. As I was getting into Das Boot, she ran up to tell me she was going to Jaycee's house.

I nodded and waved, but I couldn't bring myself to smile. I didn't want to be alone. Too much was troubling me.

Luckily Robbie sauntered over to the car. "What's up?" he asked.

I shielded my eyes from the pale November sunlight and looked at him. I wasn't sure whether or not I should tell him what was on my mind. I decided not to. It was too complicated. Instead I merely said, "I was thinking about going to Butler's Ferry park and gathering some pinecones and stuff for Thanksgiving."

Robbie thought for a moment. "Sounds cool," he said. "Do you want some company?"

"Absolutely," I said, unlocking the passenger's-side door.

"So, do you have family coming in for Thanksgiving?" he asked.

I nodded as I pulled out of the driveway, picking up speed on the open road. "My mom's parents, my dad's brother and his family. And then everyone who lives in town. We're having dinner at our house this year."

"Yeah. We're going to my aunt and uncle's," Robbie said without enthusiasm. "They'll be yelling at the football game on TV, the food will suck, and then my dad and Uncle Stan will both get plastered and end up taking a swing at each other."

"Well, they do that every year," I said, trying to inject some humor in a not-so-humorous situation. I'd heard about his from Robbie before, and it always made me sad. "So it's almost, like, traditional."

He laughed as I turned onto Miltown Pike. "I guess you're right. Tradition is a good thing. That's something I've learned from Wicca."

Soon I was pulling into the empty Butler's Ferry parking lot and cutting the engine. I retrieved a basket with a handle from the trunk. Despite the cold the sun was trying hard to shine, and it glittered off the leaves crumpling under our feet. The trees were bare and sculptural, the sky wide and a pale, bleached blue. The peace of the place began to steal over me, calm me down. I felt suddenly happy to be here with Robbie, whom I'd known for so long.

"So are there any herbs or anything around this time of year?" Robbie asked.

"Not a lot." I shook my head. "I checked my field guide, and we might see some stuff, but I'm not counting on it. I'll have to wait till spring. I'll be able to collect plants in the wild then and also start my own garden."

"It's weird that you're so powerful in Wicca, isn't it?" Robbie asked suddenly. But it wasn't a mean or probing question.

For a moment my breath stopped, and I thought about telling him everything that I had learned about myself in the past month. Robbie didn't even know I was adopted. But I just couldn't tell him. He'd been my friend for so long; he'd listened to me complain about my family, and he'd always pictured me as one of them: a Rowlands. I wasn't up to dealing with the emotional backlash of spilling the whole story *again*. I knew I would tell him sometime. We were too close for me to have this huge a secret. But not today.

"Yeah, I guess," I said finally, keeping my voice light. "I mean, it's amazing. But who would've thunk it?"

We grinned at each other, and I found a pretty pine branch on the ground that had three perfect little cones on it. I also stopped to pick up a few oak twigs that had clumps of dried leaves on them. I love the shape of oak leaves.

"It's really changed everything," Robbie murmured, picking up a likely branch and handing it to me. I accepted it, and it joined the others in my basket. "Magick, I mean. It's completely changed your life. And you completely changed my life." He gestured to his face, his skin. I felt a brief stab of guilt. All I'd meant to do was try a tiny healing spell to clear up the acne that had scarred his face since seventh grade. But the spell had continued to perfect him. He didn't even need glasses anymore. Every once in a while the whole thing spooked me all over again.

"I guess it has," I agreed quietly. I leaned down to study a small, fuzzy vine climbing a tree. It had a few withering, bright red leaves on it.

"Don't touch that," said Robbie. "It's poison ivy."

I laughed, startled. "Great witch I'll make." We smiled at each other in the deepening twilight, the silence of the woods all around us. "I'm glad there's no one else besides you here," I added. "I know you won't think I'm a complete idiot."

Robbie nodded, but his smile faded. He bit his lip.

"What's wrong?" I asked.

"Do you miss Bree?" Robbie asked out of the blue.

I stared at him, unable to answer. I didn't know what to say. But I knew what he was feeling: here we were, having fun as we'd done so many times in the past—only Bree wasn't here to share the fun with us.

"I'm in love with her, you know," he said.

My jaw dropped open. Wow. I'd had some suspicions about his feelings for her, but I'd never imagined they were so strong. Nor did I ever expect him just to put them out there like that.

"Uh, I guess I sort of figured you liked her," I admitted awkwardly.

"No, it's more than that," Robbie said. He looked away and tossed an acorn off into the bushes. "I'm in love with her. Crazy about her. I always have been, for years." He smiled and shook his head. I stole a quick glance at him, and any regrets I had about healing his face vanished. I'd done a good thing. He was handsome, secure; his jaw was smooth and strong. He looked like a model.

"Years?" I asked. "I didn't know that."

He shrugged. "I didn't want you to. I didn't want anyone to know, especially Bree. She's always gone for the dumb, good-looking types. I've been watching her be with one jerk after another, knowing I never had a chance." His smile faltered. "You know she told me about when she lost her virginity?" He turned to me, his blue-gray eyes glinting in fading sunlight. He shook his head again, remembered pain on his face. "She was all happy and excited. The best thing since mocha latte, she said. And with that loser, Akers Rowley."

I frowned. "I know. Akers was an ass. I'm sorry, Robbie."

"Anyway," Robbie went on, his smile returning, "have you looked at me lately?"

"You're gorgeous," I said instantly. "You're one of the best-looking guys in school."

Robbie laughed, sounding for a moment like his old awkward and self-conscious self. "Thanks. But, um, do you think maybe I have a shot now?"

I bit my lip. Now, there was a loaded question. I mean, totally apart from the fact that Bree might be getting involved in dark magick, it was so odd to think of her and Robbie as a couple. They'd been friends for so long. "I don't know," I said after a minute. "I don't know how Bree sees you. Yeah, you're good-looking, but she might think of you more as a brother. You sort of know her too well to put a spell on her. Or vice versa." I grinned. "Nonmagickally speaking."

Robbie nodded, kicking his boots through the leaves. His forehead was creased.

We walked deeper into the woods. We had only about twenty minutes before it would be dark; soon we'd have to turn around.

I threaded my arm through his. "There's something else," I said. I felt I needed to warn him, to put him on his guard. "Today I heard Bree and Raven talking about their new coven."

I told him the gist of what I had overheard in the bathroom, leaving out the part about my hair. That was something I had to deal with myself, with Cal's help. Besides, I wasn't even sure what the strand of hair meant. I didn't want Robbie to feel any more torn between me and Bree than he already did. But at the same time I didn't want her to use him.

"Yeah, I know they want to recruit new members," he acknowledged. "Don't worry, I'm not interested in joining them. But I am going to go and see what's going on."

Here with Robbie, in the woods, my thoughts about Bree and Raven and their coven began to seem a little paranoid. So what if they wanted to have their own coven? That wasn't necessarily bad or evil. It was just different, another spoke on the wheel. And the hair . . . well, who knew what that was about? Sky had told them no one would get hurt, and they seemed to trust her. But most of all, I just couldn't see Bree as evil. She'd been my best friend for so long. I'd know if there was something really warped about her. Wouldn't I?

I shook my head. It was too hard to think about. Then I remembered something else that I'd overheard. "Do you know someone named Thalia?" I asked Robbie. "She's in Bree and Raven's coven."

He thought and shook his head. "Maybe she's a friend of Raven's."

"Well, my informants tell me she may make a move on you," I said. I'd meant it as a joke, but the words came out sounding dark for some reason.

Robbie brightened. "Excellent," he said.

I laughed and poked him in the side as we walked along the park path.

"Just watch out, okay?" I said after a while. "I mean, with Bree. She tends to like guys she can control, you know? Guys she can intimidate, who'll do whatever she wants. They don't last long."

Robbie was silent. I didn't have to tell him all this; he knew it already.

"If Bree could care about you in the way you deserve," I went on, "it would be great. But I don't want you to get hurt."

"I know," he said.

I squeezed his arm a little tighter. "Good luck," I whispered.

He smiled. "Thanks."

For just a minute I wondered about love spells, love potions, and whether they ever worked. But Robbie broke into my thoughts, as if reading my mind.

"Don't you dare interfere with this magickwise," he warned me.

I feigned a hurt expression. "Of course not! I think I've done enough already. . . ."

Robbie laughed.

Suddenly I stopped short and pulled on his arm. He glanced at me quizzically. I raised a finger to my lips. My eyes scanned the woods. I saw nothing. But my senses . . . there was someone here. Two someones. I could feel them. But where were they?

After another moment I heard muffled voices.

Without thinking, we both dropped down behind a large boulder by the side of the path.

"You're wrong—I don't want to," someone was saying.

My eyes met Robbie's and widened. It was Matt's voice.

"Don't be silly, Matt. Of course you want to. I've seen how you look at me."

Of course. It was Raven—and she was trying to seduce Matt. It made perfect sense. I remembered how she'd said his name in the bathroom, how she'd laughed.

Without speaking, Robbie and I peeked over the top of the boulder. About twenty feet from us Matt and Raven were standing face-to-face. The sun was dropping rapidly now, the air turning colder. Raven moved closer to him, a smile playing on her lips. He frowned and stepped back but bumped into a tree. She moved in and pressed herself against him from chest to knee.

"Stop," he said weakly.

Raven wrapped her hands around his neck and stood on tiptoes to kiss him.

"Stop," he repeated, but the word had about as much force as Dagda's meowing. He resisted for a grand total of five seconds, then his arms went around her, his head slanted, and he pulled her to him tightly. Next to me Robbie dropped his head into his hands. I gaped at them for a little while longer—but when Matt unzipped Raven's coat and unbuttoned his own, I couldn't stand it anymore. Robbie and I leaned with our backs against the boulder. I heard a small moan and cringed. This was too embarrassing.

Robbie leaned closer and breathed into my ear. "Do you think they're gonna do it?"

I grimaced. "I don't know. I mean, it's freezing out here."

Robbie let out a muffled snort. Then I started giggling. For several seconds we crouched low and chewed on our coat sleeves, choking with laughter. Finally Robbie had to look. He eased his head around the boulder into the woods. "I can't see much," he complained in a whisper. "It's too dark in the trees."

I didn't want to look myself, though I knew I could have seen everything clearly. My night vision had improved dramatically; I could see easily in the darkness now, as if everything was illuminated slightly from within. I'd even found a reference to that power in a witchcraft book: it was called magesight.

"I don't think they're doing it," Robbie whispered, squinting. "It looks more like heavy making out. They're still standing."

"Thank the God and Goddess," I muttered.

I heard Matt's voice: "We have to stop. Jenna . . ."

"Forget Jenna," Raven murmured beguilingly. "I want you. You want me. You want to be with me, in our coven."

"No, I—"

"Matt, please. Quit fighting it. Just give in and you can have me. Don't you want me?"

He gave a strangled moan. Now it was my turn to cover my face with my hands. I wished I could stop Matt somehow. Of course, I was also thinking he was a total jerk.

"You *do* want me," Raven coaxed. "And I can give you what you want. What Jenna can't do for you. We can be together, and we can make magick, strong magick, in my coven. You don't want to be with Cal anymore. He's a control freak."

I stiffened and frowned. What the hell did she know about Cal?

"In our circle you can do what you want," Raven continued. "No one will hold you back. And you can be with me. Come on. . . ."

Raven's voice had never sounded so sweet and pleading. A shiver went down my spine that had nothing to do with the cold.

"I can't," Matt answered. His voice was tortured. We could hear their footsteps in the fallen leaves. Luckily they were moving away from us.

"My ass is frozen," Robbie whispered. "Let's get out of here."

I nodded and stood. As quietly and swiftly as we could,

we hurried back down the path to Das Boot. Without a word I dumped my basket of decorations in the trunk, and we hopped into the car.

"That was weird," Robbie finally muttered, blowing on his hands.

I nodded and jammed my key into the ignition. "Now we know why he's being strange," I said as I cranked the heater. I grinned. "Raven's totally hot for him."

Robbie didn't smile, and my own smile faded quickly. This wasn't funny. Not in the least. People could get hurt. I pulled Das Boot out of the parking lot and onto the road.

"Do we do anything about it?" I asked. "I feel sorry for Jenna. I even sort of feel sorry for Matt. He's just . . . lost."

"Do you think Raven's working a spell on him?" Robbie asked.

I shook my head. "I don't know. I mean, she isn't a blood witch. It would be different if she had been doing Wicca for years and was more in touch with her natural power. I don't really see it. Unless Sky did something to her that made her able to do something to Matt . . ."

"I guess it's enough to use the spell of sex," said Robbie dryly.

I thought back to how Cal had made me feel, to the few times we had been close and making out—how swept away I had been, how almost everything faded away except him.

"Yeah," I muttered. "So what do we do?"

Robbie thought. "I don't know. I can't see confronting either of them about it. In a way, it isn't our business. What if you told Cal? I mean, it's his coven they're trying to split up. Tell him the stuff you overheard at school."

I sighed, then nodded. "Good idea." I bit my lip. "Robbie—thanks for telling me about how you feel about Bree. I'm glad you trusted me. And I won't tell anyone else. But just . . . be careful, okay?"

Robbie nodded. "I will."

11

The Council

Samhain Eve, 1995.

My cousins are having a costume party on Samhain, after we do the service. I'm going as the Dagda, the Lord of the Heavens, and high king of the Tuatha De Danaan. I'm going to carry my panpipes for music, my wand for magick, and a book for knowledge. It'll be fun. I've been helping Linden and Alwyn with their costumes, and we've laughed a lot.

I saw my cousin Athar kissing Dare MacGregor behind a tree in the garden. I teased her and she put a binding spell on me and I can't even tattle. I've been looking for the antispell for two days.

Next year I'll be making my initiation, and then I'll be a witch. The waiting will be over. I've been studying long enough. Seems like all I've done is study, since I came here. Aunt Shelagh is not so bad, but Uncle Beck is a slave driver. And it's even harder because Linden and Alwyn are always hanging on to me, running after me, asking ques-

tions that I have a hard time answering. My mind is always spinning, spinning—like a wheel.

But what I think of most, still, is Mum and Dad. Where are
they, and why did they leave us? I have lost so much—my family,
my trust. The anger never dies. In a year, I'll learn the truth.
Another reason I can't wait for my initiation.

—Giomanach

"I tried to call you last night," I told Cal, pressing my face
against his warm coat. The chill air swept across the parking
lot, rustling my hair. I shivered. His hand stroked my back.

The morning bell was about to ring, but I didn't feel like
sharing Cal with the others right now. I didn't want to see
Matt and Jenna, either. My nerves felt jangled—both from the
bizarre events of yesterday and from the awful dreams I'd had
last night. Dreams of a dark cloud, like a swarm of black
insects, that was chasing me, suffocating me. I'd woken up
sweating and shaking, and I hadn't fallen back asleep until dawn.
And then Mary K. had woken me up barely an hour later.

"I know," Cal whispered, kissing my temple. "I got your
message. But I got back too late to call you. Was it important? I figured if you really needed me, you'd send a
witch message."

I wrapped my arms tightly around his waist. "It was just . . .
a bunch of weird stuff I wanted to talk to you about."

"Like what?"

For an instant I hesitated. We were leaning against his
car, across the street from school, and it felt almost private.
Not private enough, though. I glanced around to make sure

we were alone. "Well, first I overheard Raven and Bree talking in the girls' bathroom. They were talking about trying to get Matt and Robbie to join their coven. I think they want to split us up. Sky is their leader. They meet at her place, wherever that is. Then Bree said something about how she found some of my hair to give to Sky. I was kind of . . . freaked out," I confessed. "I mean, what does Sky want with my hair?"

Cal's golden eyes narrowed. "I don't know—but I plan to find out." He took a deep breath. "Don't worry. No one is going to interfere with you, Morgan. Not while I'm around."

I was amazed at how comforting I found his words. I felt like a weight had been lifted from my shoulders.

"There's more," I told him. "Later, Robbie and I were in the park, and we saw Raven and Matt actually making out."

Cal's eyebrows rose. "Oh," he said.

"Yeah. It was totally by accident. Robbie and I were walking around, gathering pinecones and stuff, and we saw Raven practically roping and tying Matt, trying to get him to break up with Jenna and join their coven."

"Man," Cal said, frowning. "So you were right—Matt is acting squirrelly, and now we know why."

"Yep."

A thoughtful expression crossed Cal's face. "And Sky's definitely the leader of their coven? That makes sense since you saw her meeting with Bree and Raven."

I nodded. But I couldn't help wondering . . . if Sky was their leader, then what had she been doing at Cal's house with Selene, participating in one of Selene's circles the night I'd found Maeve's Book of Shadows? Was she some kind of

Wiccan spy? Did Selene know Sky had her own coven? Did it even matter? My head was spinning. There was so much I didn't understand, so much I had to find out.

At that moment we heard the distant ringing of the homeroom bell, and we both groaned. Going to classes was not my number-one priority today.

With our arms around each other, we started slogging across the dead brown grass toward school. "Let me think about this," said Cal. "I need to talk to Sky, obviously. But I also need to figure out if I should talk to Raven, or Matt, or both."

I nodded. Part of me felt like a tattler. But mostly I was just relieved that Cal knew. I was thinking about talking to Matt myself, but I felt certain that Cal would take care of anything bigger, like with Sky. As we climbed the stone steps of the back entrance, I squeezed his hand good-bye. Yes, I would have to talk to Matt. He was a friend and still a part of our circle. I owed it to him.

"Matt?" I called down the hall. "Do you have a minute?"

It was after lunch and almost time to head to class. My lack of sleep was starting to catch up with me. My feet were definitely starting to drag. I would have given anything just to go curl up somewhere and take a nap. But this was the first chance I'd had to talk to Matt, and I wasn't going to let it slip.

"What's up, Morgan?" Matt asked. He stood in front of me, his face shuttered and remote, his hands in his pockets.

I took a deep breath, then decided just to get right into it. "I saw you and Raven yesterday," I stated baldly. "In Butler's Ferry park."

Matt's black eyes went wide, and he stared at me. "Uh . . . what are you talking about?"

"Come on," I said patiently. I pulled him over to one side of the hallway so we could talk without being overheard by the occasional wandering student. I lowered my voice. "I mean, I *saw* you yesterday, with Raven, in the park. I know she's trying to get you to join her coven. I know you're fooling around with her."

"I'm not fooling around with her!" Matt insisted.

I didn't even answer. I just raised my eyebrows.

His gaze fell to the floor. "I mean, it hasn't gotten that far," he mumbled, finally giving in. "Jesus, I don't know what to do."

I shrugged. "Break up with Jenna if you want to go out with Raven," I said.

"But I don't want to go out with Raven," Matt said. "I don't want to join her coven. The thing is . . . I've always thought she was kind of hot, you know?" He shook his head as if to clear it. "Why am I even telling you this?"

A couple of freshman girls passed us. Though they were only two years younger, they seemed a world apart from me. They *were* a world apart. They belonged to the world of school and homework and boys. Mary K.'s world. Not mine.

"Why does she want you to join their coven?" I asked.

"I guess they need more people," Matt answered. He sounded miserable. "A bunch of people started coming, but they all dropped out or were kicked out. A lot of them didn't take it seriously."

"But why *you?*" I pressed.

He sniffed. "I don't think it's really me. I mean, I'm nobody. I'm just a warm body."

"You're also part of our coven," I muttered. Part of me wanted to console him, but the other part wanted to wring his neck. "So what are you going to do?" I asked. I crossed my arms and tried not to look too judgmental.

"I don't know."

I sighed. "Maybe you should talk to Cal about this," I suggested. "Maybe he could help you clarify your thoughts."

Matt didn't look so sure. "Maybe," he said doubtfully. "I'll think about it." He glanced up at me. "Are you going to tell Jenna?"

"No." I shook my head. "But she's not stupid. She knows something's wrong."

He laughed distantly. "Yeah. We've been going out for four years. We know each other so well. But we're not even eighteen yet." With that, he pushed himself off the wall and headed off to his class—without so much as even a backward glance.

I watched him leave, thinking about what he'd said. Did he mean he had gotten tied up with Jenna too early and wanted to date other people? As I pondered it, a short rhyme popped into my mind. I repeated the words quietly.

> *"Help him see the way to go*
> *Help him know the truth to show*
> *He is not the hunter here*
> *Nor yet should he be the deer."*

I shook my head and headed to my own class. What did it mean? I wondered. Who knew? These things didn't come with instructions and commentary.

That afternoon when Mary K. and I got home from school, there was a gray car parked in front of our house. I didn't think anything of it—people parked in front of our house all the time. It was probably one of my mother's clients. So I just followed my sister up the walkway.

"Morgan!"

I wheeled at that voice. Hunter Niall was getting out of the car.

"Who's the dish?" Mary K. asked, arching an eyebrow.

I glared at her. "Go inside," I commanded, my heart kicking up a beat. "I'll deal with it."

Mary K. grinned at me. "Ooh. I can't wait to hear all about *this*." She pounded up the porch steps, stomped the ice off her Doc Martens, and went inside.

"Hello, Morgan," Hunter said, approaching me. How did he manage to make a simple greeting sound menacing? I wondered. His cold seemed to have gotten worse, too. His nose was red, and his voice was very nasal.

"What do you want?" I asked, swallowing. I remembered my bad dream of last night, my overwhelming feelings of being smothered, the dark cloud that had been chasing me.

He coughed. "I want to talk to you."

"About what?" I slung my backpack up onto the porch, not taking my eyes off him. I watched his hands, his mouth, his eyes, anything that he could use to do magick. My pulse was racing; my throat felt tight. I wished hard that Cal would suddenly drive up out of the blue. I considered sending him a message with my thoughts, a witch message—but then I realized I should just turn around and go in. I could handle myself. I didn't even need to talk to Hunter.

But for some reason I just stood there as he strode toward me, cutting across our lawn, leaving black footprints in the half-melted ice. He was close enough now that I could see that his fair skin was completely unblemished and there were a few freckles across the bridge of his strong nose. His eyes were cold and green.

"Let's talk about *you*, Morgan," he said, and he pushed his leather cap farther back on his head. A few tufts of blond hair poked out beneath it. "You don't know what you're doing with Cal." He made this announcement firmly but casually, as if he were simply telling me it was four o'clock and time for tea.

I shook my head, feeling the anger rise. "You don't even know—"

"It's not your fault," he interrupted. "This is all new to you."

The anger welled in the pit of my stomach, turning to rage. What right did he have to be so condescending to me?

Hunter fastened his eyes on mine. "You can't be expected to know about Cal, and his mother, and who they are," he said. "No one blames you," he added.

"No one blames me for what?" I demanded. "What are you talking about? I don't even *know* you. Where do you get off telling me anything about people I know, people I care about?"

He shrugged. His manner was as cold as the air around us. "You're stumbling into something bigger and darker than you could possibly imagine."

Rage turned to sarcasm. Hunter definitely brought out the worst in me. "Oh," I said, trying to sound bored. "Stop, stop, you're scaring me."

His face tightened, and he stepped toward me. My stomach clenched, and adrenaline pumped through my veins. I resisted the urge to turn and bolt into the house.

"Cal's lied to you," Hunter snarled. "He isn't what or who you think he is. Neither he nor his mother. I'm here to warn you. Don't be stupid. Look at me!" He gestured at his puffy eyes and red nose. "Do you think this is normal? Because it isn't. They're working magick on me—"

"Oh, are you kidding me?" I interrupted. "Are you actually telling me they're plotting against you? Give me a break!"

Who *was* this guy? Did he really think I would believe that Cal and Selene gave him a cold with dark magick? Or was he simply some paranoid nut? Maybe I should feel sorry for him—but I couldn't. All I felt was fury. I wanted to shove him as hard as I could, knock him down, and kick him. I had never been so angry, not at my parents, or Bree, not even at Bakker. I spun to go inside.

Hunter darted forward and caught my arm in a painful grip. Feeling trapped, furious, I drew my fingers together and smacked his hand. A jolt of crackly blue light jumped from my hand and shocked him. He released me at once, looking startled.

"So that's it," he whispered, rubbing his hand. He nodded in astonishment. "That's why he wants you."

"Get the hell away from me!" I shouted. "Or do you want me to really hurt you?"

Hunter sneered. "Trying to show me just what a powerful Woodbane you are?"

Time seemed to freeze.

"That's right," he whispered. "I know your secret. I know you're Woodbane."

"You don't know anything," I managed. The words came out in a misty whisper.

"Maeve Riordan," he said, shrugging. "Belwicket. They were all Woodbane. Don't act like you don't know."

"You're lying," I spat, but I felt an awful sensation

bubbling inside me, like a boiling cauldron. I wondered if I was going to throw up.

A flash of surprise crossed his face, instantly replaced with suspicion. "You can't hide it," he said. Now he sounded more irritated than arrogant. "You can't pretend it away. You're Woodbane, Cal is Woodbane, and the two of you are dancing with fire. But it's going to stop. You have a choice, and he does, too. I'm here to make sure you make the right one."

Move, I told my body, my feet. Get inside. Move, dammit! But I couldn't.

"Who are you?" I asked. "Why are you doing this to me?"

"I'm Hunter," he said with a sudden, wolfish grin that made me draw in my breath. He looked feral and dangerous. "The youngest member of the International Council of Witches."

My breath was now coming in shallow gasps, as if I were facing death itself.

"And I'm Cal's brother," he said.

12

The Future

I thank the God and Goddess for her. What a revelation she is, continually. When I was assigned to her, I had no idea she would be anything but an exercise in power. She has become so much more than that. She is a wild bird: delicate but possessing fierce strength. To move too soon would be to watch her take flight in fear.

For the first time in my life there is a chink in my armor, and it is my love.

—Sgàth

I ran up the ice-crusted steps of our house and threw myself through the door. Somehow I knew Hunter wouldn't follow me. The house was wonderfully warm and cozy, and I almost sobbed with relief as I pounded up the stairs and crashed into my bedroom. I had enough presence of mind to lock my door, and when Mary K. knocked a minute later, I called, "I'll be down in a few minutes."

"Okay," she replied. A moment later her feet padded downstairs.

My head was spinning. The first thing I did was run into the bathroom and examine my face in the mirror. It was me, still the same old me, despite the haunted look in my brown eyes and my shock-whitened face. Was Hunter right? Was I Woodbane?

I threw myself onto my bed and pulled Maeve's Book of Shadows out from under my mattress, then started flipping pages. I'd thumbed through the entries before, reading bits here and there, but mostly I'd been plodding through slowly, savoring every word, letting each spell sink in, deepening my knowledge and my only link to the woman who had given birth to me.

Strangely enough, though, it didn't take me long to find what I was looking for. It was from when Maeve was still writing as Bradhadair. She wrote matter-of-factly: "Despite the Woodbane blood in our veins, the Belwicket clan has resolved to do no evil."

With the force of a wave crashing on a beach, Selene's words came back to me: "I know what it contains, and I wasn't sure you were ready to read it."

Selene knew Maeve had been Woodbane. Suddenly my eyes were drawn to a small volume on my desk—the book about Woodbanes that Alyce at Practical Magick had wanted me to read. So . . . Alyce knew, too? Hunter knew? How did everyone know except *me*? Did Cal know? It didn't seem possible.

Hunter was a liar, though. I could feel the fury gathering within me all over again, like storm clouds. Hunter had also said he was Cal's brother. I thought back. I knew that Cal's father had remarried and that Cal had half siblings in England. But Hunter couldn't be one of them—he and Cal seemed practically the same age.

Lies. All lies.

But why was Hunter here? Had he just decided to come to America and mess with my mind? Maybe he *was* Cal's half brother and he was out to get Cal for some reason. And he was attacking me in order to hurt Cal. He was doing a damn good job of it if that was the case.

The whole thing was giving me a horrible headache. I shut the book and pulled Dagda into my arms, listening to his small, sleepy purr. I stayed there until Mary K. called me to tell me dinner was ready.

The meal was practically inedible: a vegetarian casserole that Mary K. had concocted. I wasn't even hungry, anyway. I needed some answers.

Sidestepping a whispered question from Mary K. about Hunter, I told her I'd help her with the dishes later, then asked my parents if I could go to Cal's. Luckily they said yes.

It started to snow again as I pulled away from the house in Das Boot. Of course I was still upset about everything Hunter had said, but I tried not to let it affect my driving. The wipers pushed snow off the windshield in big arcs, and my brights illuminated thousands of flakes swirling down out of the sky. It was beautiful and silent and lonely.

Woodbane. When I got home tonight, I would read the book Alyce had given me. But first I needed to see Cal.

In the long, U-shaped driveway in front of Cal's house, I saw his gold Explorer and another car—a small, green vehicle I didn't recognize. I plodded through the surface of the snowfall, feeling the ice crunch beneath my clogs. The wide stone steps had been shoveled and salted. I hurried up and rang the doorbell.

What would I say if Selene answered the door? The last time I had seen her, I was in her private library, basically stealing a book from her. On the other hand, the book was rightly mine. And she *had* allowed me to keep it.

Several seconds passed. There was no stirring inside, at least none that I could hear. I started to feel cold. Maybe I should have called first, I thought. I rang the doorbell again, then reached out with my senses to see who was home. But the house was a fortress. I received no answer. And then a thought occurred to me: It was spelled, deliberately shut off from magick.

Snowflakes gathered on my long hair, as if I wore a lace mantle that was slowly melting against my cheeks and eyelids. I rang again, beginning to feel unsure. Maybe they were busy. Maybe they were meeting with someone. Maybe they were having a circle or working magick or throwing a party . . . but at last the tall, heavy wooden door opened.

"Morgan!" Cal said. "I didn't even feel you come up. You look frozen. Come on in." He ushered me into the foyer and brushed his hand down my cold, damp hair. Light footsteps behind him made me pull back, and I looked up to see Sky Eventide.

I blinked, looking at her. Her face was closed, and I wondered what I had interrupted. Had Cal invited her here to ask her about her coven and my hair? I glanced at him for signs of irritation or wariness, but he seemed easy and comfortable.

"I should have called," I said, looking from Cal to Sky. "I didn't mean to interrupt anything."

Tell me what I'm interrupting, I thought as Sky reached for her heavy leather coat. She looked beautiful and exotic. Next to her I felt about as exciting as a brown field mouse. I had a tingle of jealousy. Did Cal find her attractive?

"It's all right," Sky said, zipping her coat. "I was just leaving." Her black eyes searched Cal's and held them. "Remember what I said," she told him, ignoring me. The words seemed to have an element of threat, but Cal laughed.

"You worry too much. Relax," he said cheerfully, and she just looked at him.

I watched as she opened the front door and left, not bothering to say good-bye. There was something strange going on here, and I needed to know what it was.

"What was all that about?" I asked point-blank.

Cal shook his head, still smiling. "I ran into her earlier and told her I wanted to talk to her about what she's up to with her coven. So she came over—but all she wanted was to be Hunter's messenger," he said, tugging on my coat so it came off. He draped it over a high-backed chair and then took my hand, rubbing its coldness away. "Hey, I tried to call you a few minutes ago, but the phone was busy."

"Someone must be online," I guessed, frowning. Was he trying to change the subject? "What kind of message did Sky have?"

"She was warning me," he answered simply. Still holding my hand, he led me through a pair of dark wooden doors that opened into a large, formal parlor. A fire was blazing in an enormous stone hearth, and in front of it a deep blue sofa beckoned. Cal sat and pulled me down to sit next to him.

"Warning you?" I pressed.

He sighed. "Hunter's out to get me, basically, and Sky was

telling me that I should be on my guard. That's all."

I frowned into the fire. Usually I felt reassured by the heat and glow of flames—but not now. "Why is Hunter out to get you?"

Cal hesitated. "It's . . . um, kind of personal," he said.

"But why was Sky warning you? Isn't she with him?"

"Sky doesn't know what she wants," Cal answered cryptically. He hadn't shaved in a while, and the shadow of stubble across his face made him look older. Sexier, too. He was quiet for a few moments, and then he edged closer to me, so I felt his warmth from my shoulder to my hip. A memory swept over me: of how it had felt to lie next to him, to kiss him deeply, to have his hands touch me and to touch him back. But I couldn't allow myself to be distracted.

"Who *is* Hunter?" I asked.

Cal made a face. "I don't want to talk about him," he said.

"Well, he came to see me today."

"What?" Shock flared in Cal's golden eyes. I saw something else there, too. Concern, maybe. Concern for *me*.

"What's the International Council of Witches?" I pressed on.

Cal drew away from me, then sighed in resignation. He sat back against the couch and nodded. "You'd better just tell me everything," he said.

"Hunter came to my house and said I was Woodbane," I said. The words flowed from my mouth as if a dam had been broken. "He said *you* were Woodbane and that he was your brother. He said I was stumbling into danger. He said he was on the International Council of Witches."

"I can't believe this." Cal groaned. "I'm sorry. I'll make sure he leaves you alone from now on." He paused, as if collecting his thoughts. "Anyway, the International Council of Witches is just what it sounds like. Witches from all over the world getting together. It's kind of a governing body, though what they govern isn't really clear. They're kind of like village elders, but the village consists of all witches everywhere. I think there's something like sixty-seven countries represented."

"What do they do?"

"In the old days they often settled disputes about land, clan wars, cases of magick being used against others," Cal explained. "Now they mostly try to set guidelines about appropriate use of magick, and they try to consolidate magickal knowledge."

I shook my head, not quite understanding. "And Hunter's part of it?"

Cal shrugged. "He says he is. I think he's lying, but who knows? Maybe the council is really hard up for members." He gave a short laugh. "Mostly he's just a second-rate witch with delusions of grandeur."

"Delusions is right," I murmured, remembering how Hunter had claimed his cold was the result of a spell. That was so obviously ridiculous that maybe I should just forget about everything else he'd said, too. But somehow I couldn't.

Cal glanced at me. "He told you that you were Woodbane?"

"Yes," I said stiffly. "And I went inside and found it in Maeve's BOS. I am Woodbane. All of Belwicket was. Did you know?"

Cal didn't answer right away. Instead he seemed to weigh my words. He looked at the fire. "How do you feel about that?" he finally asked.

"Bad," I said honestly. "I would have been really proud to be Rowanwand or even anything else. But to be Woodbane . . . it's like finding out my ancestors are a long line of jail-birds and lowlifes. Worse, really. Much worse."

Cal laughed again. He turned to me. "No, it's not, my love. It's not that bad."

"How can you say that?"

"It's easy," he said with a grin. "Nowadays it isn't a big deal. Like I said, people have sort of a prejudiced view of Woodbanes, but they're ignoring all their good qualities, like strength, and loyalty, and power, and pursuit of knowledge."

I stared at him. "You didn't know I was a Woodbane? I'm sure your mom does."

Cal shook his head. "No, I didn't know. I haven't read Maeve's book, and Mom didn't discuss it with me. Listen, knowing you're Woodbane isn't a bad thing. It's better than not knowing your clan at all. Better than being a mongrel. I've always thought the Woodbanes have gotten a bad rap— you know, revisionist history."

I turned back to the fire. "He said you were Woodbane, too," I whispered.

"We don't know what we are," Cal said quietly. "Mom has done a lot of research, but it isn't clear. But if we were, would it matter to you? Would you not love me?"

"Of course it wouldn't matter," I said. The flames crack-led with life before us, and I rested my head on Cal's shoul-der. As upset as I had been, I was starting to feel better. I kicked off my shoes and stretched my feet out to the fire. My socks hung loose. The heat felt delicious on my toes, and I sighed. I still had more questions to ask.

"Why did Hunter say he was your brother?"

Cal's eyes darkened. "Because my dad's a high priest and very powerful. Hunter wants to be that way, too. And he *is* the son of the woman my father married after he left my mom. So we're at least stepbrothers."

I swallowed, wincing. "Ouch," I murmured. "I'm sorry."

"Yeah. Me too. I wish I'd never met him."

"How did you meet?" I asked cautiously.

"At a convention, two years ago," Cal answered.

I was startled into laughter. "A witch convention?"

"Uh-huh," said Cal, smiling a little. "I met Hunter, and he informed me we were only six months apart and brothers. Which would mean that my father had deliberately gotten another woman pregnant while my mom was pregnant with *me.* I hated Hunter for that. I still don't want to believe it. So no matter what Hunter says, I say that his father is someone else, not my dad. I can't accept that my father, total jerk that he is, would have done that." He put his arm around me, and I rested my chin on his chest, hearing the steady thumping of his heart, sleepily watching the fire.

"Is that why Hunter is acting this way?"

"Yeah, I think so. Somehow he's all . . . I don't know, bent and twisted. It must have something to do with his child- hood. I know I shouldn't hate him—it's not his fault my dad's life is so messy. But he just—got off on telling me that my dad fathered him. Like he enjoyed hurting me."

I gently stroked Cal's wavy hair. "I'm sorry," I said again.

Cal gave a rueful chuckle, and I wanted to comfort him, the way he had comforted me so many times. Gently, I kissed him, trying to give him love he could be sure of. He almost purred with contentment and held me closer.

"Why was Hunter here, in your mother's house, that

night when she had the circle?" I asked softly when I stopped for breath.

"He likes to keep in touch with us," Cal said sarcastically. "I don't know why. Sometimes I think he likes Mom and me to just remember he's alive, that he exists. Rubbing our faces in it, I guess."

I shuddered. "Ugh. He's horrible. I don't feel the least bit sorry for him. I just can't stand him—and I hate what he's doing to you. If he keeps on, he'd better watch out."

Cal grinned. "Mmmm, I like it when you talk tough."

"I'm serious," I told him. "I'll zap him with witch fire so hard, he won't know what hit him." I flexed my fingers, surprised at the violence of my own feelings.

Cal's smile broadened, but he said, "Look, let's just change the subject." He kissed me, then pulled away. "I have a question for you. What are you thinking about in terms of college?"

I furrowed my brow, surprised and bemused. "I'm not sure," I said. "For a while I thought I'd apply to MIT or maybe Cal Tech. You know, something for math."

"Brain," Cal teased affectionately.

"Why do you want to know?" I asked. It seemed so oddly normal, coming right after all this talk about a Council of Witches and ancient magickal clans.

"I've been thinking about our future," he said. His tone was very straightforward, relaxed. "I was thinking about going to Europe next year, maybe taking a year off to travel. I was also thinking, maybe I could get us a little place when I come back and we could both go to the same school."

My eyes widened with shock. "You mean . . . *live together?*" I whispered.

"Yes, live together," he said, flashing me a little half grin, as if he were talking about doing our homework together or going to see a movie. "I want to be with you." He drew back and looked deeply in my eyes. "No one's ever wanted to protect me before, like you do."

My breath came fast at the thought. Laughing, I grabbed him, knocking him back on the sofa. I meant to kiss him, but we ended up toppling onto the floor with a thud.

"Ow," said Cal, rubbing his head. He smiled at me and I kissed him. But right at that moment I caught a glimpse of an old grandfather clock. My spirits sank. It was getting late. Mom and Dad would start to worry.

"I have to go," I said reluctantly.

"Someday you won't have to," he promised.

Then I was getting into my coat, melting with happiness, and Cal was walking me out. I didn't even feel the cold until I was almost home.

13

Dark Side

Litha, 1996

Until now my life has been winter. But last night, at my initiation, spring broke through the ice. It was magick. Aunt Shelagh and Uncle Beck led the rite. The coven elders gathered around. I was blindfolded and given wine to drink. I was tested and I answered as best I could. In my blindness I made a circle and drew my runes and cast my spells. The warmth of the summer night fled before the cold draughts of the North Sea, blowing off the coast. Someone held the sharp point of a dagger to my right eye and told me to step forward. I tried to remember if I'd seen any coven members with ruined eyes, and I couldn't, so I stepped smartly forward, and the sharp tip faded away.

I sang my song of initiation alone, in the darkness, with the weight of the magick pressing in on me, and my feet stumbling in the rough heathers of the headland. I sang my song, and the magick came to me and lifted me up, and I felt huge and powerful and bursting with joy and knowledge. Then I was unblindfolded and the initiation was complete. I was a witch and a full-grown man in the eyes of the craft. We drank wine and I hugged everyone. Even Uncle Beck, and he hugged me back and told me he was proud of me. Cousin Athar teased me but I just grinned at her. Later I hunted Molly F. down and gave her a real kiss, and she pushed me away and threatened to tell Aunt Shelagh.

I guess I wasn't as much of a man as I thought.

—Giomanach

On Friday when I woke up, the remnants of disturbing dreams fluttered in my mind like torn banners. I stretched several times, trying to snap myself out of it—and then they faded, and I had no idea what they'd been: there were no lingering images or clear emotions to give me a clue. I just knew they'd been bad.

I had stayed up too late the night before, reading both Maeve's Book of Shadows and the book about Woodbanes that Alyce had given to me. It was still very strange for me, knowing Maeve was my birth mother and now knowing she was also Woodbane. Throughout my entire life I had felt just a bit different from my family, and I had wondered why. The odd thing was, now that I knew my origins, I felt more like a Rowlands and less like an Irish witch.

I could tell it was cold and disgusting outside just from looking out the window. And I was snug in my bed, and I had beside me a small kitten who was completely adorable and sound asleep.

So there was no way I was getting up.

"Morgan, you have to hurry!" Mary K. shouted, sounding frantic. A second later she burst into my room and tugged at my comforter. "We have ten minutes to get to school, and it's snowing and I can't ride my bike. Come on!"

Damn, I thought, giving in. One day I would really have to act on my desire to skip school.

We made it just as the late bell rang, and I skittered into class just as my name was called for roll.

"Here!" I said unnecessarily, panting and sliding into my seat. As Tamara smirked at me, I pulled out my brush and began untangling my hair. Across the room Bree sat talking to Chip Newton. I thought about Sky and Raven and their coven, about Sky telling them about the dark side. I still didn't have a clear idea of what the dark side was except for some vague paragraphs in one of my Wicca books. I would have to do more research. I would have to finish reading the book Alyce had given me about the Woodbanes. Cal had said there was no dark side per se, there was only the circle of Wicca. Maybe I should ask Alyce about it.

I glanced over at Bree, as if looking at her would tell me what she was doing or thinking. I used to be able to look in her eyes and know exactly what was going on with her—and also tell her exactly what was going on with me. Not anymore. We spoke different languages now.

It was an odd day.

At school Matt wouldn't meet my eyes. Jenna seemed

nervous. Cal was fine, of course; we both knew we had reached a new level of closeness. We'd made plans for the future. Every time we saw each other, we smiled. He was a ray of light to me. Robbie was his usual comforting self, and it was interesting to see how girls who'd never noticed him before were now going out of their way to talk to him, to walk next to him, to pepper him with questions about home-work and chess problems and what kind of music he liked. Ethan and Sharon were still circling each other flirtatiously.

Yet the whole day I felt on edge somehow. I hadn't got-ten enough sleep, and I had too many questions ricocheting around my brain. I couldn't relax and pay attention in class. In my mind I kept going over what I had read in Maeve's book. Then my thoughts would flash to Hunter's bizarre behavior—and then to lying with Cal in front of the fire at his house, feeling so full of love for him. Why couldn't I focus? I needed to be alone or, better yet, with Cal—to meditate and focus my energy.

After school I waited for Cal by his car. He was talking to Matt, and I wondered what they were saying. Matt looked uncomfortable, but he was nodding. Cal seemed to be mak-ing him feel better. That was good. But I also hoped he was letting Matt know that it was very uncool to mess around with Raven behind Jenna's back.

Finally Cal saw me. He strolled right over and put his arms around me, pinning me to his car. I was aware of Nell Norton walking by, looking envious, and I enjoyed it.

"What are you up to right now?" I asked. "Can you hang out?"

"I wish I could," he said, holding a handful of hair and kissing my forehead. "Mom has some people in from out of town, and she wants me to meet with them. People from her old coven in Manhattan."

"How many covens has she had?" I asked, curious.

"Hmmm, let's see," Cal said, counting under his breath. "Eight, I think. She forms a coven in a new place and makes sure they're really strong, then she trains a new leader, and when they're ready, she moves on." He smiled down at me. "She's like the Johnny Appleseed of Wicca."

I laughed. Cal kissed me again and got into his car, and I headed for Das Boot. A minivan slowed next to me, and the window went down. "Going home with Jaycee!" Mary K. called. She waved, and I waved back. I saw Robbie pull away in his car, and down the block Bree climbed into her BMW and drove off. I wished I knew where she was going but didn't have the emotional or physical energy to follow her.

Instead I headed for Red Kill.

Practical Magick smelled like steam and tea and candles burning. I stepped in and felt myself relax for the first time since I had pried myself out of bed this morning.

For a moment I stood just inside the door, warming up, feeling my chest expand and my fingers thaw. My hair was slightly damp from the snow, and I shook it out so it would dry. David looked up from the checkout counter and regarded me with his full attention. He didn't smile, but somehow he conveyed the impression of being glad to see me. Maybe I was finally used to him, because it felt like seeing an old friend. I hadn't felt an immediate connection with him as I had with Alyce, and I wasn't sure why. But maybe I was getting over it.

"Hello, Morgan," he said. "How are you?"

I thought for a moment, then shook my head with a tired smile. "I don't know."

David nodded, then stepped through a curtained door in back of the counter, revealing a small, cluttered room. I saw a tiny, battered table with three chairs, a rusty apartment-size fridge, and a two-burner hot plate. A teakettle was already starting to whistle there. Strange, I thought. Had he somehow known I was coming?

"You look like you could use some tea," he called.

"Tea would be great," I said sincerely, deciding to accept the friendship he seemed to be offering. "Thanks." I stuffed my gloves into my pockets and looked around the store. No one else was here. "Slow day?" I asked.

"We had some people in this morning," David replied from behind the curtain. "But it's been quiet this afternoon. I like it this way."

I wondered if they made any money doing this.

"Um, who owns this store?" I asked.

"My aunt Rose, actually," said David. "But she's very old now, and doesn't come in much anymore. I've been working here for years—on and off since right after college." I heard some clinking of spoons in mugs, and then he ducked back through the curtain, carrying two steaming cups. He handed one to me. I took it gratefully, inhaling its unusual fragrance.

"Thanks. What kind of tea is this?"

David grinned and sipped his own. "You tell me."

I looked at him uncertainly, and he just waited. Was this a test? Feeling self-conscious, I closed my eyes and sniffed deeply. The tea had several scents: they blended together into a sweet whole, and I couldn't identify any of them.

"I don't know," I said.

"You do," David encouraged quietly. "Just listen to it."

Once again I closed my eyes and inhaled, and this time I let go of the knowledge that this was tea in a mug. I focused on the odor, on the qualities carried by the water's steam. Slowly I breathed in and out, stilling my thoughts, relaxing my tension. The more still I became, the more I felt part of the tea. In my mind's eye I saw the gentle steam rising and swaying before me, dissolving in the slightest breath of air.

Speak to me, I thought. Show me your nature.

Then, as I watched inside my mind, the steam coiled and separated into four streams, like a fine thread unraveling. With my next breath I was alone in a meadow. It was sunny and warm, and I reached out to touch a perfect, rounded pink blossom. Its heavy aroma tickled my nose and bathed me in its beauty.

"Rose," I whispered.

David was quiet.

I turned to the next steam thread and followed it, saw it being dug from the ground, black dirt clinging to its rough skin. It was washed and peeled, and when its pink flesh was grated, a sharp tang was released.

"Oh, ginger," I listed, nodding.

The third strand drifted from rows and rows of low-growing, silver-green plants covered with purple flowers. More bees than I had ever seen buzzed over the plants, creating a vibrant, living mantle of insects. Hot sun, black earth, and the incessant drone filled me with a drowsy contentment.

"Lavender."

The last thread was a woodier scent, less familiar and also less pretty. It was a low-growing, crinkle-leafed plant, with slender stalks of miniature flowers. I crushed some of the leaves in my hand and smelled them. It was earthy and different, almost unpleasant. But intertwined with the other three scents, it made a beautifully balanced whole: it added strength to their sweetness and tempered the pungent odor of the ginger.

"I want to say skullcap," I said tentatively. "But I'm not sure what that is."

I opened my eyes to find David watching me.

"Very good," he said with a nod. "Very good indeed. Skullcap is a perennial. Its flowering stems help diminish tension."

By now the tea had cooled a bit, and I took a sip. I didn't notice the actual flavors so much; I was more aware of drinking the different essences, allowing them to warm me and infuse me with their qualities of healing, soothing, and calming. I perched on a stool next to the counter. But then, without warning, all the unsettled aspects of my life crept up and made me feel like I was suffocating again. Matt and Jenna, Sky and Bree and Raven, Hunter, being Woodbane, Mary K. and Bakker . . . it was overwhelming. The only thing that was going right was Cal.

"Sometimes I feel like I don't know anything," I heard myself blurt out. "I just want things to be straightforward. But things and people have all these different layers. As soon as you learn one, then another pops up, and you have to start all over again."

"The more you learn, the more you need to learn," David agreed calmly. "That's what life is. That's what Wicca is. That's what you are."

I looked at him. "What do you mean?"

"You thought you knew yourself, and then you found out

one thing and then another thing. It changes the whole way you see yourself and see others in relation to you." He sounded very matter-of-fact.

"You mean, *one* does these things or me in particular?" I asked carefully.

Outside, the weak afternoon sun gave up its struggle and faded behind a bank of gray clouds. I could make out the hulking shape of Das Boot, parked in front of the store entrance, and I saw that it was already covered by at least an inch of snow and tiny rocks of ice.

"Everyone is like that," he said with a smile, "but I was speaking of you in particular."

I blinked, not quite understanding. David had once said that I was a witch who pretended not to be a witch.

"Do you still think I pretend that I'm not a witch?" I asked.

He didn't seem concerned that I knew what he had said. "No." He hesitated, forming his thoughts. He looked up at me, his dark eyes steady. "It's more that you don't present yourself clearly because you aren't yet sure who you are, *what* you are. I've known I'm a witch my whole life— thirty-two years. And I've also always known—" He paused again, as if making up his mind. Then he said quietly, "I'm a Burnhide. It's not only who I am, it's what I am. I'm the same thing on the inside as I am on the outside. You're different in that you've only recently discovered—"

"That I'm Woodbane?" I interrupted.

He gazed at me. "I was about to say, discovered you're a witch at all. But now you know you're Woodbane. You've hardly begun to discover what this means to you, so it's almost impossible for you to project what it should mean to others."

I nodded. He was beginning to make sense. "Alyce once told me that you and she were both blood witches, but you didn't know your clans. But you're a Burnhide?"

"Yes. The Burnhides settled mostly in Germany. My family was from there. We've always been Burnhides. Among most blood witches your clan is considered a private matter. So many people lost all knowledge of their house that nowadays most people say they don't know their clan until they know someone well enough."

I felt pleased that he had trusted me. "Well, I'm Woodbane," I said awkwardly.

David grinned without prejudice. "It's good to know what you are," he said. "The more you know, the more you know."

I laughed at that and drank my tea.

"Are there any ways to really identify the clans?" I asked after a moment. "I read that Leapvaughns tend to have red hair."

"It's not incredibly reliable," David answered. The phone rang, and he cocked his head for a moment, concentrating, then didn't answer it. In the back room I heard the answering machine pick it up.

"For example, lots of Burnhides have dark eyes, and lots of them tend to go gray early." He gestured to his own silvery hair. "But that doesn't mean every dark-eyed, gray-haired person is a Burnhide nor that all Burnhides look like this."

I had a sudden thought. "What about this?" I asked, and pulled up my shirt to show him the birthmark on my side, under my right arm. My need to know outweighed my embarrassment.

"Yeah, the Woodbane athame," David said matter-of-factly. "Same thing. Not all of you have them."

It was somehow shocking to hear so casually that I had been marked this way my whole life, marked with the symbol of a clan, and that I had never known.

"What about . . . the International Council of Witches?" I asked, my brain following a series of thoughts.

The brass bells over the door jangled, and two girls about my age came in. Without deliberately deciding to, I sent out my senses and picked up the fact that they seemed nonmagickal: just girls. They walked through the store slowly, whispering and laughing, looking at all the merchandise.

"It's an independent council," David said softly. "It's designed to represent all the modern clans—there are hundreds and hundreds who aren't affiliated with any of the seven houses. Its main function is to monitor and sometimes punish the illegitimate use of magick . . . magick used to gain power over others, for example, or to interfere with others without their knowledge or agreement. Magick used to harm."

I frowned. "So they're sort of like the Wicca police."

David raised his eyebrows. "There are those who see the council that way, certainly."

"How do they know if someone is using magick for the wrong reasons?" I asked. Behind us the girls had left the book aisle and were now oohing and aahing over the many beautiful handmade candles the store stocked. I waited to hear them come across the penis-shaped candles.

"Oh my God," whispered one, and I grinned.

"There are witches within the council who specifically look for people like that," David explained. "We call them Seekers. It's their job to investigate claims of dark magick or misuse of power."

"Seekers?" I said.

"Yeah. Wait a second. I can tell you more about them." David ducked out from the counter and headed down the book aisle. He paused for a moment in front of a shelf, then chose an old, worn volume and pulled it out. He was already thumbing through pages when he got back to me. "Here," he said. "Listen to this."

I stared at him as he began to read, sipping my tea.

"'I am sad to say that there are those who do not agree with the wisdom and purpose of the High Council. Some clans exist who wish to remain separate, secretive, and insulated from their peers. Certainly no one could fault a clan for guarding private knowledge. We all agree that a clan's spells, history, and rituals are their province alone. But we have seen in these modern times that it is wise to join together, to share as much as we can, to create a society in which we can fully participate and celebrate with others of our own kind. This is the purpose of the International Community of Witches.'"

He paused for a moment and glanced at me.

"That sounds like a good thing," I said.

"Yes," he said, but there was an odd tone in his voice. His eyes flashed back down to the page. "'One cannot help but question those who refuse to participate, who work against this goal and use magick that the council has decried. In the past such apostasy was the undoing of countless numbers. There is little strength in being alone and little joy in unsanctified magick. That is why we have Seekers.'"

There was something about the way he said *seekers* that gave me a chill. "And what do they do, exactly?" I pressed.

"'Seekers are council members who have been selected to find witches who have strayed beyond our bounds,'" he continued. "'If they discover witches who are actively working against the council, working to harm themselves or others, then they have been given license to take action against them. It is better that we police our own, from within, before the rest of the world chooses once again to police us from without.'" David closed the book and looked at me again. "Those are the words of Birgit Fallon O'Roark. She was high priestess of the High Council from the 1820s to the 1860s."

My tea was starting to get cold. I finished it all in a big gulp and placed the mug on the counter. "What do the Seekers do if they find the witches working against the council?" I asked.

"Usually they put binding spells on them," said David, looking troubled. His voice sounded strained, as if the words themselves were painful to say. "So they can't use their magick anymore. There are things you can do, certain herbs or minerals that you can make them ingest . . . and they can no longer get in touch with their inner magick."

A cold wind seemed to pass over me. My stomach twisted. "Is that bad?" I asked.

"It's very bad," said David emphatically. "To be magickal and not be able to use your magick—it's like suffocating. Like being buried alive. It's enough to make someone lose their mind."

I thought of Maeve and Angus, living in America for

years, renouncing their powers. How had they borne it? What had it done to them? I thought about my suffocating dream—how intolerable it had been. Was that what their everyday life had been like for them without Wicca?

"But if you're abusing your power, a Seeker will come for you sooner or later," said David, shaking his head, almost as if to himself. His face seemed older, lined with memories I didn't think I wanted to know about.

"Hmmm." Outside it was dark. I wondered who Cal was meeting and if he would call me later. I wondered if Hunter was really from the council. He seemed more like one of the bad witches the council would send a Seeker to track down.

I wondered if Maeve and the rest of Belwicket had been successful in renouncing the dark side. Would the dark side allow itself to be renounced?

"Is there a dark side?" I said the words tentatively, and felt David draw back.

"Oh, yes," he said softly. "Yes, there's a dark side."

I swallowed, thinking of Cal. "Someone told me there was no dark side—that all of Wicca was a circle and everything was connected to each other, all part of the same thing. That would mean there aren't two different sides, like light and dark."

"That's true, too." David sounded thoughtful. "We say bright and dark when talking about magick used for good and magick used for bad, or evil—to give it a common name."

"So they're two different things?" I pressed.

Slowly David ran his finger around the circular rim of his cup. "Yes. They are different but not opposite. Often they're right next to each other, very similar. It has to do with philosophy and how people interpret actions. It has to do with the spirit of the magick, with will and intent." He glanced up at me and smiled. "It's very complicated. That's why we have to study our whole lifetimes."

"But can you say that someone is on the dark side and that they're evil and you should stay away from them?"

Again David looked troubled. "You could. But it wouldn't be the whole picture. Are there witches who use magick for the wrong purposes? Yes. Are there witches who deliberately hurt others for their own gain? Yes. Should some witches be stopped? Yes. But it usually isn't that simple."

It seemed that nothing in Wicca was simple, I thought. "Well, I'd better get home," I said, pushing my mug across the counter. "Thanks for the talk. And for the tea."

"It was my pleasure," said David. "Please come back any time you need to talk. Sometimes Alyce and I . . . feel concerned about you."

"Me?" I asked. "Why?"

A slight smile turned up the corners of David's mouth. "Because you're in the middle of becoming who you will be," he said gently. "It isn't going to be easy. You may need help. So feel free to ask us for it."

"Thanks," I said again, feeling reassured but still not quite understanding what he meant. With a little wave I left the warmth of Practical Magick and went out to my car. My tires slid a tiny bit as I backed up, but soon I was on the road heading back to Widow's Vale, my headlights illuminating each unique, magickal snowflake.

14

Scry

Litha, 1996

Early this morning Uncle Beck and I sat on the edge of the cliff and watched the sun come up, my first sunrise as a witch, and he told me the truth about Mum and Dad. In all the years since they disappeared, I have fought back tears at every turn, telling myself not to give in to childish grief.

But today the tears came, and it's strange, because now I am supposed to be a man. Still, I wept. I wept for them, but mostly for me—for all the anger I have wasted. I know now that Uncle Beck had good reasons for keeping the truth from me, that Mum and Dad had to disappear in order to protect me, Linden, and Alwyn. That he's heard from them only once, two years ago. That he hasn't even ever tried to scry for them.

And I know why.

And now I also know what to do with myself, where I'm going, *what I'll be, and it's funny, because it's all in my name anyway. I am going to hunt down those who ripped my family apart, and I won't stop until I draw Yr on their faces with their blood.*

—Giomanach

I was barely two miles from my house when I saw the headlights behind me. First there was nothing, not another car in sight. Then I rounded a corner, and suddenly the lights were right there in my rearview mirror, blinding me, filling my car as if it were lit from within. I squinted and flashed my brakes a few times, but whoever it was didn't pass or turn off the brights. The headlights drew closer.

I slowed Das Boot, sending the message of "get off my tail," but the other car glued itself to my bumper, tailgating me. Mild road rage started to build. Who could be following me like this? Some practical joker, a jerk kid with his dad's car? I jammed my foot on the gas, but the car sped up as I did. The tires skidded slightly as I rounded another corner. The car matched my movement. A prickle of nervousness shot down my spine. My wipers were click-clicking away—matching my pulse—clearing away the falling snow. I couldn't see any other lights on the road. We were alone.

Okay. Something was definitely wrong. I'd heard stories about car jackers . . . but I was in a '71 Valiant. No matter how much I loved it, I doubted anyone would try to steal it from me by force, especially not in the middle of a snowstorm. So what was this idiot doing?

My eyes shot to the rearview mirror. The headlights bored into my pupils. I blinked, trying to clear my vision of a sea of purple dots. Anger began to turn to fear. I could barely see a thing in the darkness . . . nothing except those lights, the lights that seemed to grow in strength with each passing second. But for some reason, I couldn't hear the other car's engine. It was as if—

Magick.

The word slithered into my thoughts like a snake.

I bit my lip. Maybe that wasn't a car behind me at all. Maybe those two lights were some manifestation of a magickal force. I had a sudden, vivid memory of Hunter Niall peering under Cal's Explorer, of Cal showing me that rune-inscribed stone. We knew Hunter had tried to use magick on us once already. What if he was doing it again now, to me?

Home, I thought. I just needed to get home. I flipped up my mirror so the light wouldn't blind me. But there was about another mile and a half of road until I made it to my street. That was actually pretty far. "Crap," I muttered, and my voice shook a little. With my right hand I drew signs on my dashboard: Eolh, for protection; Ur, for strength; and Rad, for travel. . . .

The lights seemed to flash even brighter in my mirror. My left hand jerked involuntarily on the steering wheel. All at once I felt something bumpy under my wheels.

Before I knew it, I was sliding sideways out of control into the deep drainage ditch. *Goddess!* I screamed silently. Fear and adrenaline pierced my body, a slew of invisible arrows. My hands gripped the steering wheel. I had lost control; the tires screeched. Das Boot lurched sideways on an ice slick, like a heavy white glacier.

The next few seconds unfolded in slow motion. With a sickening crunch the car's nose rammed a pile of ice and snow. I jerked forward and heard the shattering of a headlight. Then silence. The car was no longer moving. But for a few seconds I sat there—paralyzed, unable to move. I was conscious only of my own breathing. It came in quick, uneven gasps.

All right, I finally said to myself. I'm not hurt.

When I lifted my head, I thought I saw the briefest flash of two red taillights, vanishing into the night.

My eyes narrowed. So . . . it *had* been a real car after all.

With a trembling sigh I turned off the engine. Then I threw open the door and hoisted myself out of the driver's seat—no easy feat, considering Das Boot was skewed at a crazy angle. It was hard to concentrate, but I called on my magesight and peered down the road in the direction that the car had disappeared. All I saw, though, were trees, sleeping birds, the faint glow of living nocturnal creatures.

The car was gone.

I leaned against my door, breathing hard, my fists clenched inside my pockets. Even though I was pretty sure those lights hadn't been magickal, the fear didn't subside. Somebody had run me off the road. Das Boot was hopelessly lodged in the ditch. A lump formed in my throat. I was on the verge of bursting into tears, shaking like a leaf. What was going on? I remembered the runes I had drawn on the dash right before the wreck, and now I redrew them in the chill air around me. Eolh, Ur, Rad. The brisk movement helped calm me slightly, at least enough for me to try to figure out what to do.

Actually, there was pretty much only one option. I had to walk the rest of the way home. I didn't have a cell phone, so I couldn't call anyone for help. And I didn't exactly feel like waiting around in the darkness on this frozen, lonely road all by myself.

Heaving open the driver's door again, I fished inside for my backpack and carefully locked Das Boot. I shook my head. It was going to be a long, miserable march to my house. But as I heaved the backpack across my shoulder, a flash of dim light illuminated the snowflakes around me, and I heard the faint rumble of a motor. I turned to see a car slowly approaching . . . from the same direction the lights had vanished.

The flash of relief I'd briefly felt at the possibility of being rescued evaporated as the car rolled to a stop, not fifteen feet from where I stood. The headlights weren't nearly as bright, but for all I knew, this was the same car. Maybe the person driving had decided to turn around and finish me off, or—

My insides clenched. The license plate, the grating of the tan BMW . . . I recognized it even before the passenger window unrolled. It was Bree's car.

Bree looked across from the driver's seat, her eyes outlined in black, her skin pale and perfect. We regarded each other silently for a few moments. I hoped I didn't look as freaked out and disheveled as I felt. I wanted to radiate strength.

"What happened, Morgan?" she asked.

I opened my mouth, then closed it. My eyes narrowed as a horrible thought struck me. Could Bree have been the one who'd run me into the ditch?

It was possible. There were no other cars on the road. She could have made a U-turn up ahead and come back to see what had happened to me. But . . . Bree? Hurt me?

Remember what you heard in the bathroom, a voice inside chimed. She gave your hair to a witch. Remember.

Maybe things had changed permanently. Maybe Bree no longer cared about me at all. Or maybe Sky Eventide had put her up to this—as a stunt to scare me, the same way that Sky had forced her to turn over a lock of my hair. A thousand thoughts pounded against my skull, aching to be let out, to be heard: Oh God, Bree, don't let them fool you! I'm worried about you. I miss you. You're being so stupid. I'm sorry. I need to talk to you. Don't you know what's happened to me? I'm adopted. I'm a blood witch. I'm Woodbane. I'm sorry about Cal—

"Morgan?" she prodded, her brow furrowed.

I cleared my throat. "I hit a patch of ice," I said. I gestured unnecessarily to Das Boot.

"Are you okay?" she asked stiffly. "Did you hurt yourself?"

I shook my head. "I'm fine."

She blinked. "Do you want a ride home?"

I took a deep breath but shook my head again. I couldn't get into her car. Not when she might have been the one who had run me off the road in the first place. Even though I could hardly believe I was having such horrible thoughts about someone who had once been my best friend, I didn't dare risk it.

"Are you sure?" she pressed.

"I'll be fine," I mumbled.

Without another word she rolled up her window and took off. I noticed that she accelerated slowly so she wouldn't splatter me with snow and slush.

My chest ached as I walked home.

*   *   *

My parents fussed over me, which was nice. I told them I'd skidded off the road on a bad patch of ice, which was true in a way, but I left out the part about the other car behind me. I didn't want to worry them any more than necessary. I called a tow truck company, who agreed to get Das Boot and bring it home later that night. Thank the Goddess for Triple A, I thought and decided to ask for a cell phone for Christmas.

"Are you sure you don't want to come for Chinese with us?" Mom asked, after making sure I had thawed. My parents were heading out to meet Aunt Eileen and Paula, to drive by several houses that were for sale in the area, then to get dinner. They wouldn't be back till late. Mary K. was at Jaycee's, and I was sure she was meeting Bakker later.

"No, thanks," I said. "I'll just wait for the tow truck."

Mom kissed me. "I am so thankful you're okay. You could've been hurt so easily," she said, and I hugged her back. It was true, I realized. I really could have been hurt. If it had happened at another section of the road, I could have gone into a thirty-foot ravine. An image popped into my mind of Das Boot tumbling down a rocky cliff, then bursting into flames—and I cringed.

After Mom and Dad left, I set a pot of water on to boil for frozen ravioli. I grabbed a Diet Coke, and the phone rang. I knew it was Cal.

"Hello there," he said. "We're taking a little break. What are you doing?"

"Fixing some dinner." It was incredible: I still felt a little shaky, even though the mere sound of Cal's voice worked wonders. "I, um, had a little accident."

"What?" His voice was sharp with concern. "Are you okay?"

"It wasn't anything," I said bravely. "I just went off the road and ended up in a ditch. I'm waiting for the tow truck to bring Das Boot home."

"Really? Why didn't you call me?"

I smiled, feeling much better as I dumped a bunch of ravioli into the water. "I guess I was still recovering. I'm okay, though. I didn't hurt anything except my car. And I knew you were busy, anyway."

He was quiet for a moment. "Next time something happens, call me right away," he said.

I laughed. If it had been anyone else, I would have said they were overreacting. "I'll try not to do it again," I said.

"I wish I could come see you," he said, sounding frustrated. "But we're doing a circle here and it's about to start. Lousy timing. I'm sorry."

"It's fine. Don't worry so much." I sighed and stirred the pot. "You know, I . . ." I left the sentence hanging. I was going to tell him about seeing Bree, about all of my terrible fears and suspicions, but I didn't. I couldn't bear to reopen the wound, to allow all those painful emotions to come flooding back.

"You what?" Cal asked.

"Nothing," I murmured.

"You're sure?"

"Yeah."

He sighed, too. "Well, okay. I should probably go. My mom is starting to do her stuff. I'm not sure how late this will go—I might not be able to call you later. And you know we don't pick up the phone if it rings during a circle, so you won't be able to call me."

"That's okay," I said. "I'll see you tomorrow."

"Oh, tomorrow," said Cal, sounding brighter. "The famous pre-birthday day. Yeah, I have special plans for tomorrow."

I laughed, wondering what plans he had made. Then he made a silly kissing noise into the phone, and we hung up.

Alone and quiet, I ate my dinner. It felt soothing to be by myself and not have to talk. In the living room I noticed a basket full of fatwood by the fireplace. In just a few minutes I had a good blaze going, and I fetched Maeve's BOS from upstairs and settled on the couch. My mom's one crocheting attempt had resulted in an incredibly ugly afghan the size and weight of a dead mule. I pulled it over me. Within moments Dagda had scrambled up the side of the couch and was stomping happily across my knees, purring hard and kneading me with his sharp little paws.

"Hey, cute thing," I said, scratching him behind his ears. He settled on my lap, and I started reading.

July 6, 1977

Tonight I'm going to scry with fire. My witch sight is good, and the magick is strong. I used water once, but it was hard to see anything. I told Angus and he laughed at me, saying that I was a clumsy girl and might have splashed some of the water out of the glass. I know he was teasing, but I never used it again.

Fire is different. Fire opens doors I never knew were there.

Fire.

The word rolled around my head, and I glanced up from the page. My birth mother was right. Fire *was* different. I'd loved fire since I was little: its warmth, the mesmerizing golden red glow of the flames. I even loved the noise fire made as it ate the dry wood. To me it had sounded like laughter—both exciting and frightening in its hungry appetite and eager destruction.

My eyes wandered to the burning logs. I shifted carefully on the couch, trying not to disturb Dagda, though he could probably sleep through almost anything. Facing the flames, I let my head rest against the back of the couch. I set the BOS aside. I was one hundred percent comfortable.

I decided to try to scry.

First I released all the thoughts circling my brain, one by one. Bree, looking at me standing in the snow by the side of the road. Hunter. His face was hard to get rid of—and when I pictured it, I got angry. Over and over I saw him, silhouetted against a leaden gray sky, his green eyes looking like reflections of Irish fields, his arrogance coming off him in waves.

My eyelids fluttered shut. I breathed in and out slowly. The tension drained from each muscle in my body. As I felt myself drift more completely into a delicious concentration, I became more and more aware of my surroundings: Dagda's small heart beating quickly as he slept, the ecstatic joy of the fire as it consumed the wood.

I opened my eyes.

The fire had transformed into a mirror.

There in the flames I saw my own face, looking back: the long sweep of brown hair, the kitten in my lap.

What do you want to know? the fire whispered to me. Its voice was raspy and sibilant—seductive yet fleeting, fading away in acrid curls of smoke.

I don't understand anything, I answered. My face was

serene, but my silent voice cried out in frustration. *I don't understand anything.*

Then in the fire a curtain of flame was drawn back. I saw Cal, walking through a field of wheat as golden as his eyes. He swept out his hand, looking beautiful and godlike, and it felt like he was offering the entire field to me as a gift. Then Hunter and Sky came up behind him, hand in hand. Their pale, bleached elegance was beautiful in its own way, but I felt a terrible sense of danger suddenly. I closed my eyes as if that might blot it out.

When I opened them again, I found myself walking through a forest so thickly grown that barely any light reached the ground. My bare feet were silent on the rotting leaves. Soon I saw figures standing in the woods, hidden among the trees. One of them was Sky again, and she turned and smiled at me, her white-blond hair glowing like an angel's halo around her. Then she turned to the person behind her: it was Raven, dressed all in black. Sky leaned over and kissed Raven gently, and I blinked in surprise.

Many disjointed images flowed over one another next, sliding across my consciousness, hard to follow. Robbie kissing Bree . . . my parents watching me walk away, tears running down their faces . . . Aunt Eileen holding a baby.

And then, as if that movie were over and a new reel began, I saw a small, white clapboard house, set back on a slight rise among the trees. Curtains fluttered from the open windows. A neat, tended garden of holly bushes and mums lined the front of the house.

Off to one side was Maeve Riordan. My birth mother.

I drew in my breath. I remembered her from another

vision I'd had, a vision of her holding me when I was an infant. She smiled and beckoned to me, looking young and goofy in her 1980s clothes. Behind her was a large square garden of herbs and vegetables, bursting with health. She turned and headed toward the house. I followed her— around the side, where a narrow walk separated the house from the lawn. Turning to face me again, she knelt and gestured underneath the house, pointing.

Confusion came over me. What was this? Then a phone began ringing from far away. Although I tried to keep concentrating, the scene began to fade, and my last image was of my birth mother, impossibly young and lovely, waving good-bye.

I blinked, my breathing ragged.

The sound of a phone still filled my ears. What was going on? Several seconds passed before I realized that it was *our* phone, not a phone in my vision. The images were all gone now. I was alone in our house again—and somebody was calling.

15

Presence

September 4, 1998

Uncle Beck hit me last night. Today I have a shiner and a split lip. It looks really impressive, and I'm going to tell people I got it defending what's left of Athar's honor.

Two years ago, on the dawn after my initiation, Uncle Beck told me why Mum and Dad disappeared. How Mum had seen the dark cloud coming when she was scrying, and how it had nearly killed her, right through the vision. And how, right after they escaped and went into hiding, their coven was wiped out. I remember all the witches in the coven, how they were like aunts and uncles to me. Then they were dead, and Linden and Alwyn and I came to live with Beck and Shelagh and Athar and Maris and Siobhan.

Since then I've been trying to find out about the dark wave, the force of evil that destroyed my parents' coven and made them go into hiding. I know it's got something to do with

Woodbanes. Dad is—or was—Woodbane. The last time I was in London, I went to all the old bookshops where they sell occult books. I visited the Circle of Morath, where they keep a lot of the old writings. I've been reading and searching for two years. Finally last night, Linden and I were going to try to call on the dark side, to get information. Since Linden's initiation last month, he's been pestering me to let him help, and I had to say yes, because they were his parents too. Maybe in two years, when Alwyn's initiated, she'll want to work with us. I don't know.

Anyway, Uncle Beck found us in the marshes a mile from the house. We hadn't even got far in the rite, and suddenly Uncle was storming up, looking huge and terrible and furious. He broke through our circles, kicked out our candles and our fire, and knocked the athame from my hand. I've never seen him so angry, and he hauled me up by my collar as if I was a dog and not sixteen and as tall as him.

"Call on the blackness, will you?" he growled, while Linden jumped to his feet. "You bloody bastard! For eight years I've fed you and taught you and you've slept under my roof, and you're out here dealing with blackness and leading your young brother astray?" Then he punched me, knocked me down, and I hit the ground like an unstrung puppet. The man has a fist like a ham—only harder.

We had words, we thrashed it out, and at the end, he understood what I wanted, and I understood that he'd rather kill me than let me do it, and that if I involved Linden again I would need to find another place to live. He's a good man, my uncle, and a good witch, though we often clash. Mum is his sister, and I know now that he desires to right the wrong done to her as much as I. The difference is that I was willing to cross the line to do it, and Beck isn't.

—Giomanach

"Hello?" I said into the receiver. I realized that I had no sense of who it was, even though I usually did before I picked up the phone.

Silence.

"Hello?" I said again.

Click. Drone of dial tone.

Okay, I knew, of course, that people get wrong numbers all the time. But for some reason, maybe because I was still caught up in images, emotions, and sensations from the fire, this silent phone call unnerved me. Every spooky movie I had ever seen came back to haunt me: *Scream, Halloween, The Exorcist, Fatal Attraction, Blair Witch.* My only thought was: Someone was checking to see if I was home. And I was. Alone.

I punched in star sixty-nine. Nothing happened. Finally a computerized female voice told me that the number I was trying to reach was blocked.

Feeling tense, I slammed the phone down on the hook. Then I began to race around the house, locking the front and back doors, the basement door, locking windows that had never been locked in my memory. Was I being stupid? It didn't matter. Better stupid and safe than smart and dead. I turned on all the outside lights instead of just the dim yellow glow of the front porch fixture.

I didn't know why I felt so afraid, but my first sense of alarm was rapidly growing into pure terror. So I retrieved my trusty baseball bat from the mudroom, locked that door, scooped up Dagda, and scampered upstairs to my room, glancing over my shoulder. Maybe it was still the aftermath of the accident, but my hands were clammy. My breath came quickly. I locked my bedroom door, then locked the door that led from the bathroom to Mary K.'s room.

I sat down on my bed, clenching and unclenching my fists. Cal, was all I could think. Cal, help me. I need you. Come to me.

I sent the witch message out into the night. Cal would get it. Cal would save me.

But the minutes ticked by, and he didn't come. He didn't even call to say he was on his way. I thought about calling him, but then I remembered what he'd said about not answering the phone during the circle.

Didn't he get my message? I wondered frantically. Where is he?

I tried to calm myself down. Mom and Dad would be home soon. So would Mary K. Anyway, it was just a phone call. A wrong number. Maybe it was Bree calling to apologize, and she'd lost her nerve.

But why would Bree's number have been blocked? It could have been anyone, though: a prank call by some pimply sixth grader whose mom caught him just before he spoke. Or maybe it was a telemarketer. . . .

Calm down, calm down, I ordered myself. Breathe.

A faint prickling at the edge of my senses made me sit up straight. I cast out my senses, searching as hard as I could.

Then I knew what it was. Someone was on the edge of the property. Fear oozed through me like burning lava.

"Wait here," I whispered idiotically to Dagda.

I crept soundlessly to my darkened window and peered out into the yard. As I looked out, the outside lights all blinked off. *Shit.* Who had gotten to them?

I could make out the leaves of the shrubs, the swooping shadow of an owl, the crusts of ice hanging on our fence.

That was when I saw them: two dark figures.

I squinted, using my magesight to make out their features, but for some reason I couldn't focus on their faces. It didn't matter, though. For a moment the night's cloud cover broke and allowed the not quite half-moon to appear. The glint of moonlight reflected off pale, shining hair, and I knew who was here. Sky Eventide. The person with her wore a dark knit cap and was too tall to be either Bree or Raven. Hunter. I felt sure it was Hunter.

Where was Cal?

I watched from my crouching position on the floor as they faded into the house's shadows. When I could no longer see them, I closed my eyes and tried to follow them with my senses. I felt them moving around the perimeter of the house slowly, pausing here and there. Would they try to come in? My fingers tightened on the bat, even though I knew it would be of zero use against witches in full possession of their powers. And Sky and Hunter were blood witches.

What did they want? What were they doing?

And then it came to me: of course. They were putting a spell on my house, on me. I remembered reading about how Maeve and her mother, Mackenna Riordan, had put spells on people. They had often needed to walk around a house or a person or a place. To surround something with magick is to change it.

Sky and Hunter were surrounding *me*.

They were circling my house, and I couldn't stop them—I didn't even have any idea what they were doing. It must have been one of them who had called earlier, to make sure I was home. And maybe they had blocked my call to Cal somehow. He might not be coming at all. . . .

I looked at Dagda to see if he was nervous or upset, if his senses had picked up on the vibrations of danger and magick.

He was asleep: tiny mouth slightly open, blue eyes shut, ribby little side rising and falling with sleep-slowed breaths. So much for the power of animals. I scowled, then looked out the window again. The shadowy figures were no longer visible but still present. Feeling terribly alone, I sat on my floor and waited. It was all I could do.

Three times Hunter and Sky moved around the house. I heard nothing and saw nothing, but I sensed them. They were there.

Almost half an hour later they left. I felt them leave, felt them close a circle behind them . . . felt them send one last line of magick out toward the house and toward me. Soon after that I heard the quiet purr of an engine as it faded down the street. The outside lights all flickered back on. But there was no way I was going outside to see what they had done. No. I was going to stay put.

With my baseball bat at my side, I went back downstairs and watched television until the tow truck driver showed up with Das Boot. Mom and Dad came home a few minutes later. I hurried upstairs to my room before they walked through the front door. I was too wrung out to act normal around them.

Cal never came.

"Hi, honey," Mom said when I stumbled into the kitchen the next morning. "Sleep well?"

"Uh-huh," I said, moving purposefully toward the refrigerator for a Diet Coke. But I was lying. The truth was, I hadn't slept well at all. I'd dozed fitfully, my fleeting dreams filled with images from the fire and the silhouettes of Sky and whoever else had been on our lawn. Finally I'd given up on sleep altogether. I glanced at the kitchen clock. Only eight-thirty. I wanted to call Cal, but it was too early, especially for a Saturday morning.

"Does anyone have plans for today?" Dad asked, folding back the newspaper.

"Jaycee and I are going to Northgate Mall," said Mary K. She fiddled with a box of Pop-Tarts, still in her pajamas. "The pre-Thanksgiving sales are starting."

"I'm going to be getting ready for tomorrow," said Mom. She flashed a meaningful smile at me. "Morgan, do you want an ice-cream cake this year?"

Suddenly I remembered that the next day was my birthday. Wow. Until this year I'd always eagerly looked forward to my birthday, anticipating it for months and months. Of course, until this year I'd had no idea that I was an adopted blood witch from the Woodbane clan. Nor, in previous years, was I being stalked by other witches. Things had changed a little.

I nodded and sipped my Diet Coke. "Chocolate cake on the bottom, mint-chip ice cream on top," I instructed, summoning up a smile.

"And what do you want for dinner tomorrow night?" Mom asked, starting to make a list.

"Lamb chops, mint jelly, roasted potatoes, fresh peas, salad," I rattled off. The same birthday dinner I always wanted. It was comforting somehow. This was my house, my family, and we were going to celebrate my birthday—same as always.

"Are you going to be busy tonight?" Mom asked, averting her eyes. She knew we usually had circles on Saturday nights.

"I'm seeing Cal," I said.

She nodded and thankfully left it at that.

As soon as I was dressed, I went outside and walked around the house. As far as I could tell, I couldn't feel the effects of a spell's magick. Which could very well be *part* of the spell, of course. Slowly I circled our entire house. I saw no sign of anything. No hexes spray painted on the house, no dead animals hanging from trees. Then again, I knew the signs would be infinitely more subtle than that.

Weirdly enough, even the snow-covered ground betrayed no footprints, though it hadn't snowed since before my visitors had arrived. I searched and searched but saw no trace of anyone's having been in our yard at all—except me, just now. Frowning, I shook my head. Had it all been an illusion? Had it been part of my scrying? How much could I trust my own perceptions? But I remembered the images I had seen—so clearly, too—the sights, sounds, and smells that had accompanied my fire scrying.

Most of all I remembered Maeve, standing by her house, smiling and pointing.

Maeve had lived in Meshomah Falls, two hours away. I glanced at my watch, then went inside to call Cal.

"What happened to your car?" Robbie asked half an hour later. We were in the front seat of Das Boot; I had just picked him up. Thankfully the car still worked, although the right headlight had been shattered and there was a massive dent in the front bumper. When I had called Cal, he hadn't been home—Selene had said he was out shopping, and she wasn't sure when he'd be back. Somehow, speaking to Selene calmed me down. I thought of asking her if he'd gotten my witch message, but my mom was in the room and I didn't want to bring it up in front of her. I'd ask Cal later.

Fortunately Robbie had been home, and he was a happy second choice for the road trip I had planned.

"I went into a ditch last night," I said with a grimace. "Slid on the ice." I didn't mention the lights I'd seen. That was something I'd only talk to Cal about. Whatever was going on, I didn't want to drag Robbie into it.

"Man," said Robbie. "Were you hurt?"

"No. But I have to get my headlight fixed. Big pain."

Robbie opened a map across the dashboard as I pulled away from his house. The day was rapidly clearing: I had a hope of actual sunshine before too long. It was still cold, but the snow and ice were melting slowly, and the streets were wet, the gutters running with water.

"You're looking for a town called Meshomah Falls. It should be north, right up the Hudson," I told him, turning onto the road that would lead to the highway. "About two, two and a half hours away."

"Oh, okay," he said, tracing his finger over the map. "I see it. Yeah, take Route 9 north until we get to Hookbridge Falls."

After a quick stop for gas and a supply of junk food, we were on our way. Bree and I used to go on road trips all the time: just day trips to malls or cool places to hike or little artists' colonies. We had felt so free, so unstoppable. But I tried not to dredge up those memories. Now they just filled me with pain.

"Want a chip?" Robbie offered, and I dug a hand into the bag.

"Have you talked to Bree yet?" I asked, unable to tear my mind from her. "About how you feel?"

He shook his head. "I've sort of tried, but it hasn't actually come up. I guess I'm a coward."

"No, you're not," I said. "But she can be hard to approach."

He shrugged. "You know, Bree asks about you, too," he said.

"What do you mean?"

"I mean, you always ask about her. Well, she asks about you, too. I mean, she never says anything nice about you, you both say mean things about the other one, but even a total idiot could tell that you two miss each other."

My face felt stiff as I stared out the window.

"Just thought you should know," he added.

We didn't say another word for the next sixty miles— not until we saw a sign for the Hookbridge Falls exit. By then the sky had cleared, and it was open and blue in a way it hadn't been for what seemed like weeks. The sun's

warmth on my face lifted my spirits. I felt like we were on a
real adventure.

Robbie consulted the map. "We get off here and head
east on Pedersen, which leads right into Meshomah Falls,"
he said.

"Okay."

A few minutes after we'd turned off the highway, I saw
the sign announcing Meshomah Falls, New York.

A shiver ran down my spine. This was where I had been
born.

I drove down Main Street slowly, staring at the buildings.
Meshomah Falls was a lot like Widow's Vale, except not
quite as old and not quite as Victorian. It was a cute town,
though, and I could see why Maeve and Angus had decided
to settle here. I picked a side street at random and turned
onto it, slowing even more as I looked carefully at each
house. Next to me, Robbie chewed gum and drummed his
fingers along to the radio.

"So, when are you going to tell me why we're here?" he
joked.

"Uh . . ." I didn't know what to say. I guess I had been
planning to pass this off as a simple joyride, just a chance to
get out and do something. But Robbie knew me too well. "I'll
tell you later," I whispered, feeling unsure and vulnerable. To
tell him one part of the story would mean telling him everything—and I had yet to come fully to terms with that.

"Have you ever been here before?" Robbie asked.

I shook my head. Most of the houses were pretty modest,
but none was immediately recognizable as the house I'd seen
in my vision. And they were fewer and farther between now;
we were heading into the country again. I started to wonder

what the hell I was doing. Why on earth did I think I'd be able to recognize Maeve's house? And if by some miracle I found it, what would I do then? This whole idea was stupid—

There it was.

I slammed on the brakes. Das Boot squealed to an abrupt halt. Robbie glared at me. But I hardly noticed. The house from my vision, my birth mother's house, stood right before my eyes.

16

Hidden

January 12, 1999

I've been ill, apparently.

Aunt Shelagh says I have been out for six days. Raving, she told me, with a high fever. I feel like death itself. I don't even remember what happened to me. And no one will say a word. I don't understand any of it.

Where is Linden? I want to see my brother. When I awoke this morning, eight witches from Vinneag were around my bed, working healing rites. I heard Athar and Alwyn in the hall, sobbing. But when I asked if they could come in to see me, the Vinneag witches just gave one another grave glances, then shook their heads. Why? Am I that ill? Or is it something else? What is happening? I must know, but no one will tell me a thing, and I am as weak as a hollow bone.

—Giomanach

The house was on the right side of the road, and as I glanced through Robbie's window, it was as if a cool breeze suddenly washed across my face. I pulled up alongside it.

The walls were no longer white but painted a pale coffee color with dark red accents. The neat garden in front was gone, as was the large herb and vegetable patch to one side. Instead some clumpy rhododendrons hid the front windows on the first floor.

I sat there in silence, drinking in the sight of the place. This was it. This was Maeve's house, and my home for the first seven months of my life. Robbie watched me, not saying anything. There were no cars in the driveway, no sign that anyone was home. I didn't know what to do. But after several minutes I turned to Robbie and took a deep breath.

"I have something to tell you," I began.

He nodded, a somber expression on his face.

"I'm a blood witch, like Cal said a couple of weeks ago. But my parents aren't. I was adopted."

Robbie's eyes widened, but he said nothing

"I was adopted when I was about eight months old. My birth mother was a blood witch from Ireland. Her name was Maeve Riordan, and she lived in that house." I gestured out the window. "Her coven was wiped out in Ireland, and she and my biological father escaped to America and settled here. When they did, they swore never to use magick again."

I took another deep, shaky breath. This whole story sounded like a movie of the week. A bad one. But Robbie nodded encouragingly.

"Anyway," I went on, "they had me, and then something happened—I don't know what—and my mother gave me up for adoption. And then, right after that, she and my father were locked in a barn and burned to death."

Robbie blinked. His face turned slightly pale. "Jesus," he muttered, rubbing his chin. "And who was your dad?"

"His name was Angus Bramson. He was a witch, too, from the same coven in Ireland. I don't think they were married." I sighed. "So that's why I'm so strong in Wicca, why that spell I did for you worked, why I channel so much energy at circles. It's because I come from a line of witches that's hundreds or thousands of years old."

For what seemed like a long time Robbie just stared at me. "This is mind-blowing," he mumbled finally.

"Tell me about it."

He offered a sympathetic smile. "I'll bet things have been crazy at your house lately."

I laughed. "Yeah, you could say that. We were all freaked out about it. I mean, my parents never told me, not in sixteen years, that I was adopted. And all my relatives knew and all their friends. I was . . . really angry."

"I'll bet," Robbie murmured.

"And they knew how my birth parents died and that witchcraft was involved, so they're really upset that I'm doing Wicca because the whole thing scares them. They don't want anything to happen to me."

Robbie chewed his lip, looking concerned. "No one knows why your birth parents were killed? They were murdered, right? I mean, it wasn't suicide or some ritual gone wrong."

"No. Apparently the barn door was locked from the outside. But they must have been scared about something because they gave me up for adoption right before they died. I can't find out why it happened, though, or who could have done it. I have Maeve's Book of Shadows, and she says that after they came to America, they didn't practice magick at all—"

"How did you get your birth mother's Book of Shadows?" he interrupted.

I sighed again. "It's a long story, but Selene Belltower had it, and I found it. It was all a bunch of weird coincidences."

Robbie raised his eyebrows. "I thought there weren't any coincidences."

I looked at him, startled. You're absolutely right, I thought.

"So why are we here?" he asked.

I hesitated. "Last night I had a dream . . . I mean, I had a vision. Actually, I scryed in the fire last night."

"You scryed?" Robbie shifted in his seat. Creases lined his forehead. "You mean you tried to divine information, like magickal information?"

"Yes," I admitted, staring down at my lap for a moment. "I know, you think I'm doing stuff I shouldn't be doing yet. But I think it's allowed. It's not a real spell or anything."

Robbie remained silent.

I shook my head and glanced out the window again. "Anyway, I was watching the fire last night, and I saw all sorts of weird images and scenes and stuff. But the most realistic scene, the clearest one, was about this house. I saw Maeve standing outside it and pointing underneath it. Pointing and smiling. Like she wanted to show me something underneath this house—"

"Wait a second," Robbie cut in. "Let me get this straight. You had a vision, so now we're here, and you want to crawl under that house?"

I almost laughed. It didn't sound bizarre; it sounded utterly insane. "Well, when you put it that way . . ."

He shook his head, but he was smiling, too. "Are you sure this is the house?"

I nodded.

He didn't say anything.

"So do you think I'm crazy, coming here?" I asked. "Do you think we should turn around and go home?"

He hesitated. "No," he said finally. "If you had that vision while you were actually scrying, then I think it makes sense to check it out. I mean, if you actually want to crawl under there." He glanced at me. "Or . . . do you want *me* to crawl under there?"

I smiled at him and patted his arm. "Thanks. That's really sweet. But no. I guess I'd better do it. Even though I have no idea what I'm looking for."

Robbie turned to the house again. "Got a flashlight?"

"Of course not." I smirked. "That would make me too well prepared, wouldn't it?"

He laughed as I slid out of the car and zipped up my coat. I hesitated only a moment before I unlatched the chain-link gate, then headed up the walk. Under my breath I whispered: "I am invisible, I am invisible, I am invisible," just in case anyone was watching from one of the neighboring houses. It was a trick Cal had told me about, but I'd never tried it before. I hoped it worked.

On the left side of the house, past the shaggy rhododendrons, I found the place where Maeve had been standing in my vision. There was an opening between the low brick foundation and the floor supports. The opening was barely twenty inches high. I glanced back at the car. Robbie was leaning against it in case he suddenly needed to come to my aid. I smiled and gave him a thumbs-up. He smiled back at me reassuringly. I was lucky. He was a good friend.

Crouching down, I peered underneath the house and saw only a dense, inky blackness. My heart was pounding loudly, but my senses picked up no people above or around me. For all I knew, I would find dead bodies and crumbling bones in there. Or rats. I would freak if I came face-to-face with a rat. I pictured myself screaming and scrambling to get out from under the house as fast as I could. But there was no sense in waiting. My magesight would guide me. I crept forward on my hands and knees. As soon as I had edged under the house, I paused to give my eyes time to adjust.

I saw a lot of junk, glowing faintly with time: old insulation foam, an ancient, dirt-encrusted sink, old pipes and chunks of sheet metal. I maneuvered my way carefully through this maze, looking around, trying to get some idea of what I could be looking *for*. I could feel the cold dampness seep through my jeans. I sneezed. It was dank under here. Dank and musty.

Again the questions festered in my mind. Why was I here? Why had Maeve wanted me to come here? Think, think! Could there be something about the house itself? I glanced upward to see if runes or sigils were traced on the bottom of the floor supports. The wood was old and dirty and blackened, and I saw nothing. I swept my gaze from side to side, starting to feel incredibly stupid—

Wait. There was something. . . . I blinked, rapidly. About fifteen feet in front of me, next to a brick piling, there was something. Something magickal. Whatever it was, I could sense it more than I could see it. I crawled forward, ducking low under water pipes and phone wires. At one point I had to shimmy on my belly beneath a sewer line. I was going to look like hell when I got out of here—I could feel my hair dragging in the dirt and cursed myself for not tying it up.

Finally I slithered out and could crawl normally again. I sneezed and wiped my nose on my sleeve. There! Tucked between two supports, practically hidden behind the piling, was a box. In order to get to it, I had to stretch my arms around the piling; the supports blocked my path.

Tentatively I reached for it. The air around the box felt thick, like clear Jell-O. My fingertips pushed through it and reached icy cold metal. Gritting my teeth, I tried to pry it out of the dirt. But it wouldn't budge. And in my awkward position I couldn't get any leverage to give it a good wrench. Again I yanked at it, scratching my fingers on its rusted, pitted surface. There was no use, though. It was stuck.

I felt like screaming. Here I was, on my hands and knees in the mud, under a strange house, *drawn* here—and I was helpless. I leaned forward and squinted at the box, concentrating hard. There, carved into the lid and barely visible under years of dust, were the initials M. R. Maeve Riordan. To me they were as clear as if I were seeing them in sunlight.

My breath came fast. This was it. This was why my mother had sent me here. I was meant to have it—this box that had remained hidden for almost seventeen years.

A memory suddenly flashed through my mind: that day not so long ago, right when we had all first discovered Wicca, when a leaf had fallen on Raven's head and I'd willed it to hover there with my thoughts. It had been nothing more than a flight of whimsy and a gesture of defiance against her for being cruel to me. But now it took on a deeper significance. If I could move a leaf, could I move something heavier?

I closed my eyes, focusing my concentration. Again I stretched forward and touched the dusty box with my fingertips. My mind emptied, all my thoughts vanishing like water down a drain. Only one thought remained: What had once belonged to my birth mother now belonged to me. The box was mine. I would have it.

It jumped into my hands.

My eyes flew open. A smile crossed my face. I'd done it! By the Goddess, I'd done it! Clutching the box under one arm, I scrambled out of there as fast as I could. Outside, the sunlight seemed overly bright, the air too cold. I blinked and stood, my muscles cramped, then stamped my feet and brushed off my coat as best I could. Then I hurried forward.

A middle-aged man was walking up the sidewalk toward the house. He dragged a fat dachshund behind him by a leash. As he caught sight of me coming around from the back of the house, he slowed and then stopped. His eyes were sharp with suspicion.

I froze for an instant, my heart thumping. I am invisible, I am invisible, I am invisible. I hurled the thought at him with as much force as I could.

A moment later his gaze seemed to lose its focus. His eyes slid aside, and he began walking again.

Wow. I felt a spurt of elation. My powers were growing so strong!

From his vantage point beside Das Boot, Robbie had seen it all. He opened the back door without a word, and I gently placed the box in the backseat. Then he slid smoothly behind the wheel, I got in, and we drove off. Over my shoulder I watched the little house grow smaller until finally we went around a bend and it disappeared from sight.

17

Treasure

January 14, 1999

I am sitting up. Today I ate some broth. Everyone is tiptoeing around me, and Uncle Beck looks at me with a coldness in his eyes the likes of which I've never seen. I keep asking about Linden, but no one will answer. They finally let Athar in today, and I caught her hand and asked her, too, but she just looked at me with those deep, dark eyes. Then they let Alwyn in to see me, but she just sobbed and clutched my hand till they took her away. I realized she's almost fourteen—three months away from her initiation.

Where is Linden? Why has he not come to see me?

Council members have been in and out of the house all week. A net of fear is closing about me. But I dare not name what I fear. It is too horrible.

—Giomanach

"What's in the box?" Robbie asked after a few minutes. He glanced at me. I had cobwebs in my hair, and I was filthy and smelled musty and dirty.

"I don't know," I said. "But it has Maeve's initials on it."

Robbie nodded. "Let's go to my house," he said. "My folks aren't there."

I nodded. "Thanks for driving," I said.

The drive back to Widow's Vale seemed endless. The sun dropped out of the sky shortly after four-thirty, and we drove the last half hour through chilly darkness. I was aching to open the box, but I felt I needed complete security to do it. Robbie parked Das Boot outside his parents' tiny, run-down house. As long as I had known Robbie, they had never repainted their house, or repaired the walk, or done any of the usual homeowner-type stuff. The front lawn was ragged and in need of mowing. It was Robbie's job and he hated it, and his parents didn't seem to care.

I'd never liked coming here, which is why the three of us had usually hung out at Bree's house, our favorite, or my house, our second favorite. Robbie's house was to be avoided, and we all knew it. But for now, it was fine.

Robbie flicked on lights, illuminating the living room, its dingy floor, and the permanent odor of stale cooking and cigarette smoke.

"Where are your folks?" I asked as we walked down the hall to Robbie's room.

"Mom's at her sister's, and Dad's hunting."

"Ugh," I said. "I still remember that time I came over and you had a deer hanging from the tree in your front yard."

Robbie laughed, and we passed through his older sister

Michelle's room. She was away at college, and her room was maintained as a kind of shrine in case she ever came home. Michelle was his parents' favorite, and they made no effort to conceal it. But Robbie didn't resent her. Michelle adored Robbie, and the two of them were very close. I caught a glimpse of a framed school picture of him up on her shelf, taken last year. His face was almost unrecognizable: his skin covered with acne, his eyes concealed by glasses.

Robbie flicked on a lamp. His room was less than half the size of Michelle's, more like a big closet. There was barely enough space for his twin-size bed, which was covered with an old Mexican blanket. A large chest of drawers topped with bookshelves was wedged into a corner. The shelves were overflowing with books, most of them paperbacks, all of them read.

"How's Michelle?" I asked, setting the box carefully on his bed. I was nervous and took my time unbuttoning my coat.

"Fine. She thinks she'll be on the dean's list again."

"Good for her. Is she coming home for Christmas?" My pulse was racing again, but I tried to calm myself. I sat down on the bed.

"Yeah." Robbie grinned. "She's going to be surprised by my looks."

I glanced at him. "Yeah," I said soberly.

"Well, are you gonna open this thing?" he asked, sitting at the other end of his bed.

I swallowed, unwilling to admit how anxious I was. What if there was something awful in there? Something awful or—

"Do you want me to do it?" he asked.

I shook my head quickly. "No—no. I'll do it."

I picked up the box. It was about twenty inches long by sixteen inches wide and about four inches tall. Outside, the metal was flaking off. Two metal clasps held the box shut. They were rusted almost solid. Robbie jumped up and rummaged around in his desk for a screwdriver, then handed it to me. Holding my breath, I wedged it under the lid and pried the clasps free. The lid opened with a pop, and I dug my fingers underneath it and flung it open.

"Wow!" Robbie and I exclaimed at the exact same time.

Though the outside of the box was worn and rusted, the inside of the box was untouched by age or the elements. The interior was shiny and silver. The first thing I saw was an athame. I picked it up. It was heavy in my hand, ancient-looking, with an age-worn silver blade and an intricately carved ivory handle. Celtic knots encircled the handle, finely carved but with the unmistakable look of handwork. This hadn't been made in a factory. Turning it over, I saw that the blade itself had been stamped with rows of initials, eighteen pairs of them. The very last ones were M. R. The ones above those were M. R.

"Maeve Riordan," I said, touching the initials. "And Mackenna Riordan, her mother. My grandmother. And me." I felt a rush of happiness. "This came to me from my family." A deep sense of belonging and continuity made me beam with satisfaction. I set the athame carefully on Robbie's bed.

Next I took out a package of deep green silk. When I held it up, it fell into the folds of a robe.

"Cool," said Robbie, touching it gently.

I nodded in agreement, awed. The robe was in the shape of a large rectangle, with an opening for the head and knots of silk that held the shoulders together.

"It looks like a toga," I said, holding it up to my chest. I blinked, seeing Robbie's questioning face. I smiled at him, knowing that I would try on the robe—but at home, behind locked doors.

The embroidery was astounding: full of Celtic knots, dragons, pentacles, runes, stars, and stylized plants worked in gold and silver thread. It was a work of art, and I could imagine how proud Maeve would have been to inherit it from her mother, to wear it the first time she presided over a circle. As far as I knew, Mackenna had still been high priestess of Belwicket when it was destroyed.

"This is incredible," said Robbie.

"I know," I echoed. "I know."

Folding the robe gently, I laid it aside. Next I found four small silver bowls, embossed again with Celtic symbols. I recognized the runes for air, fire, water, and earth and knew that my birth mother had used these in her circles.

I took out a wand, made of black wood. Thin gold and silver lines had been pounded into the shaft, and the tip was set with a large crystal sphere. Four small red stones circled the wand beneath the crystal, and I wondered if they were real rubies.

Beneath everything, jumbled on the bottom, were several other large chunks of crystal as well as other stones, a feather, and a silver chain with a claddagh charm on it: two hands holding a heart topped with a crown. It was funny: Mom—my adoptive mom—had a claddagh ring that Dad had given her on their twenty-fifth anniversary, last year. The chain felt warm and heavy in my hand.

My gaze swept over all the tools. So much treasure, so much bounty. It was mine: my true inheritance, filled with magick and mystery and power. I felt full of joy but in a way that I could never explain to Robbie . . . in a way I couldn't explain even to myself.

"Two weeks ago I had nothing of my birth mother's," I found myself saying. "Now I have her Book of Shadows and all this besides. I mean, these are things she touched and used. They're full of her magick. And I have them! This is amazing."

Robbie shook his head, his eyes wide. "What's really amazing is that you found out about them by scrying," he murmured.

"I know, I know." Excitement coursed through my veins. "It was like Maeve actually chose to visit me, to give me a message."

"Pretty weird," Robbie acknowledged. "Now, did you say that they didn't do magick while they were in America?"

I nodded. "That's what I've gotten from her Book of Shadows. I mean, I haven't finished reading it yet."

"But she brought all of this with her, anyway? And didn't use it? That must have been really hard."

"Yeah," I said. An inexplicable sense of unease began to cloud my happiness. "I guess she couldn't bear to leave her tools behind, even if she couldn't use them again."

"Maybe she knew she would have a baby," suggested Robbie, "and thought that in time she could pass the tools on. Which she did."

I shrugged. "Could be," I said thoughtfully. "I don't know. Maybe I'll find some explanation in her book."

"I wonder if she thought not using them would protect her somehow," Robbie mused. "Maybe using them would have given away her identity or her location sooner."

I gazed at him, then back at all the stuff. "Maybe so," I said slowly. The unease began to grow. My brows came together as I went on. "Maybe it's still dangerous to have these things. Maybe I shouldn't touch them—or maybe I should put them back."

"I don't know," said Robbie. "Maeve told you where to find them. She didn't seem to be warning you, did she?"

I shook my head. "No. In my vision it felt positive. No warning signs at all." I carefully folded the robe and placed it back in the box, followed by the wand, the athame, and the four small cups. Then I closed the lid. I definitely needed to talk to Cal about this, and also Alyce or David, the next time I saw them.

"So, are you getting together with Cal tonight?" Robbie asked. He grinned. "He's going to flip over all this."

My excitement began to return. "I know. I can't wait to hear what he says about it. Speaking of which, I better go. I have to get cleaned up." I bit my lip, hesitating. "Are you going to Bree's circle tonight?"

"I am," Robbie said easily. He stood and started walking back down the hall. "They're meeting at Raven's."

"Hmmm." I put on my coat and opened the front door, the box tucked securely under my arm. "Well, be careful, okay? And thanks so much for coming with me today. I couldn't have done it without you." I leaned forward and hugged Robbie hard, and he patted my back awkwardly. Then I smiled and waved, and headed out to my car.

My birth mother's tools, I thought as I cranked the engine. I actually had the same tools that had been used by my birth mother, and *her* mother, and her mother's mother, and so on, for possibly hundreds of years . . . if the initials on the athame represented all the high priestesses of Belwicket. I felt a sense of belonging, of family history—one that I knew had somehow been lacking in my life until now. I wished that I could go to Ireland to research their coven and their town and find out what really happened. Maybe someday.

18

Sigils

January 22, 1999

Now I know. Linden, my brother, barely fifteen years old, is dead. Goddess help me, I am all alone, but for Alwyn. And they say I murdered him.

I look at the words I just wrote, and I cannot make sense of them. Linden is dead. I am accused of Linden's murder.

They say my trial is starting soon. I can't think. My head aches all the time, what I eat my body rejects. I've lost more than two stone and can count my ribs.

My brother is dead.

When I looked at him I saw Mum's face. He is dead, and I am being blamed, though there is no way I would have done it.

—Giomanach

When I got home, no one else was around. I was glad to be by myself; I'd had an idea while I was driving back from Robbie's house, and I wanted to test it in private.

First, though, it was time to take some precautions. I got a Phillips-head screwdriver from Dad's toolbox in the mudroom. Then I carried the box with Maeve's tools up to the second-floor landing. Unscrewing the HVAC vent cover, I pulled it out from the wall and set the box inside the vent. When I screwed the cover back on, it would be totally invisible. I knew because I'd used this spot as a hiding place over the years—I'd kept my first diary here, and Mary K.'s favorite doll when I hid it from her after a huge fight.

Before I closed the vent, though, I took out the athame, the beautiful, antique athame with my mother's initials on it. I loved the fact that my initials were the same as hers and my grandmother's. I ran my fingers gently over the carved handle as I carried the athame downstairs.

About a week before, I'd been looking for information about Wicca online, and I'd come across an old article by a woman named Helen Firesdaughter. It described the traditional witch's tools and their uses. The athame, the article had said, was linked with the element of fire. It was used to direct energy and to symbolize and bring about change. It was also used to illuminate, to bring hidden things to light.

I pulled on my coat, then stepped outside into the frigid dusk and closed the front door behind me. A quick glance up and down the street assured me that no one was watching. Holding the athame in front of me like a metal detector, I began to walk around my house. I swept the ancient blade over windowsills, doors, the clapboard siding, whatever I could reach.

I found the first sigil on the porch railing, around to the side. To the naked eye there was nothing there, but when the athame swept over it, the rune glowed very faintly, with an ethereal bluish witch light. My throat tightened. So— there it was. Proof that Sky and Hunter had worked magick here last night. I traced its lines and curves with my finger. Peorth. It stood for hidden things revealed.

I breathed deeply, trying to stay calm and rational. Peorth. Well, that didn't tell me much about their plans, one way or the other. I'd have to keep looking.

As I circled the house, more and more sigils glowed under the athame's blade. Daeg, for awakening and clarity. Eoh, the horse, which means change of some kind. Othel, for birthright, inheritance. And then, on the clapboards directly below my bedroom window, I found the one I'd been dreading to see: the double fishhook of Yr.

I stared at it and felt like a fist was squeezing my lungs. Yr. The death rune. Cal had told me that it didn't always have to mean death—that it could mean some other kind of important ending. I tried to take comfort in that possibility. But I was having a hard time convincing myself.

Then I felt a tingle at the edge of my senses. Someone was nearby. Watching me.

I spun around, peering into the dim winter twilight. A lone streetlamp cast a cone of yellow light outside our yard. But I could see no shadowed form, no flicker of movement anywhere, not even when I used my magesight. Nor could I feel the presence any longer. Was I imagining it? Sensing things that weren't really there?

I didn't know. All I knew was that suddenly I couldn't bear to be outside, alone, for one second longer. Turning, I bolted into the house and locked the door behind me.

*   *   *

By the time Cal came to pick me up, I had calmed down enough that I was feeling excited about my special birthday celebration.

"What's changed about you?" Cal asked as I pulled the front door closed. He smiled at me, puzzled. "You look different. Your eyes are different."

I batted my lashes at him. "I'm wearing makeup," I said. "Mary K. finally got her mitts on me. I figured, why not? It's a special occasion."

He laughed and took my arm, and together we walked to his car. "Well, you look incredible, but don't think you have to wear it on my account." He opened my door and then went around to the driver's side.

"Did you get my messages?" I asked as he started the engine.

He nodded. "Mom said you called." He didn't mention the witch message. "Sorry I missed you. I had some errands to do." He wiggled his eyebrows at me. "Mysterious errands, if you know what I mean, Birthday Girl."

I smiled briefly, but I was impatient to tell him about the events of the last twenty-four hours. "I had a pretty eventful day without you. In fact, I've had *two* pretty eventful days." I hunkered lower in my coat.

"What happened?" he asked.

I opened my mouth, and before I knew it, everything was tumbling out of me like an avalanche: the headlights behind me that had made me wreck, scrying into the fire, seeing Sky and Hunter outside my house the night before. Cal kept shooting glances at me, some baffled, some shocked, some worried. Then I offered up my pièce de résistance, finding Maeve's tools.

"You found your mother's tools?" he cried. The car swerved. I wondered for a second if it was going to end up like Das Boot. Luckily, though, we were turning into his driveway.

I threw up my hands and grinned. "I can't believe it myself," I said.

He cut the engine and sat there, staring at me in amazement. "Did you bring them?" he asked eagerly.

"No," I admitted. "I hid them behind the HVAC vent. And then when I was leaving, Dad was fixing an electrical outlet in the hall and I couldn't get to them."

Cal gave me an amused, conspiratorial look. "Behind the HVAC vent," he repeated, and I couldn't help laughing with him. It was a pretty silly hiding place for a bunch of magickal tools, come to think of it.

"Oh, well, no big deal. You can show them to me tomorrow," he said. I nodded.

"So—what do you think about my accident?" I asked.

"I don't know," he murmured. He shook his head. "It could have been just some jerk who was in a hurry. But if you were scared, I say you should trust your instincts—and we should start asking some questions." His eyes seemed to harden, but then his face melted in a worried smile. "Why didn't you tell me about this last night? And about Hunter and Sky being at your house?"

"I sent you a witch message," I told him. "But you never came. I was wondering if Sky could have blocked it somehow."

Cal frowned. Then he smacked his forehead. "No, that's not it. I know exactly what it was. Mom and I did a powerful warding spell before our circle, just in case people like Sky or Hunter were trying to snoop on us. That would have blocked your message. Wow, I am so sorry, Morgan. It never occurred to me that you might try to reach me."

"It's okay," I told him. "Nothing happened to me." A shudder ran through me as I remembered my terror last night. "At least, nothing permanent."

We got out of the car, shivering, and hurried up his front steps together.

We met Selene on her way out. She was wrapped in a black velvet cloak that swept to the ground and wore shining purple amethysts around her neck and on her ears. As always, she looked stunning.

"Good evening, my dears," she said with a smile. A delicious scent wafted off her, giving me an impression of maturity, of richness. It made my own dab of patchouli oil seem naive and hippyish—girly, almost.

"You look beautiful," I said sincerely.

"Thank you, Birthday Girl. So do you," she said, pulling on black gloves. "I'm going to a party." She shot Cal a meaningful look. "I won't be back till quite late, so be on your best behavior."

I felt embarrassed, but Cal laughed easily. As Selene left through the wide front door, we started to climb the stairs to his room on the third floor.

"Um, what does your mom think we might do?" I asked clumsily. My steps were muffled by the thick carpet on the stairs.

"I guess she thinks we might make love," Cal said. Judging from his tone, it sounded like he was talking about spending the evening playing board games. He flashed a casual smile.

I nearly fell down the stairs. "Uh—would she . . . you know, be upset?" I stammered, struggling to sound calm but failing miserably. All of my friends' parents would have a cow if they thought their kids were doing that under their own roof. Well, maybe not Jenna's. But everyone else's.

"No," said Cal. "In Wicca, making love doesn't have the same kind of stigma as it does in other religions. It's seen as a celebration of love, of life—an acknowledgment of the God and Goddess. It's beautiful. Something special."

"Oh." Blood pounded through me. I nodded, trying to look confident.

Cal closed the door behind him. Then he pulled me to him and kissed me. "I'm sorry I wasn't there for you last night," he breathed against my lips. "I know I've been really tied up with Mom's business lately. But from now on I'm going to make sure I'm more available."

I reached up and draped my arms around his neck. "Good," I said.

He held me for a moment longer, then gently disengaged my arms and grabbed some matches from the nightstand by his bed. As I watched, he lit candles around his room, one by one, until there were tiny flames everywhere. The candles lined the mantel, the top of every bookcase, stood in holders on the floor; there was even an old-fashioned iron chandelier that held candles, hanging from the ceiling. When he turned off the overhead light, we found ourselves surrounded in a glowing fiery cocoon. It was dreamy, beautiful, romantic.

Next Cal walked over to his dark wooden desk, where a bottle of sparkling cider stood next to a bowl filled with perfect, amazingly red strawberries and another bowl of dipping chocolate. He poured two glasses of cider and brought me one.

"Thank you," I said happily. "This is incredible." The light, golden cider tickled my throat with its starry little bubbles.

He came and sat down next to me again, and we drank our cider. "I can't wait to see Maeve's tools," he said, stroking the hair along my temple. "The historical value alone—it's like finding King Tut's tomb."

I laughed. "The Wiccan version of King Tut's tomb. Which reminds me. I kept one thing out, and brought it with me." Putting my glass down on the nightstand, I hopped up and went to my jacket, where I took out the athame from the breast pocket. I had wrapped it in a handkerchief. Silently I handed it to Cal, watching his face as I nestled back down with him again.

"Goddess," he whispered as he unwrapped it. His eyes were shining, and an eager smile played about his lips. "Oh, Morgan, this is beautiful."

I laughed again at his excitement. "I know. Isn't it amazing?"

His fingers traced the lines of initials carved into the blade. "Tomorrow," he said absently, then looked up at me. "Tomorrow," he said more firmly, "I'm going to have a busy day. First I have to find Hunter and Sky and tell them to leave you the hell alone. Then I have to go to your house and remove all their sigils, if I can. Then I have to salivate over your mother's tools."

"Oh, that's a lovely image," I said, laughing. "Thank you."

He laughed, too, then we were leaning together, kissing and sipping cider. Magick, I thought dreamily, staring at him.

Cal kissed me again, his golden eyes intent, and then he blinked and pulled back.

"Presents!" he said, motioning across the room.

It took a second to spot the pile of beautifully wrapped gifts that waited for me on a large table pushed against the wall.

"What have you done?" I asked, putting my hand to my throat, where his silver pentacle still nestled warm against my skin. It was the first thing he'd ever given me, and I treasured it for that.

He grinned and stood, carrying the presents back to the bed and spreading them before me on the mattress. I took another sip of my cider, then placed it on the nightstand again.

First was a rectangular box. I started pulling off the paper.

"This is kind of redundant now," he said.

My face melted in a smile. Inside the box was the silver athame we had seen at Practical Magick, the one carved with roses and a skull. I turned to him.

"It's lovely," I said, running my fingers across it.

"It can be your backup," he said cheerfully. "Or a cake knife. Or a letter opener."

"Thank you," I whispered.

"I wanted you to have it," Cal said. "Next."

He held out a small box, and I held my breath as I opened it, revealing a gorgeous pair of silver earrings set with golden tigereyes. The gems looked so much like Cal's eyes that I had to glance up at him just for the sake of comparison.

"These are so beautiful." I shook my head.

"Put them on," he encouraged, "and it will be like I'm always with you." He brushed back my hair to expose my earlobe.

I held the earrings, not knowing what to say.

"Your ears aren't pierced," Cal said in surprise.

"I know," I mumbled apologetically. "My mom took me

and Bree to have it done when we were twelve, but I chickened out."

"Oh, Morgan, I'm sorry," he said, laughing. "It's my fault. I can't believe I didn't notice before now. I should have gotten you something else. Here—I'll take them back and exchange them."

"No!" I said, pulling the box close. "I love them—they're the most beautiful things I've ever seen. I've been wanting to get my ears pierced, anyway. This will be my inspiration."

Cal looked at me assessingly but appeared to take my word. "Hmmm. Well, okay." He nodded at another present.

Next was a beautifully bound and illustrated book about spell weaving. It included a short history of spell making and had a whole section of sample spells and how to use them as well as how to individualize them for your particular situation.

"Oh, this is fabulous," I said with enthusiasm, leafing through it. "This is perfect."

"I'm glad you like it," he said, grinning. "We can go over some of them if you want, practice them."

I nodded eagerly, like a child, and he laughed again.

"And last," he said, handing me a medium-size box.

"More?" I couldn't quite believe this. I was beginning to feel spoiled. Inside this box was a batik blouse in muted shades of lavender and purple and plum. It looked like a storm-shot sunset. I stared at it, touching the cloth with my fingers, drinking in the colors, practically hearing the rumble of thunder and rain.

"I love it," I said, leaning over to hug him. "I love all of it. Thank you so much for this." My throat tightened with a rush of emotion. Once again I felt a sense of belonging, of pure contentment. "These are the best birthday gifts anyone has ever given me."

Cal gave me a sweet smile, and then I was in his arms and we were lying on the bed. I held his head tightly, my fingers laced through his dark hair as we kissed.

"Do you love me?" he whispered against my mouth. I nodded, overwhelmed, holding him hard against me, wanting to be closer.

The cider, the candles all around us, the slight scent of incense, the feel of his smooth skin under my hands—it was as if he were weaving a spell of love around me, making me drowsy and full of a physical longing and ache. And yet . . . and yet. I still held the end of a line between us. Despite my love for him, despite the dark wave of yearning he had awoken in me, I felt myself holding back.

Dimly, as we kissed, I came to the surprising realization that I wasn't quite ready to give myself to him completely. Even though we were probably *mùirn beatha dàns,* still, I wasn't ready to make love with him, to go all the way in joining ourselves together physically and mentally. I didn't know the reason, but I had to trust my feelings.

"Morgan," Cal said softly. He raised up on one elbow and looked at me. He was incredibly beautiful, the most beautiful male I had ever seen. His cheeks were flushed, his mouth a dark rose color from kissing. There was no way he and Hunter could be brothers, I thought distantly—and I wondered why Hunter had even popped into my thoughts. Hunter was mean and dangerous, a liar.

"Come on," Cal said, his voice husky, his hand stroking my waist through my black jumper.

"Um . . ."

"What's wrong?" he whispered.

I let out my breath, not knowing what to say. He draped one leg over me and pulled me closer, curling his hand around my back and snuggling. He nuzzled my neck, and his hand drifted up my waist to just below my breast. It felt incredible, and I willed myself to give in to it, to let the wash of sensation carry me to a new place. I would be seventeen tomorrow: it was time. But somehow I just couldn't. . . .

"Morgan?" His voice sounded questioning, and my eyes flew to his. His hand stroked my hair away from my face. "I want to make love to you."

19

Circle of Two

They are pushing me to join with her. And I want to do it. Goddess, how I want to do it. She is a butterfly, a flower in bloom, a dark ruby being cut from dusty stone. And I can make her better than that. I can make her catch fire, so her power illuminates all who stand near. I can teach her, I can help her reach the deep magick within. Together we will be unstoppable.

Whoever would have thought this could happen? One look at her would not have revealed the tigress waiting inside. Her love devours me, her constancy humbles me, her beauty and power make me hunger.

She will be mine. And I will be hers.

—Sgàth

I stared at Cal, loving him but feeling utterly lost.

"I thought you wanted me, too," he said quietly.

I nodded. That was true—partially, anyway. But what my brain wanted and my body wanted were two different things.

"If you're worried about birth control, I can take care of it," he said. "I wouldn't ever hurt you."

"I know." I could feel tears welling up in my eyes, and I willed them to stop. I felt like a complete failure, and I didn't know why.

Cal rolled away from me, his arm resting across his forehead as he looked at me. "So what is it?" he said.

"I don't know," I whispered. "I mean, I want to, but I just can't. I don't feel ready."

He reached out his other hand and held mine, absently stroking his thumb across my palm. Finally he shifted and sat up cross-legged in front of me. I scrambled into a sitting position opposite him.

"Are you angry?" I asked.

He smiled wryly. "I'll live. It's okay. Don't worry about it. I . . ." He left the sentence unfinished.

"I'm sorry," I said miserably. "I don't know what's wrong with me."

He leaned over and pushed my hair off my neck to kiss my nape gently. I shuddered at the warmth of his lips. "Nothing is wrong with you," he whispered. "We have our whole future together. There's no hurry. Whenever you're ready, I'll be here."

I swallowed, worrying that if I opened my mouth again, I would definitely start crying.

"Look, let's do a circle," he said, rubbing the tension out of my neck. "Not a *circle* circle, but just like a joined meditation. It's another way for us to be close. Okay?"

I nodded. "Okay," I choked out.

I reached for him, and we held hands loosely, with our knees touching. Together we closed our eyes and began to systematically shut everything down: emotions, sensations, awareness of the outside world. I felt embarrassed about not wanting to sleep with him, but I deliberately released those feelings. It was almost as if I could see them falling away from me. My eyes stopped stinging; my throat relaxed.

Gradually our breathing, in sync, slowed and quieted. I had been meditating almost every day, and it was easy for me to slip into a light trance. I lost the sensation of touching Cal: we felt joined, breathing as one, drifting as one into a place of deep peace and restfulness. It was a relief.

I became aware of the strength of Cal's mind, aligning with mine, and it was very exciting and intimate. It was amazing that we could share this, and I thought of all the nonwitches in the world who would probably never be able to achieve such closeness with their lovers. I breathed a long sigh of contentment.

In our meditation I felt Cal's thoughts; I read the intensity of his passion, felt his desire for me, and my flesh broke out in goose bumps. I felt his admiration of my strength in the craft, as well as eagerness for me to progress—to get stronger and stronger, as strong as he was. I tried to share my own thoughts with him, unsure if he was reading me as well. I expressed my desires and hopes for our future together; I tried to let waves of pure emotion convey my feelings in a way that words never could.

Eventually we drifted apart, like two leaves separating as they fell toward earth. I slipped back into my self, and we remained there for a while afterward, gazing at each other.

It was the most intensely connected I had ever felt to another person. I knew it. But knowing this also made me feel vulnerable and nervous.

"Was it good for you?" I asked, trying to lighten the moment.

He smiled. "It was great for me."

I looked into his face for a while longer, allowing myself to get lost in his eyes, enjoying the silence and the glow of the candles. Dimly I became aware of the ticking of a clock nearby. I glanced at it.

"Oh my God, is it one o'clock?" I gasped.

Cal looked, too, and grinned. "Hmmm. Do you have a curfew?"

I was already climbing off the bed. "Not officially," I said, searching for my shoes. "But I'm supposed to call if I'm later than midnight. Of course, if I call now, I'll wake them up." Quickly I gathered my presents into a pile. I found Maeve's athame and put it back inside my coat. We trotted downstairs. A pang of longing welled up inside me; I wanted to stay *here,* in the warmth and coziness of Cal's room, with him.

Cold wind blasted my face when we stepped through the front door.

"Ugh," I moaned, gripping the neck of my coat tighter.

Heads down, we hurried out to Cal's Explorer. "Maybe we should call your folks and tell them you're having a sleepover," he suggested with a grin.

I laughed, thinking of how well that would go over with Mom and Dad, then carefully placed my beautiful birthday presents on the backseat. But as I was about to climb into the front, the sound of a car arriving made me pause. I glanced at Cal. His eyes had narrowed. He looked alert and tense, his hand on the car door next to me.

"Is it your mom?" I asked.

Cal shook his head. "That's not her car."

Using magesight, I squinted into the approaching head-lights, staring right past them. My heart lurched. It was a gray car. Hunter's car.

He pulled to a stop in front of us.

"Oh God, what's he doing here?" I groaned. "It's one in the morning!"

"Who knows?" Cal said tersely. "But I need to talk to him, anyway."

Hunter left his car running as he stepped out and faced us. The headlights put him in silhouette, but I could see that his green eyes were solemn. His cold seemed to have gotten better. His breath was like white smoke.

"Hello," he said precisely. Just hearing him speak made me clench up. "Fancy meeting the both of you here. How inconvenient."

"Why?" Cal asked, his voice low. "Were you going to put sigils on my house, like you did Morgan's?"

A glimmer of surprise crossed Hunter's face.

"Know about that, do you?" he said, shifting his gaze to me.

I nodded coldly.

"What else do you know?" Hunter asked. "Like, do you know what Cal wants from you? What you are to him? Do you know the truth about *anything*?"

I glared at him, trying to think of a scathing reply. But again the only thought I had was: Why is he tormenting us like this?

Beside me Cal clenched his fists. "She knows the truth. I love her."

"No," Hunter corrected him. "The truth is, you *need* her. You need her because she has incredible, untapped powers. You need her so you can use her power to take over the High Council, and then you can start to eliminate the other clans, one by one. Because you're a Woodbane, too, and frankly, the other clans just aren't good enough."

My eyes flashed to Cal. "What is he talking about? You're not a Woodbane, are you?"

"He's raving," Cal muttered, staring at Hunter with pure contempt. "Saying anything he can think of to hurt me." Cal put his arm around me. "You can forget breaking us up," he said. "She loves me, and I love her."

Hunter laughed. The sound of it was like glass shattering. "What a crock," he spat. "She's your lightning rod—the last surviving member of Belwicket, the destined high priestess of one of the most powerful of the Woodbane clans. Don't you get it? Belwicket renounced the dark arts! There's no way Morgan would agree to what you want!"

"How would *you* know what I would do?" I shouted, infuriated by how he was speaking as if I weren't there.

Cal just shook his head. "There's no point to this," he said. "We're together, and there's nothing you can do. So you can go back to where you came from and leave us alone."

Hunter chuckled softly. "Oh, no, I'm afraid it's much too late for that. You see, the council would never forgive me if I left Morgan in your clutches."

"What?" I was practically screeching. What the hell did the council care who I dated? I hardly even *knew* about the council. How could they know so much about me?

"You should know about forgiveness," Cal snapped. "After all, the council has never quite forgiven you for killing your brother, right? You're still making up for that, aren't you? Still trying to prove it wasn't your fault."

I stared at the two of them. I had no idea what Cal was talking about, but his tone terrified me. He sounded like a stranger.

"Go to hell," Hunter snarled, his body tightening.

"Wiccans don't believe in hell," Cal whispered.

Hunter started toward us, his face stiff with fury. All at once Cal ducked into the car and snatched the athame he'd given me from the pile of gifts. My pulse shot into overdrive. This isn't happening, I thought in panic. This can't be happening. I watched, immobile, as Cal backed away from me. Hunter glanced between the two of us.

"You want me?" Cal taunted Hunter. "You want me, Hunter? Then come get me." With that, he turned and sped straight for the dark woods bordering the property. I blinked, and he was out of sight, hidden by trees and darkness.

Hunter was wild-eyed as he scanned the woods' edge.

"Stay here!" he commanded me, then he raced off after Cal.

I stopped for just a moment. Then I ran after them.

20

The Seeker

February 12, 1999

    With help, now, I can walk across a room. But I am still weak, so weak.

    My trial is starting tomorrow.

    I have been telling my story over and over, what I remember of it. I woke in the night and saw Linden was gone. I tracked him to the fell, and found him in the middle of calling a taibhs, a dark spirit. It is something we had talked about in the past year, in our search for answers about our parents. But I had not counseled Linden to do it, nor would I have ever condoned his trying to summon the evil thing alone.

    I saw Linden, his arms upstretched, a look of joy on his face. The dark taibhs moved toward him, and I rushed forward. I could not get through the circle without magick, so I conjured a break in the force. The rest of what I remember is a nightmare of reaching for Linden, of finding him and having him sag in my arms, of being surrounded by a choking wraith, then being smothered, unable to breathe, and sinking down to the cold ground to embrace death.

Next I woke in my bed at Uncle Beck and Aunt Shelagh's, with witches around me praying for my recovery, after six days of unconsciousness.

I know I did not kill my brother, but I know that my quest to redress the harm done my family is what caused his death. For this I could be sentenced to death. Except that I know Alwyn would grieve for me, I would welcome it, for there is no life for me here anymore.

—Giomanach

By the time I reached the edge of the woods, it had started to snow again. While Cal and I were inside, the sky had been consumed by thick gray clouds that blotted out the moon and the stars.

"Dammit," I whispered. Cal had obviously led Hunter away to protect me, but how could he expect me to stand around, waiting to see what happened? I didn't know what was going on between the two of them. All I knew was that I would never forgive Hunter if he hurt Cal.

The woods were dense and untamed, the undergrowth thick and impossible to run through. I ran into a low-hanging branch, and I stopped. I had no idea where Cal and Hunter had gone. It was absolutely black here, and for a moment I trembled. I had to breathe slowly, to focus and concentrate.

I clenched and unclenched my fists and squeezed my eyes shut.

"One, two, three," I counted. I breathed in and out.

A moment later I opened my eyes and found that my magesight had kicked in and I could see. Trees stood out as dark verticals, the undergrowth was defined, and the few nocturnal animals and birds who weren't hibernating glowed with a pale yellow light. Okay. I scanned the area, and easily picked up the rough track Hunter and Cal had made as they crashed through the woods: the forest floor was scraped and disturbed, and small branches were snapped.

As quickly as I could, I followed their trail. My feet and nose were freezing, and snow began to fall and bleach the surroundings. Slowly I became aware of a dim, rhythmic pounding. It wasn't the blood in my veins. Then it came to me: of course. Selene and Cal lived at the edge of town; their house was practically on the Hudson River. The surging waters were dead ahead. I quickened my pace, grabbing trees to push me forward, stumbling against rocks, cursing.

"You're bidden to come with me!"

It was Hunter's voice. I stopped silent, listening—then rushed forward and came out into a narrow, treeless strip that ran parallel with the river. Hunter was backed against the edge of the cliff, and Cal, holding my athame in front of him, was moving forward. I was lost in a swirl of fear and confusion.

"Cal!" I shouted.

They both turned, their faces unreadable in the snow and darkness.

"Stay back!" Cal ordered me, flinging out his hand. To my utter shock I stopped hard, as if I'd struck a wall. He had used a spell against me.

The next instant Hunter hurled a ball of witch light, and it knocked the athame from Cal's hand. Cal's jaw dropped. I struggled to believe that this was real, my real life, and not just a screen full of computer-generated effects. Hunter leaped away from the edge and onto Cal, who was scrambling back toward the knife. As I tried to move forward, I felt like I was wrapped in a thick wool blanket. My legs were made of stone. The two of them rolled over in the new-fallen snow, light hair and dark flashing against the ground and the background of night.

"Stop it!" I shouted as loud as I could, but they ignored me.

Cal pinned Hunter on the ground, then closed his fist and smashed it into Hunter's face. Hunter's head whipped sideways. A bright ribbon of blood streamed from his nose. The redness on the snow reminded me of the spilled communion wine last Sunday, and I shuddered. This was wrong. This shouldn't be happening. This kind of anger, of long-held hatred, was the antithesis of magick. I had to separate them.

Gathering all my strength, I pictured myself breaking out of an eggshell and then tried to shove my way out of Cal's binding spell. This time I was able to move. A few feet away I saw the athame, and I lunged for it—at the very moment Hunter shoved Cal off him. We all stumbled to our feet at the same time, panting heavily.

"Morgan, get out of here!" Hunter yelled at me, not taking his eyes off Cal. "I'm a Seeker, and Cal has to answer to the council!"

"Don't listen to him, Morgan!" Cal retorted. I saw flecks of Hunter's blood on his fist. "He's jealous of anything I have, and he wants to hurt me. He'll hurt you, too!"

"That's a lie," Hunter spat angrily. "Cal's Woodbane, Morgan, but unlike Maeve, he hasn't renounced the dark side. Please, just get out of here!"

Cal turned to me, and his hot golden eyes caught mine. A fuzzy softness clouded my brain. I blinked. Hunter said something, but it was muffled, and time seemed to slow. What was happening to me? I watched helplessly as Hunter and Cal circled each other, their eyes burning, their faces stony and pale.

Hunter spoke again, waving his arm, and it fluttered through the air slowly. His voice was like the deep growl of an animal. They came softly together—as if their movements were choreographed—and Hunter's fist connected with Cal's stomach. Cal doubled over. I winced, but I was trapped in a nightmare, powerless to stop the fight. I clutched the athame to my chest. There was a small knot of heat at my throat. I touched the warm silver of the pentacle hanging there. But I couldn't move toward them.

Cal straightened. Hunter swung again at him but missed. Then Cal kicked the back of Hunter's knee, and Hunter crumpled to the ground, the blood on his face smearing the snow. Memories flashed through my mind as Hunter staggered to his feet and threw himself on Cal . . . Hunter telling me Cal was Woodbane, Hunter in the dark outside my house, Hunter being so snide and hateful.

I remembered Cal kissing me, touching me, showing me magick. Showing me how to ground myself at circles, giving me presents. I thought of Bree yelling at me in her car by the side of the road, so long ago. Sky and Hunter together. The images made me unbearably weary. All I wanted to do was lie down in the snow and fall asleep. I sank to my knees, feeling a smile form on my lips. Sleep, I thought. There must have been magick at work, but it didn't seem to matter.

In front of me Cal and Hunter rolled over and over, toward the river.

"Morgan."

My name came to me softly, on a snowflake, and I looked up. For just an instant I met Cal's eyes. They stared pleadingly at me. Then I saw that Hunter was holding Cal down, his knee on Cal's chest. He had a length of silver chain and was binding Cal's hands with it while Cal writhed in pain.

"Morgan."

I received a sharp flash of his pain. I gasped and grabbed my chest, falling forward onto the snow. As I blinked rapidly, my head suddenly seemed clearer.

"He's killing me. Help me. Morgan!"

I couldn't hear the words, but I felt them inside my head, and I pushed myself to my feet with one hand.

"You're through," Hunter was gasping angrily, pulling the silver chain. "I've got you."

"Morgan!" Cal's shout ripped through the snowy night and shattered my calm. I had to move, to fight. I loved Cal, had always loved him. I struggled to my feet as if I had been asleep for a long, long time. I had no plan; I was no match for Hunter, but suddenly I remembered I was still clutching the athame, my birthday athame. Without thinking, I hurled it at Hunter as hard as I could. I watched as it sailed through the air in a gleaming arc.

It struck Hunter's neck, quivering there for a second before falling. Hunter cried out and clapped his hand to the wound. Blood began to spout from the open flesh, blooming red like a poppy. I couldn't believe what I had done.

In that second Cal drew up his knees and kicked Hunter as hard as he could. With a cry of surprise Hunter staggered back, off balance, still clutching his wound . . . and then I was screaming, "No! No! No!" as he toppled clumsily and disappeared over the edge of the cliff.

I stared at the emptiness, dumbstruck.

"Morgan, help!" Cal cried, startling me. "Get this off! It's burning me! Get it off!"

Numb, I hurried to Cal and pulled at the silver chain looped around his wrists. I felt nothing but a mild tingle when I touched it—but I saw raw, red blistering welts on Cal's skin where it had touched him. Once it was off, I threw down the chain and scrambled to the edge of the cliff. If I saw Hunter's body at the bottom, on the rocks, I knew I would throw up, but I forced myself to look, already thinking about calling 911, about trying to climb down there, wondering if I remembered CPR from my babysitting course.

But I saw nothing. Nothing but a jumble of rocks and the gray, turbulent water.

Cal staggered up beside me. I met his eyes. He looked horrified, pale and hollow and weak. "Goddess, he's already gone," Cal murmured. "He must have hit the water, and the current . . ." He was breathing hard, his dark hair wet with snow and traces of blood.

"We have to call someone," I said softly, reaching out to touch him. "We have to tell someone about Hunter. And we have to take care of your wrists. Do you think you can get back to the house?"

Cal just shook his head. "Morgan," he said in a broken voice. "You saved me." With fingers swollen from hitting

Hunter, he touched my cheek and said tenderly, "You saved me. Hunter was going to kill me, but you protected me from him, like you said you would. I love you." He kissed me, his lips cold and tasting of blood. "I love you more than I ever knew I could. Today our future truly begins."

I didn't know what to say. My thoughts had stopped swirling; they had vanished altogether. My mind was a void. I put my arm around him as he began to limp back through the woods, and I couldn't help glancing over my shoulder to the cliff's edge. It was all too much to take in, everything that had happened, and I concentrated on putting one foot in front of the other, feeling Cal rest some of his weight on me as we slogged through the snow.

And then I remembered: it was November 23.

I wondered what time it was—I knew it was very late. I had been born at two-seventeen in the morning on November 23. I decided I must already be officially seventeen. I swallowed. This was the first day of my seventeenth year. What would tomorrow bring?